Once Upon a Time in England

Also by Helen Walsh

Brass

Once Upon a Time in England

Helen Walsh

CANONGATE

Edinburgh · London · New York · Melbourne

First published in Great Britain in 2008 by
Canongate Books Ltd, 14 High Street
Edinburgh EH1 1TE

British Library Cataloguing-in-Publication Data
A catalogue record for this book is available on
request from the British Library

ISBN 978 1 84195 868 2 (HBK)
ISBN 978 1 84767 257 5 (Export PBK)

Typeset by Palimpsest Book Production Limited,
Grangemouth, Stirlingshire

Printed and bound in Great Britain by Mackays of Chatham

www.canongate.net

For you, Mum
with love.

And in memory of Kirsty Jones
and
Lidia Fiems.

'In your town . . . people see with their own eyes what they dread, the transformation during their own lifetime . . . of towns, cities and areas that they know into alien territory.'

Enoch Powell

'Everyone, after all, goes the same dark road – and the road has a trick of being most dark, most treacherous, when it seems most bright – and it's true that nobody stays in the garden of Eden.'

James Baldwin

CONTENTS

Part One

Orford, Warrington, 1975

One

Out on the plains, the icy urban plains, a flame-haired young man was belting down the street, his two-tone shoes sliding and skidding away from his knees. His eyes were slit to the freeze, and his elbows moved freakishly fast, punching and chopping a pin-wheeling path through the night, as though his crazed perpetual motion would keep him upright, outpacing the slick of the sodium-streaked pavements.

An old lady out walking her dog heard his helter-skelter approach, saw the lad spin round the corner and flare right at her. She gasped and shrank back into a neighbour's gate, snatching up the pooch and drawing it tight to her bosom. The ice sprinter did not even see her, barely took note of the dog's startled yelp as he blitzed past in the steaming slipstream of his own breath. He was hardly dressed for the weather, wearing just a thin black shirt rolled twice at the cuffs. The top two buttons remained undone, revealing a flash of flesh as white as the snowflakes gathering in his curls.

On sight of his wild red mane the old lady's heart returned to normal, the dog was returned to the ice-bound floor. There was only one man around there with hair that hue – Jimmy Fitzgerald's lad, Robbie. There he went, running, running – always running, whatever the weather, too hot or too cold. But where was he running to? Or from what? She watched him rip round the next corner and out of sight, stood and stared at his foot-prints. The snow smothered his skidmarks so that soon there was no evidence of him having been there at all, only a tenuous ribbon of panic lingering in the air. The dog poked its snout up, sniffed at it and ran in little revolutions, yapping madly.

Robbie Fitzgerald was running for his life. He peeled another corner and at last the squat silhouette of the building lurched into view. The windows were blacked out and bore no testimony to the wildness that pulsed within. But as Robbie drew up outside and gathered his breath, the night reverberated with the rampant din of stamping feet and screeching fiddles and the braying spray of laughter. This was Orford's Irish Club, Saturday night. This was make or break. Robbie grinned to himself, took one last deep breath, swung the door wide open and plunged inside.

The heat and disorder slurped him up in one muddled flush. It was chaos in there – people were whooping and howling and whirling one another around. Dark slicks of spilt Guinness sloshed on the floor in contrast with the white of the night outside. To his right, a group of drunken men, arms draped affectionately around one another, belted out 'The Fields of Athenry'. On the small stage beyond, a fiddle quartet struggled to be heard above them. Robbie stood back and soaked it all up. He allowed himself a small smile as he stayed rooted to the spot for a moment, shaking his head at how little the place had changed. Then he got down to business. He needed those fiddle players. Without them, well – it would all turn to dust.

He pushed himself up onto his tiptoes and scanned the room for Irene. His heart kicked out with giddy relief as she ducked up from beneath the bar and flipped open one of those bumper-sized bottles of stout. She laughed her dirty, infectious laugh as she poured, propped up on one elbow, holding court to a gaggle of travellers, her huge freckled bust splayed across the bar top.

'Irene!' he yelled, and hoisted his head up so she could see it was him. He stepped through the black puddles, edging his way through a maelstrom of flailing elbows and thumping feet. 'IRENE!'

Irene O'Connor did not hear her name being yelled across the roof of noise. She couldn't hear a thing in there. It was the

4

crimson brilliance of Robbie's hair that caught her attention. Red-haired men were two a penny in her club, but Robbie's mop was such a magnificent red it almost glowed. School bus red she called it. She swivelled to meet his gaze, instinctively raking a hand through her hair. Robbie launched himself up and onto the bar. His face, his head, his hair were wrung with sweat. His eyes were big and crackling with some intense energy.

'I need you to help me,' he shouted. His words were drowned out, sucked back over his shoulder into the roistering din. His eyes flickered all over her.

'What you saying, our kid?' She moved right into him, lent her ear to his hot smoky mouth.

'Irene, this is serious, love. I need you to help us. There's been an emergency.'

She pulled back, and for a moment her stretched, anxious face ironed out its furrows, revealing the beautiful girl she once was. 'God heavens no, Robbie. Not Susheela? Has she started?'

'No, love – no. Susheela's fine. The baby's still cooking nicely. It's not that . . .'

'Vincent? It's little Vinnie, isn't it? What's he . . .'

'Vincent's fine, Iye. It's nothing like that.'

'So?'

He paused, drew himself right up and prepared himself for the inevitable rejection. He looked Irene flush in the eye. 'It's like this, Iye. I need to borrow a couple of your entertainment.'

'You what?'

'Your entertainment . . .'

'Aye-aye, love, I heard you first time . . .'

'This couldn't be more serious, Irene. I need you to loan us a couple of your fiddle players. Yeah?'

She just stared at him.

Realising she hadn't laughed in his face yet, Robbie leapt to ram home his advantage. 'It'll only be thirty minutes, darlin'.

Not a minute more. That's all's I'm asking of you. Thirty minutes of your entertainment's time.'

Irene realised then, he was not joking. She also realised she was powerless to resist. His burning green eyes were all over her, beseeching her, giving her nowhere to go. She tried to play hard to get, pulling down the corners of her mouth, arching an eyebrow, but Robbie could scent victory. He grabbed her chubby wrist, pulling her face close.

'I can tell you the whole story start to finish later on Irene, love – but this is an emergency. Everything's hanging on it. My whole life depends on it. The baby's life, the baby's whole future. I promise I'll have them back to you in two shakes of a lamb's tail.'

She looked right past him into the delirious hub of the room. Robbie knew exactly what she was thinking, and she was right. There would be a riot. But he couldn't let this opportunity slip away – not now, not with the chance of a lifetime so close he could taste it. He took her head in his hands so her nose was almost touching his, as though transmitting the urgency of his crisis to her by shortwave. He gave it one last go.

'Irene, do us a favour – listen to me, will you? I need them fiddlers, yeah? Whatever profit you lose tonight, I'll treble it for you. I'll come and sing for nothing. Do you get me? I'll do five Sundays in a row. I'll do all your favourites – whatever the punters want. I'll do a frigging Elvis night if you like . . .'

She didn't bite. A resigned sadness came over her face and, recognising it, Robbie let her go, slumping back down onto the flats of his feet. He turned to go. Irene spoke to the back of his head. She knew full well what this was about. It was Dickie Vaughan. It had to be Dickie Vaughan.

'You've got half an hour, Robert Fitzgerald. Not a minute longer. And you're to bring back my men in person, no later than . . .' She consulted her wrist, but Robbie was no longer

6

there to hear her out. She watched him bob and weave his way to the stage and silence the lead fiddle with a hand on his forearm. As he pointed across to their boss behind the bar she nodded her consent and mouthed 'good luck' to Robbie. If that boy was not a star in the making, then she'd learnt nothing through all her years in the trade. Robbie Fitzgerald was not just a prospect: he was the real thing.

Susheela perched on the cold Formica of the kitchen table, and fixed her sleepy gaze on the kitchen clock. Robbie was fifteen minutes late. She glanced at the oven where the plates were warming and wondered whether she should take them out again. Absent-mindedly she patted her globe-tight belly, then took her weight on her slender, fragile wrists and pushed herself up from the table. She held her breath. Beyond the subsonic hum of the fridge there was only the deadweight of silence. Was that snow she could sense out there? Clicking off the kitchen light, she padded over to the window above the sink and, bending forwards, pressed her face into the darkness. She was right. High above the fence in the back yard, a miasma of snowflakes whirred madly in the aureole of the street lamp. She prised herself up onto her tiptoes and unhooked the window, her belly jutting over the sink. She fed her arm out into the cold night air and just held it there. The majesty of a new snow-fall shot her through with the same childlike amazement as the first time she'd seen it, when the sheer magic of that midnight blizzard had taken her breath away. She yielded tenderly to the memory, drawing her hand back in and draping it around her hot neck.

It was December of 1971, not long after she had started her training at Warrington General. She'd just clocked off from a gruelling shift down in A&E. She'd barely made it back to the nurses' home before she collapsed into deep slumber. But something jolted her wide awake – some foreboding, a powerful sense that all was not right. The room was cold, so all she could see was her own breath – and hers was the only breath she could hear. At first she thought something terrible had happened to the other girls. They hadn't come home. They'd been involved in some accident. But then she heard a muffled cough; someone turning over in their sleep – Mata, from the obstreperous groan that accompanied it. And as she adjusted herself to the familiar acoustics of the dormitory, she managed to count the rise and fall of six pairs of lungs. She sighed her relief out loud, but still the gnawing sense persisted that something wasn't right.

And then it hit her. Outside on the streets, an eerie silence had descended. Where was the usual soundtrack to a Wednesday night? Where were the taxis, coming and going to the hospital? Where were the ambulances? What had happened to the wail of sirens, the shriek of girls fighting over men? Her heart bounced against her rib cage. All those sounds which had fed her insomnia those first few nights in the nursing home – the thrum of long-distance lorries on the motorway; the drone of the factories, pumping their bilge into the night; the low giddy puttering of the generator outside – none of this was audible. The whole symphony had seized up. Trembling, she wrapped her bedcover around her shoulders and tiptoed to the window. She hovered there, one hand lingering on a curtain, afraid of what she might see. The timorous young Malaysian girl, already adjusting to the shock of the new on a daily, an hourly basis, pictured scenes of mass destruction. In Warrington, any horror was possible. Some deadly nuclear fog could have descended during the night, sucking the life out of all who moved.

She took a deep breath, screwed her eyes tight and yanked back the curtain. When she opened them she almost passed out.

Everything was white. White and velvet and stock still. It was the most beautiful thing she had ever seen.

Now Susheela looked out from her kitchen window at the falling snow and smiled at the memory of the dark-skinned girl in her flannel dressing gown, waking all the nurses and racing down the stairs to dance in the snow. She was just a girl back then – not so long ago. A few nights after the snowstorm, Robbie Fitzgerald had been carried onto her ward and into her life. She smiled again and slid her hand across her heaving belly and thought that one day she would recount this story to her unborn child; the story of the brown girl spinning and gambolling on the pavement, trying to catch the snow on her tongue, baffled each time it melted to nothing.

Susheela closed the window and clicked the light back on. She hoped it would snow hard and blanket the landscape white. Make it all pretty. Yes, even Orford could look pretty in the snow.

Two

Flicking a clot of fringe from his damp freckled brow Robbie Fitzgerald tried to suppress the glee wrought on his face. Catching his breath, he stood dead still, stage centre, trying to revive the cool that had carried him through his performance.

When Robbie had spotted Dickie Vaughan earlier that evening he'd dropped his pint. He'd never believed that could happen – a fresh, foaming pint of Best and it had slipped right through his fingers. But it wasn't every day that Dickie Vaughan walked into your local working men's club. There was no doubting it was him, though. The legendary talent manager was sat right there in the centre of St Stephen's lounge bar, chomping contentedly on his cigar. His famous paunch took up the entire table, and Robbie Fitzgerald was rooted to the spot. Only a month ago he'd asked his young wife to read out the profile in the *MU* magazine, where Vaughan was bemoaning the death of outstanding new cabaret talent, and predicting the slow and sad demise of the working-class social club scene if things didn't change. Robbie agreed with every word. At the age of twenty-four he was already a veteran of that selfsame cabaret scene, and he'd witnessed at first hand the shabby trail of bad comedians, pub warblers and novelty acts passing themselves off as The Entertainment. Robbie could sell out any one of the clubs in the Greater Warrington area – and beyond – on reputation alone, but it was getting harder to win a crowd over. They wanted it on a plate, where he liked to build up an atmosphere. They wanted Jack Jones and Tony Bennett soundalikes, smooth easy listening, where he revered the dark, aching soul of Van Morrison and Robert Johnson. It was Robbie's dream to team up with a big-hitter like Vaughan. With a manager like that, he could go all the way – he knew he could. His bruised fusion of soul and blues with the maudlin strains of folk was not to everybody's taste, but Dickie Vaughan would see beyond the labels, right to the heart of Robbie's genius. And there could be no doubting that Robbie was exactly that – a spirit, a genius. A star.

Robbie had stopped dead in his tracks. He didn't even notice he'd let his pint slip until Barney tried to usher him back out of the room.

Barney was St Stephen's Concert Secretary, a role that brought him a certain prestige, not to say considerable power in the world of Warrington cabaret. Barney booked the Turn, compered the night, ran the show in every sense – and he could never quite resist showing he was still as good as any singer, especially after a few large Whyte & Mackays when he'd cap off a perfectly good night by treating the crowd to a Sinatra ballad. At first, Robbie thought that was behind Barney's blundering attempt to stop him performing. If there was one turn he couldn't follow, it was Robbie Fitzgerald's splintered sweet soul voice. Barney had pushed Robbie back out of the lounge, reaming him some yarn about a charity night he'd forgotten.

'Serious, Rob. Pure slipped me mind. It'll just be the stand-ups tonight.'

Robbie craned his neck round Barney's shoulder, eager to make sure that it was Dickie Vaughan. 'What? You're looking to raise money for charity and there's no music on?'

Barney shrugged, beseeching him with his 'what can I tell you' face. Robbie humoured him with an eyebrow. He was too over-whelmed with terror and excitement to get angry. The biggest talent scout in the North was here in Orford, sat right there in his frigging club. Of course there was going to be fucking music!

'I'll be going on as usual, Barney mate. Fifteen minutes.'

Barney shook his head, panicked now. 'Robbie! No.'

11

'What you on about – no?'

Barney slumped down into a cup chair, its vermillion arms singed by a hundred cigarette butts. He held his head in his hands. 'I'm sorry, Rob. You can't go on. I . . .' He glanced up at Robbie, pink, foolish and found out. 'I sent the backing band home.'

'You what?'

'Your musicians, mate. I paid 'em off . . .'

Robbie's heart slumped with his shoulders. There was no way Barney was lying. He could see it all now, and he understood why he'd done it – why Barney would have thought he had no choice. Robbie was mildly flattered. He almost felt sorry for the blustering Concert Secretary. Still, he couldn't absolve him. It was a dirty world, clubland, but Robbie had to think about Number One. This was it for Robbie Fitz and his young family, and there was no way he was letting the chance pass by. Come hell or high water, Dickie Vaughan was going to hear him sing.

He clipped the mic back into its stand and narrowed his glare into the spotlight. He bowed, once – not so much a bow as a brief incline of his head – then beckoned his backing band forward. Another swell of applause built from the back and ricocheted around the room as Robbie's fiddler and banjo player stepped forward, joined hands and took a bow grinning like they'd never seen a crowd before, let alone been feted like this. People were standing on their chairs. Euphoria swooned around Robbie's head. It hung there, dizzying him, raining sparks over the boisterous locals and then it hit him. He'd pulled it off. Whatever Dickie Vaughan thought of him didn't matter now – Robbie Fitz had just given the show of his life.

'Thank you . . . I . . . er . . . you're very kind,' he spluttered, truly lost for words now. 'I . . . em . . . I'm sure we'd all just like to thank the, erm . . . the real stars of the show, Feargal and er . . .'

He shot an embarrassed glance at the two men standing to the left of him. They laughed and yelled out their names. 'One more time, if you will. Thank you. Put your hands together for Peter and Feargal then . . . that's the spirit. Thank you. God bless.'

Robbie grazed the audience, incredulous at the response. He'd never wooed a crowd like that before, never – and he wouldn't in a hundred years have thought St Stephen's capable of such an outpouring of sheer emotion. But then they hadn't heard him sing like that and they'd probably never heard music like that. Not there, in their local club. The regulars had grown bloated on the mandatory cabaret standards, week in, week out – but Robbie Fitzgerald had blown all that away tonight. That nervous vaulting in his guts on first sight of Vaughan had crystalised into something big and magical. At first Feargal's ragged style of five-string banjo jarred with the regulars, hoping for a smoother ride. But then Robbie's vocals kicked in. His gorgeously forlorn croon seemed to flood the room with one prolonged and delirious strafe, stroking conversations to a lull. A knot of chairs and torsos, bent to their neighbours' small talk, twisted back round towards the stage. Cigarettes hovered in mid-air, never to meet the puckering lips that sought them, and by the time Robbie had reached the final refrain of Hank Williams' 'Your Cheating Heart', a stunned silence had descended upon the small and smoky salon of St Stephen's. Standing up there now, Robbie felt as stunned as they did.

Behind the veils of smoke Vaughan's eyes nettled with tears. Like the rest of the room, he was gone. Robbie Fitzgerald had him transfixed, utterly caught up in the ferocious beauty of his voice. He had never heard a voice so visceral and honest, so needy and hungry and splintered with pain. He didn't think it possible to transform the jarring, maudlin wail of bluegrass into something so profound and sensual. That voice planted a hankering in his groin, ripping the skin from his flesh in one violent tug. And as the smokescreen lifted, Vaughan appraised

13

the young flame-haired minstrel with mounting disbelief. He took in the flat boxer's nose; the wild green eyes; the litter of scars that marked his face and the fading shamrock inked between his thumb and forefinger. He observed Robbie's cheap cheesecloth shirt, his high-waisted pinstripe bags and his two-tone shoes gleaming defiantly in the spotlight, and he wondered how this crude male could radiate such beauty.

As the crowd erupted Vaughan felt that rare but shrill sensation of mad, mad excitement coursing up his spine. He'd known it on a handful of occasions, sometimes to his chagrin as record companies and publishers beat him to the catch. He wasn't letting this one slip away. He scanned the room. There was every kind of punter in the club, young and old – jazz lovers, big band fans, young stylish Motown mothers all jostled with the regular weekend drunks who'd dance to anything. Robbie's plangent, quavering voice had got to each and every one of them. With Vaughan's canny guidance, the lad had the power to seduce the nation. Dickie laughed at the random nature of his find. You walk into a club – any old club – and this! He shook his head, still emotional. He'd seen it all, Dickie Vaughan, but this wonderful business of show never failed to surprise and delight him.

Susheela glanced nervously at the kitchen clock – a china plate, with gold stencilled numerals. Another ten minutes had elapsed, and Robbie was seriously late. A slow trickle of perspiration rolled down her neck, halting in the cleft of her cleavage. She turned off the oven, feeling foolish at her disposability, her fringe role in the evening's events. Robbie was out there, living it. It was work, but he loved it. It was a life. It was his life. Susheela? She stayed at home with their son. She waited for Robbie's return. She warmed the plates. How love's young dream had delivered for her! A chaste little box at the heart of the worst estate in Orford, where she played out time, day after day, waiting for the new baby to announce its arrival. Another little Fitzgerald half-chat. Even when they were joking, the Orford people frightened her. With Robbie by her side it was different. It was grudging, but she had respect. When he was out at work she was completely and utterly alone. Even her friends from the ward found a trip into the badlands of Orford a trip too far and the first time round she'd lingered on in the cocoon of the hospital well beyond her confinement time. She couldn't tell Robbie – he was working all hours as it was – but apart from little Vincent, the only brown faces she ever saw were the doctors and nurses at Warrington General. It was all very well for Robbie; he had a life to lead. For Susheela this was the highlight of the week. Warming the plates for their Saturday night takeaway.

But when she glanced across at the slumbering figure of her Little Man, little Vincent Fitzgerald, her heart was swept away by the force and the swell of her love for him. She shuffled across and covered his head with kisses. How could she even have thought those things? She loved her time at home with her inquisitive boy. At five years old Vincent's personality was steadily forming, giving her a glimpse of the young man he might become. Already he displayed a preference for adult company, rebuffing the offers from next door's brood to come and play, choosing instead to stay indoors with his mother. He spent long slabs of the school holidays fussing around in his bedroom with only his Noddy books and the gentle puttering of the radio for company. Susheela marvelled at his quiet, industrious nature and imagined that he might become a doctor or a lawyer. The thought shot her stomach with a little frisson of delight.

She dawdled back to the kitchen, sighed hard and relit the oven. She clicked the light off again, and watched the snow. It spun around the roofs of the low-rises like the squall in a paperweight. She strained her eyes. Beyond the low-rises she thought she could make out the lights from the tower blocks, slowly blinking awake, standing sentinel over the estate. She wondered if they, too, were snowgazing. She'd come to despise Orford but she loved the different inflections of the tower blocks. Sometimes, in the summer, they'd refract the red sunset off their windows like a wild fire, and she'd ache for Kuala Lumpur – the big glass towers behind the temple which would ripple like an army of glass spaceships in the midday haze.

She tried to recapture the warm careless blush of before. It was impossible. She felt helpless. Somewhere out there the love of her life might slowly, irredeemably be slipping away from her. Typically, he would leave the club just as soon as his set ended and he'd trousered his fee, stopping only for fish and chips on the way home. He knew Susheela lit the oven at 10.45 and put the plates in at 10.50. It was now a quarter to midnight.

She tried to resist the dark thoughts lapping at her subconscious, but as the minutes toiled by she caved. She'd seen it with her own eyes, seen how those barmaids looked at him – those hot bold looks they shot him. Did they care about Susheela's feelings? She doubted they even noticed her. And she'd seen how his very presence rendered even her own friends giddy and girly. It had shocked her at first how Robbie didn't pick up on this, how totally impervious he was to their admiration. But now she was married to him, she could see that Robbie didn't think of himself as handsome. He'd stand with her in the mirror and point to his slain, pulpy nose which he saw as a tell-all about his background.

Susheela had fallen in love with that man, and that nose. Each dent and bump told out their history. She'd been there, on duty, the night they wheeled him in, barely conscious, his nose splayed across his left cheekbone pumping blood into the stung slits of his eyes. She'd sat in as the ENT consultant probed his fingers around the bloody mire and shook his head, frowning upon it as though it were an unsolvable puzzle. And she'd been there in

16

the room weeks later when his cast had peeled back to reveal his new face. She'd watched him confront the mirror and sensed his disappointment. She'd wheeled him back to the ward. He'd been embarrassed to look at her. The flirty, ebullient quips he'd lavished on her from behind his plaster cast were replaced by a sad, brooding silence. He seemed disgusted with himself, and was at pains to let her know he hadn't caused the fight. He'd been jumped by four lads. Susheela loved him for that, for his embarrassment. Saturday night dragged dozens of Robbie Fitzgeralds into Warrington General – the brawlers, the drunks, their girlfriends, their victims – often all four bound up in the one bloodied casualty. Most of them showed little remorse and took great pride in regaling the medics with blow-by-blow re-enactments of their heroics. Sometimes, Susheela would catch them post-surgery, appraising the splendour of their war wounds, surrounded by admiring comrades. Often they'd seem dejected once their gaping, gushing injuries had been swabbed and stitched so prettily they were barely grazes. Not Robbie. He seemed to shrink away from the dangerous edge his nose now lent his battle-scarred face, at odds with the tender and reticent soul beneath.

It was that contradiction in Robbie that had hit every nurse on Ward 23. Everyone flitted round the flame-haired honey, the more so when news seeped out he was a middling local song-ster. On the day of his discharge there was a frenetic scramble for his number. Susheela was faintly revulsed by the audacity of her pals, and quietly jealous, too. Oh how she wished she could exhibit herself like that: the saucy walk, their bottoms twitching as they passed, the little glance back over their shoulder making sure he'd had his fill. She couldn't even muster the mettle to reassure him about his nose! She wanted to tell him what a proud, handsome specimen it was, and how it complemented the brilliance of his eyes. Instead she had overcompensated for her nervousness by adopting a brusque, no-nonsense tone with Robbie

17

and, to the baffled ire of more worldly nurses, the ice queen act paid off. When Robbie left the ward that day, Susheela's had been the only number he took with him. He'd weaseled it out of the stony-faced matron – a feat that still made her smile, whenever she thought on it.

Those first, tentative dates and days out were as close as Susheela had come to the magical romances of her storybooks back home. Although she wanted to dance and dress up and show out, she quickly understood that Robbie preferred to avoid the crowded pubs and discos in town, and just as quickly, she came to love that in him, too. The solitary, yearning poet, striding out into the countryside, filling his lungs with fresh air. She could see the care drop away from his shoulders the further out they travelled, into Derbyshire and the Peak District or the Derwent Valley – great potholes and dripping, echoing caverns one day, heart-stopping panoramas from a crumbling hilltop wall the next.

She could understand why Robbie craved the wide open spaces and cold fresh skies. His other life was indoors; the factory by day, then, most nights of the week, the clubs. And if she thought she loved him when his great huge hands would belt her dainty waist as he lifted her, effortlessly, over a mountain stile, her heart almost stopped the first time she heard him sing. She'd had to beg him, daily, to let her come along. Then one Saturday afternoon, sat on the ridge up by Daresbury, he sighed out loud, 'If they stare, right? Take no notice.' And it dawned on her he was saying yes. Stare at her? She didn't care about that! Of course people were going to stare, she was the only brown face in town, just about. But she was going to see Robbie sing, and she could barely keep the giggles down inside.

He made sure she had a good table, made sure the steward at the Legion treated her like a VIP, but Susheela didn't even want a Coca-Cola. She'd sat there, rapt, waiting – and when her man came on, he nearly blew her soul to dust. It was spellbinding. It was heartbreaking. Nervously, at first, glancing, rather than staring at his lover, he romped through a few Motown classics: 'Band of Gold'; 'Jimmy Mack'; 'River Deep Mountain High'. And his voice just blistered right through her, turning her stomach sick. That was her Robbie, there. That was her man! And then he did it. He came to her side of the small stage, crooked his left knee and took all his weight on his right hip, closed his eyes, tilted his head back and sang 'When a Man Loves a Woman'.

And when he opened his eyes, he saw his little brown angel, streaks of mascara-black tears flooding her beautiful face.

She loved that time, those first few weeks and months. She loved Robbie, loved his heart, his dreams, his plans. She loved to cling to his waist as they raced through the countryside on his motorcycle, past streams, and glades and hillocks – the England of her dreams. She loved it when he'd suddenly pull over and race her to the top of a hill. One time, they'd stood there, drinking in the view, holding it down, his strong, thick wrists around her waist as he held her from behind, his chin resting on her shoulder.

'Ours, that,' he'd said.

She'd nodded, and gazed out upon the green, green pastures, a land of verdant plenty spread out beneath them.

'We should do it, you know. You and me.'

And she could feel, with her back to him, just exactly what he was trying to say. Within the year, they were married.

Susheela could deal with the way women looked at Robbie. She even allowed herself to feel smug. That'd be as close as any of them ever got – looks. But gazes, glances, admiring darts of the eyes belonged to the daylight. They were harmless gestures – the ritualistic extremes of daytime coquetry. It was night-time she feared most keenly. Night-time aroused them to verbal liberties and dispatched them to the flesh. Night-time meant drink, and

Susheela's time on the ward had taught her there were no limits to a Warrington girl's ambitions once she'd had a drink. Now the picture was emerging, she succumbed fully and tormented herself with its crude and rampant immediacy. Her half-sozzled husband talking, smiling with a young girl – blonde and fair and flat of stomach, her hand brushing his arm, kohl-caked eyelashes fluttering an unmistakeable promise. She buried her head. What could she do about it? She was pregnant, for goodness' sake, pregnant with Robbie's child! She pictured him with Chrissy Taylor, the barmaid with the huge breasts, always displayed to their best in a low-cut top.

She padded back to the window, bereft. Her Robbie was out there and she only had herself to blame. Her work pals had warned her all right. 'His needs don't stop just cos you're pregnant, love,' they'd jeered when she was carrying Vincent. She'd made the mistake of telling them she found intercourse uncomfortable. 'There's more than one way to milk your man!'

Her huge brown eyes had blinked back the tears, trying so hard to force a plucky smile, but their vile prognosis curdled in her ears. She'd tried to relieve Robbie, oh God how she'd tried. Many a night his hard member had pressed tentatively into the flesh of her rump, just to let her know – and she'd lain there, listening to his soft anguished whimpers, wanting so badly to comfort him. Her hand would reach down to him, but somehow she couldn't go through with it. The vulgarity of it was more than she could bear. Her husband's member would slink back, rest sadly against his thigh. Oh how she'd give anything for one more chance. Poor Robbie. All that unslaked love and desire churning his groin, raging through his veins, waiting to explode like a bomb. All those brazen blondes out there, waiting to detonate him.

Three

The moment Robbie stepped off stage Vaughan swooped on him, guiding him into the dim recesses of the back bar. Regulars hovered in speculative clusters as word seeped out about Vaughan's identity. The more hard-faced of the regulars pushed within earshot, sending back unreliable bush wires on the latest developments. St Stephen's was abuzz with the babble of excited speculation. On one thing they could all agree – Robbie Fitz was going to be big.

Eventually Robbie's beaming, half-bashful face emerged and he was engulfed by well-wishers before he'd got three feet inside the lounge. The men, emboldened by drink and swept away by this tide of communal bonhomie, shuffled over and presented him with pint upon pint of the black stuff. He sipped at one, but was still in a state of shock. Women yo-yoed back and forth to the toilets to freshen their coy smiles and plump up their décolletages. The night rang with drunken attestations as to how well and for how long each had known their home-grown hero.

Robbie just sat there, face glowing, incandescent with pride. He felt a surge of fondness for these people. He wanted to tell them everything, but superstition held him back. Nothing had been signed yet, and if anyone was going to hear his news it would be Susheela. She would be first with the low-down. He had to suppress a giggle as he pictured her eyes – easy to surprise – widening with each new opportunity: the special guest spot at the Talk of the North. The recording contract. The near certainty of a turn on *New Faces*. It was only agreed with a gentleman's handshake, but it was Dickie Vaughan's handshake, and it still warmed his palm. And had Robbie followed him out into the icy night, he would have seen Dickie Vaughan jump up and punch the air before

21

lowering his massive frame down into his snowbound E-type.

Robbie was no lounge lizard, but he was powerless in the face of all this goodwill. He was overwhelmed by it, really, and he had to admit he'd have liked to have stayed longer. As it was, it was already past eleven thirty when Robbie finally extricated himself from his woozy acolytes, his swoon of self-pleasure eventually pierced by images of his hungry and stranded young wife. He'd sipped his first sup of stardrops and it tasted delicious.

He marched through the snow, the cold night air blasting the sweat from his brow and ripping through the damp of his hair. There was a slight unease that he hadn't returned Irene's musicians as promised, but how often did nights like tonight come along? The band had been a part of the magic, and he'd left them at the bar surrounded by glad-handers, basking in his reflected glory. News would have got back to Iye by now – she'd know all about Dickie Vaughan and she'd be pleased for Robbie. He knew she would.

With each proud stride that took him away from St Stephen's, Robbie was taken over by a sense that he was, at last, walking towards something – something huge. A powerful shudder swept through him and he was overcome by the certainty that tonight was the turning point in his life. He would never, ever forget this evening: the night of the snowstorms; the night Dickie Vaughan walked into his club. He strode on through the blizzard, wanting to hang on to the feeling, that awesome sense of significance, the knowledge that he, Robbie Fitz, was at the very centre of something important.

Robbie turned a corner and saw Crossfields' two smokestacks marooned in the whiteness. A grin sliced his face as another delicious repercussion presented itself: the factory could go and fuck itself! In the very near future, he would be walking into Vernon Cohen's office and handing in his notice. That would take some of the sheen off his ingratiating face. He started to play out the departure scene in his mind's eye, but it was almost too much to take in. He'd quietly resigned himself to another forty years on the Metso Soap line, maggoting away with all the other maggots – maybe a promotion to Charge Hand if he got lucky. His head was so giddy it felt unsafe on his neck. A surge of recklessness made him want to do something impulsive and totally self-destructive. He looked across the white reach of playing fields and for a brief second thought about jumping a bus to town, really celebrating his newfound freedom! But there was an even stronger pull the other way. Susheela. Vincent. The baby.

He giggled again as he ran through the different possibilities for breaking the news to her, but one thing remained constant. The hell with fish and chips! Tonight they would be celebrating with chow mein and ribs. He patted the roll of pound notes in his pocket and hit the jackpot with a crumpled, pre-made rollie he'd forgotten about. He sparked up and pushed on.

Robbie walked right past the chippie. Some of the lads from the tower blocks were milling around in the doorway, neither really inside nor outside the place. What was it with these kids and big, lit-up windows? The off-licence, the phone box, the chippie – they flocked to them like fireflies. As he passed, their horrible mob laughter spilled out, jarring with the calm of the snowfall. Robbie felt for whomever was on duty in there tonight. He could see one of the little shaven-headed bastards leaning right over the counter, shouting something into the kitchen. His conscience warred with him. He really should go in – stand there and queue. His very presence would be enough to shut this lot up, probably see them off, too. But a glance inside made his mind up. Johny was there, too, and their paper wraps were already being stacked up on the stainless steel counter. Robbie saw the clock. He was an hour late.

Susheela would be worried by now. Even if she'd guessed he was going to Fung Ling, she wouldn't be expecting him to be this late. Perhaps he should just go straight home, but it'd be worth this minor angst when he burst through the front door with his big news and their swanky dinner, and like a gambler on a roll, he pressed right ahead. He wished he hadn't seen the skins. Subconsciously, he drew hard on his rollie as he passed them by, the sight of their harringtons and major-domo boots planting something queasy in his guts. He wasn't afraid of any of them; he'd come up against all their brothers and cousins at one time or another. He couldn't place the source of his unease, only that it was chemical, instinctive, some imminent menace they exuded just through being there. Maybe he was just experiencing the rude announcement of the new kids on the block, and he simply didn't like the shock of the cockiness their youth brought. Just like the tower blocks and low-rises realigning the skyline of his own youth, Orford was changing. But so, thought Robbie as he reached the other side of the top field, was he.

The skins filed out from the chippie and mobbed up on the corner of the road, cramming fistfuls of hot chips into their mouths as they watched Robbie go. All eyes were on Evo, the oldest of the crew, a squat, solid lad who, at nineteen, was the man among the boys. A kid no older than fifteen pushed himself forward, face twisted tight into a scowl. 'We gonna do 'im, Ev? We doing the Paki-loving twat?'

Revelling in his big moment, Evo lit up as he spoke. The flare of the lighter illuminated his burnt, stumpy hand. 'My, my! What a turn-up. English food's no good for the gypo. He's heading straight for the Chink filfth!'

The kid was almost jumping up and down. 'Let's do the cunt, then. Let's fucking roll him now and get his wedge before he fuckin' spends it. Paki-loving gypo twat.'

Calmly, and seemingly unperturbed by the boy, Evo glanced down at him – then with minimal backlift, slammed his gnarled fist into his face. The lad buckled, as much through shock as the blow to his nose. Evo pulled him up by an ear and pushed his face right into his blinking, tear-pricked eyeline. 'Who the fuck are you? You don't say nothing, you!'

There was mute sympathy as the lad slunk back into the folds of the mob, his sleeve pressed to his nose. All eyes were now on Evo. He narrowed his gaze, saw Robbie swing open Fung Ling's door and bound inside out of the cold. He could almost hear the cheery banter between the Chink and the gypo. He could see the money changing hands – notes, not coins. These immigrants were making proper money, and making sure they kept it in the family. That Fitzgerald would be smiling at the Chinawoman now, eyeing up her little sharp tits under that green smock she wore. Sex, he thought. Violence. He wasn't fooled by the lowering of the eyes, the humble, servile, willing-to-please act. She was as depraved as any of them, the Chinawoman. He'd thought of her many a night. Sex. Sex. But with even a sole chop suey roll being out of his price bracket, Evo's visits were few and far between and, still then, he felt strange in there, especially when it was just him and her. Only the Fitzgeralds of this world could eat at Fung Ling, and only then because she gave him a discount; ten per cent for fucking her up against the wall outside. Sex, sex, sex. And another ten because he was married to one of them. A stinker. One more foul, stinking alien. Violence. He watched Robbie's jaunty silhouette, and he seethed with jealousy. Violence. Sex. Violence. Sex. And then it occurred to him that he didn't have to choose. He turned to his boys.

'Come on. Cunt's too pissed to feel a hiding. We'll smack him some other time. I've got a better idea.' He started jogging back the other way – away from Robbie, away from the Chinese. 'Come on!' he rallied, a great leery grin spreading out over his dull face. 'Fuck you waiting for, you Paki-loving cunts!'

They jogged after him, leaving only Fat Brian who, after a wheezy and half-hearted pursuit, contented himself with waddling on behind them, cramming steaming hot potato flesh into his mouth.

Four

Fung Ling, their local Chinese, the only Chinese this side of Warrington, was empty. Mrs Ling hung in the window, her face pressed up to the pane, her hands clasped above her brow as she scoped the deserted streets for custom. Robbie spied her anxious face and he felt for her. Business had boomed for the Lings those first few months, but slowly the novelty had begun to wear thin and, as winter set in, the locals were shunning the exoticism of eastern spice for the doughy comforts of the chippie. Each time Robbie cycled past on his way back from work now, Fung Ling was empty.

She saw him coming from across the street and quickly re-located behind the counter, trying to look busy. As he swung through the door, she fielded an imaginary telephone order, holding one hand up to Robbie for a moment's patience. She replaced the phone, scribbled on a pad and beamed up at Robbie. 'How Susheela?' she asked in her faltering, sing-song English. She fixed him with an admonitory stare, her black-brown eyes never leaving his. 'No see long time.'

Robbie couldn't be sure if she was scolding him for witholding business, or merely enquiring about the baby. He decided on the latter and leant against the hot stainless steel counter. The heat crawled up his arms and smouldered in his pits, only adding to his all-round sense of warmth, of happiness. He was going to be a star. This woman would boast of it, soon enough. 'Robbie Fitzgerald? Eat here! Always buy duck!'

He grinned into Mrs Ling's solemn face. 'She's very big now!' Cupping his hand, he traced an arc over his tummy, unwittingly blowing out his cheeks, too. 'But she's fine. She's doing great.

She says she'll be back in to see you just as soon as she's had the little 'un.'

'And Vincent?' She said it Win-senn. She smiled hard, small gaps between each stumpy tooth. 'I save prawn crackers for your little man Vincent!' She laughed and waved a grease-stained paper bag at him. 'You tell Susheela car no go. I no go in Rusholme this week.'

Mrs Ling provided Susheela with her umbilical cord back home. Both women came from Ipoh, the seamy Kuala Lumpur quarter that became more magical the more they romanced about it. And although Mrs Ling had left KL a long time ago to live her married life in Hong Kong, the women took a childish pleasure in communicating in Malay. Theirs was not the Malay spoken in the heaving swabs of the city, but the more sophisticated variety they'd learnt in school. Had they been neighbours back home, racial snobbery would have limited their exchanges to curt, weather-based pleasantries. But here in the brash planes of Warrington, their shared tongue provided a cultural and, often, an emotional, lifeline.

When it had first opened Susheela couldn't keep away from Ling's, frittering all her wages on hit after hit, day after day. She found English food bland to the extent that it depressed her, truly. But Robbie couldn't stand Indian cuisine – it was pungent beyond his threshold, and left him with a longer-lasting and more debilitating hangover than a night on the ale. When the Lings came along, Chinese turned out to be a satisfying compromise for both.

Since Susheela had left work in November, though, her spice fix had been kept to a minimum. With only one wage coming into the household now, any extravagances had to be put in abeyance and, much as Susheela missed her chat, Robbie knew she'd never call at Fung Ling without ordering. Standing there now on the stark lino floor, with Mrs Ling cursing the fryers back to life, Robbie felt a powerful need to atone. With quick mental arithmetic, he satisfied himself there'd be enough left over from the night's earnings to see them through the week. Grinning expansively, he ordered a half aromatic crispy duck and a special banquet for two. Mrs Ling glowed at the lavishness of the order and bounced off into the kitchen where she barked instructions to an empty room. It had been worth staying open after all.

Twenty minutes passed and Robbie was beginning to regret placing such an elaborate order now. It was past midnight, and Susheela would be beside herself. At times like this he dearly wished he'd said yes to the option of a party line when the telephone company came calling in the summer. But Robbie could never quite quell the image of the hunched, ancient lady in the corner of the Indian shop in Lymm, the phone permanently glued to her ear as she yattered on and on in that indecipherable tongue. He reproached himself, but he couldn't risk a phone with Susheela – and it wasn't just the money. He didn't want her thinking of home too much.

His patience began to fray and he was almost walking out when Mrs Ling reappeared wielding two steaming plastic bags. She sang at him from behind the counter. 'All ready now Mr Fitz yeah? Good enough for a queen! Tell Susheela I missing her. Come in soon. I put small packet spice in bag – she see. Coconut milk also. And prawn crackers for little Vincent man.' Smiling her yellow smile again, she fished a crispy spring roll from the warmer. 'For walk home,' she said, handing it to him.

The gentle tick-tocking of the kitchen clock grew louder in her head. Each thrum was a blow to the heart, recalling the absence of her faithless lover. Susheela clamped her hands to her ears and padded through to the living room, swooning again at its pulverising claustrophobia. The living room was sparsely furnished. Each stick of furniture had been donated by various members of Robbie's family, resulting in a slapdash incongruity that jarred on the eye and, for Susheela, the soul. Day after day, she had to look at the monstrosity of a badly soiled, lime-green settee which dominated the room. It was too bulky for such a tight space and only added to her sense of enclosure. A trestle table draped with a large doily served as an ad hoc stand for their poky little TV. To the left of the telly, underneath the sill, was what Susheela jokingly referred to as the cultural corner. It consisted of a blue cane bookshelf filled with Susheela's nursing books and manuals. Next to that was a bulky, ugly stereogram, stacked with Robbie's records. Coming back into the main expanse of the room – or what passed for it – there was a floral lampshade and a three-bar fire (almost always switched off, though tonight it was defiantly on). A plastic-rimmed mirror above the fire amplified the general haphazardness of the room. The only item of furniture they'd bought themselves was a brown and beige Axminster offcut which they'd stretched to its limits, though not quite to the walls of the room. She felt the urge to pace up and down, worry loose some of the tightness in her chest, but the tiny floor allowed no more than two or three strides. She conceded defeat and slumped down on the couch next to her slumbering boy.

She buoyed at the sight of her son. His cheeks were puffed red and his nose stuffy from the artificial heat. She turned the fire down a bar and the room glowed apricot, but within moments she felt the dip in temperature and whacked the heat back up again. He was snoring gently on the couch, some wild dream flickering his eyelids. She smiled as she wondered what he was dreaming. Maybe it was Rama and Sita from the heroic adventures of Ramayana, or the monkey prince Sugriva. Often, when Robbie was at work, she'd light some incense sticks, rustle up a simple meal of roti canai and mulligatawny and recount the

29

ancient Hindu legends in her mother tongue. Even before Vincent could speak, she'd always spoken Tamil to him when they were alone. It was their special secret.

She lowered her head to her sleeping boy and inhaled his scent in two short draughts. His sweet, babyish smell rushed to her head, radiating through her like a glass of hot toddy. For a brief spell she was diverted from her woes, absorbed in the wonder of him. But while she marvelled at his beauty and felt weak with her love for him, the knots in her chest worked away, subconsciously tightening that constant stone in her guts reminding her of her heartache. She went through to the kitchen and sat in the dark. Not even the snow spattering the window could placate her. Her man was out there, somewhere – with another.

Five

The bitter northerly wind swept the snow right across the avenue, stacking it in huge billowing ripples. Banked ranks of council roofs were snowed under, almost cartoon-pretty in the blue-white night. Robbie felt a gush of nostalgia. It wasn't so very long ago he'd have been sick with excitement waking up to a scene like this. He transferred the two bags of hot food to one hand and bent down, scooping up a fistful of snow and hurling it at a road sign. He grinned to himself, satisfied by the thud of the snowball as it hit its target. At the bottom of Poplars Avenue he peeled off down the dark narrow cut of the walkway. A sprinkling of hoar frost blotted out the familiar daubing: 'If you want a nigger for a neighbour – vote Labour.'

Robbie marched past, singing to himself.

The walkway linked Orford's newest two estates, and cut a path right behind the low-rises. Robbie always felt odd passing so close, as though he were trespassing on people's private lives. Tonight, even later than usual, those lives seemed distilled in the late-night glow of their televisions and the dim band of yellow lighting spilling out from their windows. Yet it inspired him now, too. These were his kith and kin, and he aimed to do them proud. Passing right by a drunken argument, then a baby crying, the sweet blare of Motown, a midnight insomniac hoovering relentlessly, the clatter of a dustbin knocked to the floor, shouting and laughter – these were Robbie's people and this was the soundtrack to his life. He felt a new tune coming, and hummed it out loud, trying to keep it alive in his head.

The walkway gave out to one final clump of wasteland, and beyond it, home. Susheela. He smiled again and crunched his

31

way across the uneven padded earth, overtaking a hefty young lad cramming huge hunks of chips into his mouth. In the distance, in the town centre, a siren wailed, its howl soaring high above the tower blocks. Tonight, for once, it sounded gorgeous. Humming his tune, he tried to imagine his anthem, his hymn to the working classes with a siren as its intro. He left the patch and turned the corner into his street.

Susheela heard the front gate creak open. Her whole body slumped with the relief of it. She listened out for the clank of the gate being shut but there was nothing. He was drunk! Robbie always closed the little gate, whatever the weather. Her relief quickly gave way to indignation. Now that he was home safe, part of her wanted to punish him. She thought about creeping upstairs and feigning sleep, letting him know that she'd given up on their Saturday supper club long before he had. But the thought of him walking into an empty room and eating alone drove a stake through her heart. Besides, she could never carry Vincent upstairs in that short time. What would he think if he came home to find his little boy asleep on the couch? What kind of mother would abandon their son downstairs with the fire left on?

She pictured Robbie's squiffy eyes and the apologetic slope of his mouth as he fumbled for his keys, fingers lashed raw from the cold. She couldn't help smiling at the image, and just as quickly as it came her rash of anger slipped away. Now that he was back, she was able to find fun in the outlandish excesses of her paranoia. She slid the safety catch along its groove and set it free. She released the latch and was just about to tug the door wide open and surprise him when a menace of hushed voices stopped her in her tracks. She called out Robbie's name through the letter box. Her voice seemed to hang there, frail and scared, accentuating her feebleness, before drifting off into the night, unheard.

The voices came again and this time panic strangled her. She dared not move and was hardly able to edge towards the window. Only the tender sight of Vincent, innocent, asleep, pushed her on. Heart whamming in her ears, she peeled back an inch of curtain. She couldn't see a thing. The snow whirled around and a white crystal shimmer almost obliterated the window. She launched herself onto her tiptoes and craned her neck to spy out from the one corner of glass still free of the snowdrift, forcing her eyeballs as far right as they'd go, desperate for a view of the front of the house, terrified by what she might see. There was nobody there. But a blizzard of fresh footprints along her path confirmed her worst fears. She had not imagined it; there were people out there.

She stood stock-still in the apricot flush of the room and tried to calm herself with best case scenarios. It was kids, fired up on Saturday-night hormones and drink. They'd get bored in a moment and go. Intuitively though, she knew no teens would stay outside for devilment on a night like this. She heard the voices again. This time further away, it seemed – and fewer of them. Maybe they'd stumbled into the garden on their way home, bursting to piss away the night's beer. The sense of escape was fleeting though, immediately replaced by something much bigger, much worse. Robbie was still out there. He had not come home. The bomb had exploded.

She sighed out loud and thought about the best way to carry Vincent upstairs when all her woe was blasted away by the shock of sheer terror. There was a face. A horrible face. Pressed to the fanlight above the door, a bald, shaved dome with piggy-mean eyes glared in. She wanted to scream, to shriek out loud but nothing came. A thud at the door. They were trying to charge it open. With her hands trembling wildly, Susheela struggled to clip the safety latch back on. She left it dangling and useless, and instead turned her attention to Vincent, a shattering pain splintering her back as she scooped him up. Crazed, she looked

33

around her, took a step this way then changed her mind, stepped towards the bottom of the stairs, Vincent already starting to slip from her grasp. Boom! They were throwing themselves at the door. Her eyes fell upon the little cubbyhole under the stairs. She prised it open, heaving the vacuum cleaner to one side and laying Vincent down on the floor beside it. He stirred slightly, but did not wake. She closed the door and crept into the kitchen. Her head was racing, frantic. There seemed only one way ahead for her. With no telephone, she'd have to run out of the back door and scream until someone heard her.

Head banging with fright as she ransacked drawers and cupboards for the back-door key, she was shocked rigid by the smash of the window pane. A gloved hand reached round for the handle. Her last and only chance was to hack at the hand with the bread knife, but Susheela couldn't move an inch. She couldn't breathe. The man came in through the back door, clamped her mouth and dragged her back in a headlock. Another man came in, then another. The kitchen seemed to be full of them.

Enraged now, maddened at the invasion, she squirmed free and reached up for the frying pan. The first intruder – a stocky, ugly man – knocked the pan from her hand and dragged her back by the hair. The lino floor seemed to buffer the clang of the pan. Susheela found herself strangely grateful for that. She told herself that as long as Vincent slept through this, she would survive. She made up her mind to acquiesce, get it over with, get them out of here. Another arm held her at the belly while the pig-man squeezed so hard on her windpipe she could no longer breathe. She started to lose consciousness. She felt her eyes rolling like marbles across the ceiling, then nothing.

When she came round, she was splayed out on the living-room floor. Her arms and head hurt. Through the blur of her vision she could make out four men. The main man, the squat, pig-faced one looming over her, slowly, ritualistically removed his gloves. One of his hands was scarred, horrifically burnt. He seemed to revel in her disgust, stroking her face with his gnarled, stumpy fingers. His dome head glowed hot from the fire. Standing behind him were two men decked out in identical attire – black lace-up boots and zipped-up black jackets. A fourth boy stood guard at the curtains. He was just a boy. He was wearing this crazed expression but his eyes were fixed on hers beseechingly, almost desperate for forgiveness. As her senses reorientated, she sourced out the pains in her arms. There was a fifth man kneeling behind her, pinning her with the weight of his knees. Slowly, the night flashed before her in crystal-clear chronology. Everything suddenly made sense. Robbie was dead. She could feel the infallible certainty of this radiating from deep in her soul. These men had done him in and now they'd come for her. She knew why too. She'd seen these thugs before, around and about the estate and hanging in packs by the shops. She'd watched them file onto her bus like a small army, glowering at her and Vincent with naked revulsion. That time, she'd got off at the next stop, too frightened to stay and endure their staring. She hadn't told Robbie about it.

The man standing over her unzipped his jeans, and now her fate spun out in front of her, hurling her headlong towards its horrible and inevitable conclusion. What about the baby? They'd kill them both, Susheela and the baby, if they went through with this. She thought of Vincent growing up alone. No, no, no – not Vincent, he wouldn't make it; he wasn't strong enough, he was too soft for this world. But then her panic was obliterated and replaced by something far more ferocious – what if Vincent woke up? What if they found him? Surely there was no limit to the barbarity of men like these. She squeezed shut her eyes and made a bargain with God. She offered up her life and that of her unborn baby's in return for Vincent's safe and undisturbed passage through the horrors ahead.

35

The skinhead dipped a hand inside his trousers, pulling out a fat, limp dick. Unabashed in front of his accomplices, he kneaded his member, stretching it out and playing with it until it was harder. Whoever was squatted behind her laughed, and as he spoke she could feel the sour waft of drink in her face.

'Fuck d'you call that, Evo?' he scoffed. 'Just stick it in the bitch. Be the best she's ever had, anyway.'

There was a dull crack as pig-face, Evo, as she now supposed, leant forward and smacked him hard across his cheekbone. 'You prick! Names!' he hissed, his hot, fat head glowing red with ire. Susheela felt brief relief as his victim, the man who'd been kneeling on her arms, jumped up in pain and anger. He stormed to the other side of the room, holding his face. A young lad, who she now saw had a wound to his nose, dried blood clogging his nostril, went to his aid. A fourth lad with a spotty face stepped between the two parties.

'Come on,' he tried to reason. 'Fuck all the silly shite off. Gypo Fitzgerald's gonna be back any minute. Let's just torch the fucking joint and get out.'

Susheela squeezed shut her eyes in gratitude. Robbie was safe. He was on his way back to her. This would all be over soon and if God willed she came through it, she promised that things would be different. From now on, things were going to be good – always.

Evo stood back, his piggy eyes gleaming. 'Better and better. We'll give the IRA cunt his, too.'

'Don't talk daft, Evo.'

'Names!'

The young kid hung his head. The spotty youth spoke up. 'Fitzgerald'll fucking murder us and you fucking know it.'

Evo shook his head slowly, disappointed at the mettle of his men. 'None of you twats is going anywhere till we've taught this filthy little slag a lesson.' He kicked Susheela in the side.

She bit down hard on her lip.

'Oi! Open your eyes you fucking Paki bitch. Open your fucking eyes.' He kicked her again. Two of his mates winced and turned away. 'Look at me.'

He pushed his penis towards her face. She forced her eyeline upwards. He smiled, horribly. 'Now, see this white cock. Take a good look at it. There, good girl. That's a white cock, that is. It's quite beautiful, isn't it? Would you like to kiss it?' He looked to his gang, waiting for them to laugh. One or two of them managed a sneer. He turned back to Susheela.

'Now listen, you slag. Listen good. What I'm going to do now, is I'm going to teach you a lesson. And you must learn this lesson. You hear me, Paki? Because if you . . .' He stepped back to reinforce his sermon with another hard kick to the groin, sending a shock of pain ripping through her abdomen. She groaned, tried to swallow it, anxious not to make any noise at all. Surely Robbie would be home soon now. Surely? Evo crouched now, pushing his face up to hers. 'If you and your horrible gypo so-called husband carry on swamping this estate with your fucking mongrels, I will knife your fucking womb right out. So take a good look at this pure English cock, and make fucking sure it's the last time you ever see one.'

With a thin, psychotic smile he dropped to his knees, dragged down her pyjamas. With his coarse, hairy gut grazing her pregnant belly, he entered her hard and began fucking her, fast.

Susheela clenched her fists, willing her senses to shut down, feel nothing. All that was left was sound. As he thrust and thrust and thrust, a strange, high-pitched whimpering came from him. There was an awful slurping from between her thighs. A violent contraction deep in her womb. Her head lolled sideways as she felt herself starting to slip away. So this was it, then. They were not going to kill her after all. Robbie was still out there, alive. Susheela was already dead.

Six

Susheela told him it had been a break-in. Reflexively, instinct-ively, she knew her young husband would not be able to cope with, would never recover from, the horror of a rape. So she bought some time – Ellie's birth saw to that – and got her story straight for Robbie and the police: she'd been upstairs, removing her make-up. She'd heard a noise from outside. She came down, expecting to see Robbie. There was an intruder in her living room. He was wearing a balaclava. Fearful for her small boy, she confronted the intruder. He manhandled her, but fled. The shock had precipitated her into labour.

Robbie took it from this that she blamed him, resented him for not being there. In the days and weeks that followed, he never told her how close he got to the big time that night. What would be the point? She'd dredge up some residue of enthusiasm from what remained of her soul. She'd smile through the fear and pain, badger him, nag at him, force him out to meet his fate and make their fortune. But how could he leave her like that? Like this. She was terrified to be left on her own. How could he put on a show, knowing his frail wife was cowering in the dark back home? And even if he did tell her, told her about Dickie Vaughan's offer, would it make things better? He couldn't see it. To Susheela – and who could blame her? – it was black and white. If Robbie had got back home on time, the burglar would not have struck. It was as plain as that, and Robbie wore it on his heart like a scalding cross.

He was almost right. Susheela did blame him. She resented the part that Robbie played in her night of horror, but it was nothing to do with his coming home late. What she wanted was to be *with* him. She wanted, always, to be by his side. That night she should have been there at St Stephen's, if not only to stave off the come-ons from the local women, then at least to try and make friends of them. But instead what was happening, more and more, was that he shut her away – she was sure of that now. She understood. He wanted to protect her. And it suited him not to have to challenge all the questioning stares. If she wasn't there by his side, he didn't have to set his face hard, scare off the monsters before they struck. And the more she stayed indoors, the more she understood it had ever been thus, with her and Robbie. Those trips out to the countryside – she wouldn't change a thing about her early trysts with the love of her life, but he was able to love her out there, love her properly, because there was no one there to stop him. It was the path of least resistance. So she stayed in. She stayed indoors and wished she'd never let him fall for her. On her own, she'd be fine. She always had been. For a young man, though – for a feckless kid with all the will and the power of his own dreams – this was all too much. Could she run away and start again and set him free? But as soon as she thought it, she was crippled with doubt and grief. She could never see herself apart from Robbie – not now. But could they ever make this work? That was the part she really couldn't see at all.

Robbie sweated salt and blood to keep house and home together. It was him who got up through the night to tend to Vincent's night traumas and Ellie's feeds, it was him who bathed them and put them to bed and indulged them with enough love and fun to compensate for their mother's melancholy. Then when Susheela's maternity leave elapsed and she made no gesture to return to work he maintained a silent and supportive front. Her irrational clinginess demanded that she was not left alone after dark and so, unflinchingly, he gave up his residency at

39

St Stephen's. It had been a tidy little earner; nice money for days out, clothes for Susheela and takeaways but with another mouth to feed it formed an indispensable part of their income. Its absence meant longer hours for Robbie on the factory line. He swapped his eight-hour shift for a twelve-hour one. He worked six days a week. Robbie was exhausted. More than once, as he cycled to work in the morning, he'd be jolted out of his torpor by the white blare of a wagon as he drifted off and strayed into the other side of the road. And by the time he reached work he was too sleep starved to perform the same auto-function he'd performed for seven years. Twice in one month he'd added the incorrect ratio of treatment to the powders he presided over, causing the whole three floors of the Metso plant to stutter to a halt. Tiredness soon usurped his every bodily need. It overrode the unbearable build-up and longing in his groins, it leached away hunger causing his lean, brawny body to soften, his muscles to atrophy. His appearance and hygiene deteriorated. His bus-red hair grew lank and dull and days-old stubble sprouted in unruly spokes across his chin. His olfactory compass shut down so he could no longer smell his daughter's sick curd on the cuffs of his overalls or the fetid rot of his own tired breath. He felt himself held in suspension, waiting for some impulse to jar him from the dehumanised pulse of his life. His quiet, industrious resolve was nothing short of miraculous. Only the cruel unrealised conclusion of *that* night came close to breaking him.

During those first few weeks Vaughan had chased him like a lovelorn teenager, calling him at work, snowing him with promises of cruises and studio sessions with producers, all with glib showbiz names – Mikey Vegas, Don Emmery, Louis Lavelle. He talked about the possibility of a tour with Matt Monro and Shirley Bassey, and a season at the Talk of the North. He promised him all his aching adolescent dreams and more, and Robbie's heart warred. All of these things involved time – time away from work, time away from his babies, time away from his needy, splintered wife. But if he could just fan Vaughan's enthusiasm long enough for Susheela to pull herself together . . .

But Susheela showed no sign of improvement and gradually, inevitably, Vaughan's enthusiasm began to wilt under the weight of his own impatience. There was only so much chasing a man of his calibre could do, and when he turned up unannounced at St Stephen's one night and discovered Robbie was no longer performing, he gave up the chase. Whatever his reasons, however sick his wife, the lad wasn't devoted enough. And in the brutal and capricious world of show business, devotion was everything.

Robbie accepted his fate and backed off too. He conceded that his big moment had come and gone and cast his dreams loose to the wasteland of his youth, barely grieving for them before they shrivelled and rotted into poisoned stumps of memory. And though his heart ached for her, Robbie couldn't help but feel resentful. He simply could not come to terms with Susheela's zombie-like response, the way she wrapped herself in this punitive pall, rarely stepping outside the coop of the house. So many times he would arrive at the front door, already bent to the screams of his baby daughter inside as his key grated in the lock, her backside raw from the sting of her sodden nappy while her mother lay catatonic on the couch.

What hurt most was the gradual grinding down of any magic in their lives until what remained was drudgery, duty and work, that killing routine of early start, long days at the conveyor belt and deadly nothingness back home. He felt for her, he wanted to make it go away. But she was doing it to herself – the grudging, laboured way she toiled through motherhood, seldom smiling, rarely even seeing her children. Truly, she was a shadow of the girl he'd fallen for.

Even her accent changed. It was as though she was now looking to provoke contempt. For as long as he'd known her, Susheela had dressed like the girls she worked with. He knew she didn't love it, but she'd eat the same diet of fish fingers, mince and potatoes, Sunday roast. The more time they spent together, the more she absorbed his parochial ways. He recalled with affection the time he'd found her in front of the mirror, combing her hair, practising her local accent. The flattened vowels stretched her face so tight she looked demented – like a soprano practising her arpeggios. 'Aye-yoh, luv. Ow are yoh?' She altered the elastic pucker of her lips for the reply. 'Oh not bad yuh know. Ow about yuhself, luv?'

Robbie had thrown his head back at that and roared with laughter. But in the wake of the break-in, her adorably exaggerated colloquialisms went into retreat. Back came the sing-song staccato of her Malay-Tamil English. Her voice swooped up and down like a plucked sitar, placing its emphasis on the wrong stress – deliberately, he sometimes thought. So her favourite programme was '*Sella*'-*britee Squares*. Birthday cake was birthday *cake*. He knew it – she was making her point. She was needling him – the man who had failed to protect her.

He watched on helplessly as she receded into a world that was alien to him. She reclaimed the kitchen as her lair. She'd disappear into its cache for long brooding hours, fussing over huge cauldrons of rank-hued food that she ate in her hideout in silence. She refused to see any of the neighbours who dropped in with gifts and warm wishes for the new addition, yet she always made time for Mrs Ling. Robbie could hear them above the TV, clanging pots and muttering in some garbled language. Occasionally he would hear laughter and his heart would skitter with hope. But alone, she could barely muster a smile for him. The food she cooked would fester on the stove for days, sweating from the walls, fouling her breath, staining her fingers. Bubbling oil slimed vapours onto the neighbour's windows. She fed it to

Vincent, served cold between two slabs of bread. He could taste it in the teat of Ellie's bottle, taste it in his toothpaste. It made him ill.

He fought back where he could. He shortened her name to Sheila which, in spite of its primness, she seemed to love. It was one of only a handful of occasions he could think of in recent times when, in spite of herself, she'd given in to that radiant, face-splitting smile of hers. Suddenly she was reaching for the phone they'd had installed, making wholly unnecessary calls to his mother, or Dr Eccles, or Mrs Ling.

'Sheila here,' she'd say, then try and think of something to justify the call. But they were rare, such moments of levity. Sheila was not Sheila. She wasn't the woman he'd fallen for. Somehow, somewhere deep within, her light had been extinguished as a result of that break-in.

Oh, how he lamented it, and he'd do anything to make things right again. But the more she shut him out, the less he could find her, what there was of her – so how could he bring her back? And the more he looked into her eyes, the more he saw and felt her anger; not at a hard and unyielding England, out there, but at him. At Robbie. She hated him. And she was getting back at him any way she could.

Seven

A whole year had passed yet the events of that night seemed sorer than ever. The house seethed with triggers that exploded without warning. A sudden noise or the sweep of a shadow along the window and the whole room would foam with her attacker's presence. That patch of carpet which had been scrubbed and bleached to an abrasive scalp would leak his vile spoor into the air. Sometimes Sheila would walk downstairs into the lounge and he would be standing there, his bestial gaze rippling in the orange glow of the fire. She kept the TV on all through the day, its cathode blue beating a constancy through the morning's chat shows and the afternoon's soaps while she waited and waited and waited for a day of reckoning. Secretly, she fantasised they would strike again elsewhere but that this time they would be incarcerated, and this news, like the pulling of a tooth, would cure her completely.

Days, weeks and months dragged by. The local papers yielded nothing. It seemed she would remain stranded for ever in the horror of that one night. She would never move on. She floated around as if in a dream. At times she wondered if it had happened at all, or if it *had* only been a break-in, and the horrors she'd imagined were hallucinations triggered by the pre-term shock of pregnancy. Wasn't that how the body coped in extreme states of emergency? By subjugating physical pain to psychological suffering?

It was only in sleep when she had no power over her thoughts that the truth would peel back and expose its naked kernel. It would yank her wide awake. It was no hallucination. It happened.

In her own gentle way Sheila let it be known that she no

longer wished – if she ever had at all – to raise her children in Orford. It was time to move on. And even to a local lad like Robbie, who often struggled to see beyond the romance of his gutsy neighbourhood, a fresh start made sense. He yearned to be rid of the pall that now hung above them, and he wasn't so blinded by his love for these streets as to see how much they were changing. Sheila had a point. It hurt him to think it, but Orford was feral. He shuddered when he thought of the boots and brickbats awaiting Vinnie in big school. And did he really want the young guttersnipes that patrolled the estates pursuing his teenage daughter? The more he thought about it, the more he realised that it was the only way forward. Yes, times were hard right now with only the one set of wages coming in, but if they tightened their belts another hole, for just a little while longer, they'd soon have enough for a deposit on a house.

Since Vinnie's arrival, Robbie had been secretly salting off a chunk of his wages each week, building a little nest egg for his son's future. And then when Ellie came along he was determined to give them both the head start in life that he'd never had. As a boy, Robbie had rarely stayed in one school for more than six months. His father, an itinerant blacksmith, paid little regard for education, and at thirteen, Robbie was sent out to work. Because of this, he could barely read, and his writing – a bespoke system of hieroglyphics legible only to him – as good as determined his job on the factory line. For his babies, though, things would be different. They would see out their education in its entirety. They would be the first Fitzgeralds to go to university. But as Sheila's depression deepened and her reclusiveness began to impinge on the kids' well-being – she was afraid to take them anywhere in daylight now without Robbie by her side and even during the long hot summer months they remained tethered to the TV – his thoughts veered more and more towards the rash of newbuilds springing up on the other side of the ship canal.

45

That first time they'd ventured out into the suburbs on his motorbike, Sheila had shouted for him to pull over as they cut through one of the new estates. Robbie took it from her bewildered expression that she was as disgusted by its ready-made uniformity as he was.

'Where is this place?'

'Thelwall,' he scoffed. 'I know. Isn't it just?' He followed her gaze across the rude expanse of gleaming three-bedroom semis, gobbling up the greenbelt at breakneck pace. But far from being repulsed, Sheila was smiling her wide-eyed smile, utterly impervious to the irony in his voice. She was smitten.

'Oh Robbie! It's beautiful,' she purred.

It was all he could do to bite back his disappointment and return the wistful expression.

So when she suggested moving somewhere safer, somewhere *nicer,* a place where people wouldn't stare, where she and her babies might be accepted, Robbie knew exactly the kind of place she had in mind. And not so long back he would have told her in his half-bantering, half-chiding tone that such places didn't exist. Not in Warrington, not in England. And contrary to what she supposed, the sleepy backwaters of Thelwall would be even less forgiving to a family like the Fitzgeralds. But now he too craved the sense of constancy that this brash, northern pocket no longer yielded. Robbie was beat. He was miserable and he wanted his wife back. He knew what he had to do.

Part Two

Thelwall, Warrington, 1981

One

A Sunday, late in August. First light was starting to filter through their meagre curtains, refracting mottled shades of pink around the room. An alarm clock sputtered its fractious buzz, luminous flashing digits clashing with the mellow shades of dawn. For Susheela – Sheila, as she was now known – this creeping daylight signalled the start, not the end of sleep. Since Ellie's birth, since the incident, she had not slept a whole night, unbroken. Even after the move away from Orford she was still haunted, not so much by their faces, which by now had morphed into one mean-eyed, beastly blur, nor even their deeds, from which she was somehow able to detach herself. No, it was their words that would still drift through her subconscious, sitting her up, turning her soul cold. If she allowed herself to lapse, to drift, to take her eye off the picture for more than a moment, those deathly words would seep back into her thoughts and dreams like a final, deadly verdict. 'If you carry on swamping this estate with your fucking mongrels, I will knife your fucking womb out!'

She stifled a whimper and tried to force her eyes closed, fight off the nightmare. The alarm clock drilled on.

Robbie prised an eye open, reached out and silenced the shrill siren with a slap. He groaned as the first ripples of a migraine hit. The stale, heavy air of the bedroom snagged in his nostrils, air fouled by their slumbering emissions, the sweat and gas of too much food and drink. With an almighty heave of motivation he propelled himself up and out of bed, onto the cushioned fleece of the new carpet. His tongue was thick and dry, his mouth clogged with some glutinous moraine. He coughed up a chunky

49

stool of phlegm, stole a glance over his shoulder at his wife and, satisfied she was still sleeping, spat it into a half-drunk mug of cold coffee. His head ached madly.

Mornings were no good for Robbie. He could no longer simply lurch out of bed and steam headlong into the day after a night's drinking. Nor could he get by on the minimal sleep of his teens. As he sped away from his mid-twenties and trudged grudgingly towards his thirties these hangovers intensified. They were spiteful, draining affairs that could no longer be tempered with a fry-up and a mug of sugary tea. But at least he didn't have to work today. At least he'd be spared the claustrophobic pall of the factory line pulverising his hangover into a grey and debilitating depression. Soon he would be out there in the wide-open expanses, the lean dawn air pumping his lungs clean, leaching the impurities from his veins. And, without work to drag him down, he could almost relish the scourge of his hangover, that slightly unhinged feeling it gave him, emotions keenly vaulting from one extreme to another. A stinking hangover like this was not without its compensations. Later, he could salt himself away and take full advantage of the next-day horniness that always came after a heavy drinking session. He wouldn't have to hide himself in the shabby surrounds of the work toilets, calendars so defaced by grubby hands and minds that there wasn't a nipple to be seen. He'd be able to take his time – hatch up the plot and the cast of his fantasy in advance. After tea, he intended to leave Sheila and the kids with *Black Beauty*, run himself a hot, deep Radox bath and abandon himself completely to the ancient and venerable rite of self-abuse.

He pulled the covers back over his wife's bare shoulders. She lay dead still, a globe of white eyeball staring out from a half-closed lid. Even now, his heart lurched when he found her like this, stone asleep with her eyes open. The first time, soon after Ellie's birth, he'd sincerely believed she'd died in her sleep, and still he wasn't used to the sight. As gently as he was able, he took up her wrist in his hand, slid two fingers across the faint green vines that fed her palm and felt for a pulse. Feeling nothing, he pressed down harder, this time shocking her awake.

'NO!' she screamed.

Realising she was safe, that it was Robbie, she looked relieved, then foolish, then moved to anger in swift succession. She snatched back her arm, muttering as she flipped herself over and away from him, burying her head in the pillow. Robbie stuttered his apologies. He stooped, kissed her brow and stole softly out of the room. When he looked back on her from the doorway she was already sound asleep again, her slender shoulders once more exposed, juddering with the horror of her dreams. He hung his head in sorrow for her. The move to Thelwall was supposed to help medicate all that – the horrors, the flashbacks, the nightmares – and perhaps it would, in time. He hoped so. Without the gigs to beef up his pay, the mortgage was already more than he could afford. But the sight of Sheila lying there, tiny and scared, bore out the wisdom of his big decisions. No way could he leave her alone at night. Not even here.

Time was moving quickly – the sun would soon be rising, sloughing off the last vestiges of dawn. There'd be a brief lull, a beautiful suspension of nothingness where nature drew breath before it roused the new day. Robbie cranked up his pace. They'd need to move quickly, he and his little girl, so they could be out there, racing through the damp fields to meet it head-on.

He went to get their uniforms 'yoomifors', as Ellie called their romping outfits – two sets of identical jeans, cotton vests and lumberjack shirts hanging in the immersion heater cupboard. He grinned at the thought of his pretty, boyish girl as he slipped into his jeans and vest, leaving Ellie's clothes to warm a while longer. He continued dressing as he ran down the stairs, pausing halfway to kick his arms into the sleeves of his already-buttoned

51

shirt and pull his head through. The cool expanse of the kitchen's floor tiles shocked his bare feet, jolting him with gentle fire like the electrified fences of his boyhood. He glugged two full glasses of water, flicked the kettle on and ran the blind up. A gust was shivering the branches, pinning leaves to the window, still green. Somewhere down the road a shed door was slamming and slamming. Robbie smiled again. Ellie would be beside herself. She loved the wind. Once, last year, they'd seen a hawk, hovering on the thermals of a gust, then plummeting a hundred, two hundred feet, falling like a stone before soaring up to the clouds once again. She was entranced by it. He'd told her it was an eagle and for months that was all she could think about. Every book, every story had to have mention of the mystic golden warrior birds, preferably those that could talk and were inclined to give Ellie Fitzgerald rides around the world. Soon she'd be out there, arms spread out against the squall as she ran down the hillocks, pretending she was 'a ego'. His heart swelled with his love for her.

He squatted down and lit the oven with a match. The gas hissed, resisted the flame then, reluctantly, caught fire, limp and blue for a moment before flaring up and sending Robbie jumping from its fierce cobalt furnace. He stayed there for a moment or two, warming his hands till the heat sapped the chill from the marrow of his bones. He took a foil-clad tray of pre-baked horse chestnuts and slid it into the lower cradle of the oven. While they were warming, he filled a plastic bag with the vegetable shavings Shelia collected throughout the week, then went to wake his girl.

She was snoring gently. She slept in the way that only a child can, with her head nestled in the palm of one hand, smooth legs bent at the knees and splayed out at right angles and her mouth tilted up at the ceiling, wide open. Robbie was smitten with a strong paternal impulse to leave her sleeping. But in that strange way that one's active thoughts often seem to infiltrate the passive recesses of a slumbering mind, Ellie was suddenly wide awake, dragging her little head up, her eyes large and accusatory.

'Is it time now?' she asked, springing out of bed.

Robbie took her tiny frame in his arms and hugged her tight. He planted a kiss on her forehead and helped her dress. She wriggled into her tiny jeans and grinned her gappy smile at the toasty warm touch of her socks and vest. But when it came to the ritual of her shoes, his little caramel kid had a point to prove. She pushed him away, and head bent studiously to the task, her careful little fingers picked at the laces of her imitation Nature Trekkers. 'My can do it-ah!' She twisted her head round to it, seeking his approval. 'My am a big boy!'

Again, Robbie's heart swooned as he fished up his little girl in one arm and blew raspberries all over her tummy. 'Big girl, Ellie! Yes? Ellie is a big girl!'

The partners in crime tiptoed downstairs, shushing each other theatrically at each creak of the floorboards.

They shut the door quietly and headed off. The light was still weak as Robbie squinted up to see what the day had in store, the first strains of sunlight presaged by lean skies and streaky cloud, stretched chewing-gum thin by the receding winds. A milk float whirred past and Ellie raced to skip alongside it, a bag of chestnuts and a bag of shavings flapping from either hand. These early morning adventures with Ellie were the very best thing in his life right now, but they always came with a heady, heavy nostalgia, a sense of the best already galloping by. Not just a mourning for his wild youth, but a realisation that these golden moments with Ellie were priceless, too. Even as they crossed the main road and headed for the fields, he squeezed her little hand, keenly aware that this couldn't last for ever.

Vincent perched on the sill of his bedroom window tracing tenta-

53

tive shapes in the condensation. He made a heart, then changed it into a flower. He watched his father and sister head off down the street, bruised yet vaguely happy for them. They'd have much more fun together, just the two of them. He'd only hold them back. If it wasn't his asthma it would be the hay fever, or his pungent allergy to horses or some other ailment sure to blight their progress. He watched the balmy summer wind breathe softly into Ellie's carrier bags and smiled for his little sister, feeling a faint but heroic throb of martyrdom. She'd been born lucky, Ellie. She wasn't even brown – not really. Whereas Vincent had always felt the sting of the glares, or the mere frisson of curiosity his mother and he provoked with each trip out to the shops, Ellie's colouring was subtle, exotic, beautiful. She was going to be a beauty – if ever she'd let herself. With her grazes to the knees, her bruised shins and bitten nails, her hacked, boyish haircut, self-styled and delivered of her own blunt scissors, Ellie Fitzgerald was a tough little tar baby. Yet with her pale green eyes, her father's button nose and her long, slender, Caramac limbs, she had it all. Vincent's eyeline stayed with them right to the very end of the road where they faded into finger puppets and slipped out of sight. He wiped the flower away and stepped carefully down from his sill, lying on his back on his bed, hands behind his head, deep in thought.

Robbie and Ellie passed through a battery of newbuilds, each identical to their own – streets and streets of three-bedroom semis, neat and compact and safe. All the curtains were drawn. Apart from the low moan of the morning wind, everything was still. Ellie chattered gaily, pausing only to take breath or wipe a slug of snot from her nose, sending carrot and apple peel spilling from the carrier bag. Her father listened solemnly, fists shoved deep in his pocket, his head bowed in deference to the rising sun.

They picked up the ship canal path, the water black and

fathomless as though the night had sunk into it. They followed the lichen-strewn path through the stinking shanks of factory land where the ground was flat and charred, littered with crushed cans and burnt-out bonfires, the detritus of another Saturday night. They passed under the motorway bridge where the air was cooler and the water rippled with each passing rumble from the carriageway above. A little further on, the path curved away from the canal, and the landscape shook itself free from the dirty grip of Warrington's industrial heartlands. Ahead, a green and yellow counterpane of fields led gently up to the knoll and the woods beyond, which, to Ellie, were heaven.

From the little knoll the only evidence of that other, man-made world were the tower blocks that studded the horizon. When he'd first arrived in the suburbs, Robbie had found those bleak grey silos oddly reassuring, a reminder that all he knew and loved was a bus ride away. Now, he chose not to see these sedentary giants, as though his mind and its windows were closed to that chapter of his past. Sometimes, like now, he was able to think back on it without regret – the night that Dickie Vaughan came to town. He'd had to make a decision and, by and large, he was satisfied with it. How could he not be out here, out in the elements with his plucky little dreamer? Would he have had this if he'd been away on tour somewhere, off being a star? No, he wouldn't. Robbie Fitzgerald was glad of the sacrifice he'd made.

He stood back, inhaled hard, dragging the distant vista inside of him and holding it down. Once, not so long ago, this had been him and her – Robbie and Sheila. Now it was father and daughter, and he couldn't quite fathom how, or why, or when. It was happening, though. It was happening all around him and somehow, today, it no longer daunted him. Breathing in the sights and scents of the awakening earth, Robbie felt inspired. This, right now, was how freedom tasted.

The sun finally burnt off the cloud, sending the new day smashing down on them, at last. The fields flickered silver and the air reverberated with the lowing of cattle and birds singing their swansong to summer. They stopped at a hollow for their final treat – sweet, baked chestnuts, and a hand-rolled cigarette for Robbie. He winked at his small girl as he fixed the papers and tamped down the tobacco. Ellie picked up a short twig, pretending to light it so she, too, could end the morning with a smoke. She lay back in the hollow and turned towards Robbie, twig poised carefully between two fingers, her face glowing with the absolute certainty that only she was privy to this furtive pocket of his universe.

Every Sunday lunchtime Sheila cooked Robbie his favourite dish of mixed grill – or London grill, as Jean Bishop from next door had corrected her. To Sheila the sizzling platter of egg, tomatoes, mushrooms and the various meats looked pretty much like the standard British fry-up, but Jean had been good enough to enlighten her. 'It's all about quality and aspiration,' she'd smiled. 'If you want it to be a fry-up, a fry-up it shall be. If you want it to be any old mixed grill – fine. But if, like the head chef at the Savoy, you aspire to serve the perfect London grill . . . well. For starters, never source your meats from the Co-op. Ideally, you should only use a master butcher for your sausages, gammons and so on. I mean look at . . .' Unable to finish the sentence she'd jerked her head towards the Andersons next door and fluttered her eyelids in disdain. 'Everything's pre-packed or out of a can. Honestly!'

Sheila had blinked and nodded, but nothing was sinking in. She was staring at the whisker springing from the mole on Jean's chin.

'Are you listening to me, Sheila? Never overwhelm the plate . . . plenty of space between the meats . . . give them their own identity within the blend . . . use a bigger plate if necessary . . . that way each component gets its own say. Your palate is drawn to them as discrete culinary entities, it tackles them as distinctive flavours yet each pulls its weight towards the overall, unified ideal of the London grill sensation. It's all the rage in Didsbury.'

Sheila's head had spun as she tried to process these rapid bullets of information. She'd left the Bishops bewildered, but with a beginner's grasp of the rudiments of London grilling nonetheless, and in truth, she liked the sound of it. She brought out the biggest plates they had – only ever used for Christmas dinner previously, but whose appearance was welcomed by Robbie for the dual stroke of deriving extra value for money from their additional use, while simultaneously allowing more room for more meat. She elaborated by adding black pudding, pig's livers and special jumbo frankfurter sausages sourced from Loke's, the venerable butcher's shop in Latchford village. She'd serve it all up with oven-hot cob bread and a fry-up of onions, mushrooms and diced potatoes.

Robbie had beamed with real pleasure the first time she presented him with her new discovery. He loved it, and quickly made clear that this would now be a Sunday fixture. Indeed, the only thing he couldn't quite come to terms with was the fancy new name she'd bestowed upon it. 'London Grill!' The nose had wrinkled up in snarling disapproval as he spat the words out. 'Where d'you get that one from?'

'Don't be shooting the messenger,' Sheila had protested, turning away from him and ducking back down to the grill to avoid the stab of his sarcastic gaze. She'd spooned up the remainder of the splitting, bubbling grilled tomatoes, sprinkled a little chopped parsley on top and brought them to his plate. She could tell from his face he was sorry. He hated hurting her. She'd taken a breath and given it another go. 'That's just what they're calling it at the Savoy, that's all.' She looked up, melting big brown eyes pleading with him to come round, agree, see what everyone could see. 'It's all the rage in Didsbury.'

A pregnant pause had followed, and with it she knew she'd lost. Far from joining in with the bright, mobile folk of Hayes Close, Robbie was slamming the shutters closed, blinking angrily, cross at his wife's gullibility, her innocence, her willingness to like these people and give them credence and space in her life. Willing him to let it go, turn his attention to the succulent gammon and hissing sausage, she'd rattled the grill pan, turned over imaginary slices of bacon, her shoulder blades clenched together in anticipation of Robbie's new attack.

'That's what they're calling it where? Who's *they*, She? Hey? When I can meet them? Cos they must be a pretty clever bunch, changing an old classic like mixed grill into . . . what d'you call it? Savoy Sizzle? Didsbury Dip? By God, Sheila . . .'

And she had realised that, far from being intimidated by him it was she who was angry. She'd put time and love and plenty of planning into that meal and he hadn't even taken a mouthful. She'd banged the grill door shut and, jutting out her jaw, she'd turned to him, ready to fight back. But she couldn't. Seeing that wrinkled, furious nose and the reddening face she hadn't so much feared him as pitied him. And without being able to compute it or articulate it, she'd been able to work out the nature of his contempt and, in a way, empathise with it. In simplest terms, she'd sensed her husband was scared. Sheila had raised a neat, puckish eyebrow and, as she did often now when she needed to combat his ire, she'd humoured him. 'Call it what you want, darling. Whatever's easiest to swallow.'

Mixed grill, London grill, Fitzgerald fry-up – Vincent and Ellie came to relish the Sunday treat as much as their father (even if they did obliterate it with ketchup). But for her own part, Sheila might as well have been chomping on cardboard. Her palate still remained impervious to the charms of English cuisine. Its blandness, quite frankly, depressed her. But aside from fretting about her own palate, Sheila was starting to worry for her family's health. Since she'd moved to this country she'd endured three fillings, two abscesses and at least four bouts of flu. Her hair was starting to lose its newspun glossy sheen and, if she left it unpampered for more than a day or two, her skin would dry as scaly as a snake's. Back home in Malaysia she'd been taught to gauge her health from the residue on her tongue. Amah made them scrape regularly, in front of her: a transparent and slender deposit usually denoted good health, while anything too white or gluey saw you hauled off to the local *bomoh*. Since moving to England her tongue had told its own story, and she became more and more convinced that diet was to blame. Vincent's entire childhood had been blighted by poor health – eczema, asthma, hay fever, colds, tonsillitis, glandular fever. Every bug and virus saw him poleaxed. She was no dietician, but she felt certain that a little chilli, a pinch of garlic and a sprinkling of ginger formed a better barrier to lurgies than chips, tinned sausage and those beans they had to have with everything, livid vermillion and tasting of nothing but sugar. But Robbie's palate had become so frigid of late that he could now smoke out even the pinch of chilli she sneaked into the bolognaise. He seemed determined to reject anything remotely exotic and, given that he'd even begun prodding at his plum tomatoes with suspicion last Sunday, exotic was a broad church indeed.

The more Sheila had to tailor the family meal to suit Robbie, the more she craved the kick and rush of spice. She was like a heroin addict, publicly abasing herself to feed her cravings. And it was an addiction – the more spice she consumed, the more she needed to slake her hunger. There was no rationale to it, no pattern. A craving could overcome her as she was doing the dishes, walking Vincent to school, brushing her teeth. Her attacks were so invasive, so all-consuming that she carried around with her a bottle of West Indian pepper sauce. On the top deck of the bus, she'd dip into her bag, eyes darting around her, stealthily unscrew the cap, trace the rim of the bottle with her trembling finger and, head hung low for secrecy and out of the sheer shame of it, she'd bring the smarting fix to her already tingling lips. The high was instantaneous, supreme – and all too brief.

Today, though – today she would try. She'd prepare the mother of all grills for the whole family, for today was a landmark day, a very big day indeed in their developing life as the Fitzgeralds of Hayes Close, Thelwall. Today, Robbie and Ellie would be coming home from town in a car. Careful not to spoil the surprise, she hadn't pushed him too hard on the basic information. So long as it started first time, didn't guzzle the petrol and wasn't too dull in colour, Sheila was happy. A nice Vauxhall Nova would be close to her dream car or, if they could push the boat out, the big Citroën family saloon like the Gibbs' would be perfect. This, as far as Sheila could discern, was the key prerequisite: it had to be a saloon car. To her heart and mind, that beguiling word summed up everything one could desire in a vehicle – space, comfort, reliability, economy. Soon they too would own a saloon. She could hardly stop giggling at the thought of it. Wait till Jean Bishop saw their new car – she wouldn't be able to hide her envy!

Two

Robbie and Ellie returned from their walk, retrieved his bike from the shed and took from beneath the tool box a brown envelope packed with notes. Robbie was giddy as they set off towards town to purchase his first car. He'd passed his test easily, first time. Unlike his pals and fellow apprentices though, Robbie could never quite bring himself to pay good money for a boxish old banger; if he couldn't afford to put some romance, some beauty into his choice of wheels he'd rather not bother at all. If he couldn't have a Jag, he'd have a BSA, or a Triumph motorbike instead. And if he hadn't made that choice, then he'd never have won Sheila's heart. It was that simple, and he smiled at the thought.

He'd spotted it on his way back from work last week, gleaming nobly, if rather tucked away in the furthest corner of the dealer's forecourt. Surely it couldn't be? Not for that price! He checked there were no predatory salesmen around and freewheeled over to the car – a beautiful, regal, pebble-grey XJ6. It was love at first sight, a magnificent, pristine, feline 1970 Jag with a sumptuous, red leather interior and a mahogany finish. He'd always fantasised that one day he'd find himself cruising through the Dingle Peninsular in the racing-green E-Type the royalties from his chart-topping record had afforded, roof down, the damp and peaty air thrashing through his tousled hair. But the longer the holidays between that particular daydream, the more remote his chances seemed of ever laying his hands on a Jag. He'd given up on it, more or less, and had never even considered the more practical XJ6 as a possible compromise – until he found himself gazing upon a pebble-grey Series One with red leather interior! She really was the answer to all his prayers. With her spacious interior, low-slung bumper and rare manual overdrive gearbox she was a family car as much as she was a wayfarer's plaything. She was roomy, comfortable yet elegant, mature but with a hint of the family's bohemian bloodline. And she was nine hundred quid – money he could just about lay his hands on.

Ellie rode on her cushion, strapped to the crossbar with a tie. In spite of his general good cheer, Robbie pre-empted the stares from the straggle of passing cars with his customary glower. Drivers and passengers always reacted in the same way. Before they could check themselves, there was always that moment of stark, unstinting honesty as their aesthetic sensibilities were thrown into revolt. They could never quite decide what was confronting them – deformity, or exquisite beauty. The combination of Robbie's shock-white skin and vermilion hair snagged the eyeline like a flare in the sky. It seized their attention for a split, instinctive second then let it go in a flash, too. But alongside his little girl, Robbie became a spectacle. The pair of them, side by side, held people transfixed. Next to her father, Ellie's fudge skin seemed to darken deeper brown, and Robbie's alabaster face blanched yet whiter still. They clashed viciously, but their crude physicality soldered them together, as though they'd been hewn by the same sculptor and painted by different artists. Both had the same heart-shaped face, the same small upturned nose spattered with freckles. They shared the same wide mouth that tugged down at the corners and, at close quarters, Ellie had a weaker version of her father's light-proof pupil that didn't dilate. Caught in a certain light, it looked like a glass eye. Robbie and Ellie looked nothing like each other – yet they could only be father and daughter.

From nowhere, the rain began to fall in large, single, heavy drops, bouncing off the road. Lorries thundered past, spraying cold water up Ellie's dangling limbs. She tightened her grip around the handlebars, the colour draining from her rain-dappled knuckles. She could see the wet shanks of her father's denim-clad thighs pummelling down on the slippery pedals, and the streaky slick tarmac made her feel sick as it raced by below.

Another lorry thrashed past, ripping the air from her lungs. Passing windscreen wipers slashed water at her. People swerved and beeped, but still her dad ploughed on.

The rain seemed to get warmer, splashing up and smattering their faces with the muddy fomentation of the overflowing gutters. They passed a scruffy sprawl of travellers' caravans banked up by Victoria Park, and as the carriageway peeled left and the show-room loomed ahead, Robbie was once again dizzy with excite-ment. The thought that he'd be driving away in a Jaguar, a Jaguar for Christ's sake, filled him with a boyish frisson. He eased up on the pedals, patted the wad of notes in his breast pocket and grinned into the grey scrim of Saturday morning traffic.

But as they pulled into the showroom and he dragged out his foot to help slow the bike, he had his first misgivings. The accent for Sheila had been all about 'modern' and 'new' and right now she imagined he'd be at Howarth's, haggling for a new Vauxhall. Since moving to Thelwall, Sheila began to pride herself on her possessions, cleverly managing the HP repayments on all their mod cons – the fridge, the washing machine, the Hoover, the Moulinex mixer. All Robbie had to do was hand her the money each week, and Sheila would make it last for ever.

He'd done everything for Sheila and the kids since Orford days. He'd given up on his own dreams and taken every bit of overtime the factory could throw at him instead. He'd got them this house in an avenue he could never call home, full of people he could never like, and furnished it, top to bottom, with brand new furni-ture and brand new 'things'. He'd even bunged Sheila money for new clothes and he'd bitten back his dismay when she'd come back from her shopping spree with only a pair of Gloria Vanderbilt jeans to show for the fifty quid he'd coughed up. Surely, surely she wouldn't begrudge him this one thing? Once she saw this beauty, once she came to understand the prestige of owning a Jag of what-ever age, she'd be as bowled over as him, would she not? And if

63

he didn't indulge himself in this passion, then what would be the point of it all? Where would be the sense in the six, often seven shifts he did each week? It would just be purgatory. He was buying himself a Jag. End of story.

'Amah! Amah!' Vincent ran into the kitchen, beaming. 'They're back!'

A reflexive panic that made her pull out the grill pan hurriedly and begin laying out slices of gammon and steak gave way to a splinter of excitement. 'Have they got it?' she said.

Vincent craned his neck at the window. Sheila peered around him. There was no new car, just Robbie and Ellie, dismounting from his bike. An instinctive torrent of anger surged through her at the sight of their soaked and filthy clothes, but was extinguished as Ellie burst in and flung herself into her mother's arms. 'We've got a new car!' she shouted, wriggling free and running over to Vincent.

Sheila looked to Robbie. 'So?'

'Monday,' said Robbie. 'Pick it up Monday.'

His lips were pressed in a thin, indecipherable smile. She knew her husband. He was holding back. Something was wrong here. She barely dared ask. Refusing to believe anything bad could have come of this, she forced her most radiant smile and put her arms around him. 'Come on! Tell me about it. Tell me all about our new car!'

Again he flashed the humbled grin and shrugged. 'What's to say? It's . . .' Suddenly his eyelids began to flicker, his face twitched. Sheila went to him, but he turned and went back out, wheeling his bike round to the shed. Sheila dropped to a crouch and took Ellie's face in her hands.

'Ellie? Did something bad happen?'

Something very bad had happened. Even now, hours after the shattering realisation that the showroom manager had thought *that*, Robbie couldn't stop thinking about it, every nuance of it, from that first moment they'd freewheeled into the garage forecourt. The cloudburst had ended and in its place the sun came out again, high and strong. As Robbie dismounted, gently lifting his excitable daughter to the floor, steam was starting to rise from the gleaming roofs and bonnets of all the pristine sports cars on display. He wheeled his bike towards reception, Ellie in tow. From behind the big display window, two eyes locked on Robbie. He felt it, somehow, felt the presence and squinted through the misty haze to see who was there. The sun glanced off the glittering window, blinding Robbie for a second, and then the manager, or at least someone in a suit, was standing in front of him. Robbie leant his bike as gently as possible against the window then, thinking better of it, laid it flat down on the floor.

'Can I help you?'

This was the worst bit for Robbie, in flashback. He winced at the recollection, angry not at the showroom manager – no 'please', no 'sir' – but at himself for simply not getting it. Robbie, nervous, threw the guy a big smile. 'I've come to see about the Series One.' He ran the back of his hand across his glistening top lip and cast a proud, proprietary gaze towards the pebble-grey beauty.

The manager looked him in the eye for a second – sense of commerce overcoming common sense for the briefest of instants – then turned, brutally, and walked away.

Robbie stood exactly where he was, flabbergasted. Ellie tugged his hand. 'When can we wide it?'

Before he could answer, there was another fellow blocking his path, this one more than happy to call him 'sir'. 'Sir? Can I help you?'

As the sun disappeared behind a cloud, Robbie now saw a line of baffled salesmen studding the window. All wore the same bleached expression, somewhere between contempt and middling terror. At first he thought their revulsion was aimed at his Ellie – her light-brown hair blackened by the rain, her green eyes peeled back by the pure black of her excited irises and her fudge-brown skin spattered dark by the dirt slung up from the wet carriageway. She'd been shaded in by the journey and the walk this morning, and the horrified Jag sales platoon were recoiling at the arrival of this half-breed kid. They'd sent out their stockiest bloke to dispatch them.

Robbie had drawn himself up, injured, irate, ready to go and bust heads. But then the revolving door spat out a lady customer whose unambiguous glare was directed at Robbie, and Robbie alone. He shook his head in silent anger, looked at the floor, then looked up again and caught sight of himself in the reflection of the plate glass window. He saw what they were looking at, saw the whole picture – and flinched. His hair was wild, flayed to crazy tumbleweed by the lash of the wind and the rain. His face was sprayed in mud, his clothes sodden. And his little dark-skinned baby was just another prop, one more gypsy kid dragged along for the sympathy vote.

The salesman had gestured with one arm, simultaneously indicating the way out, and that he wanted no trouble. Robbie stood there a moment longer, dreams in tatters, the realisation consuming him. Travellers. They all thought he and Ellie were from the site down the road. Fate sealed and heart broken, Robbie dragged up his bike and hauled it around. Ellie knew something bad had just happened, but she asked no questions. As they made their way back along the carriageway, past the straggle of caravans, the sky blackened and bore down on them again. Ellie saw a fat tear welling in his eye. 'It's OK, Daddy,' she said.

She only called him Daddy when she wanted something, these days – or when she sensed he needed her most. Robbie bit back the waves of vitriol and despair crashing through him and forced himself back into his favourite role, one he could still fulfil. He became Dad again, with all of his everything channelled into making Ellie grin and giggle. It didn't take much. He rang his bell at strangers walking by, swerved up onto the pavement and attempted a wheelie and by the time they were pulling into the forecourt of Howarth's Motors, Ellie was a kid again, shielded from the world out there.

And for as long as possible, Robbie wanted to keep it that way.

And so it was that, foolish and found-out, his soul drained of all and any hope, Robbie took his little tar-baby to Howarths and, after a detached and cursory inspection of the gleaming box, shook hands on HP terms for a brand new family saloon. The world had reached its verdict on Robbie Fitzgerald, and they'd found against him. He was a vagabond, an outsider, a threat, a menace; and Jaguars – even well-loved, elderly ones – were not for the likes of him. And that was that. Sheila was right. They should do as others did, set their sights on what was do-able, get-able. Keep their sight lines low, and do things by the book. How could he have thought any different? How could he have deluded himself so? A Jaguar! For *him*. Hurting and hungering now, he bypassed the Fords, the Vauxhalls – even a Citroën would bestow too much dignity upon one such as he. If this was how things were then so be it – he'd go the whole hog for them, open up his own veins and bleed martyrdom. Barely listening to the salesman, he accepted the colour they had in stock rather than wait for the now-fashionable metallic shades. This would be the sack-cloth that he'd wear now, day in, day out. He popped Ellie back on the bike, mugged a delighted face for her and set about the merry pedal ride home. But how his heart ached.

'Ellie?' Her mother continued scouring her mud-speckled face for answers. Robbie came into the room and Susheela turned her questioning gaze onto him. 'What has happened? Tell me, somebody.'

Ellie jumped up, clapping her hands for joy. 'We've got a Lar-dar! A norringe Lar-dar!'

Susheela had never heard of this make. She paused and, hesitantly, edged out her question, afraid of the reply. 'A . . . a new one?'

Robbie did his utmost to force a smile. 'Yep. Brand spanker!'

He stood there, holding the pose, smiling hard as he fought back the tears. Sheila didn't notice a thing. She hugged him tight, heart thumping with joy as she gleefully imagined Jean Bishop's face.

Three

Sheila had had misgivings right until the first of the ladies rang the front doorbell, and now she knew for sure it had all been a wretched mistake. How could people be so nice to your face, smile right into your eyes then be so cruel the moment your back was turned? She froze against the kitchen wall, tray in hand. She could still hear the two of them – at least Jean had not got involved – giggling in there. Served her right. Served her right for being so ridiculous as to take them up on it and host a coffee morning in the first place. Robbie would wring her neck if he ever found out. The one time she'd ever ventured the subject, he as good as laughed in her face. 'Women's Institute,' he called the ladies in the close. He seemed to hate all of them, but reserved a special contempt for Jean Bishop – or Emily Bishop as he insisted on referring to the neighbourhood Avon Lady. 'Just want a nosey, She,' he poo-pooed, when she'd gingerly enquired about having some friends around. 'These types aren't your friends, love. Just want a good look at what you've got.' Or haven't got, she'd thought, but didn't say.

But vanity got the better of her and, after an avalanche of praise and encouragement from Jean, she'd agreed to the little get-together. She would have liked to have waited till her new curtains were back from the tailor, but this was the only week she had the run of the house. Partly in an attempt to lure Vincent from the cocoon of his bedroom – since breaking up three weeks ago, he'd barely set foot outside the house – and also to gently acclimatise Ellie to the six-hour school day before she started at St Mary's next month, she'd enrolled them both at a week-long summer school the local community centre was running.

So, it was just the five of them – Jean, herself, Marge Wallace from Number 17 and her pretty sister-in-law Penny, who everyone said looked like Sheena Easton (but who had to be at least thirty, surely). And Liza was coming too. Of all the young mums at Ellie's playgroup, Liza, with her long, gazelle legs clad in Gloria Vanderbilt jeans, was the star. Everyone wanted to know Liza Cohen.

Marge and Penny arrived together, ten minutes early. Sheila was in a flummox, unsure whether to trim the crust off the sandwiches or if chocolate eclairs were vulgar. That was all she'd heard off Marge all week – 'vulgar'. Those all-in-one boiler suits she loved were, apparently, vulgar. The beautiful Cotswold stone-effect cladding on the Harrisons' house opposite was vulgar. Their regular bus driver was vulgar. This last, at least, gave Sheila an opportunity to boast about their new car. 'We went for a saloon car. It made sense, what with Ellie starting school in September.'

Marge contorted her face into that tight, terrifying mask that was intended to demonstrate pleasure but gave off only the most virulent envy. 'Really?' She smiled through gritted teeth. 'A *sal*-oon car?'

No sooner had Sheila seated Marge and Penny – who declined both tea and coffee and asked if she had 'something naughty' – than they were picking things up, turning them over, nudging one another. Sheila went off to the garage in a fug of panic. What did they mean, something naughty? Well, it was obvious – they meant drink. But where did Robbie keep it, if he kept it at all? And suddenly, triumphantly, she spotted it up on the paint shelf. Of course! He'd been given it by his workmates for his birthday and he was keeping it for Christmas, but she could easily get another before then. Robbie would never know. She got right up onto her tiptoes and started, inch by inch, to ease it towards her. From back within the house came the sharp single drill of the doorbell. By the time she'd lugged the booze back into the front room, Marge had already let Jean in. She was standing regally in the centre of the Persian rug, hair heavily lacquered, surveying the turnout.

'Oh!' she said, clearly disappointed. 'I thought you said Liza Cohen was coming?'

Sheila fidgeted with her pendant, unsure what to say. 'She *said* she was coming.'

All eyes fell upon the object Sheila was struggling to keep hold of – a Party Four can of Tartan Ale. Surely that counted as naughty? Penny jammed a hand across her mouth, twinkling eyes giving away her hilarity.

Sheila moved it from the table down to the floor, trying to contain a mounting irritation. 'Here. Somebody open that while I bring the coffees in.'

No sooner had she left the room than the snort of derision erupted. Stung, she couldn't help stopping dead in her tracks nonetheless. The first voice she heard was Penny's, still breathless with laughter. 'Imagine Liza's face if she saw that!'

'Come off it! As if Liza Cohen's going to be coming *here*.'

'I don't know, darling – they do like to rough it, 'specially that husband of hers. I hear he's a proper commie.'

Blinded with anger, disappointment, grief and betrayal, Sheila nevertheless found herself thinking only two things. She did know Liza Cohen – she knew her well. And what, if you please, was a commie? So it was with particular delight that, for a second time, the shrill note of the doorbell snapped her out of the doldrums. And it was with nothing other than a childish glee that she introduced her friends to the smiling and immediately likeable Liza Cohen.

Four

For all Robbie's misgivings and insecurities about the people of Hayes Close – some of which had been duly vindicated, although she could never admit to this – Sheila had no doubt that moving to Thelwall had been the right decision. It was a huge leap forward for the Fitzgeralds. And for her, too. Yes, people still stared – although they weren't the same disapproving lip-curling glowers she'd endured in Orford; this was more harmless fascination – and yes, some of the locals hadn't been as hospitable as she'd hoped for. But for the most part she felt safe out here in the suburbs. She could venture outside the womb of the house without deference to the dizzying fear of what lay around the corner. She was happy. And yet more and more, she was aware of a growing sense of tristesse in her soul that was nothing to do with the events of that night. Sheila was starting to question if the cache of family life was enough to sustain her alone. She loved that she was a source of constancy for her babies, and until Ellie was old enough and for as long as Robbie's income permitted, she would continue to relish her role as stay-at-home mother. But in recent months, a dark haze had crept over her world and not even the love of her children could shift it. What she craved, as she came to understand, was friendship. Companionship. And not the kind that was on offer from the women of Hayes Close. She yearned to be close to Liza, but not even a kampong girl like Sheila was so naive as to assume that Liza's loveliness was born out of anything other than just that. She was a good egg and she liked Sheila – this much she knew for certain – but there was an unambiguous air of charity to her affections. What Liza wanted was to help. That's what the cookery lesson was about. Liza had been badgering her about it ever since the coffee morning. She'd visited Goa as a student and was desperate to learn the rudiments of Indian cuisine, and Sheila was the ideal teacher. It was lovely of her, it was, but Sheila knew the reasons why and really, Liza didn't have to.

The simple truth was that Sheila was beginning to lament the friendship she'd once shared with Robbie, viewing it as a period in her life that was bound up with the first flush of newly-wed romance, one that could never return, not even when Vincent and Ellie left the nest. She missed their conversations, their laughter, their Saturday night supper club. But it was what it was, and not only did she understand it completely, she was in awe of how far they'd come. She loved that they were now the guardians of these amazing little people. But that was all they were these days and she couldn't help wonder how it was for Robbie and if it was enough.

Five

The school holidays were drawing to an end. The carefree haze Vincent had floated through these last five weeks seemed to dissipate into the balmy, mottled heat of late August and in its wake came the gradual return of all those tics and nerves, the instinctive inner tension, niggling reminders of what lay just around the corner. First thing in the morning he'd wake with that familiar tightening in his guts, a strangulating grip around his sternum that made him car sick while still in bed. He'd get a tingling in his hands that caused the pads of his fingertips to swell and flare out. Then on the bank holiday Monday, his bowels seized up – packing his stomach tight and fat, like an unpricked sausage. He'd had five blissful weeks of respite from all this, five weeks in which he'd barely been aware of the mishaps and malfunctions of his own body. It had all been fine. Even his shits had come thoughtlessly and naturally once he'd fallen into stride with summer. But now that careless utopia was being leached away by the looming return to school. It was a matter of days, now. He was a nervous wreck.

Vincent sat on his window sill, Ellie by his side. It had been much the hottest day of summer. Outside on the street, the heat hung low in cloying drapes, languid enough to step through. Nothing stirred but for the lazy ripple of the heat haze where the end of the road met the ship canal. Looking out through the open window, it was hard to discern any movement at all, any sign of life other than the distant thrum of the motorway flyover. Ellie dragged a Matchbox car up and down the sill. Vincent patiently shushed her while he pondered, forcing her to make the requisite 'brmmm' noise in her head. While his mother

73

respected his solitude, Ellie burst it like a grape, over and over again. Vincent adored his little sister unconditionally though, and each time she bounded into his bedroom, grinning her gappy grin, he put himself to one side, smiled and made space for her. And Ellie knew it – knew she didn't have to work hard for his affections. She could monopolise them just by being herself.

This time, though, he ignored her tacit clamouring for attention and continued to scribble into a nearly full jotter. He hesitated, absent-mindedly sucking the tip of his pen as he looked to the window for inspiration, staining the corners of his mouth until he could taste the sweet, acidic ink and spat it out. He always wrote in the same position that he read in – knees bunched up, shoulders pushed forward, head almost horizontal to his desk, tongue protruding and a delicate frown rippling his brow. He could remain in this pod-like pose for hours, moving only to knead the cramp from his legs or push his glasses back in place. His books, and there were many of them, heaved from all four walls of his room. The white synthetic shelves his mum had put up were already buckling under the weight of all those books, from Hans Christian Andersen to Jules Verne. In recent weeks, his mum had been forced to find another home for the spare blankets and towels so that the small airing cupboard above his bed could be fitted with yet more shelves. Most of his books were second hand, bought at school jumble sales – and often just to have, rather than to read immediately. But he had a collection of new editions, which he displayed in pole position above his bed. He arranged them categorically – sci-fi, nature, classics, historical – and alphabetically, too.

The discovery during the holiday of a main library, only a few bus stops away in Stockton Heath, was a boon for Vincent. The local branch library only had a smattering of serious titles among the *Biggles* and *Just William* staples. But junior membership of the Stockton Heath branch led him into a whole new world, and only inspired him to acquire more books, rather than simply borrow them from the library. His poky little room just couldn't accommodate them all. Once every six weeks he would rotate his books ninety degrees clockwise so the books in the airing cupboard didn't curl up at the corners, and the books on his window ledge didn't get damp with condensation.

Whereas once he would zip through almost any work of fiction, Vincent had taken up the pen himself now, and writing had altered his experience of books for good. He now read fiction with a critical eye. The simple delectations of reading – of empathising, repelling or losing himself completely to the story – had been usurped by a higher art. Vincent sought gratification in the pleasures of language; he was fascinated with how words collided and burnt to form sentences, to form images and worlds. He marvelled at the process, and the art. He developed a liking for lean, stripped-down prose – though not exclusively. But if a writer took too convoluted a path to convey something simple he would find himself striking a line through it with a pencil.

Just before lunch there was a knock at the door down below. Ellie and Vincent peered over the flat asphalt roof of the porch and saw a trio of heads with sticky-out ears. Boys' heads; boys' ears. Standing off behind them, minding the bikes, was a fourth kid – a fat lad.

'Go on then, off you go.' Vincent smiled at his little sister. A second later he saw her burst out through the porch door. She went into a huddle with the boys, disappeared down the side of the house and emerged a moment later, pedalling madly on her tiny kid's bicycle, chin jutting forward, elbows flaring as she zipped in and out of the bigger bikes.

Vincent watched them go. Ellie's legs were already too long for the bike, and she rode with her knees almost knocking the handlebars as she pushed to the front of the group. Vincent smiled to himself, yet the sight of them heading off like the

Famous Five on some big adventure planted a little pip of envy deep within. He hopped down from the window sill and picked up his pen again.

Sheila and Robbie were downstairs in the kitchen.

'What'd you like for your tea, Robert?'

That sealed it. She'd called him by his full name – her last throw of the dice, half a warning shot across the bows, half a plea for moderation. But he was having none of it. 'Why d'you ask? There's not much chance of me getting it.'

He wanted a fight. She knew he wanted a fight, and she wasn't giving it to him. Not over Vincent. She looked at Robbie's face, twisted with self-pity and disgust. Again, she tried to soothe the situation. 'Ask. Who knows . . .'

Robbie stood and, slowly, very deliberately, padded across to Sheila. There was sadness in his eyes. He fixed his gaze on her – his hurt, baffled, angry gaze – and took hold of her wrists.

'Ouch! Robbie – there's no need to squeeze so tight!'

She was by no means a silent victim in these showdowns – when pressed she could give as good as she got, but Sheila knew the limits of Robbie's temper. She was quick to work out what was eating him, quick to distinguish between the real killer rows and those that could be easily mitigated. Robbie, on the other hand, was impossible. Once he'd lost control, there was nothing he wouldn't say, no incident he wouldn't dredge up from the past, no matter how long forgotten. He'd been spoiling for this. Almost from the moment he and Ellie came back from the car showroom two weeks ago, he'd been walking around under his own black nimbus, and today it was ready to burst. Eyes bubbling with self-righteous ire, she knew there was no going back.

'What d'you think, She? What do you think? That's what I'm asking you. Do you think it's right that there's lads Vincent's age knocking for his little sister instead of him? Out on bikes, out climbing trees, out playing football!'

76

'Vincent doesn't like football.'

She might as well have produced photographs of Vincent in a ballerina's tutu, for the effect her words had upon her husband. Enraged, he crashed his fist onto the kitchen table. 'Jesus! I don't know what you think you're doing to him, She, but it's certainly not mothering. You're turning him into a right Mary Ellen, and I'll tell you another thing for nothing. He's going to get battered! Believe you me, Sheila – this might be suburbia but it's still fucking Warrington.'

'Robert!'

'No! I know this place. It's going to be hard enough for the lad going on to high school next year the . . . the . . . the way he is, right?' He was exhausted by his own anger, breathing deep to regulate his message. 'Right?'

She nodded, heartbroken.

He took her wrist again – just one this time, and gentler. 'But Sheila, darlin', if he doesn't get his nose out them books and start acting like a lad, he's gonna get the shit kicked out of him—'

A creak on the landing floorboards, and the crash of Vincent's bedroom door slamming prevented either of them from saying more. Sheila grazed Robbie's face with her big, moist eyes, shook her head and went to console her son.

Six

The school holidays had finally come to an end. Robbie sat there, the sounds of the kids getting ready for school upstairs throttling his guts with dread. He closed his eyes and willed himself to the point in the next hour or so when, duty done, Ellie safely seen into school to start her new life, he could get on with his own stagnating one. But there was a treat in store – one little oasis he'd stumbled upon, a buffer for Robbie between now and then. He'd clock in, swerve the canteen ritual, the syrupy tea, the leery chat and let himself up onto the roof of the Metso plant to lap up the lands of his youth. The weather was still glorious, and every day of the last week's heatwave he'd taken himself up there first thing and sat back over a blissful smoke before the horn sounded, tracing the pathways of his life. On a day like this, you could see it all; see Orford, see the houses he grew up in, see the town centre where he'd gotten into that senseless brawl that had delivered him to Warrington General, to Sheila. He could see the Irish Club and, if he stood on his tiptoes, he could mark out the route he'd taken back that fateful night – the night of Dickie Vaughan. But in this balmy Indian summer, he couldn't stay too down about much for too long. It was just life. It was the same for everyone. Every ginnel, every towpath, every little shortcut behind every estate was taking someone somewhere, or taking them back again. He'd found himself thinking about it more and more.

Last night, vaguely drunk, he'd started talking himself out of Ellie's first day at St Mary's. Once again, he fell back on the rationale he'd used to duck out of Vincent's big day – that he'd be the only parent there in overalls, the only labourer among

78

them. Not that he was bothered about that – fuck them, to be honest – it was more about responsible parenting. All it would take was for one of those poker-faced Belindas in their Barbour jackets to make some quip over dinner about Robbie Fitzgerald's work suit and Ellie and Vincent's lives would be made hell. He was preoccupied with this – his children, their colour, the lives they'd lead. A lot of the time he'd brush it off, revel in Ellie's button-nosed cuteness. But a lot of the time, too, he'd sit back and curse himself for his vanity, for his irresponsibility in bringing them about in the first place, and bringing them here.

Tipsy on his two pints after work, he'd raised his concerns again with She. Was he placing Ellie in the firing line, turning up at school in his factory overalls? With Vincent, it was tough – he was browner, he wore glasses, he hated rough games; Vincent couldn't really help himself. But Ellie could more than look after herself. She was a fighter. She was a winner. Wouldn't he be doing her down by turning up outside that school with all its pretensions to being the area's 'prep school without fees', and opening her up to ridicule?

But this time Sheila was having none of it. She'd been way too lenient last time, even buying into his paranoia herself – when the other mothers had asked what line of work her husband was in, she'd said, 'Chemicals.'

So it had been assumed, for a while, that Robbie was some kind of a research lab technician. But they'd lived in Hayes Close for three years now, and Robbie's background was no longer a secret. Until the Lada came along the neighbours saw that he went to work on his bike in overalls, butty box strapped to the back, yet still the invites to fondues and fancy-dress parties dropped through the door. He'd shortened her name and banished all trace of Asian exoticism to help her assimilate. Yet, if anyone risked ostracising the Fitzgeralds it was her husband. So when he'd started into his martyred spiel last night, she simply coshed

79

him with a look. There were no extenuating circumstances, no reason whatsoever why he should not chaperone his little girl to her very first day at Big School. He'd be walking his daughter up that school path with all the other parents, and that was the end of that.

As they approached the school gates, Ellie broke free from her dad's hand and seamlessly insinuated herself into the surge of small people gravitating towards the school gates. Instinctively, Vincent went to follow, but found himself tugged back.

'Keep an eye on her, Vincent lad, will you?' Robbie gave his shoulder a decisive little squeeze.

Vincent nodded, thrilled then dejected by the shock of his dad's touch – excited by the magic of the connection and the promise of bonding it brought, but crushed by its rareness and the reality of his father's remoteness towards him. But as he watched his sister's tiny frame blazing a trail through her new buddies, he found himself smiling. Who could blame his father for loving Ellie so much? Not Vincent.

He wrestled his way through the mêlée and caught up with her. He had a strong sense that things would be different for Ellie, that she wouldn't have to go through the same rituals, the baptism of fire that he'd endured. Ellie reminded him of one of those characters in the cartoons she watched, swaggering blithely down the street while bombs exploded all around her. He wondered if it was luck or fate, or if she simply possessed what Jane Austen called 'savoir-faire' and his dad called nous. Instinctively, she always knew the right thing to say or do, as though there were some inner amulet steering her helm. Like when the townies came over from across the locks and demanded a stake in her trick-or-treat spoils, she knew exactly what to say, and what savage accent to employ in order to send the young thugs on their way. And then there was the absolute precision with which she could read their father. She seemed able to sense out each and every shifting inflection of his moods. Effortlessly, she knew when would be a good time to ask him for new trainers or football boots. Innately, she seemed to understand his silences, his voids, though she hadn't yet cultivated the vocabulary to explain them to her brother. He on the other hand possessed none of this *nous*. He was forever misreading his father. The townies from the nearby estates terrified Vincent, and some of them were two years younger than he was. One time, galvanised by his sister's battle stories, he told them to piss off when they hustled him for money outside the library. He drew himself up, looked them flush in the eye and snarled his lip, just like Ellie. But as with every big decision he'd ever made it had been a duff one. He came away with a bust lip.

Still, he felt the heavy grind of guilt wrench at him as he watched her waif-like frame struggle with the bulk of his old school bag, its broad straps winging out like Sue Ellen's shoulder pads. If the rucksack overwhelmed his own slight frame then it engulfed his sister. But palming the bag off onto Ellie had been a necessary means of self-preservation. For four years it had offered itself up as a target, a taunt, exhorting others to jerk it downwards and pull the Paki to the floor. The bag had been a vivid symbol of Vincent's peculiarity. It was the opposite of cool – bulky, practical, unwieldly. He'd spied it in the window of the Army & Navy store and become smitten with its pockets and zips and military allure. It had been another duff choice.

Towards the end of last term, he'd delicately planted the idea in his mum's head that he'd be needing a new bag for next year – a Le Coq Sportif bag, like the hard lads had. Harrassed at the time, Sheila made a tentative promise to take him down to Warrington market, but back-pedalled when she saw the military kit bag was still as good as new. And so it was onto his contingency plan. Over the course of the summer holidays, he set about soft-selling it to Ellie, duping her into believing that the entire school footie team favoured this exact model. He goaded her into coveting it that little bit more by refusing to part with it, come what may. His chicanery paid off. By the end of the holidays, Ellie was threatening to leave home if Mum didn't make Vincent give her the 'sojer's bag'.

Vincent had traipsed around the market with Sheila, knowing exactly what he wanted but, of necessity, having to go through the ritual of considering and rejecting his mother's cheaper options. She was enjoying herself, dragging the day out, lingering at every single market stall and fingering dresses, curtain fabric, towels and wall clocks she had no intention of buying. Vincent loitered by her side, loyally offering an opinion on every gaudy bathrobe, every useless kitchen gadget, hoping no one he knew was down the next aisle. Eventually they located the right stall and he opted for a small, black Le Coq Sportif sports bag, identical to those that littered the corridors and cloakrooms of St Mary's. He got what he wanted – and hated it from the moment he got it home. There were no grooves to slot his pens in for a start, no inner labyrinth of pockets and pouches to store his secrets. But what he hated most about this slight, impractical bag was the way it demanded to be carried. It had two stout handles, located in such a way that the bag could only be suspended from one hand, or slung awkwardly across a shoulder. Unlike his rucksack, it allowed no symmetrical distribution of its weight and, as a consequence, it upset the rhythm of his feet and the rhythm of his thoughts. Yet as he scurried after Ellie, Vincent believed he'd made the right decision. He felt a strange surge of optimism as he mingled with the other kids, dangling his bag so they'd see that he had the right badge, too. He straightened his neck out from the hunch of his shoulders and stood tall. Maybe, just maybe this year would be different.

*

Standing shoulder to shoulder with Sheila, Robbie watched his small girl scudding a dauntless passage through the sweep of bodies, her big bag bobbing her head in the tide. His son scuffed along behind her, his uneven gait counterpointing with her easy, agile rhythm. Robbie's love for Vincent was intense, yet it always came with a sense of tragedy. Often, it felt like he was loving someone who could not be loved. There went his son. There, too, went Ellie, making her way down the path, eyes dancing. Robbie's tummy sank with the deadweight of some nameless emotion. As though she knew, Ellie turned for a second and smote him with her gap-toothed grin. Robbie held up a hand and tried to wave. It was like he was waving goodbye to something other than his little girl – something huge and impossible to comprehend. The school bell pealed out across the yard and with its shrill finality, something ended, and something new began.

As Ellie's bob swished out of sight, Robbie became aware of the other parents thronging near the railings in mawkish clumps, their clipped accents making him self-conscious once more. How he despised them – the fathers rigged out in cheap suits and ties, their wives in their prissy Thatcher outfits, all sensible, matronly skirts at the age of twenty-nine and not a decent pair of calves between them. Robbie might well be the only man there in overalls, but at least his wife had a waistline to be proud of.

He turned and caught a couple of dads off guard admiring Sheila's slender silhouette, accentuated by her tight denims. He recognised their faces, or thought he did – they all looked the same. Found out, they cowed and looked away immediately, that overconfident glow draining from their faces in a sobering flush of self-knowledge. They didn't want to be making eye contact, not with a man like Fitzgerald.

Robbie, too, felt uncomfortable and little flickers of chagrin licked at his nape. He'd long been aware of the effect he had on strangers. Even when he was happy, his face couldn't help displaying a certain ferocity. As a teenager, that look, that glowering, menacing, half-sneer had often won him scraps without a single punch being thrown. But since moving to Thelwall, that was currency he didn't want to own, let alone use. It was another stigma, one more telltale tic that gave away his past, his background. Robbie had come to despise the savage warning signs his uneven dial sent out. There was something about the alignment between his unblinking, glassy left eye and his pulpy boxer's nose that said: 'Beware. Hard Man.' And he could have been, had he not had music in his soul. The truth was that Robbie Fitzgerald was a poet ruffian, a soul man who looked hard. He could grow his hair long, part it this way or that, but there was nothing he could do about it: other men didn't want to look him in the eye.

The other parents – those who'd had to go right up to the gates with their children – were now streaming back down the path towards them. Robbie was keen to get away, but Sheila stood on her tiptoes and continued waving fiercely at the backs of Vincent and Ellie's heads.

'They've gone, She. Come on.'

A couple of fathers from their street nodded over to him. He saw his face perfectly reflected in the nervous wells of their eyes. He forced his shoulders down into a slouch and tried to look easy, normal, like any other dad, when he saw him. Vernon Cohen. Slowly, his boss was coming down the path towards him. Rooted to the spot, he caught Robbie's eye and beamed before Robbie had a chance to make his getaway.

When Robbie started work on the Metso plant fifteen years ago, Vernon Cohen was already a legend – a boss serving his time on the shop floor. His great-grandfather built Crossfields in the 1880s, and the plant had stayed in the Cohen family ever since. Vernon was something of an enlightened despot, generally

84

held in esteem by the shop stewards. His token sop to being management – his tie – was worn loose, top button undone. He was, in every sense, A Good Bloke. Under his aegis, the factory's working conditions improved above and beyond TUC guidelines. Cohen lifted the bar on how many times workers could leave their line to go to the toilet, he gave all workers and their immediate families a private health care plan and, crucially for a chemical plant like theirs, installed state of the art ventilation systems. Most important of all, he acknowledged the monetary worth of overtime. Up until Cohen's regime, overtime was time and a half, Sundays and bank holidays only. Crossfields was a 24-hour, 365-day-a-year, perpetual productivity site, but the night shift and the Saturday had always been treated as 'regular' pay days. Vernon Cohen changed all that, unbidden. The night shift went time and a half, Saturdays were double pay and Sundays and bank holidays paid at three times the regular rate.

Yet Robbie couldn't warm to the man. It was typical of him that, with all the wealth he had, he should send his girls here, when he could well afford any one of the Cheshire prep schools that were just as near to his Stockton Heath mansion. Somehow, it made a fit with his egalitarian self-image. And he made Robbie nervous, too. Too many times over the years Robbie had found himself in the urinals, or crossing the factory quadrangle, when there was Cohen, almost gurning he was smiling so hard, ready with some matey quip about Dalglish, or Elsie Tanner or the latest Bond girl in the news. There was something over-eager, something forced and almost desperate about his chuminess that made Robbie both anxious and equally eager to take his leave.

Robbie dug his chin into his chest and pretended he hadn't seen him. That was all he needed – word getting round that his kids grazed from the same pastures as management's. He slipped an arm around Sheila's hip and rotated her 180 degrees but, just as they got their backs to Vernon, something caught Sheila's eye

85

and she spun back round again, eyes sparkling, face lit up with an almighty grin. 'Liza!'

She was waving over to someone. Robbie's pulse was hammering like a road drill. Even before he tracked her eyeline he knew who his wife was waving to. He hissed in her ear. 'She! I've got to get off.'

Sheila didn't hear him. She only had eyes for the lady bearing down on her now, smiling gaily, her balding husband in tow. 'Helleeew,' said Sheila, in an accent that was nothing less than extraordinary. 'How are yi?'

Gobsmacked, Robbie turned away and picked out a distant poplar tree, anything to focus on while this nightmare unfolded around him. His wife was talking to the boss, and there was nothing he could do about it. Up close, Cohen's shiny bald head looked like it had been Pledged. He looked as stunned as Robbie, but pleasantly so.

'Hello, Robbie mate,' he said, his face opening up into a beam every bit as dazzling as his beautiful wife's.

Robbie turned slowly, raking the woman of whom Sheila spoke so gushingly. In truth she was more pretty than beautiful – pert and slender, and, no denying it, sexy in the way fine women always are when they no longer have sex. Sheila followed Vernon's smile back to Robbie's shifty grimace, stepped back, shrank her head into her shoulders and put her hand to her mouth. 'What? Yi ti know each other?'

Robbie felt his neck burning up as it all clicked horribly into place. This was Liza Cohen. Sheila had been boasting about her new pal all summer long – her Range Rover, their timeshare in Spain, the boat they kept at their weekend house on Anglesey. She reeled this stuff off to Robbie as though they were her own spoils. Yet still the penny had never dropped with him. Liza Cohen. Lady Lever. Sheila was positively swooning as Vernon clapped Robbie on the back.

'Old comrades, me and your husband. Isn't that right, Robbie?'

Robbie smiled without parting his lips.

'Com-rades. Yi ti work together? Yi and my Robbie? Golly, that is am-aaazing.'

Robbie's eyes fixed on his wife's lips as they produced more and more of this hideous meld of Mrs Elton and *It Ain't Half Hot Mum*. He felt dizzy.

'Isn't it though, Sheila? Isn't that too extraordinary?' Liza spoke for the first time. Even her voice was beautiful.

Robbie turned, realising he was keen for another, longer look at the lissom Mrs Cohen. She was tall and svelte, her slim calves just visible below her knee-length trench coat. She had bright blue eyes, a hue so sharp you could nick yourself on them, and a lovely, clever smile. These were the qualities she exuded – intelligence, wit, compassion, niceness – and Robbie was getting a boner for her. He hadn't expected the boss's wife to look like that, hadn't expected such a young, attractive woman. A trophy wife, he sneered to himself, trying to square it all up. She was lovely, and she had finesse but Robbie knew well that that was an expensive act to run. No way would she be with Vernon Cohen if he was from the shop floor rather than going through the motions of presiding over it. He waited for her to look back at him and held her gaze, trying to pull back the balance of power. She blushed, and a flicker of something skittered across her eyes. Instinctively, her hand shot up to her neck, concealing a brief but hot flush of colour.

'God! I just can't get my head around it though! What a co-in-cid-ence, Liza? All this time and we never ni our husbands worked together.'

'I should've guessed when you said chemicals.'

Sheila flashed a guilty look at Robbie and, aware of the spiky rash bristling across his face, bustled the conversation in a different direction. 'So, how was Marlborough?'

This baffled the Cohens. They mugged up to each other for clues. Sheila sensed she'd made a faux pas, but drove on regardless.

'Spain? Were you not going to your place in Spain?'

'Oh! Mar . . .' Liza stopped herself, and the faintest glimmer of a smile passed over Vernon. But if he felt any sense of impropriety at all it was towards himself, and he quickly self-censured for even thinking of correcting the innocent, smiling Malaysian woman Liza had become so fond of. Liza's elegant hand delved from her neck to Sheila's shoulder, affectionately guiding her out of the school gates. 'Yes – yes, it was lovely, thank you, She.'

Robbie and Vernon brought up the rear, scuffing their soles as they went.

'What about you, Rob? How was France?'

'Eh?' He stopped dead in his tracks. Sheila turned, eyes haunted as her husband's furious, twitching face glowered at her, betrayed. She leapt in, fighting the fire, fanning the flames.

'Well, we had talked about France! But with the weather being so lovely here and with, you know, having a brand new *sal*-oon car we thought we should exploit the joys of the English countryside more.'

'Oh my fucking God!' Robbie nearly said it. He could hear his bewildered tone, hear the hurt and the shock and the dread in his voice – but somehow he strangled it. He needed to sit down.

'Well . . .' said Vernon, stretching ostentatiously, and glancing at his watch. 'Better make tracks.' He held his hand out to Robbie and, as he reluctantly, sullenly shook, winked conspirationally at his beet-red charge. 'She's lovely, Rob. You're a lucky man.'

That Cohen had tuned into his agony was bad. That he was seeking to neutralise it was worse. 'Yeah. Ta-ra then.'

Robbie turned and walked away, not even glancing in Liza's direction. She shot Sheila a compassionate smile and mouthed the words 'go on', eyes twinkling sadly at her hapless friend. Sheila smiled back, turned and ran after Robbie, knowing she'd killed him, totally ignorant as to how or why. She caught him, briefly, but struggled to match his angry stride.

They got to the car. He wrestled with the door in bitter silence, his violent twists of the key only making the lock resist yet more. Sheila stood back as Robbie wiggled and jabbed with the key. She knew the form, by now. She'd wait for Robbie to go first. He got his breath back, made a conspicuous effort to breathe deeply and evenly, then let her have it. 'Are you determined to make a fucking twat of me?'

His voice was beyond anger. He was wounded, horribly, mortally. The lock gave way. He got in and slammed the door. He stared directly ahead for a moment, then leant over and began struggling with the passenger door's window. Sheila dipped her head down, eyes puzzled. Robbie could barely look at her.

'I've no time to run you home. You'll have to walk.'

Her throat started to pound. He fired the engine. She scurried round to Robbie's side and rapped on his window. He wound it down a couple of strokes. He wouldn't look at her, stared wildly and blankly ahead. His face was dead still, but his eyes burnt with rage and hurt.

'Robbie! For goodness' sake – what did I do?'

Still he wouldn't look at her. It was a long while before he spoke, voice laden with grief. 'What have you been saying, She?'

She started to speak but he steam-rollered right over her, eyes shining on the brink of tears.

'Christ's sake! It's gonna be all over fucking Metso by now.'

'What will? I've done nothing wrong.'

He cut her dead again. 'Just for the record, you dumb fucking mare, it's Marbella.'

She'd never heard him swear like this. He was barely in control. She tried to lean closer. 'Robbie?'

'Marfuckingbella. See, even a daft twat like me who's never been further than fucking Blackpool knows that.'

Her face crumpled. A rare tear dribbled down her cheeks and Robbie knew then that he'd gone too far. They had an under-standing, he and Sheila, one that had never been spoken of, and didn't need explaining. He'd just crashed right through the perimeter fence and had a horrible misgiving he'd never find his way back again. Heart set like a cold metal in his guts, he peeled out of the car park and away from here, out of this bloody mess. Through his rear-view mirror he watched his forlorn wife traipse off into the distance, utterly uncomprehending what had just taken place. But he couldn't go back to her. He swung onto the main road, and sped away from the wreckage.

The new arrivals began streaming through the school doors. The headmaster and his secretary stood in the foyer, smiling, waving them in. The sun smashed down on Ellie's crown picking out wisps of claret red. Her unruly boy's crop glowed like a bauble spot-lit to start the show. She bounded through the doors, beamed back a big fearless hello to the headmaster and threaded herself into the heart of the scrimmage massing in the corridor. Two fifth-formers were swooping around the nervous herd, worrying them into an orderly queue.

Vincent made his way to his classroom. As always, he was first in. Automatically, he began lifting chairs down from the tables but checked himself. How would that look to the other kids? He put them back up and snagged himself a window seat at the very far corner of the classroom. He arranged his bag so that it jutted out from under his desk with the cock motif on display, then patted the left breast of his blazer and felt for his trump cards.

When he'd first found them in the undergrowth of the old building site, the pack was warped from the rain and sunshine but you could still make out the curve of a sharp, bronzed breast. Some of the cards were soaked through and tore as he eased them out of the packet. But the images – those mysterious, air-brushed curves and peaks – were there by the dozen. It was nothing a hairdryer and a lick of Pritt Stick couldn't fix. Later that night, Vincent lined up the refurbished goodies, some of them still sticky from glue. One by one, he studied them under the weak beam of his torchlight. Nothing happened. There were breasts of all shapes and sizes, dark, fat nipples and pale, almost invisible pink ones; pouts and poses and alluring, limpid eyes; bottoms, and thighs, and taut, narrow tummies. None of these images stirred the kind of response he'd been expecting – the pulsating heart, the quickening groin, the anxious, voracious gnawing in his solar plexus he'd read so much about. None of this happened. But he was glad he'd found the cards. They'd serve another, higher purpose further down the line. These cards would buy Vincent some time, maybe even some credibility. They might even help him stave off the boots and fists.

He heard the whistle outside bring the school day to its start. There was a brief suspension of noise as the playground emptied, the distant stampede of feet building to a deafening crescendo as they piled down the corridor towards him. Vincent felt his bowels loosen, his heart start to thrash. For six weeks he'd lived like the heroes in his books. He'd slain bad men – he'd travelled and conquered. He'd been lionised by whole nations, but now he was small and pathetic once again. He stiffened himself and drew back his shoulders in preparation for the looming moment of reckoning.

They rioted into the classroom, bumping each other along, fighting for tables, pulling down chairs and dragging them along the floor, scratching and shredding the new shell of varnish. The noise fizzed away for a moment as they stumbled upon Vincent and there was that excruciating wait for whoever was going to

91

say something first. The suspense snagged his heart, making him gag. He could feel them, raking him over, sussing his new bag. Reflexively, he felt for the cards in his breast pocket, rehearsed what he was going to say. But more faces, more raggedy bodies spilled in through the door and saved him, for now.

Loud and raw, they swept across the room, fighting over desks and chairs, tugging friends or rivals away from favoured spots. Vincent barely dared make eye contact, watching the scene unfold through the window's reflection. There was something especially menacing about the way the unruliest of them rode the legs of their chairs right back, reclining at such precipitous angles. The sun ventured out from behind a cloud and cast a blinding shield across the window, obscuring his vision. But he knew what was coming and steeled himself, a thin lip of ear poking through the feathered slant of his hair listening out for the first signs, those conversational threads that, sooner or later, would find their mark. Him. He flexed himself, awaiting the buzzwords. Market. Curry. Mini bus. Corner shop. Any of these, even innocently muttered, could quickly flare up into an onslaught. Just as bad were the silences – the pauses between sentences, the semicolons, that deadly hitch of breath, each inducing a jolt in his tummy. But so far fate seemed to be scheming in his favour. They were all too wrapped up in the boastings and toastings of their holidays to notice him, just yet. Simon Hewitt had got to second base with Kevin Lawson's sister. Louis Taylor had been signed up by Stockport County's youth team. Paula Dee was going on *Jim'll Fix It*. Kerry Young had started her periods, and was gleefully passing around a blood-specked towel to prove it, revelling in the horrified reactions of the boys. If things continued like this, their teacher might arrive before the jousting started. Maybe it wouldn't, this year. Maybe they had better things to do. Maybe they'd all grown up.

Vincent allowed himself a sidelong gaze at their bags. His heart stopped dead. No! Not one black bag, and not a cock motif to be seen! A quick gander around the room revealed an overwhelming plurality of these slightly crinkled, leatherette bags with a fat sort of tick on the side. One or two bore the name Patrick, but most of these new, compact sports bags displayed the tick on their side and one beguiling word on the frontispiece: Nike. Crushed, Vincent slid his foot out, hooked his bag and dragged it back under his desk. It was not yet nine o'clock and already he'd made another duff choice.

Their voices grew more and more obstreperous. From the corner of his eye, he could see the Cohen twins sat on the edge of their desks, nudging each other. He knew who they were talking about. The fatter of the two – and they were both bursting out of their horribly shortened school skirts – spied a blonde girl sashaying through the door. Isobel Cohen flashed a look at Vincent and called across to her, 'Hey, Lucy? Where d'you get your tan?'

The pause. The deadly hitch of breath, the stifled sniggering – and then the kill.

'Been knocking round with Gaylord?'

Storms of nasty, raucous laughter erupted, punctuated by disgusted 'eughs' from the girls and horrified 'as ifs' from Lucy herself. Vincent fixed his concentration on the slow chug of the lawnmower on the field outside. But in the reflection he saw more arrivals, and these two spelt danger. It was his arch-tormentors, Simon Blake and his weasly sidekick, Anthony Young – and how they'd grown. They were men, almost! How could they have grown so much in six weeks? His heart whammed faster and faster. He looked up at the clock. It was already past nine. Where the hell was the teacher? He didn't even know who they'd be getting this year. He hoped it was someone hard. Someone who would stamp their authority from day one.

'Oi!' He didn't even need to look up. He shot a quick desperate glance over to the door. 'Gaylord! I'm talking to you.'

Vincent turned round and slipped right back into his trad-
itional mask – a shit-eating, self-mocking grin. His antagoniser
was a stout lad with an angry face. His reconstructed harelip
had once made Blake a target for playground jibes himself, but
that had all been forgotten when his dad had picked him up in
a Porsche. Isobel Cohen sidled next to him and leant back, arms
folded across her fat breasts. Simon winked at her – two uglies
in league together.

'Where d'you go on hols?'

Vincent shrugged, his deflective shield already up. What could
he say? What would cause least offence? France? Too flash for
a spaz like him. Lake District? Too boring. Blackpool? Too povvo.
'Cornwall,' Vincent replied, as casually as he could.

'Cornwall, *Simon*,' he said, coming closer, eyes wide and
menacing.

Vincent's thorax tightened. Discreetly, he pulled out his inhaler
from his trouser pocket and held it between his thumb and forefinger, primed for action.

'Wha-is-wrong-with-Bleck-pull?' Blake taunted, rolling his
eyeballs and mimicking an Indian accent.

Laughter ricocheted around the classroom. Vincent set his face
in a jovial, sporting grin. He was grateful for the brief diversion.
He took a quick, sharp draught on his inhaler. Simon waited for
the laughter to subside.

'So, Gaylord. Cornwall. You go on the A1?'

'No.'

'No, *Simon*! Jeez, you're fucking slow learners, you curry-
guzzlers . . .' He came closer, turned briefly back to Isobel, put
an arm around Vincent's shoulders then theatrically jerked it
away, brushing it self-consciously as though he'd caught a rash.
'Abdul. I mean Gaylord . . .'

Vincent tensed himself. He didn't reply.

'Know who built the A1?'

He chanced the most bored, deadpan answer he could muster. He knew, now, there was no hope. Best get it over with. This year was going to be like any other year. It was going to be hell. 'The Romans built the A1, Simon.'

'So they did, Gaylord. So they did.' He turned again to face his audience, winked once more and returned to his quarry. 'Know why they built it so straight?'

A hiccup of giggling from those who'd heard it before, from their brothers, from uncles, from parents. Vincent knew the punchline, too. He weighed up the pros and cons of stealing Simon's thunder, but elected to bow down and take his medicine instead. 'Erm, no – not sure. To get there quicker?'

'No, Gaylord. Wrong. The Romans built straight roads so the Pakis couldn't build corner shops.'

The room exploded with lusty guffawing. And as with last year and the year before, it was Vincent who laughed hardest.

Seven

Robbie rolled back his head and let the putter-putter-putter of the factory line claim him. He was numb with misery from the events of the morning. Shattered by the hurt he'd caused his own wife, he still could not get Liza Cohen off his mind. She enraged him, and he took himself off to the cubicles to fix it. But he could barely sustain a hard-on, let alone the fantasy. A woman like Liza Cohen was intangible to a man like him. Her flawlessness only made him more aware of his own bad design. No matter how tight he screwed his eyes and tried to abandon himself, the fantasy was so unattainable he couldn't even get into the first act. So he tucked himself away feeling bad about it all. Bad about Liza, bad about Sheila but above all else feeling intensely sorry for himself. What was so wrong about wanting the simple things in life? A drink. A sing-song. A shag. And by God, how he wanted a shag!

As the morning slithered on, his thoughts veered away from his own sad plight to the wrecked, broken face of his wife. Ashamed of everything he'd thought and done, he excused himself from the line and called her from the payphone outside the canteen. A lump pushed up against his throat. He felt utterly, utterly wretched – yet even then, as he dialled home, he still felt a residue of resentment towards her smiling haplessness. He was disgusted at himself for pulling her up for her innocent mispronunciations, but kowtowing to the Cohens? Now that was unforgivable.

She wasn't in – or she didn't pick up, at least – and by the time lunch came round things didn't seem half as raw. He knew Sheila well enough to be sure that it would all be forgotten by the time he got in from work. She might cling on to a silent and dignified sense of injury for a few hours more, just to let him know he'd done wrong, but she'd never bring it up again and that suited Robbie just fine. All he wanted now was to forget the whole thing and move on. If only Vernon Cohen would let him.

Robbie saw him cutting across the works' canteen, but he was already too late. Vernon always ate his lunch with the men – or among them – but, a creature of habit, it was easy enough to swerve him if you timed your run late enough. The siren sounded at 12.30 and at 12.45 Vernon Cohen would walk in with his chip-shop dinner, sit himself down on the nearest bench to the door and spread the *Daily Mirror* out as he munched. He was respectful in that he never forced himself upon anybody, didn't even make eye contact – yet his very presence, however well-meant, was an affront to the men. But today was unlike every other day. It was almost one o'clock and Vernon was still not seated. He was scanning the room, looking for someone and Robbie knew that somebody was him. It was futile pretending he hadn't seen him so Robbie mitigated the damage by heading back outside, thinking that, at worst, there'd be fewer witnesses to his pow-wow with The Boss. Vernon followed.

'Robbie, mate – you got a mo?'

Robbie cringed. His tone was so jaunty. He found himself succumbing to anger once more. Why him? What was this? Why couldn't he just be left alone to do his job, for fuck's sake? He lengthened his stride across the quadrangle, putting distance between them briefly, but Cohen went into a trot to keep up with him, his stout legs working overtime. He got within a pace of Robbie and, satisfied he had his ear, went into his spiel.

'Just wanted to run something by you, like . . .' He was panting as he speed-walked, and his shortness of breath made him speak louder, in gasps. 'Thing is . . . dunno if Sheila's told you . . . but Liza and I are fanatical curry fans. Love our tuck, we do . . .' He rested a moment, bent double, the flats of his hands glued to his ample thighs. He started after Robbie again. 'The thing is, Rob . . . our lot still think Italian's exotic. Couldn't sell a curry to our brood for love nor money.'

Robbie slowed himself, vexed at Vernon making free and easy about curry. The very word made him recoil. And here was Vernon Cohen tossing it about like it was just another meal.

'So, how's about it, yeah? How's about a curry night round at ours?'

Robbie felt himself coming apart at the seams. What the fuck was going on here? He was being harassed by his fucking boss! He stopped dead in the middle of the quadrangle, turned to his obliging employer and stopped him in his tracks with a glower. 'What?'

Cohen backed off, holding up the flat of a palm. 'Not to worry, mate. Some other time.'

One or two workmates passed, stopping to see what was going on.

Keen to show his understanding 'of the way things are', Cohen raised his voice, as though chiding Robbie. 'Put yourself in my shoes – how can I pay you overtime if you keep forgetting to clock off? Think about it, Fitz.' Pleased with himself, he winked at Robbie and bustled away. He couldn't have made it any more obvious if he'd been reading aloud from *Cole's Notes on Hamming It*. Robbie felt his face burning up. He didn't need to turn round to see what his workmates had made of it. It would be all round the plant by now. Fitzgerald was going to Cohen's for a curry night.

No worse sight could have greeted Vincent as he entered the hothouse. His bag, his blazer and all their contents had been emptied out all over the floor. Scattered on top of them were several dozen blistered playing cards with fading nudes. Nudged on by Simon Blake, Isobel Cohen swallowed hard and threw herself into character. Scuffing at the nudie cards with the sole of her shoe, she circled Vincent, her face twisted in contempt. 'What d'you call this, you freak? You fucking pervert!'

Suddenly, a thunderball flew past her, throwing itself into Vincent's chest and driving him to the floor. He blinked and gasped for air. Sat on top of him, reddened by fury, was Victoria Cohen, the quieter sister. She pinned Vincent's weedy arms back and let a glob of spittle drop onto his face. He wriggled this way and that, trying to get some purchase on her, when a splintering pain caught him in the ribs. Isobel was leering over him.

'Spazzy 'ead!' She kicked him again. This one didn't hurt so much. 'Crappy hair!' Kick. 'Shit, crappy hair pervert!'

Victoria jumped up, threw herself back down onto Vincent and set about him, peppering his face with angry digs and smacks. 'Spaz-hair sicko!' She punched him, full, flinty knuckles this time, right in the mouth.

'Ow!' A feeble reaction, but he couldn't stop himself. He put his hand to his mouth to check for blood.

'Go Vicky! Go Vicky!'

A crowd gathered around them. Throughout the din, the fury and the pain, Vincent was aware of Tim Butcher, the class dunce, trudging in, confused, as ever, by everything. As though the moment were being slowed down for his own benefit and his higher education, Vincent heard every word of the exchange.

'Who's getting it?'

'Some lad with a shit haircut.'

'It's Gaylord. The Paki lad.'

'What's he done?'

'He's a pervert.'

'With crap hair.'

Izzy slammed her foot into his face. A string of bloody snot shot out as his nose burst. Vincent passed out, not through the pain or the blow itself, but at the sight of his own blood. When he came to, there was a teacher on the scene, holding one of the girls by the wrist. The other girl picked up a fistful of playing cards and held them up to the teacher. 'He had these, miss! He was making us look. He's a sicko!'

'Yeah! He's a pervert, miss!'

For Vincent, it wasn't the physical beating that hurt. It wasn't the fact that it was two girls who'd attacked him, nor that the whole class had stood around and cheered them on. It wasn't the shouts of pervert or sicko – though he could scarcely see how one boy's crowing machismo made him cool while another's stab at sexual integration made him sick. No, a whole hour after the blood flow had been staunched and the braying, stomping catcalls fled his inner ear, the one pitiful remnant of their attack that hung around to haunt him was the spite they'd reserved for one specific aspect of his being. His hair. He sat in the secretary's office, reinvented for the occasion as an ad hoc sick bay, still trying to quell the occasional sob. What could be so awful about his hair? He was more than familiar with the anti-Paki drill, and greasy hair was up there with lime-green flares and fuck-off collars and smelling of curry . . . but the sisters hadn't mentioned anything about grease or dirt. It was his actual *hair* they hated. Something about the styling, the lack of style, some offensive thing about the way his hair made him look had driven them over the edge. There was much more to their onslaught than common-or-garden bullying. They'd wanted him to really suffer out there. He stared directly at his reflection, trying not to blink. True enough, his hair was thick and somewhat shapeless. More lenient observers might call it a genius cut. Perhaps it did give him a know-it-all, somewhat smarmy look.

Vincent took a step closer to the mirror and made his mind up. The visiting nurse had said he should go home. As soon as the secretary came back with her cup of tea he would tell her he'd managed to reach his mother and she was on her way to collect him now. Another child, and they'd probably make him wait inside. Intuitively though, he knew the secretary would have no objection to him waiting for his Amah at the school gates. So he'd slip away, take himself down to Les's and let him do what he was always begging to.

Self-conscious about his split lip and the fact he wasn't in school, Vincent drew himself up, strode into Les's and asked for a skinhead. Part of it was he wanted to look hard – or harder, anyway, as hard as a diminutive, bespectacled Paki lad can look. But it went beyond that. Skinheads fascinated him. The look, the aura – something about all that excited him. But camp, fussy Les was having none of it.

'A *thkin-head*!' he lisped, eyes wide with horror, hand clamped to his mouth. 'Don't you dare ask me to butcher this beautiful little face with a thug's cut!'

Beautiful! Had he *really* just said that? It was the first time anyone other than his mother had complimented him. Shocked, then immediately flattered, Vincent's eyes met Les's in the mirror. He felt a vague and gentle throb of affection for the world-weary hairdresser with the peroxide mop. 'Well – I don't know. I just *hate* my hair. What can I do with it?' It was a straightforward question, but it had the effect of hurling Les into inexplicable delirium.

'You leave this to me, gorgeous,' he exclaimed.

Vincent swooned. He'd never been called gorgeous before – and whether Les meant it or not, it didn't really matter. He felt high.

Les set to work, hips banging into Vincent as scissors of various shapes and sizes clipped, trimmed, thinned and layered, flurrying and nipping away at his tousled thatch, graduating it into a slick, precipitous fringe that fell away right across his face, occluding one eye altogether. And when he showed him what he'd done at the back, it was nothing less than genius. Again, with intricately stepped gradients, he'd built a staggered wedge, bulbous at the

101

skull and dropping away to nothing as it tapered into the neck.

'There! David Thylvian eat your heart out!'

Vincent knew his father would kill him, but he loved it straight away. He couldn't stop staring at himself, beaming and flirting into the mirror as though it were a complete stranger looking back at him. Les laid one gentle hand on his shoulder, pleased with his work and even happier at the effect it was having on his young client.

'You look thtunning, Vinthent – even if I do thay-thow methelf!'

He ran outside in a staccato burst of joy, a sudden hunger for life. But where to go? He still had an hour and a half until home time. Then it came to him. Matt. Matt from the library. He'd only really found the courage to start responding to his gentle prompts and suggestions those last couple of weeks of the holidays, but already he saw Matt as a soulmate. To Vincent it was a definite plus that Matt was as softly spoken and as introverted as he was. Although they'd spent pretty much the entire summer nodding awkwardly then scurrying off to opposite corners of the library, bit by bit – and in the most unobtrusive way possible – Matt had gradually struck up a nice, understated kinship with the bookish young boy. Vincent loved having someone to show off to. Matt approved of the books he loved, and pointed him in the direction of other similar things he might 'get'. That's what Vincent loved best of all – when Matt would look him the eye, pat him on the shoulder sometimes and say, 'You'll get it, Vin. You'll *definitely* get it.'

He couldn't say which was more of a thrill – his being deemed worthy of Matt's personal tip-sheet, or his bestowing of a nick-name upon him. Only rarely had he ever felt the cosy swoon of inclusion that a 'Vinnie' or a 'Vin' could bring. And though Matt was sparing with his endearments, each new familiarity brought a fulsome flush of pleasure with it.

He ran, head down out of habit, clutching his blazer shut as always as he loped his awkward, leggy gait towards the library, eating up the yards with his long, silly strides. There he was. Perched on the wall outside, always in black whatever the weather, idling in the sunshine. He stopped for a second. A brief flash of panic and fear and, yes – jealousy. Matt was larking about, grinning and chortling with a friend. From the top of the street, Vincent could pick out the man's hennaed hair, a purplish nimbus hovering above him. A bloodrush of inadequacy, a cloying sense of threat that this new guy was so . . . weird-looking, so radical and challenging in his otherness. Yet, for all his sudden feelings of smallness, Vincent wanted to see more – and to be seen. As he got closer, he quashed his mild hurt at seeing a cigarette dangling from his mentor's hand, concentrating instead on suppressing the grin he could feel radiating out from within him as the two men became conscious of his approach. On seeing him, Matt did a Disney-style double take, tossed his half-smoked rollie to the floor and came bounding towards him. 'Wow!' he purred. 'Look at you! You've got yourself a Romantic's cut.'

Vincent almost fainted at the word.

'Jim! This is my book buddy, Vincent. Vin – this is James.'

Vincent was still tingling from Matt's initial declaration: a Romantic's cut. It sounded impossibly glamorous. And now, to cap it all, Jim or James was gently appraising him. He had a similar hairstyle himself, though his brown fringe was less jagged, and flecked with reddish splinters. He stepped forward, hand held out to shake. Gingerly, Vincent allowed his hand to be taken, pumped and squeezed, rather than offering any shaking motion himself. He just stared up at James. Dressed in black shirt, tight black Levis and black, school-style pumps, he looked slick and stylish.

'Top swede,' he said, nodding at Vincent's hair and sending little electric currents probing his tummy. Vincent took a deep breath and held it down. He didn't have to do anything – just stand there, being appreciated. Being cool. It felt delicious.

*

Robbie could not go home. He drove aimlessly through the town, turning this way and that, one vague plan nestling in his subconscious only to be supplanted by another. The sun was a huge glowering disc in the sky. It hovered above the factory rooftops before slipping off into the beyond. Robbie put his lights on half-beam. The petrol gauge nudged red. He drove on. It was growing dark. He pulled up at a phone box. Vincent answered, sounding curiously upbeat.

'Put your mum on will you, love?'

Sheila came to the phone. 'Robbie. Is everything OK? I was starting to get worried. Ellie's driving us up the wall asking when you'll be back.' Her voice was cracked and tiny. 'Are you OK? Is everything OK?'

He couldn't say. What could he say? 'Yeah. I'm fine. I'll be back a bit later.' He hung up and got back in his car, happier. He had an idea.

It was dark now as Robbie drove through the sodium-studded streets of his boyhood. He was gripped by a blistering nostalgia, rootless but overpowering. He lingered outside the terraced red-brick of his birth, dimly recalling the noises, the smells. He started choking, hit the accelerator and pushed away, past the wind-chafed wastelands, past the watchful tower blocks where he'd smoked his first fag, past the meagre corpse of an old Capri where Orford's eager lasses had lain down under the cover of the night. How he wished he hadn't dragged poor Sheila into all this. How much harder he had to try, to make things right for her – and how little difference it made. Any pretty Orford girl – and he could have taken his pick – they would be delirious, just to be married to Robbie Fitz. There'd be none of this overtime. None of this constant strife and struggle and heavy churning of the soul.

He came to, looked up, and blinked to clear the sting from his eyes. He was right by the Irish Club – the last landmark in the elegy of his youth. Smiling now, feeling something warm and generous and curiously fatalistic wash over him, he pulled over. He shut down the engine.

The walls had been given a lick of paint. The torn upholstery had been stitched back up. The heady waft of a simmering stew hit him as he walked through the door. He stopped, took a deep breath, and just stood there a while, taking it all in. A few old men were stooped into a well-stoked fire. A couple of youths were setting up the pool table. A TV simmered above their tender Dublin brogue. Some of the faces had changed, but it was the same old place. He padded across to the bar, pulled up a stool and ordered a pint of Guinness, his eyes stinging as he remembered how much he loved this place and what a big part of his heart it owned. An old fella at the end of the bar called over without so much as looking up. 'Titz? Bluegrass singer from the thirties?'

Robbie looked back at the old man, thin lips stained blue at the corner where he'd been sucking his biro as he tackled the crossword. Robbie was momentarily shocked – not just at hearing his name but the casual, almost throwaway manner in which it was uttered, as though he'd never been away from there – and for a moment the drudgery of his world was suspended.

'Come on well, Robbie. If you can't get it, no bastard can. Had a hit with "Song of the Sierras". You *know* him, so you do! First name begins with a J. Second name ends with a Y.'

Robbie smiled and lifted his pint to his lips as though mulling the question over. He knew it, knew it off by heart, but he wanted to tease out the moment. 'Jimmy Wakely,' he said.

The old man nodded, pushed his glasses back up his nose and filled in the answer, perfectly content for their intercourse to end forthwith. Robbie signalled to the barmaid.

'Hello, stranger,' she said. He vaguely recognised the pretty, round face, the huge freckled charms.

'Hiya,' he said, and it was evident in his eyes that he didn't know her in the way she knew him.

105

She held his embarrassed gaze for a moment, then laughed and let him off the hook. 'It's me, *Helen*.' 'El-on', she pronounced it.

Helen. Helen. The cogs of his memory spun rapidly, yielded nothing. She laughed again, flirting with him now.

'Irene's daughter?'

He saw the unmistakeable resemblance then, and he remembered the bashful chubby teenager who had hung by the small stage at St Stephen's, desperately trying to catch his eye. She'd grown into a beautiful woman. He half wanted to tell her so. Maybe later he would – he'd tell her just that. For now, he acted like he'd known all along, smiled and half turned himself around to face the club, leaning his back against the bar, eyes glistening as he remembered the Guinness-sloshed floor, the roistering din, the snowstorm outside.

'Mum's still waiting for you to bring back them fiddle players, you know.'

Robbie felt a lump in his throat. He turned back to face her. 'Irene? She's here?'

'No. She has the Irish club in Runcorn now. Still talks about you, mind.' She gave him the same bashful smile from all those years ago.

'Hey, Helen. Listen. Give us a shot, will you. The Tulamore Dew.'

'You celebrating, then?'

'Hah! I am, sort of, yeah . . .'

He sipped gently at his dram and felt it all come seeping back through him, the feeling, that wonderful, gut-tingling feeling of being here, being home. And, from nowhere, a huge swell of nostalgic grief washed up from inside of him and had him biting on his bottom lip to keep the tears back.

Eight

Sheila sat on the living-room settee, holding the letter between two limp fingers. It had been there when she eventually got home, tired, and still stung from her husband's wrath at the school gates. Instead of making her way straight back to the house and putting out the washing she'd walked and walked. None of this made sense. Robbie was angry, Vincent was more and more reclusive and Ellie, well – Ellie was just Ellie. Bolshie. Resourceful. Inquisitive. She'd be fine, Ellie. But Sheila, she was drowning. All she was trying to do was her best, for everyone.

Not even the thought of her precious boy keeping watch over his sister on her very first day at school was enough to drag her from the slough of despondency. She sat by Lymm dam, and tried to imagine how it was, life for her Robbie. He loved his babies for sure, if he was not a little hard on Vincent – and he loved her. But she was unable to love him back in the way a man needed to be loved. Occasionally, she would concede to his pleas for sex, but she could never initiate the act herself, not since the break-in and really, if she was honest with herself, not since she became pregnant with Ellie. Was it that important though? Sex? Did it mean so much to a man that it could fill him with sadness and bitterness and ultimately resentment? She felt faintly pathetic that she had no one to confide in, at least whom she could trust.

Sheila had had a sudden rush of panic and only got herself home with a few minutes to spare to wash – she was hot and tired and sweaty – before dashing back out to collect the children. She swept up the letter with the airmail sticker and the fastidious, unmistakable handwriting – the rigid marshalling of

107

blocked capitals, so precise it looked like typescript. She stashed the letter in her bag until she had time, real time, to take it all in.

The temperature dropped acutely as the cool September evening drove in and, once she'd got the children off to bed – actually quite relieved that Robbie wasn't there to witness Vincent's new, exotic haircut – she'd taken a deep, hot bath, soaked away some of her cares, wrapped herself up in her fluffy dressing gown and gone downstairs, pulled up her chair close to the coal-effect fire and settled down to her brother's letter.

She stared blankly into the mottled firelight, her eyes wide and unfocused. It was only the slicing sensation of her skin burning that snapped her from her stupor. Disbelieving, saddened and curiously calm, she digested the news a second time. Amah was dead. She'd already been buried.

Sheila folded the blue letter in two and turned the fire down a notch. She stood up, her shin stinging from the heat, and made her way slowly upstairs. She brought down her large black vanity box from the top of the wardrobe and took out her little Ganesha elephant. Placing it on the dresser and lighting some incense sticks, she drew the curtains, knelt down and prayed, starting with her mother. 'O Supreme light, lead us from untruth to truth, from darkness to light and from death to immortality . . .'

For the last couple of years she had gently relinquished any hope of ever again seeing her family back home. She wrote often to her mother and to Rasa, right up until the move to Thelwall. No answer. No reply. Not a single message, or card, or anything. She'd understood, innately, that this would always be a big ask for her mother – a leap of sympathies and ideologies that, in truth, she hardly dared ask of anyone back home. She had said she'd come home after nursing school and instead she'd fallen in love with an Englishman and let them all down. But still she wrote, told them her news, hoped they'd be happy for her until

108

one day she found herself sitting there, looking at Ganesha, and it suddenly struck her that that was that. And she stopped it all. She packed away her statues and her artefacts and she ceased sending the letters and the pictures of young Vincent and Ellie.

But what she couldn't get over, no matter how hard she strived, was the loss of her adored brother, Rasa. She missed him like a hole in the heart. With only eleven months between them, they were inseparable as children. As teenagers they'd behaved more like partners than siblings. She would iron his shirts in the morning, giggle over some foolish thing as she cut his corns or prepared him a simple lunch of roti and dhal to take to work; and he'd meet her off the college bus each evening and walk her home, stopping off at one of the stalls along the way to stand her a mango and lychee milkshake. It was Rasa who'd spotted the advert, insisted she go after the post and helped her apply for nursing school in England. When she was accepted, it was Rasa who unflinchingly plunged himself into debt to present her with her plane ticket. At the airport his face was lit up with smiles as he made her promise that she'd write as soon as she got there, write every single week. Then he turned and went home to break the news to Amah.

She wrote, regularly, passionately – and she never once heard back from him. Now she realised why. When they came to take away her body, Rasa wrote, they had found all of her letters under Amah's mattress. Sheila was happy to hear that each one of her letters, he'd found opened. And though the realisation that she'd never made peace with her mother filled her with regret, the fact that she'd seen her two beautiful grandchildren before she passed away gave her hope, too. It was a start.

She read on. Rasa was married to Usher, a quiet girl from the village who, she now recalled, used to sit and watch their skipping games, knowing she was too young to join in. It seemed impossible to imagine, but she and Rasa were expecting their fifth child! Things were good, he sounded happy – but money was tight. He simply couldn't afford to bring his family over to visit. He hoped that one day, her rich English husband would bring his niece and nephew to see them. He missed her so much. Sometimes, he forgot and he went to her bus stop to meet her. He hoped she was happy, too.

The grate of Robbie's key in the front door made her jump. She tidied up the ornaments, tucked Rasa's letter away in the casket and slumped on the bed, a Jackie Collins left open, pretending to be asleep. Robbie was whistling downstairs. She heard the fridge door open and close, heard a satisfied 'aaah' as he glugged on cold milk. The whistling got closer and closer. She concentrated on keeping her eyelids still and breathing regularly, hoping he'd just be quiet, come to bed, fall asleep. But he didn't. She was aware of him, leaning over her. For one nasty beat she thought he was about to hit her. But instead he started stroking her hair, whispering in her ear, kissing her neck. 'I'm sorry, She. I'm so sorry, my love. But I promise, I promise . . . it's all going to be OK. We're going to be right as rain, me and you . . .'

His breath was sour, his hair fuggy with smoke. She turned slightly, as naturally as possible, sighing and stifling a yawn. His kisses became more urgent. He slid a hand inside her dressing gown, coaxing her nipples, stroking her belly, reaching between her legs. She willed herself to relax, succumb, let it happen. She wanted to, but at the same time didn't want to at all. She stayed tense and, aware now that it couldn't work, affected the best, contented grunt she could conjure and rolled away from him, as though dead to the world. She heard his deep, deep sigh of frustration. She heard him undress, felt him drop like a stone into bed. She heard and felt the bed shudder as he beat himself off as quietly as possible.

Nine

November arrived suddenly, bringing forth winter's first cold snap. Robbie stepped out into the factory yard, wincing as his gloveless hands ignited. He stared up at the rinsed-out bitumen of the sky, a monstrous, stabbing pain at the back of his eyeballs. It was impossible to gauge whether it was yet another hangover or the first shards of the vicious influenza gripping the town. Whichever, standing out there with an almighty chill shredding his lungs to ribbons was pure folly. But he couldn't go back inside. With nothing much to do, the day was dawdling more begrudgingly than ever. He heaved himself up onto the low wall and, fingers numb with cold, set about rolling a fag.

One of the hoppers had jammed up during the night shift, and all three floors of the Metso plant had stuttered to a halt. Of the twenty-three men who had clocked in this morning, all had been reallocated temporary work. Those who could drive a forklift truck were dragooned to the warehouses and the yard, while the remainder were sent off to the Cormax plant. Robbie had started out his working life there on the Cormax plant, and he hated it: hated the smell, hated the routine, hated the smarting, itchy side effects of the detergent against his skin. In spite of the standard issue rubber gloves, the Cormax always found a way through, chafing at his hands and wrists, leaving him sore and blotchy. Cormax was bad enough at busy times but with orders at an all-time low anyway, and with a spare fifteen men shuffled onto the factory floor, there was no real job for them to do. The day slithered on, crushingly slowly.

Robbie groaned as he spotted Cohen's Jaguar turn, tank-like, through the factory gates. Every glimpse of Vernon, every hopeful nod and wink, reminded him that, sooner or later, he was going to have to confront this matter of the curry evening. Sheila was mentioning it first thing in the morning, last thing at night, now. She was obsessed by the idea – or obsessed by Liza fucking Cohen, anyway.

Locked away in some meeting at head office in Liverpool all morning, Robbie realised that Vernon was yet to discover the pandemonium afoot. Not only was the unprofitable Metso plant on shutdown, speculation that Cohen was away discussing redundancies was rife among the workforce. Wait till he tuned into the anger, resentment and sheer hostility starting to brew up from the shop floor, Robbie thought. He'd be all matey and gurning as he parked up and spotted him out there. Robbie was sat outside on company time, having a smoke, but Vernon would just waddle over and ask for a light. Robbie hauled himself back down from the wall, preferring the drudgery of the Cormax line to the cheesy simpatico chat of Vernon Cohen.

Vincent ducked his way round to the garbage sheds. He wedged himself between two giant aluminium bins. Too close, the feral screams of the playground pack echoed all around, the otherwordly boom emphasising the huge emptiness of the two containers. The garbage sheds had been his secret lair these last two months since starting back at St Mary's. It was the only place they didn't look for him now, its putrid stench warding them off like evil spirits. But always, he had to be on his guard. One over-hit ball, one over-zealous pursuer and they'd smoke him out.

He was only grateful that Ellie had been spared the torment that had dogged him. That first day back, as the bell for morning break reverberated through the corridor, Vincent had shot up and flown out of the classroom before anyone could get to him, burrowing his way through the raucous throng towards Ellie's classroom. He'd stuck his face up against the pane. He could see her classmates filing out through the side door, out into the playground. He scanned the diminutive knot of heads and spotted her. He couldn't help but smile. She'd ditched her cardigan, and her tie knot was pulled tight like a pea, just like the roughs in his class. She was sandwiched between two boys, one of them Liza Cohen's youngest, a hand gripping each of their shoulders. The three of them were laughing convulsively. Ellie was going to be just fine.

When Vincent wasn't reading or writing in his hideout – although the recent blast of cold weather was making this an impractical and painful diversion – he was deep in thought. Often he would be thinking about how it was, how it had come to pass, that a boy as clever and good-natured as himself came to be stuck here – hunted and hiding – in these fetid surroundings. He reflected that since moving from Orford, life had only become more unpleasant for him – and it wasn't just on the school front, either. His father's feelings towards him were now rudely conspicuous. He was embarrassed of him, that much was true. What he coveted was a son like Simon Blake, a 'rum 'un' who could stand his own with the guttersnipes that came over the locks and gathered on the wasteland flicking their baby wedges and pulling on ciggies. What he'd got was Vincent. Shy, bookish, reclusive and physically incompetent. A son who cowed at the first sight of such boys. His father wanted a miniature version of himself; a son who took an interest in their local rugby team, the Wires; someone with whom he could horse around on the rug before hunkering down to watch the big fight on *Sports Sunday*. That first Christmas they'd moved here was surely testimony to that. Robbie had ignored Vincent's pleas for a desk with an inkwell and instead bought him a punch bag. He'd hung it from the roof of the shed and in the blitz of a snowstorm he'd dragged him outside and had him dance around it, jabbing left and right till the gloves on his hands fell like weights from his wrists. But a combination of the plunging temperature and the rare exertion had precipitated a monstrous asthma attack and put paid to the brute bonding session. The bag hung there for the rest of the winter like a stuffed animal, soaked through with his father's crushed aspirations until one day Vincent came home from school and it was gone.

But at least he was free from the nightmares that had tortured him in Orford, jolting him awake and forcing his fevered head to relive the night of the break-in again and again. In the aftermath of that evening, his mother had probed him often and rigorously, and he'd told her the truth, kept nothing back: the sound of her screams had woken him, it was dark and unfamiliar and he couldn't work out where he was. He'd pushed open the door and there she was, on the floor, his father stooped over her as the wail of a siren carried close above the rooftops.

But then the nightmares came, distorting everything he held true about that night. In them, he'd edge out of the cubbyhole, curl up behind the couch and watch it all happen. And it wasn't his father bent over his mother but a man with a mean piggy face and an ugly hand. Even though his mother had been adamant, right from the start, of there being only one intruder – a *masked* intruder – there were four of them in this dream, their hideous, beastly faces leering down at her in the fire-flushed glow of the room. The nightmares were so lurid, so persuasive, that at times they were impossible to separate from his own lived version of events. But since moving to Thelwall, the regularity and intensity of the dreams had eased up. The simple reframing of space seemed to cure them completely. He stopped wetting his bed. He slept right through. And now, with the clarity of hindsight, Vincent was satisfied that that's all they ever were. Bad dreams. And he was no longer afraid.

*

Robbie came to. He'd been sat there, in a trance, staring at the engraved design on the ornamental mirror above the rickety old cast-iron till they still used in the club. Something about the cosy Celtic bonhomie of the imagery – a blissful, ruddy-faced, fattened-tight pig dancing on its hind legs as a trio of fiddle-playing felines urged him on – chimed with Robbie's recent and growing nostalgia. He'd been let off just after lunch and had come straight here. The Metso line would not be up and running till tomorrow and Cohen had used this as an opportunity to curry favour with his disenchanted floor. 'No point kicking your feet, comrades. Might as well get yourselves off.'

Comrades! It was said in jest, punctuated with a stentorian wink – just in case you didn't get the gag first time round – but it only made Robbie hate him all the more. He tilted his head back and opened up his throat to demolish the sour dregs of his fourth and final pint. Darkness shrouded the windows but Robbie could tell by the procession of headlights sweeping past that it was still early.

The odd assortment of daytime drinkers killing time and suspending reality drifted out in ones and twos after the five o'clock horn. Greenhalls had been laying off men by the hundred, and the Irish Club was, more and more, a daytime refuge for those who couldn't quite digest that their job for life was no more. Robbie could well understand the lure of the club's womb. Everything in here seemed constant, somehow harking back to better times. He examined his empty pint glass, reluctant to leave. Should he have another? Probably not. Probably best get off. Helen was whistling and bustling around, holding glasses up to the light, checking their rims for stains. He picked up a limp newspaper, damp and stained with the blackened rims of count-less pint glasses. He turned to the back page, vaguely taking in the photo-action from the Wires' weekend win while his animus overrode his conscience and drove him on to order another drink.

115

'Terrible, that . . .' Helen was leaning on the bar, nodding at the paper. Flushed as he was from the booze, Robbie could still feel his face reddening.

'Yeah. Awful.' He hadn't a clue what she meant. She seemed to fold her arms too tightly, pushing her breasts even closer together and exposing yet more enticing, freckled cleavage to his gaze. He gulped and tried to keep his eyeline on hers, but she looked away.

'I don't know. Rapists. Here. What on earth's the world coming to, hey?'

'I know.' He wanted to ask more – but how could he tell this girl, this pale beauty who was going to fuel his fantasies back home tonight that he couldn't read? He didn't have to. The ghoulish sprite that beguiles girls like Helen to gather round glass fights at Mr Smith's and pick over the bones of every macabre folk tale had her wide-eyed already.

'Imagine that, hey? If it's not bad enough, you know . . . what happened. The bastard had a withered hand 'n' all.'

'A what?'

She snapped out of it and bundled the paper open, ripping damp pages as she looked for the passage. 'Here. See?' Standing back as though she were no longer a part of the ritual, she poked a telescopic finger at the page in question. 'Bald. Beer gut. Withered hand. Can you imagine how terrifed she must have been?'

Robbie nodded sagely, as though he, too, were taking in the full gruesome horror of the rape in the park. Only once Helen had shuffled off to serve another customer did he lay the paper down again. She was only right. What, indeed, was Warrington coming to? At least his own brood were safe and sound in dull, doleful Thelwall. But still – one more for the road and he'd head back there.

Outside, the sweep and din of traffic faded to nothing, only making it more cosy inside the snug. The silent factories gave off a sepia aura, as though they, too, were already old-time movies. Not even Crossfields operated a night shift these days. The industrial clutch lay cold and quiet, and useless. He signalled to Helen for a dram. Robbie Fitzgerald was not a man who drank to get drunk. Inebriation was always a consequence, never his intention. What he loved was the getting there, starting with the intoxicating kick of that very first sip – was it really possible to feel so stoned after just one glug? He smiled at the thought, wished it was four o'clock again. His first pint was always his best. He liked to be alone with his thoughts as the virgin liquid soaked right through him and the night reinvented itself as a blank canvas, opening the mind up to the dreams and possibil-ities that were smothered by his daytime routine. Over that luxurious first pint, Robbie's dreams could take flight. He'd project himself onto an imaginary stage and reduce the room to a spellbound awe. By his second pint though, his dreams had smashed free of the fetters of plausibility, and he'd be singing to a ram-packed Talk of the North. In the audience a young, pale, firm-breasted redhead would be moved to tears. Clapping and sobbing, she'd wait for him backstage, clear green eyes full of promise. They'd roar off in his silver E-Type Jag, pulling over along the highway for wild, explosive sex. But he could never quite bring himself to invent a world without Ellie and Vincent. They were always there in the audience, too. And in these tipsy bar-room reveries, Vincent and Ellie adored his new girlfriend, and Sheila was wonderfully supportive of the whole thing.

He downed the nip and sat back, letting it burn through him. That was better. The whiskey was doing its job, soothing him, settling him down. He was ready, now. Ready for another long, silent evening of being and nothingness. If he put a spurt on, he'd get back in time to give the kids a story. Not that Vincent would be that bothered, but Ellie still loved his labyrinthine yarns. Then he'd have his tea, and have a look what was on the telly. Sheila'd want to watch *Coronation Street*. Rubbish. That Brian Tilsley? Dickhead. Made him mad the way her eyes widened every time he was on, with his fluffy blond perm and his sly eyes. Twat. At least they'd have something to talk about tonight, what with this rapist going round. Then it'd be bed, alarm clock, same thing all over again. And he'd be back here.

He put on his coat and sparked up his final rollie of the evening. Vaguely conscious of someone, a girl, idly observing him from the other side of the room, he flicked at the *Warrington Guardian*. He never, as a rule, eyed women up. He'd never needed to do so and besides, it struck him as . . . well, wrong, that's all. If someone was there to enjoy a drink and a bit of head space, let them be. He rolled both elbows across the bar and exhaled a valedictory spume of smoke into the bar-room mirror. His fingertips tingled pleasantly from the slow-burning tobacco and that shot of Tullamore Dew was still radiating gorgeously deep down. Everything was just lovely.

Blissfully inebriated now, and heavy on his feet, he was at last ready to commit the night to memory and head home. It was still early enough and hopefully Sheila would not yet have made a start on his tea. That's what he'd do! He'd bell her from the call box outside, tell her to put her feet up – he was bringing back take-away and a bottle of Cinzano. He slipped on his coat, felt for his keys and waited for Helen to reappear so he could bid her adieu.

'This paper done with?' The girl who'd been sat across the room from him was now next to him. He glanced into her pretty face, pale as a harvest moon. Close up, she was younger than his cursory glance over had suggested an hour before. He couldn't look her in the eye.

'Yeah-yeah, take it. Weren't even mine . . .' He hesitated, lost for words, then overcompensated, fishing out his keys, tossing them up a couple of inches and swiping them mid-air. 'Got 'em!

Right . . .' Only now did he turn and face her, forcing a half-grin as he spoke. 'So I'll be seeing you then!'

She met his stare and held it. 'Couldn't leave us a smoke, could you?'

He sighed out loud and glanced at the swing doors, shaking his head mockingly. 'I don't know.'

He feigned impatience with her, sighing again as he stitched together papers and tobacco. He shot her another glance. Who did she look like? There was something, if not deranged then shambolic about her. Her clothes were a little frayed at the edges, yet it suited her elfin look. She was wearing one of those mod parkas with the fur-trimmed hood. It swamped her.

'Light?'

He held out the flame and as she leant in to suck, he realised where he'd seen her before. It was Holly Golightly – the Audrey Hepburn of *Breakfast at Tiffany's*, but with one of those bloody one-eye haircuts like Vincent's. Admittedly this was a young, edgy Hepburn who gave every appearance of living on pure adrenalin. She certainly hadn't slept in a while. Her eyes were like two back-lit, slanted wounds, black circles surrounding them like perfect bruises. Her mouth was small, a perfect strawberry, her lips cracked. The two fingers now nursing the rollie he'd made her were dirty, their nails bitten to stumps, and she squeezed at the fag, eyes darting everywhere. She needed a bath, and yet her beauty knocked Robbie sideways.

'Can I buy yorra drink?'

Yes, thought Robbie. He yearned to say yes. 'I was just on me way out. Ta anyway.' Home. Why had he not said home?

'I'm not stopping myself. I've a bus to catch. Just wanted to suss the place out before I dived in head first.' She gestured with her eyes to a note pinned on the wall above the jukebox.

Robbie felt flummoxed for a moment, then thinking quickly, squinted hard and said, 'You can see that far?'

119

She shot a quick glance over to Helen, then turned back to Robbie, dropping her voice right down. 'They're looking for a new barmaid,' she said. 'Lol's OK but it's a bit out the way and it's not exactly jumping, is it? I mean how much d'yoh reckon I'd pull in in tips?' Before he had a chance to answer she added, 'I dunno. I'll 'ave a think on it.' She held out her tiny hand. 'Jodie, by the way.'

And when she smiled it got him, right between his lungs.

Waiting in the queue at the Chinese, bothered by the squall of teenagers foraging in their pockets for coins, Robbie made his mind up, turned abruptly and headed back to the car.

Jodie. Little Holly Golightly. He had to see her again. He didn't necessarily intend to bother her with conversation, with any further contact at all, really – he just wanted to see her, before he took himself off to bed. He was in luck. Driving up Liverpool Road one way, then the other, he caught sight of her inside the southbound bus shelter. Her casual posturing seemed rehearsed, as though she'd spent a lifetime performing this skewed take on beauty. Robbie pulled over on the opposite side of the road, his tummy looping backwards and forwards, a mad sickening sensation that he was teetering on the edge of something massive. It felt dangerous. He felt wonderfully, fervently alive.

Moments passed and no bus came and still he sat and watched. From the other end of the street, men's laughter fractured the still of the scene. In company, now, he suddenly felt foolish. He chided himself for this idiocy, this pure . . . Robbie-ishness. For being so easily seduced by the sorcery of the whiskey. What only moments before had hit him as a wild and tangible romance now seemed absolute insanity. What should he do? He could park up and walk back to the Irish Club and finish the job off, blot out the night altogether with another pint and another rollie, and fuck the consequences. He could smooth it out with Sheila when he got in – if she was still up. Or, no – he'd drive back, pick up the takeaway, just as he'd planned so excitedly before. He did neither. Gripped by the same queasy ripple of panic and recklessness that blindsided him back in the bar, he found himself locking the car door, hand trembling; stepping out into the road, pulse thumping; and walking towards her.

It came together, all at once. The bus appeared at the end of the road, lit up, completely empty. Robbie was still ten paces away. He was drunk. He should ditch the car and get the bus. It was late, too. With that rapist bastard out there somewhere, how could he stand by and let this lovely young thing make her way home alone? If she were there, Sheila would be telling him the same thing. It was innocent. It was chivalrous. It was common sense. But Robbie knew that it was none of these factors driving him on. It was the fact that the bus was empty. She hardly acknowledged Robbie as he drew up beside her. She brought her flat palm right up to her face, squinted to see the coin denominations before picking out six two-pence pieces. The sight of her hard-bitten fingernails made him swoon – some woozy brew of love and desire and a will to look after her, to protect. He took a deep breath and tried to inject playfulness into his voice. 'You're never a half.'

He wasn't expecting the vehemence of her response. 'Who's fucking counting?'

The lamplights stared him right in the eye, stared him down so that he had to make a show of searching for his own fare. She stepped out into the road to wave the bus down, making sure the driver had seen her. It was make your mind up time. He couldn't do it. Just as with all his plans – grand designs to get back singing, get on stage, take things in hand, master his own dreams once again, he faltered in his resolve. He wasn't too far gone – he could just walk, now, walk away without further ado.

She got on and didn't look back at him, and Robbie felt it hard in his guts. She smiled at the driver, paid and lurched for the staircase.

Robbie bounded onboard. He followed her up the narrow, curving stairway, steadying himself against the sway of the bus. He was at eye level with her slender calves, cutting in and out of her clumsy parka as she mounted each step. She was wearing DM ankle boots, and the combination of leather and skin socked him right in the groin.

The whole of the top deck was empty. She headed straight to the back seat, slid along its shiny torn upholstery and huddled up against the window, drawing her knees close to her chest. She made no gesture for him to sit, just stared out of the window. But he knew she was watching him. As the bus juddered forward, sending him reeling, briefly, he caught sight of his car. Symbolic and utterly final, the sight thrilled him. He was doing it. All sense of guilt and any lingering reservations were abandoned now, and instead he felt adrenalised and full of mad good feeling for the night and nights ahead. Jodie looked up at him, that twisted grin making him want to kiss her, hard and urgently.

'You got more baccy?'

Robbie smiled, pulled out his pouch and tapped it with one finger. She, too, smiled – warm now, and full of promise.

'Yoh better sit down than, ant yoh?'

Silently, and once again making an art form of it, Robbie built her a rollie and flashed his lighter. Jodie tugged hungrily on her fag, sucking it down as though it were a joint. She tipped her head right back and blew her smoke up at the bus's tinny ceiling, its fuzzy green light pixelated by the brilliant cold air filtering in through the slats. He watched her quietly in her window image. When she passed the smoke to him, he unwittingly turned to meet her reflection instead. She laughed her deep hoarse laugh, throwing off her hood in the action. He didn't mind the mockery, not a bit of it – just so long as he could be with her. He took a drag on the ciggy, its end flattened by her fingers, wet from her lips. He could almost taste her.

She unzipped her parka. She turned to face him, pressing her back into the window, and took back her smoke. Inhaling deeply, she stretched a boot across his lap. His dick pulsed.

'Where d'you get off?' he asked.

'End of the line.' She paused and examined the butt end of the fag, before looking into his eyes. 'You?'

He shrugged and smiled. He wasn't being enigmatic, he just didn't want to speak. He wanted to sit back and succumb to her mannish voice, and just be with her, lap up her loveliness, her boot pressing into his dick. Feeling her so close to him, his cock swelled up. Any more, and she'd feel him. He shifted slightly as he spoke. 'You live in Thelwall, then?'

Now she shrugged. Without a word she took the tobacco pouch from him, swiftly skinned up another smoke, lit up and observed him with narrowed eyes. 'I mean, we been here a while. But if we need to move, we'll move. Do you get me?'

Robbie didn't have a clue what she was on about. 'I get you, kid.'

'Kid! Who says kid any more?'

'Well? You are.'

'I'm nearly twenty!'

'Oh aye!'

'I *am*.' She rolled her eyes. 'I've done eighteen month inside.'

'Where?'

'Styal. And you've gorra be eighteen to go there . . .'

He didn't care what she'd done. Didn't care if she was reaming him. He was happy just to sit back and listen, watch every little pucker of her nose, every dimple of her cheek and her chin. He loved how her face danced as she talked, and he didn't want her to stop. There was a connection here, an instant, visceral tug

123

that went way beyond physical desire. It triggered the same gorgeous freefall inside that used to keep him up on his guitar all night, pasting words onto the melodies his fingers plucked.

She stopped talking to check out of the window and his guts shrank in panic at the realisation they were nearly there. This could be over before it had even begun. She'd be stepping off the bus and out of his life. This split, tender moment, right now – it was already history. Things were moving too quickly. He wanted to claw back the night. He needed for Jodie to feel that same devastating pull that he did. He needed for her to know that he wasn't just some chancer who'd followed her onto the bus. If only she knew him, she'd know he'd done it out of romance. He needed her to know that he was a singer, a dreamer. He wanted so badly to tell her what the Irish Club meant to him; about the night when fate had deserted him, all those years ago. And the night, only a few weeks ago, when it had transported him back there, deposited his shipwrecked soul at its doors and displayed to him the possibility of a way ahead through a vision of his past. Going back there, just walking through those doors and seeing the men, men of his own kidney stooped over their pints, had been his salvation. And now the club had delivered Jodie to him. It was meant to be, and he needed her to know that.

She took him by surprise by jumping up at the next stop. When she'd said end of the line he thought she'd meant just that. But he was relieved. They were a comfortable way away from Hayes Close, and she hadn't made any big deal about farewells. She was expecting Robbie to follow her. He made an apologetic leer at the bus driver and scampered along after her.

They walked in silence down a terraced street that gave onto the ship canal towpath. On the other side of the placid black drink, the safe routine of Thelwall bore on, lights already extinguished as happy families committed themselves to sleep. His own little family was over there, tucked up, tucked away. All over Thelwall, people were choosing to sleep rather than stay up. To lie down, instead of carrying on standing. To turn over, rather than face. All those good people were choosing silence over noise.

As though reading his thoughts, Jodie linked him, her wrist touching his. The sensation of skin upon skin shot up his arm and jolted him in the chest, leaving him gasping. He tried to pull her closer, but she pivoted him round and pointed to the boxy silhouette of a pub. 'That's my local,' she said. 'At the moment.'

At last circumstance had thrown Robbie a bone. Inside he smiled, and made the most of the ceremony. 'Is it? I used to gig there,' he added casually.

The revelation hung in the night sky, waiting to come home to roost. And then it came. She turned right round to face him, eyes wide. 'What? You're a DJ?' But she sounded more shocked than seduced. Robbie felt his throat tighten.

'Singer, doll,' he said authoritatively. 'That's what I do. I'm a singer.'

'Do you write your own songs?'

'I do. Aye.'

She ran a cursory eye over his overalls, but she wanted to believe now. Robbie was offering her a splinter of glamour, and she was keen to see it. 'How come you're in workies' gear, then?'

At this, Robbie was so well-versed he had to force himself to breathe slowly, make it sound off the cuff. 'A true artist doesn't perform for money,' he growled with all the weary gravitas he could muster. He fingered his overalls as he spoke, looking down at his boots. She nodded and nuzzled her cheek right into his arm.

'Can I . . . can I come and see you sometime? Hear you sing, like?' Her voice had lost some of its granular bite. For that moment, she almost sounded girly. Robbie responded in kind, his gruff modesty so affected he almost forgot to charm her.

'Don't see why not, kid. Yeah.' And as he said it, even though he hadn't stood in front of a crowd in almost five years, even though he hadn't thought up a single refrain, there was a delirious tingling certitude coursing through his veins that this time, he would. He was definitely coming back.

'Where, though? When?'

He couldn't falter here. This was crucial. Any stalling at all and the moment was lost. Where the fuck, where could he say, quickly? Where was he certain to get a gig? Even now, even after all these years away from it, who would have him back like that? And then it came to him. Of course. Where had Helen told him her ma had moved on to? 'Week Saturday. Think it's Runcorn, have to check.'

She hugged him. 'And I can definitely come?'

'I said so, didn't I?'

Everything was hyperreal, saturated with the shadowlands' weird half-light, making even the rooftops intense and heightened against the blue-black canvas of the night sky. Robbie had always thought the filthy bitumen water of the canal ugly. Now, he marvelled at the way the glossy black strip merged with the navy dome of the pin-wheeling sky, the squat black iron bridge crouched low beneath the weight of the moon. He rolled them a smoke as they walked. They continued along the towpath, past the last clutch of houses. She was taking him onto the wasteland. His dick was already stabbing out at the thought of it. And no sooner did he think it than he was overcome with terror. This young, infallible, beautiful girl was going to lie down with him and, for the first time in years, Robbie was going to have sex with a woman who desired him. He was suddenly scared shitless. What if it went wrong? What if he was no good?

'So. This is me, here.'

Robbie looked round into the spume of darkness. How was

126

this going to happen? Who would make the first move? Where was it going to happen? Eyes wildly trying to locate an obliging spot among the rubble, the tyres and the potholes, Robbie reckoned the best bet was to stand up against a tree. She read his thoughts and laughed, directing his gaze towards two phosphorescent lights glowing like wolves' eyes. He stared hard until the distant outline resolved into focus – a solitary caravan, surrounded by scrub.

'You live in a caravan,' Robbie blurted, then added, 'That's amazing.' He felt foolish. There was going to be no sex. Not tonight. She'd toyed with him all along, let him think his thoughts, make his assumptions.

'I like it. It has its up sides. Means we get to move house whenever we want.'

Who's we? Robbie was dying to ask. But he didn't. He stood, awaiting the verdict. Was this going to be it, or would he maybe see her again? A few minutes ago she'd seemed truly besotted by the revelation that Robbie was a singer. He could kick himself for sliding straight back into that act of his: yeah, I'm a singer. So what? Given the time again . . . But it was hopeless. She was looking at him, if not with scorn then certainly wicked amusement. She'd played him and she'd won.

She took one last hungry pull on her smoke and flicked the butt out onto the scarred scrubland, watching the embers fizz to nothing. Robbie followed her eyeline across the horizon. Chimney stacks, telephone cables, factories lay dormant in the distance. She was feeling it the way he did, he could tell. She felt things huge and hard. He shuffled behind her, putting his arms around her waist and resting his chin on her frail shoulder so his lips grazed her earlobe. He felt her shudder. She backed into him, and she sighed, not with her lips but with her body. He could feel her succumbing. Whatever he said now, it was going to have to be something wondrous. His words and his message would

127

have to be eternal, because this was going to be their first kiss. But Jodie spoke first. She straightened, throwing him off. 'Is she pretty then?'

'Who?'

Any playfulness was gone from her voice. There was only acid as she spoke out to the magic night. 'Your wife.'

Robbie stalled a moment, striving for the right tone. 'Who says I'm married?' he asked, trying to sound jaunty.

'You. Everything about you.'

He couldn't speak. Jodie turned to face him.

'So. Is she? Is she pretty?'

Robbie paused, no longer worried for himself, him and Jodie, any of that. He thought of Sheila, his always-smiling wife, back in their house. He felt a flush of guilt. What could he say? 'Yes,' Robbie said softly. 'Yes she is.'

He saw the sting of hurt silt up in her eyes. She turned back round and looked out across the water. He wanted to slit the silence. There were a hundred things he wanted to tell her. He wanted to tell her that it shocked and terrified him, what was happening now. And it was happening. Jodie was still here, still with him, and in spite of everything, it was all going to happen. He needed her to know that – that it wasn't a whim. He wasn't some married fella looking for a bit of strange. Instead he turned the spotlight on her.

'What about yourself?'

'What about me?'

'You got someone?' He felt his stomach sinking in anticipation. The blow she delivered was even worse.

'I wouldn't be stood here if I had someone, would I?' She turned to him, fiddled with the clip on his shoulder strap and gave him a rueful smile. 'You best go,' she said. 'Your tea'll be getting cold.' She swallowed hard and, smiling briefly, she kissed him on the lips and ran towards the caravan.

'Jodie!' he shouted. Her bunched figure stopped for a second. A silhouette appeared in one of the caravan windows. A vested torso.

'What?'

'I'm mad on you,' he mumbled.

'WHAT?'

He cupped his hands around his mouth and shouted, 'I'M MAD ON YOU, KID!' Even in this half-light, he could see her square, babyish stained teeth, smiling. 'WHEN CAN I SEE YOU AGAIN?'

She shrugged her shoulders, blew him a kiss and ran. Robbie watched her disappear into the band of light as the caravan door opened then closed. He stood there under the leaking moon, willing the night to suck her back out again. When his heart and his loins could stand it no more, he ran back towards the bridge. Hidden in the echoing chamber, he squatted down on the towpath, unbuttoned his overalls and let his dick spring free. Feasting on her, hard and urgent, Robbie almost passed out with relief as powerful jets of spunk sprayed out against the damp brick wall, again and again and again. And he was spent.

Ten

Sheila's mood deteriorated over breakfast. She rarely allowed a squabble from the night before to bleed into the new day. She rarely allowed a difference of opinion to flare into a squabble at all. But on this one occasion, she was standing her ground. She slapped his breakfast on the table, wincing at the children to let them know they were absolved of any blame. All the evidence of her righteous ire was splayed across Robbie's plate in the slapdash pile of sausage, eggs and beans, and the charred underside of his toast. She hadn't bothered to thaw the butter before applying it and it had torn great holes in the bread.

Robbie pretended not to notice. He'd met Jodie and he felt good about life. He felt guilty for it, too. He wanted to make things better for Sheila and, therefore, better for himself – but this? Liza Cohen? He prodded the egg and let its yellow current spill all over the sabotaged toast. Even without looking up, he could sense Sheila, pushing a sulky fork around her plate, head hung so low that her nose was almost grazing the yolk. His throat tensed with each mouthful of food, then eventually, he snapped. 'Be reasonable, She,' he pleaded. 'She's my boss's bloody wife! You can invite the whole bloody street round if you want, and I'll dress up in a shirt and cravat and wait on you like Soft Joe. But there's no way Liza frigging Cohen sets foot in this house. End of.'

Sheila sighed and shook her head, lost for words. She shouldn't have asked him last night. She should have just gone ahead and invited Liza over anyway. She couldn't see why he was being so unreasonable. It wasn't like she was angling for a weekend at their Anglesey retreat for God's sake. All she wanted was to coach

Liza through the basics of a simple chicken curry. She cursed herself now for being so foolish, so bloody upfront about everything. Thinking on it, she could easily have had Liza round early, like she'd done the coffee morning, which would have bought her the rest of the day to fumigate the spicy evidence from the kitchen before Robbie returned from work. But she wanted to run it by him, to do the right thing. As ever she wanted his blessing.

Only Ellie's dogged attempts to imitate her daddy's angry facial expression brought any levity to the table. Vincent winked at her and pushed his cereal bowl away to make room for his scrapbook. He'd located great new pics of Adam Ant in the *Record Mirror* and they were going straight into his album. Robbie cocked his head and appraised the androgynous pop star clad in pirate's regalia. Unwilling to make an enemy of the kids too, he let his disapproval be known to his wife with a curt shake of the head. Eyes down, tongue protruding, Vincent carefully secured the cut-outs in place, penning in a vignette beneath each picture. Every few seconds he'd pause to push his glasses back up his nose. Ellie pushed herself up in her chair and craned her neck across the table.

'What are you doing?' she asked.

'An exercise in character building,' he replied, without looking up. He continued to scribble away.

'What's that?'

Vincent sighed. Reluctantly, he prised himself away from Adam and fixed his specs on Ellie. 'It's a bit like role play, Ellie. You know – what you do with Mrs King in singing and drama?' Robbie and Sheila both looked up, now. Vincent continued with renewed self-importance. 'It was Matt's idea.'

'The library man?'

'Well – he doesn't like to be called a librarian.' Vincent shot a glance at his father, fairly certain he wasn't going to like this. 'Matt says librarians are just curators.' He drew himself back, smiling back at the recollection, and announced: 'Mothball curators of fusty tomes.' He stopped so everyone could laugh at his mentor's witticism and, when no one did, continued with his explanation. 'Matt prefers to see himself more as a facilitator, do you see? He's a facilitator of knowledge and yes, he's been helping me with my stories.'

Robbie grimaced at Sheila as though she'd engineered all this.

Vincent went on. 'Matt says that basically I have great characters but my stories are a bit one-dimensional. So what I'm doing is using one character – Adam Ant – and taking him through a whole load of different, everyday things. Like, say, a walk in the park. Or a trip to the pictures. Matt says . . .'

'Matt says!' minced his father, surprised by the venom of his own outburst. 'And how do we know this Matt's not, you know?'

Vincent pushed his specs back up his nose. Sheila intervened. 'Robert! Don't!'

'Bloody load of . . .' Exasperated, and unable to pinpoint exactly what he found so irksome about this mysterious new book person who was taking over Vincent's life, Robbie stormed out, slamming the door. Sheila smiled sadly at Vincent.

'Take no notice. Your father just feels . . .'

'I know,' said Vincent with a smile.

'Come on!' shouted Ellie. 'What happens?'

Pleased to have such a rapt, captive audience – albeit only two strong – Vincent rolled his eyes and leant forward. 'Well. What happens is that Adam comes home from his walk in the park and finds his dear, lovely old mother all white and sick in bed. She says to him, "Son, my time is near now. You must abandon me and follow your dreams."'

Ellie launched herself at his scrapbook, desperate for a closer look. 'But do pirates even have mothers?'

'He's not a pirate, Ellie. He's Adam Ant – King of the Wild Frontier. Emperor of the New Romantics.'

'Sounds stupid to me,' said Ellie. But she snatched the book from her brother and sat back down. Within moments, her eyes popped up above the cover. 'Wow!'

Vincent took his scrapbook back.

'I want a-Adam Ant sticker book,' she bleated.

'No, Ellie. You already have a sticker book.'

'It's full.'

Sensing that argument would get her nowhere, she pushed on, small brown arms folded defiantly. 'And I don't like football sticker books any more! They don't *do* anything!' She scowled in jealousy at Vincent's album. 'Want one like that.'

Robbie returned to the room, his brow still wrinkled by his defensive snarl.

'Dad. Can I have a Ant book?'

Unable to stay cross in the eye of his daughter's pot-bellied cuteness, Robbie winked at her and sat down at the table again. 'We'll see.'

She offered him a conspiratorial smile, a smile of unconditional love. But he felt wretched. In the midst of this family breakfast scene, a portion was fenced off, for Jodie. As soon as he could easily do so, he was dashing off to see her.

'Dad!' He jerked back out of his reverie. 'I want a-outfit like Adam Ant's. Can I have one? Can I?'

Vincent groaned. 'Ellie, an outfit like that is not something you can buy. The Adam Ant look is something you put together.'

Robbie's face tensed. 'Just give it a rest will you, son? D'you hear me? Pipe down and finish your breakfast.'

Vincent muttered into the tablecloth, 'You can't just switch off. Not if your muse doesn't want you to.'

'You what?'

But as Vincent went to answer, his glasses slid from his nose, plopping neatly onto his plate. Sheila stifled a smirk, and for a moment she found herself revelling in the discomfiture and panic

133

her clever young boy was starting to instil in his father. She picked them out, wiped them down and went across to the tool drawer, dipping inside for a small screwdriver.

'You wouldn't understand,' yawned Vincent, rubbing away the dents either side of his nose.

Robbie couldn't look at him without experiencing a sharp stab of disappointment these days – betrayal, even. Where had he gone wrong? All he'd wanted was a son, a boy – someone to muck around with. Instead he got this. Mentors. Curators. Muses. And the cheek of him, by the way – 'wouldn't understand'? If that lad knew what he'd forsaken to let him grow up out here, with his books and his libraries and his tart's hairdo. The sight of his son's mole-like face blinking helplessly against the kitchen's strip light stirred an irrational anger in him, and he got up sharply, tapping into his anger to help him make The Call. Robbie hated the telephone, but the sooner he spoke to Irene, the better. He was failing, here. He had to do something.

Eleven

Top of the Pops was due on any minute. Vincent gave himself a final once-over in the mirror. He liked what he saw. It had been well worth the effort. He was wearing his mother's gold shimmery tights, her brown suede tuck boots and a braided, military-style jacket they'd picked up for a pound in a charity shop, not unlike the type the Beatles wore for the cover of *Sgt. Pepper*. He'd made a tricolour cummerbund from three silken neck scarves which he'd plaited around his waist, and to top the whole look off he'd daubed his eyes in eyeliner and struck a bold band of white eyeshadow across the bridge of his nose.

The theme tune pealed out and Ellie ran in front of the TV. Vincent gently tugged her to one side. It amazed him that a programme dedicated to showcasing the cream of British pop could get away with such a monumentally crap signature tune. These were swashbuckling times for music, and the best they could come up with was some crusty old electric guitar solo. Weren't the BBC supposed to act as arbiters of good taste? Wasn't that why Mum was always threatening Dad with the ignominy of the big white van pulling up outside the house when he kicked up a fuss about paying the TV licence, because the BBC knew what was best? There was no debate, the theme tune was rubbish and this, along with why the Prime Minister had taken their school milk away when everyone said how good it was for you, and why his father called his haircut 'puffy' when his own hair was almost down to his shoulders, was just another of life's great conundrums.

Sheila popped her head around the door with the earpiece of the phone pushed into her chest. She rolled her lids back revealing

135

the whites of her eyes and brought an admonitory finger to her lips. Vincent gave her the thumbs-up and slid the volume down a notch. But no sooner had his mother left the room than Ellie banged the sound back up again.

'Ellie! Mum's got an important phone call. She told us . . .'

'Antman's going to be on in a minute!' She pouted decisively, arms firmly folded, and that was that. Ellie pushed her paper pirate hat into place and pulled down the elastic dangling across the tip of her nose. Antman. Vincent snorted to himself. He resented this action hero sobriquet she'd bestowed on him, but even worse, he was starting to lament the folly of bringing her into the Romantics fold. He should have known better. In just one week, she'd managed to make a mockery of the profound ideals of this passionate, yet puritan movement. He'd tried, belatedly, to steer her towards something more poppy. He'd dangled Duran Duran and Michael Jackson. But her loyalty to the fearless half pirate, half Apache was unswerving. Adam Ant was her first pop crush, and there was no going back now.

The pair of them waited with bated breath for the top ten countdown, wondering if Adam had managed to nudge Buck's Fizz off the top spot. For a few tense seconds Vincent forgot his gripe and they were joined as one, united under the credo of Antmania. Then they came on, and his deflation at the fact they'd dropped a place – the galling Toyah Wilcox had leapfrogged the Ants – alloyed to Ellie's dancing made him cross. He looked at the spectacle of his little sister, gyrating her hips violently, each thrust launching the horse brass she'd commandeered as a makeshift pirate's buckle and dragging her waistband down below her knickers.

'It's not punk, Ellie!' he screamed, although he couldn't be entirely sure if he knew what punk was. 'It's not for everyone!'

Ellie ignored him, snapping her pelvis as though working a hula hoop.

'For God's sake, Ellie. At least get it right. That's not even an Ant move.'

'Yeah, it is a-Antman move! You're just jealous because you haven't got a pirate hat. Everyone knows that's what the real Ants are wearing!'

''Scuse me, real Antpeople come up with something original.'

'Hah! At least I've not *bought* my costume,' she hissed back. 'I've pieced mine together!'

Vincent stepped back, winded. Wounded. He looked at his little sister, jacking madly along with the studio audience, and shook his head. So soon, so soon. Was this really the kind of pantomime that Antmania had been reduced to? Christmas-cracker hats and cardboard swords? Last week it seemed as though he was the only boy in town who'd even heard of Adam Ant. Now this – one TV appearance and already the movement had reached its nadir. He wanted to snap the elastic on his sister's hat; with its smiley skull and crossbones and cheap gold cardboard, that hat seemed to flag precisely the moment where the movement had turned on itself. He was all for going back upstairs and taking off his make-up, but again that sense of guilt prevailed. He watched the cameras pan across a sea of flailing arms and plastic muskets, fastening on the snarling face of his idol, Adam Ant, lit up in a shower of gold and scarlet light bulbs. How could he abandon him now in his hour of need? It was simple – he couldn't. With his credibility in danger of being sabotaged by little sisters all over the country brandishing weapons made from cereal boxes, Adam needed the likes of Vincent Fitzgerald like never before. First thing tomorrow he was writing to the fan club to strategise their rearguard action.

Sheila came into the lounge grinning and seemingly in mild shock. Vincent turned, grateful for an excuse to miss Ellie's last, triumphant chorus of 'Antmusic'. Sheila flopped down on the sofa. She grinned over at Vincent and nodded 'aah' at Ellie's clumsy dance routine. Vincent arched an eyebrow. 'What's happened, Mum? Good news?'

'Well – not really. But yes. I suppose so . . .'

'What then?'

She beckoned for Vincent to come and sit next to her. 'So. You know the nice lady who you see me talking to sometimes? When I pick you up from school?'

Vincent's heart sank. He knew exactly who she meant. 'Mrs Cohen?'

'Liza. Yes. Lovely lady . . .'

Vincent wanted to tell her; how lovely could a lady be who brought her piggy little daughters up to scratch, bite, tease, punch, snitch, lie and kick? He looked into his mother's eyes – and he knew he couldn't do it to her. She had that enchanted, faraway look he only rarely saw in her these days. He didn't know what brought it on, or made it go, for that matter. All he knew was that, sometimes, his mother was on top of the world – and this was one of those times. 'What about her?'

'Well . . .' She puffed out her chest as she let him in on the news. 'Liza has asked me to host the next fund-raiser . . .'

'Fund-raiser?'

'Yes. What's so funny about that?'

'What're you raising funds for?'

'I don't know,' she giggled. 'Forgot to ask her!'

Vincent tried to keep the scowl out of his voice. 'Well. It'll be some good cause, I'm sure . . .'

As excited as she was at the fun and hard work that lay ahead if she were to repay Liza's faith in her, even Sheila couldn't have missed the hurt in her son's face. She wrinkled her brow and touched his leg. 'What is it, baby? Hey?'

'Nothing.' He looked away from her, out of the window. The rain outside, of which he'd only been faintly aware, rose to a roar. Vincent chanelled everything into just keeping his breathing regular. He was all too familiar with this sensation, and knew how it would end up. Whenever he felt wronged he couldn't speak without bursting into tears. He couldn't let that happen. Not now. Not over the Cohen sisters. He composed himself, swallowed his anxiety, set his shoulders straight and started to feel he might be OK.

His mother's face softened into a smile. She walked her hand towards him along the ragged polythene that still clung to their settee and ran her fingers along his cheek. He turned his face away, eyes troubled. 'Don't be silly, darling. Tell Amah!'

Penned in, his teeth started to chatter as he built himself up into a state. 'I can't,' he cried, jumping up and standing in front of her, wronged and betrayed.

She tried to smile and cajole her way out of it. 'Come on . . .' She patted the seat next to her. 'Tell Amah what's eating you.'

Furious, he pointed a finger in her face, hoping and praying that the words wouldn't come. They came. 'You should know without me having to tell you,' he spat. 'You're a crap mother.' And with that he flounced out of the room. Never one to miss out on a drama – and the potential lure of a conciliatory treat – Ellie joined the show of strength and stormed out in his slipstream.

Sheila was gazing absent-mindedly at the TV when Robbie arrived home. She started when he walked into the lounge, saw the time on the wall clock, jumped up and apologised. 'Robbie! I don't know where the time's gone! I've not even put the oven on.'

Robbie gripped her gently around her shoulders and pushed her back into her seat. His eyes were squiffy, his voice mellow and he wore his careless, drowsy, four-pints glaze. Yet there was more. There was something different about Robbie, something beyond the half-drunk figure that rolled home most evenings, equally ready to squabble or chatter. Tonight, he seemed . . . high. She'd heard a lot about drugs and addictions, but surely

139

not her Robbie? He plonked himself down next to her and focused woozily somewhere in between her eyes. 'You,' he said decisively, 'are not lifting a finger!'

Sheila felt too sapped by the evening's events to question either his mood or his motive, but it planted something unpleasant deep within her. As though sensing her unease, Robbie hauled himself up and went into the kitchen, keeping his back to her questioning eyes. He dug around and, pleased with himself, retrieved a heavily stained menu from under the bread bin. Ellie appeared at his side. Robbie scooped her up and sucked her whole ear into his mouth. He kissed her on the tip of her nose then pulled back to get a proper look at her. Her eyes were spring-loaded like she wanted to tell him something.

'Hello, little smasher! Who loves you, hey? Who loves ya, baby?'

Her face buckled. 'Vincent sworn-ah!' she said – and promptly forced tears.

Robbie shushed her, kissing her forehead. 'Hey, little fella, shush-shush! Tell me . . .'

Manfully, she quelled her sobbing shoulders and looked her father in the eye with full melodramatic confusion. 'He said a very wrong word.' She paused, sticking the knife in with exquisite timing. 'To Mum.'

Robbie bit back a smile. With Ellie still wrapped around his waist, he reached down into the fridge and retrieved a can. He measured its temperature against his cheek. 'Did he now. Well we can't have that sort of nonsense going on, can we, poppet?' He put her down and stepped into the living room, snapping back the ring pull.

Ellie poked her head around the doorjamb then scurried back into the kitchen. She paced the floor restively, nipping her inner lip with her lower teeth. When she could stand the tension no longer, she ducked under the kitchen table and huddled herself in a cosy ball against the radiator, safe against the maelstrom

140

that would follow. Now she'd set things in motion, she was eager to distance herself from the action.

Robbie sat down, casting his eyes over the menu out of habit rather than curiosity. He knew what he'd be having. Duck. He licked the icy droplets off the side of the can and ventured a glance at Sheila. She was looking at him funny.

'Go on, then. What's he been up to? Our Vincent?' He slurped on the can and passed her the menu. His mouth had a sneering curl to it which she did not like. She knew how much it would please him to be able to reprimand their son for something worthy of the name – to have the neighbours knocking at the door, dragging their bloodied sons with them. But Vincent's bad behaviour rarely ventured beyond putting his light back on after bedtime, or forgetting to flush the toilet or, worst of all, picking at his food. She wanted to tell Robbie what had happened, but only as a way into the bigger issues. Liza. The curry evening. Her life outside Hayes Close.

Sheila pored over the menu. She wasn't hungry, but the roof of her mouth now tingled in anticipation of spice. These days, take-away tended to mean something from the chip shop, or a tea-time special down at the Little Manor – scampi and chips, chicken in a basket. Tasteless cardboard, whatever name they gave it. She knew he'd started drinking after work – but that drowsy, dreamy face he was wearing took her back to their early days of courtship. She wasn't inclined to quiz him though – not tonight, and it just wasn't worth it, anyway. She opted for the chicken satay, by no means her favourite oriental dish, but without a doubt the hottest. She ordered some prawn crackers for Vincent too, in the hope that the spicy aroma might lure him down from his sulk. The breaded chicken fillet and the glass of dandelion and burdock she'd left outside the bathroom door had not been touched last time she looked, and there was still no sign of him coming out of there.

Robbie dialled up the order, adding a half duck and beansprouts

141

for himself, then settled on the floor in front of the fire, pulling out tobacco and papers, and started to build a rollie. Sheila watched him with mounting suspicion. He only ever smoked outside – even in the fiercest scourge of February he'd go out back, squat down on the cold concrete and nurse his dirty habit in solitude. The kids were well aware that their father smoked – they smelt it on his breath and sometimes the wind kicked up his long-dead butts and spat them across the lawn – but Robbie was always at pains to stress to his children that smoking was bad for them. For him to light up right here could only mean his mind was elsewhere. Sheila brought two weary hands to her face and tried to rub loose some of the anguish that was tightening it to tears.

'Oh Robert,' she sighed. 'There's something wrong with Vincent.'

Robbie looked at her, serious for a moment. 'How like?'

Sheila felt a slow wave of guilt for the panic strafing her husband's eyes. She'd made it sound more grave than it was, but she had his attention now, and she didn't want to lose it. 'Just lately, I don't know, he's receding even further into himself. He's so uptight . . .'

Robbie looked relieved. His attention had already wandered back to his tobacco and papers. Sheila felt a staccato stab of anger. She strived for his attention once more.

'He's been wallowing there in the bath now for hours. I left his tea outside the door for him. Not touched it. Stone cold. I'm telling you, Robbie, something's not right.'

Robbie jumped to his feet, flushed, his nose wrinkling up with anger. 'What? He's not eaten his tea? Vincent!'

His shoulders squared for confrontation. Sheila felt an awful clawing in her tummy. She'd played this one badly, and it was only going to get worse. 'Robbie! Robbie! Please don't! Leave him . . .'

He swung round in the doorway, his face puce with rage. He pre-justified his actions out loud. 'We'll see about letting his tea go cold.'

Sheila made a feeble lunge, trying to pull him back into the room. He shrugged her off.

'The big Mary Ellen. You need to toughen up, you! Taking his fucking tea up to him . . .' He stormed out of the living room, slamming the door shut behind him.

The pounding of her father's feet on the stairs dragged Ellie out from under the table. She came running into the lounge and took flight in the hot ravine of her mother's breast. Sheila pulled her baby in close, wrapping her hands around her little ears. Ellie began to sob. As the evening's drama lurched towards its conclusion Ellie wished more than anything she could wind it back. She didn't mean it to happen like this.

Vincent was wallowing in the bath, in the mellow dark, thinking about things. All sorts of thoughts skittered across his consciousness – clothes, records, Matt, Mum, the Cohens, school. In particular, school was on his mind. School was hell – it was purgatory – but he was used to it and, like a gazelle in the wild, he was skilled in avoiding his hunters. At worst he'd been kicked, punched, bitten, slapped, tied up and, once, last week, tortured with cigarettes and matches. In a way, it seemed normal to him or, if not exactly normal, it was easily explained away. He could make sense of it. Only the Cohen girls seemed to actively hate him. But how could he tell Mum that? She positively idolised Liza.

He checked on his wrist to see how the blistering scab was coming along – he'd suffered worse from being tied up so tightly, although the flame on his palm stung for days afterwards. All of this he took as par for the course, and took it easier for the knowledge that Ellie was sailing through school unscathed. He

143

topped up the tub with more hot water. Every time it started to cool, he'd pull out the plug with his toes, let the tepid water drain off, add more hot and nimbly replace the plug. But now the pipes were reverberating with a stentorian drone that told him the tank was dry, and the bath was dangerously full.

It was this spectacle that greeted Robbie as he barged the bathroom door open, snapping the flimsy lock: his son, almost wholly submerged in an overflowing bath, face streaked with gold flecks and runny mascara, humming to himself as he stared up at the ceiling.

Vincent, ears deliciously warm and pulsing under the water, didn't hear his father come in; didn't hear his shouting or his feet on the stairs. He didn't hear any of it, just dimly registered the vibration of the door banging against the bath. Only the sudden snap of the light and a vague sensory perception sat him up. He blinked at the sudden flurry of movement; through weak, squinting eyes, he just about made out his father's vermilion hair. He felt out along the rim of the tub for his glasses, causing a great slosh of water to crash onto the floor. He managed to locate them just as they were flung into the water by the force of the mighty crack of a hand slapping his wrist. Another blow got him hard and fast across the cheek. He ducked down into the water so Robbie couldn't hit him again, the violent flailing of arms and legs heaving another great torrent of water over the side of the bath. But this just enraged his dad further. His huge hand delved down into the bath water and dragged Vincent up by the hair, up and over and right out of the bath. He stood there dripping, shivering, both hands clamped pathetically over his privates.

Blinking and scared, Vincent still hadn't worked out what he'd done wrong. He'd been in trouble for using up the hot water before, for filling the bath right up, but nothing like this, ever. He could feel the rancid paste of his father's beer breath, hot on

144

his face. He could hear the vicious squeaking of the mirror being rubbed clear with a bare hand. But he couldn't see a thing. He could just make out the bleary outline of his father's arm groping around in the water – then he handed him his glasses.

'Look at yourself!'

Vincent was dimly aware of Ellie crying downstairs.

'Just look at you!'

Vincent pushed his nose right up against the mirror, right into the naked leering truth of his reflection. He let out a nervous laugh. He looked like a painting that Ellie might bring home. The steam had fleshed his eyes out into two kohl bruises and the sticky gold lipstick now clung to his lips like a second mouth.

'Do you want me to start dressing you in a skirt as well, hey? Is that what you want?' His dad let go of his head with a final thrust and stood back, panting. 'That what it is, hey? Put on your mam's make-up and . . .'

The injustice of it, rather than the violence, got to Vincent and he felt the onset of tears. He couldn't speak. His throat, swollen and sore, throbbed harder with each breath he snatched. He hung his head low, and his glasses slid down his soapy face and onto the floor. He felt puny – squalid and ridiculous; a skinny, pathetic, found-out nude, shivering in shame in front of his father. He turned away, seeking his freedom by looking elsewhere, finding his own spot.

Robbie snapped off the light and went to his bedroom.

Twelve

After Sheila had seen Ellie and Vincent off to school she took a bus to Lymm. She sat at the window, her eyes slatted against the pale November sun, thinking it all through. Vincent had stayed in his bedroom this morning till he'd heard his father's car pull away from the drive. She'd taken his breakfast up to him. He'd managed a conciliatory smile. Without having to say a word, she knew intuitively that he didn't blame her. Robbie, in comparison, was unaccountably chipper, almost as though it hadn't happened. He even promised them the rare treat of a pub supper out in the country. Whether this was a sop to his conscience or an olive branch held out to Vincent, she couldn't be sure, but she felt the same queasy foreboding she'd felt last night when he'd come through the door with that dreamy look about him. Something had caused this shift in constitution and she ached to know what – or who – was responsible.

The bus deposited her outside the ancient parish church – even that seemed hunched against the cold. Closest to its banks the dam was frozen hard, with odd plaques of ice slopping on its surface and the old willows lapping at its edges dusted with a silver sheen of frost. It was postcard pretty, just like the paintings in her school back home. Without permission, but knowing he'd never miss it, she'd brought Robbie's Instamatic to snap some scenes for Rasa. Now she'd found her brother again, she was making up for lost time, getting together a package of news and photos and little treats. Just inexpensive little things – clothes from the market for his kids, a packet of Hamlet cigars, Club biscuits. But as she framed and snapped the idyllic English winter scene, the thrill of the venture was at once weakened by the thought of Robbie. She still hadn't told him about Amah. The right moment had not presented itself the evening she'd received the letter, and in the days that followed, Robbie's drill of rolling in squiffy-eyed and sloppy from booze had acted as a bulwark. Yet it was more than that. Most of the time Sheila was able to keep a handle on her grief. The sheer, surreal distance between the world Rasa wrote of and the here and now of her life in Warrington enabled her to hold it off, push it far, far away. But the moment she drifted, dropped her guard, the stinging reality of Amah's death would pounce on her unbidden, eliciting a truth that left her cold and hollow. The fact was that more and more Robbie was seeking to efface all traces of the life she'd lived back home. It had come to such a pass that she could barely mention KL these days without him looking betrayed and bustling the conversation elsewhere.

But Sheila only had herself to blame. She understood his reasons, and rather than challenge them, help him see things from her point of view, she'd taken the path of least resistance and become complicit in this gradual whittling down of her culture. The few remaining relics of a previous existence – the Ganesha statue, her tongue cleaners, her incense sticks – she kept hidden away from him now, and it was only when Robbie worked the late shift that she would be so bold as to throw open the windows and rustle up a small pot of sweet, spicy nasi lemak, always heedful of disposing the evidence with candles and lavender-scented Haze air freshener.

In forcing herself to confront the situation head-on Sheila realised that far from postponing Amah's death she was actually postponing the bigger issues it cleaved open. The simple truth was that Sheila was homesick. She badly needed to go back, if not to see Rasa and the siblings she'd left behind then to pay her respects to her mother. Only then could she start to grieve for her properly. To this, she knew Robbie would never agree.

She would have to present and package Amah's death neatly to him. He would allow her to mourn for her mother, but not for her motherland. Sheila zoomed in on the lake and made a decision. If she couldn't tell it as it was, she wouldn't tell him at all. She continued snapping. If she was lucky, the swans might deign to glide this side of the dam.

She cut through the church's graveyard, exhaling cold quills of vapour as she picked her way carefully between the mossy slabs that marked the dead. A couple of girls in Loretto School blazers were hunched up at the furthest end of the graveyard, next to an uprooted birch, smoking furiously – sucking and blasting, tugging and blowing, bandying the ember from one to the other. Sheila hung back and watched them for a while, wondering if she dared steal a picture for her brother – England, old and new. The smell of their tobacco drifted on the cold and she smiled, remembering how she and Rasa would go down to the banks of the river to smoke their mother's miniature cigars. He'd let her light them while he slouched back and smoked like an American mobster, the wedge of tobacco squeezed tight between his thumb and fingers.

The young girls started when they saw her, instinctively lashing their smouldering cigarette butt and flinging themselves over the cliff ledge. Sheila gasped in horror and sped after them, halting suddenly as the land dropped away. Gingerly, she inched herself forward. She was steeling herself for the worst, for the sight of the girls' bodies lying flat and lifeless, splayed like shadows on the dam's cracked roof. But the girls' yellow and green striped blazers bobbed into view directly below her, stealthily negotiating themselves down the tricky flank of cliff. Sheila, bursting with a queer mix of empathy, relief and excitement, wanted nothing more than to shout down to them, say 'well done' and let them know it was OK; they needn't have run away. She wanted to tell them that she was a teenager too, not so long ago. Not so very long ago at all.

She descended by the broad wooden steps that had been cut into the cliff face, marvelling at the water rippling silver behind a flotilla of ducks. No swans today. Up on the bridge she saw the mobile food van parked up. Slowly, still at peace with herself, she took herself across, unhurried and without her typical worry – worry that he'd pull away before she got there, worry that school might be trying to get in touch, worry that Robbie was drifting further and further away from his son. She bought a styrofoam cup of tea so hot she could barely hold it, and sat down on a bench overlooking the dam, blowing at the surface of the tea until her lips could stand contact. Nevertheless the first sip blistered the roof of her mouth.

Warmed by the scalding tea and buoyed by the sunshine, she crossed the road to Sintah's. Sintah's had been a real find – an old-style village grocers in the centre of Lymm, recently taken over by a young Indian family. At least Mrs Sintah was young enough; her husband was a proud, rather disapproving man of forty-five or so with a small moustache and a perfectly round stomach, clad in the gold-embroidered dhoti of the Brahmin. Sheila couldn't help smiling at him. As was often the way with the higher caste, he sat perched on a stool behind the counter, half-spectacles perched on his oddly leonine nose, back perfectly straight as he perused the *Daily Mail*. Out of the few times she'd gone in there for their Patak range, or fresh limes and ginger, or coconut milk, Mr Sintah let her wait at the counter, ignoring her until his wife came out, peering down his nose at John Junor's cloying memoirs of Auchtermuchty. But Sheila couldn't take offence – quite the opposite. It seemed fitting that this absurdly arriviste fellow should have found his spiritual home here in Lymm, the epicentre of the Cheshire set.

But Sintah's was boarded up. As Sheila got closer, she spied shards of glass on the pavement. Behind the temporary hoardings shoring up their shattered plate windows, the shop was in darkness. On the main, whitewashed wall were two daubed words: PAKIS OUT. Underneath, there was a crudely drawn swastika and another symbol, like a B and an M in a circle. In spite of the bile rising within and the bang bang of her pulse, Sheila continued across the road. A small, handwritten note was tacked to the security hoarding: 'Due to vandalise the store will remained close today. Open as usual in morning. Thank you to all customer for understand. Yours, Mr Sintah.'

'Disgusting, it is.'

Sheila jumped back, and turned to face the voice. It was an old man, carrying rather than walking a small Pekinese.

'This is the third time now in a month. Every time they open up again.'

Sheila caught her breath and spoke. 'Do they know who's doing it?'

'Oh, they know all right. It's that Hitler lot from up Partington. Young bucks think they're clever with all the *zeig heil* and wogs out.' Seemingly oblivious to her colour, her feelings, to anything but the anger that convulsed inside, the man tightened his face and shook his head. 'I fought alongside Gurkhas to keep this country great. And now this. Thank God I haven't got long.'

Sheila nodded, unsure what to say. She found herself staring at Mr Sintah's sad, strangely dignified note. She turned to the old man again. 'But they're not giving in to them. They'll open up again tomorrow.'

The pensioner gave her a sad and knowing look. He shook his head once more and shuffled off, carrying his panting, lazy dog. Sheila headed back to the bus stop, looking all around for the dark force that was suddenly encroaching her world.

Thirteen

Saturday night. Robbie sat backstage. This was it, then. In five minutes he'd be on. Out there, an expectant mob had gathered in Runcorn's Irish Club, a mixture of ecstatic former acolytes who remembered Robbie Fitz from the old days – and still couldn't quite believe he was really going to be appearing here – and their sons, wives, second wives, boyfriends, nieces and nephews, all on board for the promise of a great night out.

Word had spread quickly. From finally forcing himself to make the call and convincing Irene it was really him, Fitz, live and raring to go, to the sudden proliferation of posters around the Widnes–Runcorn area and his surreal run-through last night with only a backing track for company, Robbie had thrown himself right in at the deep end. Little by little he'd found first his range, then his soul. By his fifth free Guinness and his umpteenth whiskey chaser, it was evident to Robbie that folk thought he'd hit the big time. It was funny at first – old men pumping his hand and congratulating him, telling him in all sincerity how much they loved him – but the truth, as the whiskey revealed to him, was that he'd let them down even more than he'd betrayed himself by taking his talent home and locking it away. Whatever the situation had required of him back then, he should never have given up singing. It was him. It was his life. And, more than that, it meant something to all these everyday people. Robbie Fitzgerald was their boy up there. They loved him, and they loved that he was back among them at long last.

That he would deliver for them, Robbie had no doubt at all. His sole concern was Jodie: that she'd remember; that she'd find the place; and that, plunged into the thick of a Saturday night in the hardest part of Runcorn's old town, she'd manage to remain in one piece – at least until she'd heard him sing.

A flake of him was troubled by the possibility of Sheila turning up. She'd seemed genuinely delighted by the prospect of him picking up his mic again, although Robbie fancied it was born more out of the extra money he'd be raking in rather than any concern that his talent was going to waste. Since moving to Thelwall Sheila had seldom broached the subject of his music, she'd never questioned the ease with which he'd let it all fade to dust. He only ever sang to Ellie these days and even that he did in private, when it was just the two of them, out on their walks. His guitar sat forlorn in the attic along with the unpacked crates of records that had once upon a time formed the focal point of their evening's entertainment. As Sheila's confidence had grown and she was happy to be left alone of a night, Robbie had secretly hoped she would nudge him back to the stage. Now, he couldn't shrug off the feeling that she'd given up on his dreams long before he'd given up on himself. Robbie pushed away the splinter of anxiety worming its way into his thoughts. There was no need to worry. Sheila would not be making an appearance tonight.

The club itself was a glorified wooden chalet. It looked as though it had arrived ready made on the back of a lorry and dumped on the first scrap of wasteland. In the shadow of the bridge and serenaded by the rattle and hum of trains and traffic, this part of Runcorn was riven with folklore – classic northern badlands and a law unto itself. Surrounded by new estates populated mainly by Scousers and Mancs, Robbie could relate to the type of old-school hardcases who still lived in the terraced red-bricks of Old Runcorn. The Irish Club here was less of a beacon to the Celtic diaspora, more of catch-all community centre. On any given morning it might host a Fight the Flab class or serve as polling station or a temporary signing-on centre. But every day without fail, from four o'clock onwards it was back to being the Irish Club – purveyor of cheap ale and good times. Tonight, for the first time in a long while, Robbie Fitzgerald *was* Mr Good Times – and it was all for Jodie, who'd come to see him, he hoped.

Jodie was there all right. She'd tucked herself away in the furthest corner from the bar, but with the best view of the poky little stage. She set her mouth in a half-scowl to deter any suitors, and dug her back in against the drinks ledge, an elbow splayed out and behind on either side so she was leaning uncomfortably on the corners of the six-inch-wide ledge. It was a look she'd practised and honed to perfection and it came from endlessly having to fend off the advances of drunks. But she needn't have worried; there was more than enough spare to go around the local roughnecks, an alarming abundance of cleavage and leg. Jodie's gamine beauty was unlikely to tempt them into making a move anyway. To the uninitiated she looked more like a junky, all cheekbones and lips and hollow, haunted eyes. One of the brassy women at the nearest table threaded her foot through the strap of her handbag and slid it closer to, where she could keep an eye on it.

The men in here scared Jodie – and she didn't scare easily. They were no older than twenty-five, some of them, and they were already bald, their complexion slain by drink and bad diets and the poisons and gases that coursed unchecked in the chemical skies of the Lower Mersey estuary. There were some of the hardest faces she'd ever seen, with that certain disconnect in the eyes that presaged unpredictability, volatility, extreme unflinching violence. She'd grown up with it, and she knew the syndrome too well – the flickering eyelids, the nervous energy, the lack of concentration. What chance did Robbie have, performing in front of hillbillies like this?

Here he came now – so white, so calm in the spotlight. She'd

153

only met up with him twice since the night they'd taken the bus but already she had a strong sense that he was her man. That was her fella up there. Her heart was in her mouth as, without eye contact, without intro, he adjusted the mic. She saw him gulp. Only she would have noticed that. He swallowed, once, raked the crowd and, seeing her, allowed himself the briefest half-smile. Then he nodded to the band, closed his eyes – and blew her away.

She had never, ever heard anything like this before. Not live, not this close up. He sang 'When a Man Loves a Woman' and it tore her to shreds. Innately, she'd known he'd be something staggering – immense, yet fragile, too. But nothing could have prepared her for this. He broke her heart and she couldn't wait to get him off there and in her arms, thrusting and panting between her thighs.

By the time he finished his third and final encore and made her feel a hundred feet tall by hopping off the stage, coming straight over to her and giving her a chaste kiss, and before she got too big for her boots when he slipped her a fiver and nodded to the bar with a sloppy grin, Jodie had fallen hopelessly, helplessly in love.

Queuing at the bar she tried to make sense of the path that had led her here tonight. He was a married man, many years her senior, but when she'd first clapped eyes on him, she fancied him in that immediate, animalistic way. She'd have shagged him ten minutes after meeting him, if he'd pushed it. However, if he hadn't followed up, hadn't waited by the caravan for her the next evening, she'd have forgotten about him soon enough. Things were different now – now she'd heard him sing. Her heart was vaulting and it was all she could do to keep the grin off her face long enough to get served. She had to have him. For keeps.

Through the softly swirling canopy of smoke she watched the blousy local women eyeing him from a respectful distance, insufficiently drunk enough yet to be bold with him, their ruddy faces all giddy with arm's-length lust. They were no threat to her, these relics. Their breasts had collapsed almost as soon as they'd blossomed. But seeing her fella indulge them now with his coy, half-bored smile, she experienced a little flutter of jealousy. Robbie's talent was wasted on women like that, and she couldn't wait to get back and tell him so. She didn't believe for one moment that he touched them in that same visceral, gutwrenching way his voice touched her. All he was was the bloke on stage. They saw this hard-looking, handsome male, with his taut body, those green eyes and masses of thick red hair, and they went to bits. They fell for the romance of the pub singer, hook, line and sinker – hard shell, sensitive soul. Robbie could have been singing Abba for all they cared. They still would have followed him outside and tried to get in his car with him. All they were bothered about was nailing this week's turn. For her, it was so much more than that. Jodie was totally gone on him.

Jodie sat down and slid him his Guinness. She handed him his money back.

'Thanks,' he said, and offered her the smoke he'd prepared for her.

Her mouth broke into a thin smile as she sparked up. 'Don't thank me. On the house . . .'

They made a big thing of sipping their drinks and examining their glasses, rearranging and turning them round, awkward while the silence went unbroken. Robbie caught her sneaking a glance at him as she took a hit of her Southern Comfort. He was waiting, if not for a direct compliment, then at least for some kind of reaction from her. He'd come back after all these years – for Jodie – and he'd rocked the place. He'd knocked them out. And he wanted to hear it, from her.

Still she played with her drink, darting him quizzical little looks. Robbie tried not to notice. When they finally made eye contact, it was almost a war of nerves. Jodie caved first – but not in the way he was counting on.

'So. How come you gave it all up?'

'How do you mean, like?'

'This. Why did you stop?'

He was taken aback and tried to cover himself with a slug on his pint and a reflexive dip into his tobacco pouch. 'Don't get your drift.' He took another deep slurp, averting the drill of her eyes as he rolled out the tobacco. She flicked her head at the bar.

'Yer man there. The barman – one with the sidies. He was saying you could have been massive.'

Robbie cocked a swift glance over to the bar. Jodie reached for his Rizlas, eyed him as she rolled.

'Coulda been the next Joe Cocker, he reckons . . .'

Robbie slammed his pint down. 'That's crap! Cunt doesn't know what he's talking about! If I'd wanted to be on *Top of the* fucking *Pops* then fair enough, but I never. It was only ever music for me . . .' He lowered his eyeline, lowered his voice. 'I told you that.'

She looked at him for a second, lit her fag and snorted the smoke out through nose and mouth simultaneously. 'That's fucking bollocks!'

He shrugged his shoulders. Jodie leant closer, trying to force him to look at her.

'Fuck off, Robbie. I seen it in you, tonight. You're up there. Something happens inside of you. I felt it – the whole room fucking felt it. What d'you want me to say?'

Again the shrug, and he drained off his pint.

'Fancy another one, Robbie?' But she wasn't laughing. She flashed her eyes off to the side, impatient with him. She drew her knees up to her chin, scraping at her jeans with her lower teeth, deep in thought. 'You selfish cunt.'

'You what?'

156

'You know! You know that's no ordinary voice you've got – what you do to people when you get up there . . .' She had tears in her eyes now. Robbie tensed his face, giving nothing away. Jodie grabbed his wrist, making him look, making him listen. 'It's like some people have this big mad fucking need to do something, yeah? To leave their mark before they meet their maker. But they ain't got the talent to do it. They got fuck all. But you have, Robbie. You've got it all – and you don't give a fuck. And that's fucking selfish . . .' She dropped her blazing eyes now, dropped her voice to a whisper. 'That's proper fucking selfish that. Think what someone else might have done with all that . . .'

Robbie looked at her. Her eyes were smarting with a wired breathless intensity.

'What happened to you, Robbie?' Her tone was more tragic than accusatory now.

He stubbed out a cigarette and straight away set to building another. He lit it, turned his stool right round, took the room in and, as though thinking about it for the very first time, popped out his lower lip and shrugged. He turned to her, looked at her for a second, then dropped his eyes. He changed the subject, back to her, back to them. 'You sure your ma and her fella are deffo out tonight then?'

'Oh yeah. They're out all right.'

'All night? Like you said?'

'All fucking night.'

Under the table, he touched her leg, gently slid a knuckle up and down her denim-clad thigh. She tossed back the dregs of her drink. Robbie edged further towards her, pushed his thumb a little further into the heat of her groin. He could feel her yield, see the anger and the adrenalin leach from her face, taken over by the swell of desire.

'Come on then,' he said. 'I need to see you. Properly.'

The caravan was a pit. He'd only seen it from the outside before, and not even the streaks of rust and muddied windows could have prepared him for this. Roughly split into two living areas by a makeshift curtain strung from a piece of washing line, it smelt and felt damp. On one side were her mother's quarters which also encompassed the lounge, the kitchen and the bathroom cubicle. The main door in and out opened directly into Jodie's room which occupied about a quarter of the overall living space. She had a small single bed that pulled down from the wall, and a battered Formica chest of drawers which could only be opened when the bed was packed away. The surface of the chest was littered with the spent relics of old make-up – kohl shavings, sticky lipstick butts, the neon voids of eyeshadow pots. In the middle of the blitz were three or four tea mugs jam-packed with ash and ciggie ends and chocolate wrappers. The entire room was a moraine of junk and dirty plates and unwashed vests and knickers.

'So this is where it all happens,' Robbie joked, feeling anything but cheerful, and as far removed from sex as it was possible to feel. He did a sweep of the room, taking in the forlorn intimacies of her life, trying to reconcile this juvenile tip with the girl he had fallen for. He just could not square it. He tried to tell himself that none of this mattered, but to Robbie it mattered very much. Whatever romantic notions he'd fostered about his wild gypsy waif and her makeshift life on the road had been dealt a death blow.

She left the room then came back with a half-bottle of supermarket Scotch. He took a slug, winced and kissed her on the mouth, tasting her sour whiskey breath, getting hard in spite of himself. She squeezed him through his trousers and pulled away, smiling. She flitted around him, briskly shoving things into drawers. Teacups were taken out. Space was created. She straightened the bed covers, pushed Robbie down and, in silence, pulled his boots off, one then the other. Robbie craned his head up at her. 'You sure your ma and her fella are out for the night?' he asked again.

She fixed a patient, if slightly disappointed, look. 'Yes. I'm sure.'

He still could not relax – not here, on her bed, within such close proximity of her mother's bed. 'Where did you say they'd gone again?'

She humoured him with an eyebrow, stood up and clicked the deadlock on the caravan's front door. 'There y'are. That better?' She disappeared behind the curtain, popping her head back round the hem. She attempted a coquettish smile. 'Come and gerrus in a minute, yeah?'

Robbie sat up on the couchette and appraised himself in the dusty pane of her bedroom mirror. His reflection leered back at him, revealing the unsightly jowl of flesh above his hips. Where the fuck had that come from? No Sunday grill for you this week, Fitzgerald, he sighed. It was on with the trainers and off down the canal path first thing before he woke Ellie. He sucked in hard and held his breath, exploding after a moment. What did it matter anyway? She fancied him like he was, didn't she?

He rolled himself a smoke, turning away from the mirror. The dank, fetid stench of the bedroom smothered him. He sucked on his fag, trying to keep the mood alive. His head hummed with disconnected thoughts on a similar theme. Sheila. The house. The kids. Their life. His conscience had sat easily enough on the back burner. He was a good man, he worked hard, he had talent to burn and he felt he was due something back. However, in this poky, musty sex pit the sheer profundity of his actions, his choices, the thing that he was doing right here and now slapped him heavy in the face. Out there, across the canal, sat his life, just waiting for him to step back into its shoes and walk away in them. The stench and claustrophobia of Jodie's life here was

159

something he was unwilling to take on. Why? What for? Why did he continue to move forward, to meet this fate head-on? It went beyond folly. This was destructive, and he knew it, and it scared him shitless all of a sudden. He should put his boots on and walk out, walk away right now. But frightened and disgusted as he was, Robbie was already hooked.

He heard her brush her teeth in the cramped toilet next door, felt it through the wobble of the thin hardboard wall. The flush of the Elasan toilet crashed through the caravan, pasting a caustic waft of detergent through the squalid air. He could hear her fussing around in the bathroom now. He pictured Jodie primping and preening herself, getting ready for sex. This was it, then. He'd go through there, in a minute. With a glug of whiskey, he lay back and tried to calm his vaulting mind.

He heard the creak of her mother's bed. Robbie pushed back the curtains and gasped. She was splayed out, legs slightly apart, in a school uniform. Her shirt was undone exposing the white lace of a bra. He stood there, unsure how to go to her. In passion, or with tenderness? She snapped off the light and a scimitar moon shone in through the window onto the bed. She parted her legs wider. Again that rampant desire and revulsion that came with Jodie swept through him, the need for sex swamping the other.

She kissed him as a teenager would, chomping on his mouth. Yet still he felt himself hardening, an involuntary response to the wrongness of it all, the dirty piquancy of sex in a caravan with a kid. He pulled back, started unbuttoning her schoolgirl's blouse. He touched the fabric of her bra, running his finger around the frayed, jaundiced straps. Already on fire, she dragged off his belt, pulled his jeans right down so his dick shot out, pulled him towards her by his arse. He entered her hard and fast and the whole caravan seemed to shake with them. He'd had rough, untrammelled sex before when he was a teenager – the kind of needy, cathartic, behind-the-garage sex that had smashed his world right open. But never like this. Jodie was biting and slapping and tearing at his hair, crying out for him to do the same.

'Hurt me! Fuck yes, Daddy! Tear my fucking hair out!'

He gave as good as he could, but even in the purest resin of desire, he could not bring himself to hurt her – he didn't have it in him to hit her.

As she convulsed towards orgasm, she called out again. 'Daddy!' she whimpered. 'Oh Daddy, baby! Fuck me like that, Daddy!'

They lay there, side by side, exhausted, sweating, unable to speak. It was Robbie who came round first. He had to know. He just couldn't let it go. 'Jodie. What's with the . . .' He couldn't bring himself to say it. He held her by the jaw, gently. 'Why was you saying that?'

She rolled over onto her front, propped her face up in her palms and gave a curt laugh.

'Jodie?'

'Fuck's sake, man . . . you don't think? My God, you do, don't you?' Now she was amused. She sat right up and poked him, every other syllable, with her forefinger. 'God, Robbie! Surely you – a performer – should know better than anyone?' She jabbed harder, face close to his now. 'Don't tell me you never done no role-play shit with your wife?' No answer from Robbie. He played with a crust of sperm, drying in the hairs on his groin. 'Jeez, Robbie! Even my mum and Bob . . .'

'All right, Jodie. Let's . . . let's just leave it, shall we?'

She rolled over and curled into him, wrapping a long arm and a skinny stockinged leg around him. Robbie turned his head away from the truth of the moonlight and peered into the dank, yeasty room. He was burning all over. He felt foolish and old and alien, totally estranged from the body lying next to him. All he wanted now was to get his clothes on and get out of there.

161

If only he could wash this away, make things right again – the cleansing safety of his own bed, his own woman, all that he knew so well. But the gentleman in Robbie Fitzgerald told him that he should wait a moment, leave a decent interval before making off. So he lay there stiff and stoic, while the young girl with the young boy's body moulded herself to him. Disgusted with himself, he could not return the intimacy, but he couldn't bring himself to wholly reject her, either. He moved his face away from her hair and stroked her head, distantly, and waited for her to fall asleep. Only then would he leave. She twitched and muttered like a child as she drifted in and out of sleep. Finally, at long last, her breathing slowed right down, and she sighed and rolled away off Robbie's chest, dead to the world. Robbie's eyes throbbed painfully as they flickered to stay awake. The air was cold now, and he shivered at the reality of getting up, getting dressed, getting the car started and waiting for the engine to heat up and demist the frosty windows. His thoughts began to buckle and scramble, surreal fragments of memories pulling him back down. Just a snooze, he told himself – a little nap to clear my head, chase the last of the booze away.

When he woke, it was morning.

It was with a certain sadness that Sheila finally gave in to sleep. At 2.40 a.m. she heard a car's engine getting closer and hoped against hope. But just as she started allowing herself to believe that yes, this was Robbie, the car throbbed down to a purr, engine in neutral as a door opened and slammed shut again, a voice shouted 'Ta-ra' and the car was reversing and heading away. It wasn't him. She stroked his pillow and turned onto her back and stared up at the ceiling and she really, truly, could not work out how she came to be here, in an empty bed in Thelwall, Warrington, Northern England.

162

Fourteen

'Mum!'

Dimly, the voice penetrated her troubled sleep. She tuned in to Vincent's anxious voice.

'Mum!'

She shot upright. No! Oh, no, no, no – let it not be so. Robbie. The police were on the phone to tell them Robbie had fallen asleep at the wheel . . . she half rolled, half hopped out of the bed and bumped into Vincent on the landing. He gave her his look and, quietly, said, 'Liza.'

'Liza? What time is it?'

'Nine. You slept in.'

Not even the unexpected fillip of Liza on the phone could drag her from the sadness that gripped her as she knuckled the sleep from her eyes and registered fully that Robbie had not come home.

With no wish for a repeat of last time's outburst, Vincent bottled up the resentment he felt towards his mother's growing friendship with Liza Cohen, put on his parka, his gloves, his balaclava – at least the winter's sting allowed him to cover every telltale patch of brown he might otherwise have to display – and made his way out towards the old railway bridge. It was his place, these days. He'd happened upon it on one of those long treks home from school, taking the most circuitous route to avoid the boots and knuckles of the ambush squad. There was a certain satisfaction in outwitting the yahoos, especially so since he'd found the disused railway bridge over the canal. It spoke to his heart, directly, on first sight: the mossy, overgrown, mighty slab of the disused docking stage, the dank and placid calm of its green-black depths; the bridge itself – beautifully bent, studded iron, unloved and unnoticed these days as it straddled the still black waters. He could sit and stare at that for ever.

The other evening after school, overcome by some lusty sprite, some inner vim he'd never felt before, Vincent had the urge to climb the bridge. It wasn't so high – a hundred feet, perhaps, at its collar. The dip of its spine was gentle, one huge, head-sized, rounded rivet studding every yard of its broad and smooth back. Giddy with the thrill of what he was about to do, Vincent placed his left foot against the nub of the first stud and, taking the next but one in his right fist, hauled himself up. He fitted his right foot on top of the next rivet and tried to gain some purchase, but slipped, hanging on for a second, then giving in to the ugly drop. He grazed his knee and bruised the top of his thigh, but it was nothing. He'd seen enough. He was going up there again in daylight.

This morning he brought along the bare essentials. Some water and a cheese sandwich – in case he got stuck and the locals were disinclined to trouble the emergency services for a Paki lad – and his jotter. More than anything he wanted to describe the view from up there; and not just the view – the feel. The closer he got, picking his way through the frozen wasteland to the back of the house, the more he was taken over by this senseless onrush of exhilaration. He wanted to preserve it, know it, savour it – then write it all down. Smiling within himself, he got out beyond the damp copse and swallowed up his first view of the hunched iron bridge.

It took a while getting up there. It was wide enough to take him comfortably, but, with his slim feet slipping on the rounded rivets and his hands only gripping once he'd pocketed the gloves, it was slow, piecemeal, step-by-step progress. Halfway up he made the mistake of glancing down at the canal beneath and, for a minute or two, he was frozen to the spot by the shock of its infinity. Regaining the beat of his breath again, he inched his way upwards until the gradual arc flattened out and he was perched on a broad, wrought-iron sill, looking out at the flats and fields of his homeland. And, perversely, it felt like home, from here.

He sat for hours, only dimly aware of the occasional shout from passers-by below.

'You OK, kid?'

'You wanna be careful, you know.'

One old fellow stood stock-still with his hands clamped to his waist and, head tilted slightly back and mouth agape, he started laughing. '*Jump!*' he shouted. 'Only messing . . .' And then he was on his way.

Vincent barely noticed them. His eyes, his heart and mind were drinking it all in, holding it down. He could see for miles. The Runcorn bridge, the oil refineries at Stanlow and Rocksavage, and, tracing his pathway back, the gaunt, towering viaduct and the caravan site beyond. He swooned at the realisation of how high up he was, how far away from home he'd come. The people in the streets below were rolling around like marbles. Licking his gaze over the tiny ranks and rows of miniature caravans, with their awnings and dinky cars outside, his eyeline was snagged by the only moving vehicle, its progress cumbersome as it hesitated at the gates before heading down onto the main road. It was a square, boxy orange car. A Lada. It looked like their car – his tormentors at school had made it abundantly clear there weren't too many orange Ladas in Thelwall – and right there in his solar plexus he knew it *was* their car. But where was he going at that time? Where had he been? That morning he hadn't been around to take Ellie on their Sunday walk. Mum had cranked out some feeble alibi about his gig involving an overnight stay, but Vincent had a strong sense she was reaming. Not wanting

165

anyone to think badly of her dad, Ellie had put on a brave face and sloped up to her room where she immediately succumbed to huge, shuddering sobs. Vincent had tried to jolly her out of her tears with the promise of all the Christmas presents the extra work would buy. But not even the mention of a Tonka Truck could lift the heaviness from her stung face. Her daddy had stood her up and it was almost too much to bear.

And now everything came to Vincent all at once. How it was. How it would be. His father's secret. His mother's sadness. The night of the break-in. The nightmares that followed. He pushed it out to the very pits of his soul and told himself it wasn't there at all. He picked up his pen again and scribbled as fast as the revolutions of his mind.

Fifteen

There were little things about Liza Cohen that made Sheila certain about her, in that innate, instinctive way. One of these things was the way Liza pre-empted and pre-navigated any potential awkwardness in terms of their relative wealth. As though reading Sheila's misgivings through the vibrations of the phone line the other morning, she'd bounced an extra level of jollity into her voice in declaring: 'And we'll go by bus, of course. The bus to Rusholme is half the thrill of it.'

So they were going to the Curry Mile, and no one was to know of it, and Sheila didn't need to fret about not driving – though she planned to take lessons soon – or the fact that their Lada was neither a thing of beauty nor a source of envy, after all.

Making her way past the shops to the stop for the Manchester bus, a distant playground chirruping reminded her of Vincent and Ellie. It wasn't that far out of the way – she could easily pick the bus up two stops further down the road – and, now she'd envisaged her babies at play, she had to go and check on them. Briskly, she checked the time and injected a little brio into her stride.

She hooked her fingers through the rusty wire mesh of the fence, and pressed her face close. It took no time at all to pick out the lusty cut and thrust of Ellie, on the fringes of the central tumult of the playground where the big boys played and fought, but right at the very heart of her own little gang. She could see it in their eyes and in their actions; Ellie was loved. Two buttons popped open over her round pot belly, she was barging around, explaining their roles to them, telling them what to do. Even the

167

tough-looking boy with the sticky-out ears and scruffy uniform was listening intently, giggling nervously as the game was about to start. They split up and ran off to three corners of the playground, ready to hunt each other down. There was no sign of Vincent, though. With the same certainty of instinct that told her Liza was a goodie, Sheila knew her boy was safe. She knew he was OK. And yet she felt his sadness keenly, in a way she now felt her own.

Since the night Robbie had stayed out, four whole days ago, she'd been moping around in a fug of gloom. He'd stolen in the next morning, sheepish, the worse for wear. He'd held up his hands in instinctive protest and cranked out a clumsy apology. But even then his tone implied that it was she, not him, that was at fault. That she was being unreasonable. 'It was too *late* to call. It was one in the morning for Christ's sake. Irene took my keys, didn't she? Said there was no way I was driving home in that state – that she'd never forgive herself if anything happened . . . And I was done in. First gig nerves and all that . . . you remember how it was.' And then, as though to pre-empt any further comeback, he dropped his eyes, lowered his voice, seemingly hurt, and said, 'Well then. Are you not going to ask how it went?'

And she did want to know. She wanted to know every little detail; what the venue looked like, what songs he sang, did he bring the house down? But her soul was heavy with fear and sadness and she couldn't dredge up the words. She wanted to believe him – it hurt too much not to – and yet none of this made sense. Something indefinable and ominous now lay between them and it seemed to emanate from him and not her. Week nights he stayed back later and later at the pub and when he did stumble in, sozzled and inattentive to his children, he floated around as if in a dream. Could it be possible that Robbie had found someone else? A woman who could love him properly?

168

The drag of weary sorrow in her heart almost kept her from making the bus, and only a shout from Liza, mouth pressed to a tiny gap in the sliding window, snapped her back into action.

Vincent sat in his cubbyhole, flicking through the Alty Grammar brochure. He'd found the den by accident. Waiting in the dining hall, which doubled as the gym, though they hardly ever used it, about to hand his sick note to the games teacher, he found himself precipitated into a store room as the door he'd been leaning on nudged open. Though it was completely dark at first, he could sense the room was large. He blinked to acclimatise himself to the light. He could make out its furthest extent, cluttered with boxes and gym apparatus and bits of stage and set from the school play, before he could see directly in front of him. Vincent checked outside, shut the door firmly behind him, and came inside for a proper look. The light switch didn't work, but he could see just fine, the longer he stayed in there. In the weeks that followed, it became his second home. He made a little hollow behind the gym horse, hung a stretch of curtain up for added seclusion and lay odd costumes and beanbags and bits of sports kit out for him to flop down on. It was warm, insulated, safe and comfortable. As Christmas beckoned and the days got colder, he got a real thrill from stowing away there. If he was careful, taking nothing for granted and always, always checking thoroughly before coming and going, this bolt-hole could see him through till he left St Mary's.

Initially, his mother had been pushing for Tower College, St Ambrose or North Cestrian. But unless he could bag a free place, such seats of learning were way beyond his parents' means. So they'd gone for the next best thing – or the best if the Avon Lady was to be relied upon. Altrincham Grammar, according to Jean Bishop, was far better than any of the fee-paying schools. Oh yes! Her entire face was trembling with self-righteousness as

169

she boasted how her eldest, Charles, had scored within the top one per cent of A-level results in the country. Sheila looked into it, and for once Jean's outlandish vaunting seemed to carry some credibility. Fact: for the last twenty years, Altrincham Grammar had been among the country's top five schools for both O and A-level results. Fact: the school dispatched the highest number of students to Oxbridge outside of the network of top public schools. Fact: 99 per cent of all its students went on to university. A cursory flick through the brochure revealed Alty Grammar to be pretty much like the other posh schools in the area; lots of very uncool lads wearing thick-rimmed glasses, stooped over Bunsen burners. What mattered most of all to Vincent was that he would be able to start afresh.

If he got into Altrincham Grammar, he could reinvent himself from scratch. And, reassuringly, the brochure was smattered with other brown faces, though these were glaringly the very uncoolest of the uncool. This, too, gave him a glimmer of hope. Maybe, at Alty Grammar, he'd be cool! There was no good reason why not. Why, with its plethora of brown students, you could almost call the school Balti Grammar! There would be an abundance of gaylords and Pakis who'd deflect attention from him and maybe, just maybe, he'd make friends. In a school like that there'd be kids who were into books, into image, into music. He was tingling at the thought of it – at the thought of his new life. But first he had to pass the entrance exam. He stowed the brochure under the threadbare Trojan horse, safe till he came back at first break.

Sheila forgot her sadness as she stepped off the bus. She'd never seen anything like this – not here in England. Not on a Wednesday, on her doorstep, a bus ride away. As the bus had slowed to a stuttering chug up teeming Wilmslow Road, Liza sat back in silent satisfaction as Sheila's eyes widened. It was a bazaar out there. Every single face was brown. Liza had to nudge her friend twice, then prod her hard to jerk her from her trance.

Sheila was torn. She wanted to stop at every stall, touch every bolt of fabric, finger the silk, smell the fresh spices, relish the bantering ebb and flow of the barter. But this was Liza's gig. Happily amazed to know that Sheila had never been, Liza was revelling in the theatre of bringing her to Rusholme – and bringing Rusholme to Sheila. Lunch was on her mind and, until they'd done the curry thing, there was no prospect of a real go-around the street market. Sheila committed every little nuance to memory, made a pledge to herself that she'd be back, as soon as possible, and followed her nimble leader up the road, past dozens and dozens of wondrous-looking cafés and curry houses until Liza stopped and led her by the hand into the Rhani. Taking in the draught and the waft of the spice stream, separating each delicate frond of the aroma and feeling dizzy in its sensual rush, Sheila couldn't keep the big grin off her face.

Liza lit a cigarette and gave a cursory sweep of the menu. 'Shall we have red?'

Sheila raked the menu once, twice, unsure of what her friend was referring to.

Liza tuned into her indecisiveness – or unworldliness – and gave her a helping prod. 'Do we think we'll be eating lamb or chicken?'

So she was referring to the meat then. 'Mutton,' Sheila replied, her eyes dancing childishly to the suggestion. 'I haven't had mutton since I was back home.'

Liza tilted her head a fraction and rolled her eyes across the room to where a small huddle of men congregated expectantly. With the faintest smile she crooked a finger and summoned one over. 'We'll take a bottle of Shiraz. And a jug of iced water.'

Sheila realised her faux pas and flushed red. And when the diminutive waiter filled her glass with the crimson poison, she

171

daren't concede that she didn't drink, not really, and on the rare times she did it was under duress – typically a glass of lemonade shot through with a sliver of Advocaat or Cinzano. Instead she followed Liza's lead, inhaled at the heavy waxy surface, sipped reflexively and made the requisite facial gestures. She pretended to like the taste. She summoned up all her reserves of strength, trying to banish the sense association she always had with alcohol – of the time, as a young girl, she'd got drunk on home-brewed toddy with her cousin Navamalar. She took another sip, barely supressing a retch. It seemed to get worse with each taste.

'So. I mean. How did it happen?'

'What?'

'Kuala Lumpur. That's where you're from, right? How the fuck do you come to end up in a place like Warrington?'

Sheila had never heard Liza swear before. It made her giggle. 'You really want to know?'

Maybe it was the wine – all three paltry sips of it – but she felt more relaxed with Liza now and instead of reeling out her usual response, that she came here to do her training, met Robbie and stayed, she teased out the moment, delved deep inside herself and spoke from her heart, like she'd seldom done before.

'When I was eleven, my sister and I found a purse by the railway line on the way home from school. We kept it. There wasn't a lot of money inside but, to us, it was a fortune. We knew the police would never hand it back and we were each just waiting for the other to say: come on, let's keep it. We ended up splitting the money. Java, my sister, was older, but she was the nearest of my sisters to me in age and we were more like best friends than anything. She took her share and bought so many sweets. Oh blimey, Liza – there were enough sweets to last her a year, all the fancy imported American rubbish, too: chews and jelly snakes and all that . . . crap.' Sheila put her hand over her mouth at the filth she'd just spouted. Liza didn't seem to register.

'Know how I spent mine? I went to see a movie. That wasn't allowed, you see – too many girls got big ideas from going to see the English films. My mother would have killed me if she'd found out.' She pulled back a moment, sipped on her wine. She liked the way it was starting to feel around her belly, in her limbs. She took another sip. And then another.

'It was Christmas time – there are lots of Catholics in Malaysia, you know? Oh yes. Lots of Malay Catholics, lots of expatty British types, too. They used to put on all the old classics for them – didn't matter how old the film was, there used to be queues around the block. I went to see *It's A Wonderful Life*.' She gulped at the recollection, swallowed it back down with her last mouthful of wine. She looked at the empty glass, almost rueful.

'Go on . . .' Liza replenished it.

'Sounds so stupid now . . .' She looked up for encouragement. Liza gave it with the very slightest incline of her head. 'The film changed my life. All I could think about after that was how to get to Britain.'

'But . . . it's Hollywood, isn't it?' It was out before Liza could stop herself. She put a hand to her mouth. 'I'm so sorry . . . I didn't mean to . . .'

Sheila shushed her with a smile and squeezed her hand across the table. 'Liza, to me, it *was* England. They spoke English. England was the country you could get to. And anyway . . .' The drink was beginning to ripple through her now. She hoped she wouldn't lose her thread. Muff her lines. 'Anyway, it wasn't that that got me. It was that thing of looking in on your life from the outside. I'd never really thought about my future or anything important at all. But suddenly, well – I just didn't want to be like all my cousins and aunties and all the women around me in the kampong. I didn't know what I wanted, but I didn't want to end up like them. Everything I did after that, the subjects I studied at school, the books I read, the sort of jobs I thought I could do – it was all about getting away.'

'You ran away?' Liza was wide-eyed.

'Well, not quite. It wasn't a midnight bunk or anything like that. My brother, Rasa, he was my angel. In a way now I realise he was doing it – what's the word?' Liza opened her mouth instinctively but then checked herself. 'He wanted me to escape as much as I wanted it myself. He took extra shifts and he saved and saved, and he bought me my airline ticket. I couldn't have done it without him. He helped me through the whole thing – money, finding nurse's training in England, everything . . .' Sheila dropped her eyes guiltily. 'I think he thought – I think he hoped . . .' She looked her right in the eye again. 'That I might come back. I think he hoped that England wouldn't be the promised land I'd been dreaming about.'

'But you never went back, right?'

'No.' She hung her head. 'That only happens in the film.'

Liza was mesmerised by her story. The cigarette she had lit remained untouched, just one long flute of ash. Sheila sighed and looked out onto the bustling street.

'Rasa saved me. He worked so hard to pay for me to come over here. One day I would like to pay him back the money. But I guess that's just the guilt that England has taught me. Back home you do not need to pay anybody back.'

They ordered mutton kari and mopped up the ghee with peshwari naan and, tipsy from the wine, swapped intimacies about their husbands. Some of Liza's revelations Sheila found shocking; Vernon was close to bankruptcy. He refused to throw the towel in, claiming the workers relied upon the likes of himself for their livelihood. Her father was trying to hand over his chain of South Manchester pharmacies to him, joking that valium and methadone were future currencies of the UK. But most shocking of all was her throwaway confession that, since the troubles started, since

174

he'd had to start laying the Cormax workforce off, Vernon had ceased to pay her any attention. Sadly, eyeing Sheila through the mist of her wine glass, Liza added, 'But I suppose that happens, hey?'

After a moment, Sheila realised it was a question. All she could offer back was a shy smile but, this time, Liza wasn't letting it lie.

'Yourself and Robbie. Do you . . . ?'

Now she thought about it, it didn't seem such a taboo at all. She *wanted* to talk about this sort of thing. She wanted to know what was normal, and what things were like for other girls, too. She took a timid sip and, keeping her eyes on the wine glass, responded in kind. 'Only sometimes. Hardly ever, these days . . .'

Liza seemed more dejected than relieved. She turned her brilliant blue eyes on Sheila. 'Look at you, though. You're gorgeous! What man wouldn't . . . ?'

'Like you say, Liza, I think it's just what happens. They're tired. They have preoccupations.'

'I know.'

She sighed, hard. 'It's just . . . I don't know. Don't you ask yourself what it's all about, sometimes? How you end up together? Why you stay together?'

'More than you could ever guess.'

Sheila laughed, but her eyes were prickling now. She forced a giggle. 'I'm sorry. I'm not usually . . . The wine must have gone to my head. This is all so . . .' She sat back, took a deep breath and tried again. 'I haven't talked like this. Not in a long while. Not since leaving the nurses' home.'

Liza manoeuvred herself to the edge of her chair, narrowing the space between them. She cupped a hand around Sheila's wrist and left it there. She made to speak, her plaintive, needy look suggesting she was about to share a secret of her own, but she seemed to change her mind and instead turned the spotlight back on Sheila. 'Whatever it is you *can* tell me you know.' She smiled, dug deep into the wells of Sheila's eyes as she tried to divine her thoughts, then added, 'In absolute confidence of course.'

Sheila hung her head, stared into the oily receding surface of her wine.

'I see a sadness in you. Most of the time you conceal it well, but it's there and I can see it now.'

Sheila looked up, her eyes shining on the brink of tears as she struggled to batten down the heave of sweet-sour emotion in her throat. As though sensing the imminence of some kind of outpouring, Liza edged a finger under Sheila's cuff and began to stroke her. Little shockwaves of pleasure darted up Sheila's shoulders and smouldered in the pits of her arms. The moment hung over them, huge, alive, suspended.

It was Sheila who broke it. She was anxious, suddenly – denuded by the stream of confession that sat on her lips. For all she trusted Liza implicitly, this was still the boss's wife, for God's sake. She should not be confiding in her – in anyone – about matters so intimate, and whatever had happened just then was over. She leant back across the table, reclaimed her wrist and returned to the menu. 'Room for rasmalai?'

Liza was still eyeing her intently. 'It'll all be fine, darling,' she said. 'You'll work things out.'

Sheila couldn't bring herself to meet her gaze and as she drained the last dregs of her glass, she found herself wondering if they really would.

After walking Ellie home, changing out of his school uniform and cramming a small selection of treats into the pockets of his parka – namely a packet of Wotsits, a Viscount biscuit and a Twix – Vincent headed for his bridge under the mantle of dusk. From up here, in the falling light, his street seemed scarcely to exist, but closer, a little way up the dirt track that flanked the canal, the lights of a caravan became apparent as the gloaming hardened around it. Vincent's heart grew heavy as he sank deeper into his thoughts. He'd tuned in to his mother's turmoil the morning his father hadn't come home and how he wished he'd had the fortitude to speak to her, to lend her his support. More and more his father was giving vent to his disapproval about this or that, his latest *bête noire* being her friendship with Liza. Yet his mother remained keen to please him. She nourished and nurtured family equilibrium by way of a conspiracy of silences, of sacrifices, of putting up and shutting up – and it made Vincent seethe. Sometimes, his dad would come home from the pub a little earlier than usual, stumble into the living room where they'd be snuggled up watching *Coronation Street* or *Dynasty* and he'd screw up his nose in disgust and spit, 'Jesus, She! You're not watching this, are you?'

The inference was that he, the worker, had been grafting at the coalface while they, the dilettantes, had sat around painting their toes and smoking opium. This was Sheila's cue to shuffle off into the kitchen and tend to his tea. Without fail his mother would pull the same hurt face, instantly transforming it into an embarrassed, caught-out smile, and off she would scuttle. How he wanted to race over and slam his fists into his father's face. Of course they were watching *Coronation Street*! They'd been looking forward to it since Monday night's episode. It was something they did – together! Why didn't he just stay down by the canal or the caravan site or wherever it is he went when he was pretending to work overtime? God, how he would have loved to say that – to stop his reddening father mid-sentence and say to him, 'Was that you I saw down at the caravan site, Dad? No? Oh, nothing – just wondering. Don't see that many orange Lada Rivas round here, do you?'

That would make him think twice before he came barging into his bedroom, wanting to catch him out, always thinking the worst of him. But it was his mother Vincent most wanted to shake. She seemed unwilling or incapable of recognising her own worth in the relationship. She was the one who cooked and cleaned and helped them with their homework and got them ready for school and went to parents' evenings when Dad cried off with some last-minute excuse. She did the shopping and dealt with the bills and prepared their packed lunch and looked after the garden and bathed Ellie and read her bedtime story. All their father contributed was a sullen attitude, a brooding, resentful presence and a brown envelope at the end of the week. Vincent was beginning to despise him. Mum was the heart of the household and her blood fuelled all of them, not least their father. Sheila was his iron lung, and without her Robbie would crumble. Without him, she'd survive. It was as simple as that. He'd looked at his mother's anguished face that morning and he wondered how they'd all be without Dad. Happy. Happier.

When Vincent got in that evening there was an envelope waiting for him on the kitchen table. He snatched it up, made straight into the living room and slowly prised it open. He could hear Ellie behind the sofa, the fat snooping syllables of her breath, imagining herself invisible. He ignored her and slipped the letter out of the envelope. It was something official, something formal. He digested the ordered typescript and speed-read the print, barely taking it in at first. Sentence by sentence his pulse lurched with an exultant bang as he began to comprehend the detail. This was no mailshot; it was an entry form for a young persons' writing competition. It was being channelled through the Libraries Commission. The prize was fifty pounds of WH Smith book vouchers and the winning piece would be published in an anthology. The deadline was the 10th of December and there was a hand-scrawled note from Matt asking him not to do anything or send anything off until they'd met up to plan it through.

Vincent perched on the window sill and read through the letter again and again, drinking in the magic and the majesty of every word. Deep in his subconscious, a delicious and jittering excitement was brewing. It was nameless and formless right now, impossible to marshal into words, but it shot through him, electrifying him to the core. And the more excited he became, the more he sensed that this could be it. This was the start of it all – the beginning of his way out of this shallow travesty of a town. There was nothing that mattered more than winning this competition right now. He just had to win.

Sixteen

Vincent devoted himself, body and soul. When he wasn't writing he was down at the library, flicking through their meaty thesaurus in search of new words. He floated sentences in the back of his jotter. 'The night was callow.' 'The wind seethed.' 'The stars were sozzled.' He shared his ideas with Matt and, under his patient aegis, bit by bit he let go of the unicorn story he'd started.

'I just don't feel this is you, mate. Just – don't force it, yeah? It'll come. I promise you, Vin. It'll come . . .'

But the first week in December wore on without his story even getting beyond the planning stage. Each time he made headway with an idea, Matt would open his eyes to its weaknesses. He wouldn't help him out, either. He just kept patting him on the shoulder and telling him to wait for the Voice. His head whirred, but his fountain pen lay dormant in the groove of his bedroom desk. Vincent began to despair, and came close to tearing up the entry form more than once. And then the unthinkable happened.

Robbie came home drunk one evening, well after midnight, to find the light seeping out from under his son's bedroom door. Angry in his drink, and imagining his profligate, disappointing son had fallen asleep, uncaring of how much electricity he wasted, he barged into the room, ready to snap off the lights, hoping to wake him in the process, maybe scare some remorse into the drip. But Vincent was very much awake, hunched over his desk, pen poised, the tip of his tongue protruding as he wrote. He had his earphones on, head nodding gently to his latest love, John Foxx.

Robbie stood and watched, taken aback by the sudden and enormous jolt of love that shot through him. Vincent ducked

180

down so his ear was almost touching the paper as he scribbled. He sat back, swooped up the sheet of paper and analysed his prose, reading it back to himself. He hissed and shook his head and screwed the paper up into a ball. Robbie watched him do this, and he was overcome with a rare stab of pride for his son. He knew the signs here, recognised the symptoms oh so well. He'd been there a thousand times before, himself. He went over as casually as he was able, sat down on the bed next to him.

Vincent yanked off his headphones, his whole body tensing in anticipation of the telling-off he expected to follow. But his father surprised him. His face was mellow, twinkling.

'We'll have no forests left at that rate, son. Here . . .' He took the headphones from him, and laid them gently to one side. 'What is it you're trying to say?'

Vincent, caught out, sat there in dread. If he told his father, he'd only bring the giddy vim of all his thoughts and dreams crashing back down to earth. All his father would have to do was stress one single word in a certain way: *writing* competition? He wouldn't even have to wrinkle his nose – he'd wring all the disgust he could muster out of that one word. Instinctively, Vincent shoved the entry form behind his back.

Robbie tried a sympathetic grin on him. 'Come on, son! Fucksake – I've wrote lyrics all my life, lad! I know . . .'

Reluctantly, Vincent handed his dad the entry form.

He sank back onto the bed, trying to focus on the application details, before handing it back to Vincent. 'Bit pissed, son. You read it?'

In a heady rush of truth it dawned on Vincent, there and then, that his father couldn't read. He was entering a new writing competition – no, worse – he had aspirations of becoming a novelist, a writer, a story composer, and his own father couldn't read! But far from feeling crushed by the revelation, Vincent was energised. For the first time in a long, long time, he felt something other than fear and contempt for his dad. He read the terms and conditions out to him. Robbie lay back, chewing all this over. He sat up, gave him a squiffy look, and pronounced: 'Thing is, son – don't really matter what you write. Yeah?'

Vincent nodded, unsure where this was going. Robbie continued, his face set straight.

'Whatever you write, you got to write it from here.' He slapped his heart passionately to emphasise his point but only looked comical, almost disintegrating the value of his words. He drew himself up for the climax. 'If it ain't got heart it ain't got soul and if it ain't got soul then it ain't got nothing.' He dispensed this with something approaching a country and western twang. He got up and placed his hand on Vincent's shoulder. 'I'm proud of what you're doing here, son. Just . . . write, hey? Write. Write what you know. That way, it'll ring true.' He smiled wistfully, loitered a second then turned and walked out of the room. The stink of booze and smoke lingered long after he'd gone.

Write from the heart, write what you know. The more Vincent thought about it, the more it made sense. The boozy spore his father left behind was real to him, too. All of a sudden, in a tumbling, torrential freefall out of nowhere, the idea came to him. And though he was weary to the marrow of his bones from the fretting and the relentless setting up and setting back down of new and better stories, he sat up straight and wrote his story in one seamless draft.

Seventeen

Robbie woke, instinctively groping for an alarm clock that wasn't ringing. He hauled himself up into a sitting position, disorientated but vaguely aware that things were not as they should be. There was no Ellie charging across the landing, shouting and shrieking and imitating her He-Man action heroes; no pipes keening as Vincent ran another hot bath; and what nagged at him with a quickly intensifying anguish was the lack of clatter of pans and dishes from the kitchen below – no signs of Sheila preparing breakfast. The familiar weekend hum of related lives busy on their separate tracks was absent. All he could sense out there beyond their bedroom door was the doleful still of an empty house – the metronomic beat of the clock on the landing, the low burr of the fridge. Outside, the sound of a car's wet tyres hissing along the main road obeying the new speed limit only accentuated the emptiness of the house. Where was everybody? Cross and confused, Robbie stumbled downstairs.

Vincent was curled up in a blanket on the sofa, head bent to a book. Making no reference to last night's paternal tête-à-tête Robbie stood over him and asked, 'Where's Ellie and your mum gone?'

As though sensing the underlying irritation in his father's voice, Vincent didn't look up from his page. 'A picnic with Liza.'

'A *picnic*? It's the middle of frigging winter.'

Vincent shrugged his shoulders, giving away nothing.

Robbie advanced into the kitchen. It was rank with the stink of freshly baked spices, ineptly buried under the tang of air freshener. She'd left a window wide open in another lame attempt at covering her tracks, but Robbie was starting to get the picture.

He leant across the sink and slammed it shut, cursing his wife as he did so. What was she playing at? She knew what he thought about cooking that shit in this kitchen! Her cooking smells would be stinking out the whole street by now. He made himself a cup of tea but, convinced some malignant spice had contaminated the milk, chucked it back down the sink after one sip.

His stomach clenched tighter and tighter. Wallowing in the righteous bitterness of victimisation, he returned over and again to her name – that sly, calculating bitch who'd insinuated her way into their lives. That . . . *toff*. Sheila would jump into a furnace for her if she crooked her finger. And it was clear from his wife's decision not to run this picnic by him first that she was trying it on here. She hadn't so much as even hinted that she might have plans – of course she hadn't! She knew full well what the answer would've been. If Sheila had had the grace to sit him down and put it to him that she fancied a day out with Liza – and that she planned to take Ellie with her too . . . well, there'd be no way, end of story. It just wasn't on, splitting up a father from his kids of a weekend. He'd have had to look her in the eye and tell her sorry, love – no way. So she'd just gone ahead and done it anyway, come what may.

He jerked the fridge open, immediately confronted by the ingredients of his breakfast – Manx kippers wrapped in cling film on a plate. Here was further evidence of her calumny. She had gone so far as to unpack the fish from its packaging before voting against it – and against him. He stared at the fleshy pungent fish. She must have taken the food out, got it all ready when the call came through from her. Little miss pert tits, the wide-eyed, do-gooder blonde princess! How fucking dare she turn Sheila's head away from her family? How dare she interfere with their plans, their system, their fucking happiness! And he could strangle bloody Sheila for being too weak to say no to her. He could see her stupid, grinning face now, all pleased at

184

being asked out, all too willing to drop everything and cook up an 'ethnic' feast for that slim-hipped, smiling supermum. No – instead of finishing off her work and getting the family breakfast sorted, she'd packed it back into the fridge and jumped to the task of rustling up whatever filth that Cohen one had demanded of her. Curry. Samosas. All of that. Robbie unwrapped the fish and deposited it into the bin. There! Martyred and self-conscious now, and beginning to feel a little foolish, he took his tobacco pouch from his coat pocket and perched on the lounge window sill, seething, thinking it all through. Vincent, all too aware of his anger, must have taken himself out of the firing line and up to his bedroom.

The grim futility of the situation terrified Robbie. As he looked out into his empty living room he felt horribly estranged from the trappings of family life: the framed pictures lining the mantelpiece; the carefully centred doily on the genuine reproduction mahogany coffee table; the leatherette settee. None of it had done the trick. At one time or another, these were items they'd conned each other into believing they wanted, badly – that they would bring some elusive quality to their domestic lives. But they hadn't done, not for Robbie, at least. None of it had made him happier.

He sighed hard, smoke billowing from his mouth in reckless plumes. He'd be seeing Jodie tonight, at the gig – and she made him happier. Up there on the stage he could put on a show and let her see at first hand how magical a muse she was, how fortunate she was to have him. But it'd be over in a flash and all the rebuffed advances and the scribbled and screwed-up phone numbers of others would be replaced by the harsh reality of her musty caravan, or a quick one in the car. He was in love with Jodie, possibly – but where could it lead?

Then it came to him. If Sheila could make her own plans this weekend, then so could he. Tonight's gig was in Lytham. So why, oh why, should he have to belt back down the M6 in the wee small hours to sleep next to, but not with, the woman who cared not a glimmer for him? Sold on his blamelessness, he dug under the cushions for an old *Sunday Mirror* and looked for guest houses in Blackpool. He felt not a jot of guilt.

Between her feet, Sheila's tartan shopping bag was stuffed with tupperware containers, packed tight with her curries and spicy fancies. She couldn't help feeling bad about Robbie. She should have just come out with it – told him she was going to Walton Garden's Winterwonderland and dealt with the consequences. She knew he'd be furious, come what may, and now it felt like no good could come of it.

The gentle throb of the bus wheels below, and the sensation of passing by these familiar front doors and shops and lives, led Sheila back along the route that brought her here. She could still recall the bus ride from her mother's front door to the airport, the day she left home for good. The bus ran right past her school, a journey she'd lived for thirteen years of her life. And this time, in spite of its cloying familiarity, she'd devoured each and every pulse of the hurtling landscape with fresh eyes. She'd drunk in the endless stretch of hawkers' stalls, already bustling with trade in the early rinsed-out light of morning; the new motorway flyover, almost built – as it had been for most of her life – and the small ghetto of tin houses accommodating the workforce in the cooling shadows beneath; the squat and blackened stumps of the durian trees, some of which had been hewn into rough effigies of Hindu gods. With a tearful nod, she'd passed the factory where Rasa had slogged through long hot nights to buy her plane ticket; and the deep, dank, rain-filled tin mines where her youngest brother, Jadi, had died swimming their black lagoon. The horror of it, the sheer, unrestrained agony and sadness of the sight of his slim lifeless body, carried back to the village. She'd closed her eyes and breathed deeply, living the last leg of the journey as the bus passed the mangrove swamps, whose glittering spores drifted in through the open windows and settled on her, stinking her clothes.

She'd committed that whole journey to memory because, even then, she sensed she may never be back to pass through it again. Those were the moments and that was the trail that led to this, her latest journey. As the bus toiled through the familiar, everyday beats of her life she was overcome with a similar, deep-seated certitude. Things were changing. She was changing. The world might not look the same, the next time she travelled this way.

Eighteen

As soon as they checked into their poky Blackpool B&B, they dragged each other down onto the bed, hungry and needy. Robbie plunged into her, giddily in love with her, and the freedom and the possibilities of all that lay ahead. With Jodie, he could cut loose.

A little later, he sat on the shelf of a window sill, knees tucked into his chin, smoking as he looked out onto the wild grey toss of the stormy Irish Sea. The famed promenade below was deserted, just a blur of wind-whipped neon and odd, struggling silhouettes, heads bent down against the gust, getting nowhere. He smiled at Jodie, asleep, only her face and lightly freckled shoulders visible. He wanted to scoop her up in his arms and let her know his love all over again. He kissed her awake, softly on the lips, handing her a rollie. 'Come on, you.' He smiled.

And she knew. There was drinking to be done.

They took a tramway past the Pleasure Beach to Hardy's, at the Lytham end of the prom. Hardy's was a small, smoky drinkers' joint Robbie knew from its former life as a cabaret lounge. Years and years ago he'd hitched up there to see Christy Moore play, before he was well known even on the Irish scene. Like all great bars, there was something about the layout, the people, the atmosphere – something indefinable that made it arcane and magical from the moment you stepped inside.

It was still the same in there, more or less. Not that busy out of season and on a night like this, but there was still the doughty band of regulars and one ribald hen party. It was hard to make out whether the manly buxom blonde on stage was the main attraction, or one of the party girls trying it on with a glib-faced suit, flashing his cash about. Robbie eyed up the sturdy thighs straining against a sequinned cabaret dress and nudged Jodie. 'Looks like a butch mermaid!'

'A mer-man!'

They checked no one had heard their little in-joke, and ordered pints and whiskey chasers. Jodie was keen to sit at the bar but Robbie ushered them into the furthest, darkest armpit of the room, where the tinny boom of the club's PA couldn't quite smother their talk.

'Never fails that one, ay?' said Jodie with a smile. She could look so feminine, in a certain light. So innocent and pretty and lovely, he just wanted to drink her up. He nodded, hearing her voice but not her words, and carried on smiling at her. She flicked her head up towards the ropey blonde, splintering the microphone with her anguished warbling.

'I will survive . . .'

She nudged him and glanced around the room at all the hefty tattooed lasses belting their lungs out mightily, their faces rippling with contempt for any man who caught their eye.

Robbie laughed. 'Proper marriage wrecker, that one.'

'Serious though, Robbie. Put Gloria Gaynor on and the loveliest birds in the house are suddenly stabbing their fellas. I mean it. It's the anthem, man. It's our ladies' call to arms.'

He checked to see if there was any glint of fun in her eyes, and couldn't be sure one way or the other. 'Like I say. It's banned in our house.' As soon as he said it, he regretted it. Bitterly. Jodie used the entrée to steer the conversation towards her new obsession – Sheila and the kids.

'Really? She'll stand for that?'

She was doing this more and more – usually when they were drunk, or after sex, when everything between them was easy and honest and devoid of agendas. She'd throw in a little comment, innocent on the face of it but as provocative as ever. And Robbie was learning hard and fast – with Jodie there was always an

189

agenda. Every expression, every little comment demanded close scrutiny. Sometimes his mind would ache from always trying to second guess her. What did she mean by that? What *did* she mean? She was complex and contradictory, Jodie. Nothing was simple with her, not even sex. And that was exactly why he'd fallen for her. That's why they were sitting here now. He flashed her a teasing grin. 'She'll take her cue from the master, aye.'

She, too, was succumbing to the sheer wild romance of a stormy December night away with her lover – but she couldn't let it go. She had to know. She had to know more. 'But . . .' She hesitated and ran her slim fingers across his chest to let him know this was curiosity, not war. 'What's she like, Robbie? I mean . . . I just can't picture you as the family man, you know? I can't picture you and her together. Do you get me? I mean . . . what kind of stuff do you two talk about? Say, when your havin' your tea together, right? Fuck do you say to each other?'

Robbie twinkled back at her, but he knew better than to take the bait. He made sure not to use Sheila's name or, if he did, to use it in as dismissive a tone as he could muster. 'We don't have our tea together. She eats with the kids.'

'OK. When you're watching telly or whatever. What do you chat about?'

Again, he told her exactly what she wanted to hear. 'We hardly see each other, tell the truth. And when we do, it's more . . . well, it's not like this, if that's what you're wondering. We don't talk about life and music or anything big like that. It's all the bare necessities, really. It's all stuff to do with the kids.'

She liked what she was hearing and cut him a little slack. 'You really love your kids, don't you?'

His instinct was to gush, but with Jodie he knew there was always a trap, a tripwire, somewhere. He shrugged his shoulders, pulled the 'never really thought about it' face. 'Dunno. They're my babies, aren't they?'

190

'So . . . how old's little Vincent, again?'

Robbie was starting to tense. This one felt like a trick question. 'Our Vincent. He's almost twelve.'

She smiled and ran her finger around the rim of the whiskey glass. 'Is he like you?'

'Vincent? Oh God aye, yeah. Mirror image of us when I was his age. Proper little scoundrel, he is. Always scrapping, always getting into trouble at school.' He looked up briefly, snorted and smiled at the same time. 'Kids down the street are frigging terrified of him.'

'And can he sing an' all?'

'He's too much of a lad to say if he could.'

She paused, treading carefully. 'How come you chose that name, like?'

'Vincent?'

'That's his name, isn't it?'

Robbie smiled, bashful now. 'Don't suppose you'll remember it, like. It were me favourite song when me and She was, you know . . .'

Jodie stared at her glass, picked it up and rotated the sliver of ice, creating a mouthful of whiskey-water.

'Don Maclean. "Vincent",' he said.

Eyes still lingering artfully on the table, Jodie pulled a sad smile. 'I love that song. It's about Van Gogh.'

'Who?'

Her wild gaze punched up at him. 'Never mind.' She stood up. 'N'other one?'

'Of course.'

They drank more and, once again, grew carefree, in love with the night and the pure gorgeous immediacy of it. Jodie wrapped her arms around Robbie, licking his neck. 'C'mon, then. Get up and show them. Sing, Robbie!' She looked at him and added quietly, with a flicker of resignation, 'Sing . . . for me.'

191

She had him and she knew it. Robbie got up and, as he stepped onto the low stage, decided he'd do the first one unaccompanied. He filtered out all the background noise and looked out beyond the smattering of bodies until he could see her clearly. He took a deep breath and with the clearest, most searing and heartbroken timbre, he sang: 'Every time we say goodbye, I cry a little . . .'

The room fell to a hush. He sang, without a backing band, for forty-five minutes. The end of each song brought wilder, more passionate applause and by the end, they were thrusting drinks into his hand as well as shirts and napkins for autographs. The manageress of Hardy's came bounding over to him. 'You can see how we're fixed here, love. It's six hundred max even during the August bank holiday. But you can name your price, love. Within reason.'

Robbie thanked her and promised he'd definitely get his agent to phone, but he only had eyes for Jodie right now. He was overcome with love for the girl. He had to get her back to the B&B.

Outside was wild. Unhinged by the violent wind, bins and shop signs cartwheeled down the prom, belting into the sides of cars, crashing into bus shelters. A tumultuous sea was pummelling the promenade walls, spuming up high and smashing down onto car roofs and bonnets. Giggling and yelling, Robbie and Jodie ran out of the pub and dived into the hub of it, hand in hand. The trams had closed down for the night and they staggered through in the angry teeth of the wind to the taxi rank. The wooden hut of an office was closed. More people came up behind them, huddled and soaked and frozen. Nobody spoke a word to one another, but they gave each other faith that something would turn up soon.

Dim yellow headlights turned the corner, burning through the drizzle which seemed to be turning to snow. Robbie refused to get his hopes up. Jodie stuck out an arm, then a leg. The car slowed to pick them up. Robbie opened the door for Jodie to jump in first, wishing she'd be quick about it, but no sooner had he ducked his head down inside than Jodie, bug-eyed with disgust, or contempt, he couldn't quite make out, was pushing him back out into the ferocious night.

'What! What's up? What'd he say?' Robbie bent down again, ready to take it up with the driver. Jodie pulled him back.

'I'm not getting in there, no fucking way.'

'What. The fuck. Has happened?'

But she was already beckoning for the women behind to take the cab. Robbie held on to the door doggedly. Seizing their lifeline, the two women muscled their way past Robbie and ducked down into the taxi. Jodie marched away, head held rigid and aloof, out into the wild night. Robbie ran to catch up with her, pulling her back by the arm. 'Tell us what that cunt said, Jodie! I'll nut the bastard . . .'

Jodie swung round, her face wriggling with disdain. 'Robbie, I don't care if we fucking drown out here. There's no fucking way I'm getting in a car with any Paki.'

Nothing could have prepared Robbie for that. In saying so little about Sheila, he'd told Jodie nothing. And looking at it now, though there had been little hints and nudges – off the cuff remarks about gypsies and foreigners stealing all the jobs and all the usual bullshit – he'd always been quick to steer things away. And in his shame now, he had to accept that he'd even insinuated Sheila was a blonde. He should have guessed. But how could he have known? Devastated and utterly drained, he trudged behind her, back towards the B&B, hoping it would be hours before they got there. His head was swimming. He needed to think. Think it all through.

Nineteen

For the second time in three weeks Robbie did not come home. And this time, Sheila only had herself to blame. She lay awake, shivering. Propped up on one elbow, she observed his empty space. The man who had slept by her side for thirteen years was somewhere out there, slowly, irredeemably slipping away. She felt a keen anger at him, underscored by an enormous tristesse. Where had they been, she and Robbie? Where were they going?

She could tell there was snow without having to go to the window. Beyond the rasp of Vincent's snoring in the next room, Sheila tuned in to the merry peal of drunk lads, pelting one another with snowballs. She smiled and thought fondly of her early days at Warrington General. How very long ago it seemed. She stared up at the ceiling, too cold to get up and go downstairs. The flashing green digits of the alarm clock taunted her: 3:00, then 3:30, then 4:00. She heard the low-pitch whine of the milk van, skidding in the road. Then nothing.

She dragged herself out of bed, sat on the toilet, too cold to go, and padded downstairs. She lit the oven. She pulled back the curtains and stared out into the garden, already levelled by fat white snow. Beyond it, the white saddle of wasteland loped down to the frozen canal. Everywhere, as far as the eye could see, the landscape was drugged. She stayed at the window, enchanted by the sight of the whirling, white-speckled air, moved by the memories it evoked. She shuffled to the table, resting her weary head on her forearms, and drifted quickly into a white, swirling sleep.

A vague consciousness of footfall woke her. Her neck was stiff from laying her head on the table. She sat up and squinted into the heat-flushed darkness. Wide-awake whites of eyes glowed back at her from the stairs.

'Ellie?' Even now in the chaste safety belt of Thelwall, and especially in this kind of weather, Sheila could find herself gripped by an irrational slash of panic. 'Ellie? Is that you?'

'It's snowing!' bleated a tiny voice. A face jammed itself between the spindles of the staircase. 'I want to go outside.'

'It's too early, Ellie! Go back to bed, darling. Go on! I'll wake you when it's time. Promise.' Sheila's tone was soft but non-negotiable. Ellie negotiated.

'But . . . but . . . I want to be first! I want to be the first out in the snow.'

Sensing an opening when her mother didn't immediately chase her back upstairs, Ellie drew in her head and came quickly down to the kitchen. She reached up for her mummy to lift her onto her knee. Sheila couldn't resist her. One side of her face was impressed with the pattern of the carpet, where she'd fallen out of bed and slept half the night on the floor. Sheila lifted her onto her lap and smoothed down her herringbone cheek. Ellie pushed her face up close, trying to look adorable. She stared right into her mother's eyes. 'Please. Oh pleeease,' she beseeched. 'I haven't got school today. Why can't I go out? Oh can I?'

Sheila smiled, trying to fight back a familiar sensation – that this was her husband staring into her, trying to talk her round. Her daughter's eyes reminded her so much of Robbie's, when they'd first met. Robbie could never, would never sit still. He was always pacing and flitting, always changing his mind. He'd lunge headlong into one quixotic enterprise before abandoning it halfway through to pursue the thrill of another. She hadn't noticed how or when Robbie's eyes had stopped darting and glistening, only that they no longer did.

Sheila looked deep into the ambit of her husband's emerald eyes and, smitten all over again, her heart danced to the thought that she still had the power to transform. 'Come on!' She smiled, and kissed her beautiful little girl hard on the head.

Ellie's bottom lip was already quivering, ready for the rejection she anticipated. She peered up at her mum, disbelieving.

Sheila bumped her down onto the kitchen floor.

'Really?!'

'Yes! Really. Come on! Let's do it! Me and you. Let's make a great big snowman out on the lawn.'

Twenty

It was the week before Christmas and on Liza's suggestion, Sheila had bitten the bullet and taken herself off to Minsky's in Stockton Heath for a 'radical new look'. Liza herself had just had a complete overhaul – five days in Tenerife with her sister and a stunning, pixieish, short spiky cut with highlights that only she could pull off, Sheila thought. Where other women might look hard or brash with such salt and pepper contrasts in such a rude crop, the cut only accentuated Liza's cheekbones, her dazzling blue eyes, and her light, healthy tan. She looked beautiful. Whatever the point of the mini-break – and she'd pretty well told Sheila how the land lay, back at Cohen Central – it had worked. Even in late December, she was a svelte honey-hued beauty. Sheila found herself admiring Liza's slim calves and taut bottom and it took no persuasion at all when she suggested a change might be as good as a rest for Sheila, too. They spent a lazy Friday afternoon in the Stockton Heath Wine Bar with a bottle of wine, flicking through *Vogue* and *Harpers*, but it was from the glittering pages of *Cheshire Life*'s Society section that Liza found her inspiration. Tucked away on the last page, after the Bowden Women's Guild's Yule Fayre, was a brief photo spread about a medics' ball in Tarporley. Three radiant young wenches were mugging up to the camera, each still desirable in spite of tightly curled tresses.

'Oh, darling! Look! Yes!' trilled Liza.

'Curls?'

'A perm! Oh, darling – you have the sweetest little face! You'd look adorable!'

'Do you think so?' Sheila couldn't keep the pleasure out of

her voice. But she'd got way, way more than she'd bargained for at Minsky's. The camp coiffeur, stroking her elegant neck and teasing her tresses up in bunches, had suggested that not only was a bubble-perm the very last word in Cheshire glamour, but if she lay back and let him have his way with her – lowlights at the back graduated through to bold, unapologetic, gold and copper highlights up top – she'd have a queue around the block. He complimented her pretty face and swan-like neck. He even said he'd give her her money back if she didn't like it. Still unsure, she twisted her head round to her style guru for her verdict.

'Do it, Sheila! Forget about him! Do it for yourself . . .'

She took it that Liza was talking about the hairdresser, who stood to take tewnty-five pounds off her for a full perm and highlights. But Liza had spent the walk back to the bus stop steeling her against her husband's likely response.

'If Robbie doesn't take one look at you and just faint with the wonder of your beauty . . . if he doesn't realise how *lucky* he is . . .'

'But are you sure it's me, Liza?' With Robbie out singing that evening, Sheila had invited Liza back to the homestead. They stopped off en route to pick up two bottles of excellent wine. She threw off her coat, her tanned arms slim in a tight green vest top. ''Cos I really can't get used to it myself . . .'

Liza followed Sheila into the kitchen, cooing. 'Oh, darling, yes! Yes!'

While Liza uncorked the first bottle and slid the other one into the fridge, Sheila hung in the doorway and tilted her head. She took a chin-length spiral of hair and pulled it down to her shoulder. 'It just takes a bit of getting used to, I suppose. It just feels so . . . short. Like all my neck's on display.'

'You do realise the Japanese would worship you for that neck. And I mean *worship* you. I still think you could have gone for something shorter. You've got such a pretty face – you don't need to hide behind all that hair.'

Sheila blew through her cheeks, unconvinced. Liza surprised her with a close, lingering hug. Her breasts were firm as they dug against her.

'You're beautiful. Don't you forget that, you . . .'

Sheila pulled away, still toying with her brittle, springy curls. 'Anyway, Marco said it would drop after a while. And the high-lights will not look so orange after a few washes. And I mean . . . my hair grows really quick – that's the main thing. I could have it back to its natural length in no time.'

Liza shook her head, indulgently amused. 'Natural length?' She smiled. 'I'd love to know, actually – what is a person's natural length?'

'Well, you know, the length I've always been used to.'

Smiling and feeling faintly childish, Sheila went to check how the curry was coming on and, swooping to straighten a lopsided Advent calendar, she now noticed the scruffy lattice of sellotape criss-crossing the nativity scene. She couldn't help smiling. Every single door had been jemmied open, looted of chocolate and hastily patched back up again. Ellie.

A while later Liza followed Sheila into the lounge with a bottle of chilled Pinot Grigio and poured two ample glasses. They sat down on the floor by the coal-effect fire, and both took a long, thirsty slug, parched from the curries and savouries. Liza half reclined so she was propped up on her elbow and forearms. She stifled a little yawn, stretched and extended her long legs. She turned to Sheila. 'Can I ask you something?' Her tone was light, but Sheila was panicked.

'Course. What?'

'Do you . . .' Liza gripped her with her bright eyes, fierce and unblinking. 'Do you ever wonder if Robbie's got anyone else?'

'What?'

Seeing the sudden anguish in Sheila's face, she switched to a more soothing tone. 'It's not such a crazy question, She. Most of the men we know have got someone on the side . . .'

'Do you know something? Is that what you're trying to tell me?' Sheila looked anxiously to the ceiling, where Ellie was stomping about.

'God! No! No, no, no – not at all. It's more . . . I'm just . . . It's nothing, really. Just something I'm thinking about a lot at the moment. Ignore me!' She tried an ironic smile, but she just looked tense and drawn.

Sheila sipped on her drink. The two friends said nothing for a moment. Liza gazed off into the middle distance, lost in her thoughts. For all her tan, and her tight, aerobicised body, her careworn complexion was starting to show her age – or her distraction. She came to, quickly flashing another apologetic smile at Sheila.

'Sorry. Miles away.'

'You look tired.'

'Oh. No. Still adjusting back from holiday time.' She forced another smile but her eyes were troubled. Sheila took another deep glug. When she put the glass down, Liza was looking at her intently.

'What is it, Liza? You can tell me . . .'

Liza glanced down at her glass, gave a little snort while she made up her mind but then, clearly and decisively, swallowed the urge to confess – whatever it was. 'It's nothing.'

'Is it Vernon? Is everything OK?'

She seemed to bridle at this. 'Well, your husband's job is safe, if that's what you mean. For now . . .' Liza gulped hard.

Sheila got to her feet, went to her. She took her hand and looked into her eyes. 'No. That's not what I meant at all.'

Liza gulped again, her eyes watering over. 'Sorry.'

Sheila took the glass from her hand, leant across for the bottle but Liza caught her wrist. She put her arms around Sheila and hugged her.

'Oh God, darling. It's such a mess.'

Unsure how to react, Sheila felt the sinews of Liza's arms and neck pressing into her, tight to snapping point. Keen to extricate herself from the hug, Sheila sprang up, poking at Liza's upper arm. 'Here,' she soothed. 'Sit back. Let's see if we can loosen this up a bit.' Positioning herself behind Liza's narrow back, Sheila dug her thumbs into her friend's shoulders, kneading and plying the taut muscle. Gradually, she let her neck fall slack, drifting off in a reverie while Sheila probed and caressed.

'Wow, yes . . .' she said. 'That is really doing it for me . . .' She let out a girlish chuckle and tilted her head right back so her scalp was grazing Sheila's breasts. 'I'm drunk,' she whispered.

Sheila continued to manipulate her tense lower neck, her earlobes. With minimal restraint, Liza began to writhe beneath her touch. Sheila scratched behind her ear, aware she was making love to her now, not caring, wanting to make her purr again. Liza strained back, lifting her lithe hips from the floor. Sheila could see right down her top to her breasts, freckled from the sun, straining against the fabric. Lightly, only grazing her skin with the membrane of her lips, she kissed her neck. And when Liza did not object she kissed her again, scraping her scalp with her long fingernails. Liza went limp now, letting it all happen to her. Instinctively, Sheila went to slide her hand across her stomach. Liza's hand clamped down, stopping her. She sat up, hair tousled, eyes squiffy. She looked Sheila up and down with a mixture of love and fear. A second's hesitation, then the two women tore into each other in one crazed, impassioned kiss. Then Liza was pulling away again.

'Oh my God! God. Sheila. Where the fuck did that come from?'

Sheila couldn't look at her. There was a long, loaded silence.

201

Liza got to her feet. Sheila could feel her eyes pleading with her to meet her gaze, but she couldn't look up. She picked out an amber-glowing plastic coal and fixed her eyes on it and sat there, dead still.

'I . . . I can't. I'm so sorry. I'm so, so very sorry, Sheila. I'm going to go now.' She paused in the doorway again. Sheila didn't move a sinew until long after she heard the door click shut behind her.

Twenty-one

Robbie's head thumped wildly as he pulled into Hayes Close. The gig at Blackburn had been a success. They'd offered him a residency, good lol too and to cap it all off he and Jodie had pulled into a lay-by on the way home and had the best sex of his life. But now, his mind was spinning. It was Christmas, he should feel merry, he should feel something. But all he felt was trapped. Trapped by the aspirations of his wife and kids; trapped by what was expected of him, especially this time of year. It was all about stuff – stuff that he had to get, stuff he had to deliver else he'd have failed. All the other fellas at work seemed electrified, convincing themselves they could buzz off their kids, mad excitement. But not Robbie. It all seemed wrong. And part of what made it wrong – a big part of it – was himself. His failings. The way he'd let his family fall away before they'd even got going. He'd let that happen. He'd allowed it. He'd be sat there on Christmas Day, carving a big, succulent turkey, with a cheerful brood he cared little for, wishing himself elsewhere.

Robbie was trapped more than anything by his own refuge from all this. His escape from reality was Jodie. But she was his jailer now as well as his sometime lover. Lover – hah! Time and again since Blackpool he'd tried to shake her off, but she was always there, knowing where he'd be, knowing how to get to him: a drink, a roll-up, a bunk-up, a silly joke, sure to make him guffaw; and how he needed to guffaw these days, the primal and cathartic release of a man pent up. His bladder seemed to swell as the house came into view, reminding him all over that here his children slept, excited for Christmas, unaware that their father was slowly killing himself. He stopped outside the Bishops', steadied himself against the lurch of his hangover and fired a dark, polluted stream of Jodie's whiskey into the thick of their holly bush. He smiled as he zipped himself up.

He hesitated outside the house. The silence and the dirty sepia light flushing the mottled windows gave out a sense of a safe, secure, family unity. If only. He inserted his key quietly, careful not to wake Ellie. The last thing he needed was her expectant little face, beseeching him to take her out walking. He wouldn't be right for the day until he'd had at least a few hours' kip. He'd do the usual – bed himself down on the sofa until dawn broke, then slip upstairs to his guilty limbo next to Sheila.

Robbie didn't see her at first, sitting dead still on the couch, staring out at the nothingness of the garden. He snapped on the light and jumped back, shocked. He stared at her, knowing it was her but unable to grasp how that was his Sheila sat there. 'Fuckin' hell! What have you done?'

Sheila's heart raced away from her. Her first thought was that he knew – knew what had taken place in this very room, only hours before. But then she followed his eyeline, and remembered. Laughably, out of sheer habit she found herself explaining, apologising. 'It'll drop. It'll grow out.'

'Jesus. What happened? What did you do . . . ?'

She glanced at herself in the mirror, the dim light picking out the whites of her eyeballs, her teeth. She looked like a savage. Weirdly disembodied from the moment her eyes flickered back over Robbie's puce-red face. But this time she made no attempt to placate him, to diffuse the imminent dispute. The fact that he felt entitled to an opinion enraged her. Yet she didn't shout. She crushed the vitriol and said, 'What do you care, anyway?'

'What do I care?' He steeled himself up. 'You're my fucking wife, Sheila!'

She eyed him, bitter, disappointed. 'Am I?'

He was not expecting that. He sat down.

She carried on glaring at him, cold and furious. Hating him. 'Who else is your wife?'

He stared up at her, eyes on the verge of popping. He'd never been a great liar. He looked away. 'What you on about, stupid?'

She knelt down in front of him, looked right into his eyes. 'Who else, Robbie?'

He wouldn't look at her. He shut his eyes tight.

'Who is she?'

Robbie got up, went to say something and paced back out into the hall. Ellie was sitting on the stairs.

'Is it time?' She grinned. Robbie scooped her up, smothered her with kisses and placed her gently back down. He let himself out, walking on, out through the dull grey cold, no notion where to go. All that was important was to have a target, a focus, something to aim at next. The canal. After that could wait. He pushed on, head and throat clotted with hurt.

Everything was grey and grieving, the sky streaky and miserable. The canal was starting to thaw. Dirty icebergs bobbed along the oil-choked flow of the narrow waterway, groping to stay afloat among the debris of crushed cans and cellophane chip trays – the dregs of last night. Robbie was desperate. Every house wore lights or decorations, singing out the joys of Yuletide. He felt none of it. None. He headed over the locks, aching and hungry for Jodie's musty embrace, the lover he no longer loved.

Twenty-two

It was the last day of term. From his store-room lair, Vincent heard the scrape and shuffle of chairs along the dining-hall floor and the clang of plates being stacked away as the noisy diners emptied out into the playground. He heard the giddy whispering of boys who had managed to sneak back into the corridor sail past his cubbyhole and pause at the tuck shop, trying to rattle its shutter free. The braying laughter of teachers welled up in the pipes that ran from the staffroom. All of these sounds seemed magnified and hyperreal, and with them came the faintest whiff of some remote shard of misgiving – so slippery, so tenuous that it would ebb away before he could properly register it.

Vincent put down his jotter and looked around the room with new suspicion. There was nothing tangible to point to intrusion, yet the hollows and silences of his lair were suddenly stained by something nearby. The smell appeared again, softly spreading like a rustle around him. A stretch of silence where nothing stirred, not even the pipes, but then the fresh beat of footsteps from the corridor beyond. The steps seemed to quicken with his pulse. The smell drifted all round him once more, thickening to a soup. As the footsteps grew louder and closer, he suddenly recognised the smell. It was him. It was the stench of dread.

The creak of the door handle being pulled down shot through him like a current. He snubbed the light from his pocket torch and shrank back into the muggy silence, stiff with fear. The door opened, cast a band of light across the floor, then closed and sucked the room back into darkness. Vincent felt his lungs seize up, his chest clenching with terror. He bit hard on his lip, and tried to master the old man's rasp of his chest. His inhaler was

206

way out there, out of reach, in his desk. He saw two silhouettes advance across the room. A boy and a girl. They stopped at the gym horse, giggling, whispering. And he recognised the voices then. It was Simon. Simon Blake and Isobel Cohen. His heart banged out of kilter. Then a flame shot forth and lit up the room.

The flame tilted back then died. Vincent squinted through the slats of half-light. He could no longer see them, they had receded into the groggy shadows of the room but he could see the talons of smoke streaming from the red eye of the fag they were sharing, dancing from mouth to mouth. Vincent's heart beat louder and faster till he could no longer hear anything else in his ears. There was a long breathless moment and then the room was suddenly flooded with light.

He heard his name being dragged out from the pits of her stomach. Had the boom of his heart given him away? Or had he simply called out in the reeling oblivion of his fear?

'It *is* you! Fucking Gaylord, would you believe it? You were *spying* on us!'

Vincent pulled himself up, his legs buckling to jelly. 'I wasn't,' he stated weakly. 'And just so you know, I haven't seen a thing.' He mugged a smile. 'Mum's the word.'

Simon came flying towards him, kicking his way through the rubble of old Christmas decorations and medicine balls. 'What *you* saw? And what *did* you see, Bud Bud?'

Isobel lurched towards him, grabbed him by the collar and shook him violently. She'd tossed away the cigarette but its incriminating stink poured all over him. 'Cos I know what *I* saw. We saw what *you* were doing in here, didn't we, Simon?'

'Yeah. You were playing with yourself.'

Vincent peered out at her from beneath the cowl of his fringe, angry now. 'Whatever,' he mumbled and muscled past them.

'Pervert!' Isobel screamed at him then pushed him out into the corridor.

Vincent had nowhere to go but the playground. He hung by the doorway, cowering against the fierce silvery light like a hunted animal smoked out of its den. The refuse sheds and the safety of the bins lay on the other side of the school. There was no way he could make it there, not now the playground was in full throttle. If he could just make it through till the end of lunch though, he could get a plan together. If he could get through today, the last day of term, he'd go back to spending the rest of next term hidden away in those stinking, freezing sheds.

Skirting the walls like a shadow, Vincent was able to steal round the infant block to the blind side of school by the playing fields. He shrank back into a crevice and contemplated his watch. Fifteen minutes to survive. Fifteen minutes for them to find him and flog him. Time dripped by. He slid his head around the corner, willing the dinner lady to brandish her whistle. That same foreboding funk hung over him, bringing him out in goosebumps. He could feel it deep inside, that animal sense of danger – and survival, urging him to flee across the playing fields, deep into the woods. He looked out across the battlefield. Would he make it? What would happen if he just went to ground, out there? Would the police be brought in?

He rose to a half-crouch and inched towards the lip of the fields. He was edgy now, jumping back and forth, unable to make a decision. He threw his blinking eyes up to the heavens, scouring the roiling hulks of cloud for some kind of sign. And it came. A ball rolled round the corner, stopping centimetres from his foot. The slap of chasing footsteps pushed him back into the hollow, flattened him to the wall. A lad came tearing round the corner, a diminutive little ginger nut with his two front teeth missing. He was nothing, but Vincent was instantly at his mercy, pleading with his eyes. The lad gave Vincent a reassuring close-lipped smile, retrieved the ball and capered off. But Vincent already knew. The heroic buzz of leading the mob towards its victim was going to prove too delicious for this small boy to resist. He cocked an ear and waited for the signs: the clamour, the mounting stampede from the far reaches of the playground, the hooves and cries steaming closer and closer. And it didn't seem so bad. Just like that, he came out and began to walk easily towards his fate. In offering himself up he was at least denying the mob the thrill of the chase. As he came round the corner, they were already roaring towards him, their battle cries carried high above the playground.

Sheila waited for Vincent at the school gates, heart pounding. The bell sounded and the school exploded into the playground. A cold knuckle of fear pressed up against her neck. All day long she'd been clutching the envelope, madly excited for him, anticipating the celebration party she was going to throw for her son – Vincent Fitzgerald, the writer. Not once had she stopped to consider the possibility that he might not have won. Standing at the school gates now with the wind licking her damp neck cold and the moment of truth so terrifyingly imminent, she wasn't so sure all of a sudden. She was sick with dread.

Vincent looked shocked to see her. His hair was ruffled, his top lip encrusted with a faint trail of blood. He walked quickly in front, refusing to answer her questions, eager to march round the corner and out of sight. Sheila pressed Ellie, her tone soft and encouraging. 'Do you know anything about this? Has Vincent been in a fight, honey?'

Ellie shrugged her shoulders, looked away guiltily. Then unable to resist the lure of another drama, she reneged on her pact with Vincent and told. 'It wasn't *his* fault.' Her bottom lip quivered.

'It's OK, honey, I know that. Just tell me what happened? How did it start?'

'It was one of the twins. I don't know which one.'

209

There was a long loaded pause while Sheila digested the unthinkable.

'Not *Liza's* twins?' Her heart boomed. She could barely keep the dread from her voice. Ellie nodded. 'Vincent was fighting with Liza's girls?'

'Not just them, there were big boys too. But they were the ones who were kicking him the hardest.'

'*Kicking* him? Why on earth would they do that, Ellie?' Panic and rage had crept into her voice. Ellie dropped her head, afraid she was in trouble. 'It's OK, Ellie, I'm not mad at you. Just tell me what happened.'

'I don't know what happened. They were kicking him and calling him a name and then the dinner lady came and everyone ran away.'

'A name? What kind of name?'

Ellie focused on removing a stub of gum from her sleeve, reluctant to meet her mother's gaze. 'Vincent said I'm not to say it again. It's a very bad word.'

Sheila didn't need to ask what it was, she knew instinctively. But surely this couldn't be happening here, not here in Thelwall? She curbed the impulse to head back up the school path and thrash this out with the headmaster. Had the culprits been reprimanded? Why hadn't she been called in? And as for Liza, did she have any idea? She would have to be told. But not now and not today. She put on a smile and forced some levity into her voice. 'Well, whatever it was, Ellie, I'm sure it will have all blown over by the time you come back to school next term.' Then, with her heart smashed to a thousand fragments, she caught up with Vincent. Resisting the urge to reach out and touch his wrecked, broken face, she handed him the envelope.

He refused to open it in front of them. He ran ahead with the house key while Sheila carried his school bag. She felt certain he'd be unable to hold out that long. She pictured him rushing round the corner, hunkering down against a wall and tearing it open. She half expected his head to bob back round any moment. But with each step that didn't happen and with every step closer to home, she began to fear the worst. How foolish she'd been. How silly, just to assume. And today of all days. When she turned into the close and saw his bedroom light on, her heart sank further. It was over. He'd have come out to tell them, if there was anything to tell. He'd have been halfway down that road, grinning. She squeezed Ellie's hand – and Ellie wondered what was wrong this time.

The front door was wide open. Vincent was sitting on the bottom stair. He was holding a sheet of paper in front of him. She could see his eyes behind his spectacles, blurred with tears. He lowered the letter and she could have cried. It was the most beautiful, rapturous smile she'd ever seen. The only time she'd seen her boy succumb to joy like that, ever.

Sheila made a decision not to probe Vincent about the Cohen twins, at least not till Christmas was out of the way. The three of them told Robbie his good news over tea. It zapped the yellow drain of last night's hangover from his face. He was up and out of his seat, swooping on Vincent and lifting him out of his seat. Vincent looked as stunned as his mother. Checking himself, Robbie sat down and checked his delight, before it broke free again and thrashed back, redoubled. He leant across the table, bombarded Vincent with questions, then demanded he get his story and read it out to them. Vincent shot a slow sheepish glance towards his mother. 'I didn't have time to copy it out. We'll have to wait until the anthology comes out, I suppose.'

Robbie sat back, shaking his head, beaming wildly. 'Did you do what I said though, lad? Did you write from your heart? Did you write what you know?'

Vincent nodded self-consciously, his cheeks flaming hot beneath his chocolate hide. Sheila reached over and clutched her husband's wrist, eyeing him affectionately. The news had drawn a temporary armistice, thawed all bitterness between them. Vincent didn't know quite where to look. He averted the mawkish green burn of his father's eyes, unable to return the sheer unconditional blaze of approval.

'So. Does this mean I can have contacts now?'

On the toilet, the next morning before he left for work, Sheila heard Robbie talking to himself.

'Our Vincent, hey? Would you fucking believe it!'

The phone rang and Ellie snatched it up without a second's thought. 'It's for you, Deenius,' she trilled.

Vincent came to the phone, the corners of his mouth tugged down, eyes still disbelieving. 'What do they want?'

Ellie hung by his side, trying to listen in. Vincent mumbled, said 'mmmm' once or twice. He broke off, clamped his hand over the receiver and hissed, 'Mum, it's the *Warrington Guardian*!'

So that was that. Perhaps even more than her husband, Sheila equated the celebrity with achievement – and to her, the *Warrington Guardian* was *The Limelight*. Vincent flitted round the house, punching the air, doing little robotic dances on the spot, but his excitement quickly gave way to a sartorial quandary. He raked through his wardrobe, desperate, demented. He yelled down to his mother in the kitchen, 'Can somebody please help me? I'm having a breakdown up here!'

When she went up he was flinging different interpretations of the same black jeans/black T-shirt combo onto his bed. 'I mean, God! How's a writer s'posed to look?'

Sheila laughed and pulled him in close to her bosom. She kissed his head. She had a strong sense that whatever had happened in the playground yesterday was already behind him. Not for her though – as difficult as it was, come New Year, she was going to have to pick up that phone and speak with Liza. 'Oh, Vincent! Just go as you.'

That seemed to find accord with him. He looked at himself in the mirror and smiled, liking what he saw.

Twenty-three

Robbie parked round the corner from the Irish Club and legged it to the paper shop. What a day. What a fucking weird, topsy-turvy day. Summoned to see Cohen. Phoney handshakes and man-to-man stuff and see-how-it-is-for-me stuff, and 'best all round, in the circumstances' stuff. But the bottom line was he'd been sacked – and he couldn't feel better about it. All that shit about downsizing and facing up to economic realities – they'd all seen it coming months ago. Years, really. It was just a matter of hanging on in there for the pay-off, and he had to admit it was generous. Whether he and Sheila made a go of it or not was anybody's call. More and more, he fancied she was better off without him – and that was when he was sober, when he was thinking straight; thinking for her and the kids, not for himself. They'd just have to see what happened. For now, he had just under two grand in cash in his pocket. He'd be locking all but a tenner in the boot of the car, buying the *Warrington Guardian* and giving himself an entire selfish night in the Irish Club to salute his gifted son, and be saluted for him.

Boy, was he going to toast the little weirdo! He felt giddy as he snatched a sly glimpse of the *Guardian*. He almost crumbled as he handed over his twenty pence to the timid Asian shop-keeper, every fibre of his hand quivering with the onslaught of pride and pure emotion that surged through him. There it was, blazing from the masthead, Vincent's mugshot – the front frig-ging page! He could only guess what they were saying about the little genius. He could recognise his son's name but that was about all, but there were plenty of fucking exclamation marks, that was for sure. He grabbed the newsagent by his slender brown

214

wrist. 'See him, yeah? That's my lad, that.' His eyes welled up as he jabbed a finger at Vincent's headline. 'He's one of you, an' all!'

He tucked the paper firmly underneath his arm, and broke into a trot as he fine-tuned his countdown to the big moment. What he was going to do was roll himself a smoke, order himself a pint of Guinness and a Tullimore Dew chaser, then perch at the far end of the bar and take his time over it. He wasn't going to go tearing through the paper, looking for Vincent's spread – he'd let it find him. He was going to turn the pages serenely, from front to back, in chronological order – just sit back and wait for his lad to jump out and surprise him – and then he was going to get Helen to read it out to the room. A delicious thought sidled up to him, winking: Cohen'd be reading this now. That'd show the conceited little cunt. He could sack him if he wanted. He could put him on the dole, but he'd never keep him down for long, because Robbie had what his son had, in buckets. Raw talent. He was going to take a few days off, then it was his turn. Robbie Fitzgerald – back with a bang.

He took his seat at the bar and reflected on how much he and his bookish son had in common. It was round about Vincent's age that he himself had composed his first song. Unable to transcribe the words onto paper, he'd had to memorise it. He smiled to himself and took a tender sip of his malt as he recalled it, word for word. He raised his glass and toasted himself in the mirror. Who would have thought it, though – him, their Vincent, following in his old man's footsteps? How often did you get that, hey? Robert and Vincent Fitzgerald. He could reach out to his boy now – guide him along the way. As things stood, he, Robbie Fitzgerald, the great wayfarer, wrote from the heart about his life's experiences. Vincent, it seemed, wrote to experience them.

'What's with you, then?' Helen asked, eyebrows raised in suspicion. He stood there beaming back at her like a simpleton.

215

'Ah, nowt. Everything and nothing. Do you know?'

'Christ sakes, Fitz! Spill the beans before you give yourself a hernia!'

Robbie needed little encouragement. He could hold back no longer. Picking up the newspaper, he slapped it down in front of her and pointed to the small picture on the masthead. 'That's our Vincent, that. Me lad.'

Helen snatched up the paper and turned it round to face her. '"Local lad wins prestigious . . ." What? That's your Vincent? Christ, Robbie. Your lad a writer, an'all! You kept that one quiet didn't you?'

Robbie grinned back at her. She'd turned to the middle of the paper, where the main story was laid out. There was already a throng of heads bobbing over Robbie's shoulder.

'What was that, 'Elen? A writer? Your lad is it, Robbie?'

Helen found the page and started reading. '"Eleven-year-old Vincent Fitzgerald . . ."'

Robbie could scarcely contain himself. 'Come on then, 'Elen! Loud and clear, will you! I'm frigging dying here . . .'

She was staring blankly into the paper. All the excitement had bled from her face. She turned to Robbie, perplexed.

'What's up? What's the face for?' Heart swelling up with some grim, queasy foreboding, he snatched the paper out of her hands. The gaggle of men lapping round him drew in closer for a better look. They were onto it before he was.

'Jesus Christ! Lad's wearing make-up!'

Robbie felt his face explode beneath the billows of laughter that blew around him. It hadn't been visible before, but blown up to half the page, it became apparent. Everything around him faded out. His sole focus of attention was taken up by the boy staring back at him – the wedge of kohl underlining each eye, the hint of lip gloss on his smile and, worst of all, the slicked-down nancy boy's fringe. He slapped the paper shut, glowered

216

the company to silence and downed the remnants of his malt. He took his Guinness into the snug and tucked himself up in a corner with his back to the bar. Occasional chuckles rang through from the bar beyond. He supped greedily at his pint, trying to mollify the hurt and anger that was starting to devour him. He opened the paper up again, this time sitting back and letting the full impact sear right through him. Helen's broad hips nudged the brim of his table. She placed a good measure of Talisker down in front of him and signalled with her smile – it was on the house. Robbie snapped the paper shut. He couldn't bring himself to look up and thank her. She put a hand on his shoulder.

'He's just a kid, Robbie. Just a lad who's into his music, hey? Don't tell me you never dressed up like Bowie when you was a teenager?'

'I was never into Bowie,' Robbie mumbled.

'OK. Elvis then. Jim Morrison. You name 'em. They all wore eyeliner . . .'

But Robbie was on a mission. He wanted to suffer now, and he was willing to spare himself nothing. 'Bit bevvied, 'Elen love. Will you read it us? Haven't got me gigs with me.'

She eyed him carefully. 'You sure, Rob?'

'Aye. Let's have it.'

He left his Guinness on the table. He left the paper, too. Head throbbing and ears ringing – one long, drilling, high-pitched, underwater note – he surged out into the night, dizzy. He turned into the side street where his car was parked and staggered right past it. He carried on walking and walking, choking up with hurt and confusion.

It was past eleven when he finally came to. He found himself in town, sat on one of the benches in the Golden Square, up by the little enclave of daytime drinkers' pubs. Men had started stumbling out into the night, momentarily sobered by the slap

217

of cold. Robbie pulled his own coat more tightly around him. He was sober now. His head was clear. And the clarity of his thoughts only made things worse. Perhaps if his son's writing had not been so beautiful, the truths it yielded up would have been easier to deny. But Vincent's words had reached inside him and taken a grip of his soul and squeezed the life out of him. His writing was straight from the heart all right – it was straight from the guts. Robbie had got it so wrong about his son being a writer who lived through his imagination; this corrosive, lyrical prose was grounded in a terrible, lived experience. He wrote and told it exactly how it was. Raw. Untrammelled. Unsparing. He wrote without thinking. The fury of his pen was driven on by what he knew. What he'd seen.

He'd disguised their names, called them the Potters. He'd even made him, Mr Potter, a white-collar worker in a pale attempt at throwing him off the scent. But this imaginary family could only be them. The Fitzgeralds. Vincent was the all-seeing eye, and he had seen everything. That night. Vincent was five. He had to have seen it. The pregnant mother, attacked in her own home by a gang of thugs in boots and jackets which, the way he described them, could only be harrington jackets, the uniform of the racist boot boys that patrolled the estate.

Robbie curled up on the bench and gave way to the anguish in his heart. He lay back and looked up at the winter stars and bawled out loud like a baby. He opened up his coat to the freeze and wished for the night to slay him dead, to still his heart before he woke. There was no hope. There was nothing left for him.

Part Three

Thelwall, Warrington, 1989

One

It's not going to work. From the moment Sheila steps inside the crammed, chaotic bar she knows she won't be staying long. This isn't her. She shouldn't have come.

In the run-up to Christmas she's come close to caving a few times, and joining the girls on the work nights out. Last time though, Enid, one of her dearest patients, took a turn for the worse and, as ever, it was Sheila they called first. But they got paid yesterday, and this time there's been no getting out of it. Dana the receptionist, all cleavage and mascara, had given her one of those piercing looks and sighed, 'I don't know, She. It's like you're punishing yourself, hiding away there all by yourself. Don't you want to meet no one?'

Harmless as the question was meant to be, it had taken Sheila aback. It struck right to the core of her situation. What *did* she want? Was she punishing herself? Did she blame herself on some subliminal level for pushing Robbie away? In the most basic sense she knew she hadn't adapted herself to his needs. She knew that, and God how she lamented it sometimes. But what did he expect? What could anyone expect? She'd been raped, for God's sake. Did she want to try again? Don't know. Don't want to think about it. Did she want to meet anyone? *Did* she? Well, yes, actually. Maybe. Not romance, necessarily, but . . . she wasn't sure what. A friend. Someone to talk to, spend time with. She made herself busy with her patients, and that's why they all adored her so – but they were men and women in their dotage, keener to talk than to listen. More and more, she wanted a pal to confide in, especially now her weekends were so lonely. She was happy Ellie had found nice friends at last, friends from nice

221

families; and she had to be pleased her cosy Saturday nights in with Ellie and a takeaway had, inevitably, been passed over for sleepovers at Jemma's and Sara's. But she certainly didn't want to spend her weekends running Ellie here and there for ever more, waiting for her to phone for a lift home, waiting for Vincent to get in, waiting, waiting.

And so rather than dart back behind the usual excuses and camouflage, Sheila had found herself smiling back at the brassy receptionist and saying, 'OK, then. You're on. Where we going?'

From what she'd gleaned over the two and a bit years she'd worked at Blackbrook Clinic, the girls enjoyed a good blast on their nights out. One or two of them weren't too choosy about the men they accepted – the wretches who'd call in at work were testimony to that. By and large, they went out, ten or twelve of them, got smashed, had a dance and a sing-song and, depending on who was left standing, they'd round it all off with a curry. It all sounded innocent enough, actually, just what she was looking for – some fun. They were all big drinkers and Sheila wasn't completely green: she knew they'd find it funny trying to get her loaded. Her first Christmas at Blackbrook – she'd only been there a month and didn't feel confident putting her foot down – she'd been woefully sick on Martinis. But so long as she stuck to spritzers this time, she'd be fine. As she got herself ready that night, paying particular attention to her still-devastating eyes and brushing her black mane to a glossy sheet, she was child-ishly excited about dancing again. With Robbie, they'd never gone out into town at all – too many 'head the balls', he always said. She'd been once or twice when she first started at Warrington General all those years ago but, other than that, it had been so long ago.

Vincent hears the shrill, braying laughter around the corner, and crosses the road. It's the laughter of a gang of women out on the town, humiliating themselves, throwing down their challenge, their right to party. He keeps his head down and walks quickly in the shadows. It is a mistake, this. Breaking his own rules, coming into town, risking the wrath of strangers – pure stupidity on his part. He's asking for it. If he gets there in one piece, he'll steady his nerves with a double, then he'll be off, and he won't be back. Fuck the band. All the bands at the Barley Mow are shit. Yet Kenny said he'd be there – and for Kenny, he will risk Warrington on a Friday night.

It was a mistake coming here. For Sheila, this place is simply terrifying. It's full of kids. Some of them are not much older than Ellie and they're out of it, up on the tables, up on the bar, their faces gone, their eyes screwed up, their arms in the air. They're hardly wearing anything at all. Some of the girls have great legs and she can appreciate they want to display them – but those shorts they're wearing! They're barely more than lycra knickers, and in this weather! Two girls are leaning back against either side of the big central pillar and there are three, four, five boys molesting them. The girls are letting them. There's no doubt about it, the girls are willing it, gyrating and writhing as hands disappear down their pants, down their tops. Everybody's grinning, everybody's having a time of it. This isn't her.

She looks around. Most of the girls from work are by the door, talking to the two bald bouncers. They seem to look up to these men, seem to think they're important. Robbie never had anything good to say about doormen – 'plastic gangsters', he called them – but Robbie, if she's honest, didn't really like anybody. She smiles at the memory, but it's gone in an instant.

Dana has obviously forgotten her. She went to the bar and hasn't come back. She might only have been gone minutes, but it feels like an hour. She is totally alone here, and she wants out. The music threatens her. Lately Ellie has begun banging out this selfsame demonic throb from the cloisters of her bedroom, and it drives Sheila to distraction. It's not that she doesn't want Ellie finding her own identity, but this stuff just isn't music! It's one repetitive driving disco track – no words, no tune, just a weird, synthetic drone. She would *never* have agreed to come if she'd known the bar played this kind of trash. Dana told her they all got up and danced to Abba and the Bee Gees, all the old Motown classics, but there's none of that. She looks around now, starting to panic. Every single person is white. And here, at night, at play, it frightens her.

She spots Dana at last and, relieved, begins to push her way towards her, smiling in that apologetic, frigid way of hers to the people she moves through. It says: 'I know. I'm really, really dark. But give me a chance. I'm nice.'

She checks herself, not for the ingratiating smile, but for the hatred in her heart. The people in this bar – she hates them. She gets a step closer to Dana but the spectacle has her baulking. An old guy in his forties is kissing Dana passionately; he's moving his head round in full circular sweeps as he kicks a rhythm into his kissing, and he's pressing his groin right into her. With his left hand, he mauls her breast – not merely through the fabric of her flowery dress, but right inside the neckline, his gnarled hand fumbles under her bra. Sheila can see her white flesh dimple as he squeezes hard – and it sickens her. In his other hand the guy holds a pint of lager, which he is spilling all over himself. Sheila turns and picks her way back through the throng and out of the bar.

The slap of the cold shocks her for a second but, as she makes her way to the bus station, she feels better and better. So strangely elated is she by her escape that she stops in her tracks, turns and heads for the taxi rank. She's hardly spent anything tonight. She'll go home in a cab.

*

Kenny isn't in there. He hasn't turned up once since they struck up the friendship. Not that he definitely said he could make it, but Vinnie had held out real hope Kenny might show tonight, see the band, whatever. Accepting it, he tucks his fringe behind his ear and enjoys the frisson that everyone in the place is looking at him. He's getting curious stares, but it's good curiosity. He looks cool, all in black, thin and beautiful and exotic. People want to know who he is. He smiles at his glass and tosses off the last of his Jameson and suddenly there's a shriek of excitement from the end of the bar. 'It is! I told you! It definitely one hundred per cent no back answers is him!'

Two fat blonde girls have been giving him the eye from the moment he walked in there. He's not a fan of body mass, but there is something even more loathsome about these girls. They both have identically mean, tiny, calculating eyes. Piggy little eyes in fat faces, faces he can never forget, and they're beaming across at him.

'It's Gaylord!'

'My God . . .'

'He's gone gorgeous . . .'

'I'm going over . . .'

She swallows her drink and she *is* coming over. Her face betrays everything – indulgence, complacency, entitlement. For her, this is someone she knows. She knows his name, they have things in common, she has a claim on him and, by staking that claim, she will have him. This is what happens. This is how it works. Vinnie can't be sure which of the Cohen sisters this is, but it doesn't really matter. She smiles, making her eyes disappear into slits. She has perfect teeth. Vincent would like teeth like hers – small, indecently white.

'Vincent Fitzgerald! How are you?'

He looks her up and down, slightly dismayed. 'Do we know each other?'

225

She gasps slightly, turns to her sister at the end of the bar, then turns back to Vinnie, bracing herself as the distant possibility of rejection enters her orbit. 'It's me! Izzy Cohen! We . . .'

Vinnie looks her up and down again, very slowly, making evident his displeasure. 'Nope . . .' The sneer on his face leaves no room for ambiguity. 'I wouldn't forget a face like yours.'

And though there's nothing left in his glass he necks the ice water, places the glass gently down on the counter, turns and leaves. As he reaches the door, he can barely suppress his glittering smile.

The closer they get to Thelwall, the more tense she gets. They're almost there now. The little Pakistani driver has been disapproving from the moment she stepped into his cab, tutting at her appearance, muttering to himself all the way. She's used to this from Asian men. The men at the market were happy enough to sell her a miniskirt for Ellie, but what a huddle of fury and disdain if she dared to walk past in it. The shame! An Indian girl – dressed like that! Dressed like *them*. Where was the respect, these days!

The cabbie's curiosity gets the better of him. He fires off his questions – where is her husband tonight? Where did they meet? Where does he work? Sheila is in no mood to soft-soap him. Politely, but firmly, she confirms his darkest suspicions – that, of all the horrors, she is single. Sheila is a single mother. This dressed-up, made-up, fluffed-up tart was married to a white man and, worse, he has left her – as they do. He can contain himself no longer. He stamps down on the brakes and slams his fists down on the steering wheel. 'You are a whore! Get out!'

'I . . . don't you dare . . .'

'Do not answer back to me! Get out!' Sheila goes to get out. The driver pulls her back. 'Ten pounds!'

Sheila turns slowly to the driver and calmly speaks into his beady eyes. 'You'd take money from a whore?'

The driver cannot look at her. His black eyes gleaming with contempt, he stares straight ahead.

'Get. Out,' he spits.

Without allowing her eyes to leave his face, Sheila drops a five-pound note on the passenger seat and, head held high, she makes her way back to her empty house.

Two

Last night is all forgotten now. Sheila is over it. The taxi driver, Dana, all of them, they mean no harm. It's just what life does to you, if you let it.

She waves Pat and Enid goodbye, gets into her car – the old orange Lada, still going strong, left, along with all the other stuff that Robbie never came back for and which Vincent, bit by bit, is shunting off into the garage, or the loft, or just out – and reverses away. She bites on her lip as she smiles back at old Pat, waving from the window of their small, terraced house. She's been visiting them since her very first day on the district; Pat with his respiratory problems and now Enid, his wife, with her ravenous cancer. Sheila cares deeply for all her patients, but of the twenty-five, sometimes thirty clients that make up her weekly rota, Pat and Enid are her favourites. Enid hasn't long now. Through Sheila's ministrations, in part, she has been allowed to come home to die in the house she's lived these past forty-odd years. She will be dead soon, and Pat will be utterly alone.

Sheila sighs as she heads away, promising herself that she will take care of Pat. It'll be nothing – an extra visit after her day's shift to make sure he's comfortable, a phone call over the weekend. She glances in the wing mirror. Pat's still there, forlorn. She's choking up now, feeling Pat's fear and his anguish acutely. What has he to look forward to? Nothing. Yet in spite of her sadness there's a selfish sense of relief too, that she's finished her last visit of the day and is finally going home. She's taken on Saturdays and Sunday mornings to help manage all the extra costs that come with Ellie's schooling these days – extra kit, drama club, excursions to Chester and Jodrell Bank and Liverpool. But they're worth it all, her babies, and compared with how things were that first year after Robbie left, they're doing fine. As a unit she and Ellie and Vincent are doing just fine.

For now, for the next few hours, her time is her own and she's looking forward to having the house to herself. Once she's dropped Ellie at her friend's she's going to soak all her aches away in a deep, hot bath, then she'll settle down to a selfish evening with her latest squeeze – Terry Wogan. Her work friends have been teasing her ever since she ventured this little crush. Michael Parkinson, they could half see the attraction; Des O'Connor, well, in his day . . . But Terry Wogan? That was just wrong! Sheila didn't mind that they jibed her, but it was futile trying to justify the attraction. They just didn't get it. The soft brogue, the twinkling eyes and, most of all, the sheer niceness he exuded, only made them all the more wary. 'Sheeela!' they'd trill. 'You need to get out more!'

Sheila smiles to herself. No, thank you very much. I'm just fine as I am.

For a moment, her thoughts switch back to Pat and Enid and a lifetime of loneliness, but her train of consciousness leads her on to her babies, and she wonders what they're doing right now, and what they'll be doing this time next year. She does it all the time, fantasises about what Ellie and Vinnie will make of their lives. They're only thirteen and eighteen, and already they've done so well, achieved so much. They're both bright kids, each on a scholarship at two of the best schools in the North-West and, in their own distinctive ways, each is turning into a remarkable young person. Vincent with his writing and his poetry, one of the brightest stars of Alty Grammar's sixth form. As for Ellie, there is no limit to her possibilities. Since starting her third year at Culcheth, she's blossomed. Not just physically, though with her long legs and caramel skin she could be a model if she weren't so boisterous; but with her interest in music and drama and every-thing on the arty side at school, Sheila could see Ellie as a concert pianist, training at the Royal Academy. It was costing her a fortune in extra lessons and specialised sheet music, but what of it? What else was she to spend her money on?

She allows herself a smile as she cruises on past the canal. Surely she won't be jinxing their good fortune if she allows herself to dream out loud for a second? Her heart bumps along wildly as she pictures her little man leaving for university. She and her elegant young daughter will head off to Rusholme together, sharing secrets over an intimate meal, maybe even a bottle of wine. But much closer on the horizon is the pilgrimage back home the three of them will make next year. Vinnie and Ellie will visit Kuala Lumpur for the first time in their lives.

There is much to look forward to, yet still she feels sad for Robbie. It was never on, he and she. She can see that, now. And she no longer blames him. She's never hated him and of late she's started to sympathise with him. She wonders what the world holds in store for the hopeless, shambolic romancer. Above all else, she hopes for some equilibrium in his relationship with the kids. She wishes he could make his peace with Vincent. Each of them needs to give way a little, yet Robbie is even more childish than his boy. He was eleven for goodness' sake, and Robbie can't get over it. Won't get over it. Yet the more he drinks himself into oblivion in Blackpool, the more besotted his daughter becomes. She'd visit him there, regularly, until a few months ago. With so much going on at school though, even Ellie can't be everywhere all at once.

As she approaches the swing bridge, Sheila is taken unawares by the depth of her sorrow for him. She sees the flame-haired man racing along the towpath with the five-year-old Ellie. She sees him running, always running. It's all too sad. She has a strong sense that Robbie is still roaming, still searching the waste-land of his youth as he chases the splintered echo of a dream. And she can't shrug off the cold, probing finger that points at her. Deep down, she feels that somehow she is to blame.

Three

Vinnie keeps a wary eye on the two young lads prowling closer towards him. They're nothing, just a pair of townies from Orford or Bewsey. They're bottom rung too, the whey-faced, glue-sniffing skins in the worst of naff, market shell suits and big, overbuilt last-year's trainers. Even Vinnie knows that no one wears Travel Fox any more. These two are just guttersnipes, glueheads on the prowl. Furtive and instantly guilty like all teen nightcrawlers, they ram their solvents deep down into their shit, shiny, black tracksuit bottoms. He can hear the clank of the click-ball inside the aerosol. Warrington has its fair share of baddies, but these lads are nothing. Vinnie has learnt what to look out for. They pass him by, trying to look hard, only looking very young, very bored, very ugly.

They get right down the far end of the overpass.

'Hey! *Paki*!'

He hears the death rattle of their krylon spray paint as they whip it back out, give it a good shake and drag their handiwork all over the perspex easel. The pair of them work quickly. They've done this before.

'Look and learn, raghead!' They back away, cranking out a half-hearted one-arm salute, turn and leg it.

Vinnie could not be less disturbed by them. Almost feels sorry for them. He sighs hard, cranes his neck and squints at their graffiti. BNP. He fishes out a roll-up from his empty ten-pack of Lambert & Butler and sparks up, smiling. So this is the public face of the great white menace, then? Fourteen-year-old ferrets in shell suits with hideous acne. Somehow the Aryan ideal has been lost in translation.

He presses on towards the bus station at the end of the walkway, pulling his famous blue raincoat tight around him. Time is leaking away, and he has to move quickly. He should be in Rusholme by now, sat there in Abdul's, perched in his favourite upstairs window pew, watching the dusk wend its way along the pulsing artery of Little India, flickering the street lamps to life. He should be there with his leather-bound notebook, tracing the shifting inflections of night as it rises up beyond the solemn tower blocks that stand over Moss Side, dreaming up stories that, later, he'll go in search of. It's Saturday night and the main drag of Rusholme will soon be coming alive without him. He has to be there before the Indian sweet stalls and the grocers pack away their rare, plump 'fayre' – their yams and their pickle and their little tubs of cumin and turmeric and their bunches of fragrant coriander; before the silk and cloth stalls shut down and remove the gaudy shock of their extravagant colours and patterns; before the clanking, twinkling bracelets disappear from the trinket stands, Bollywood film scores drifting out and up and away down the tide of the street. He has to get to Rusholme before they all close up, fold away and stand back for the main attraction. The restaurants. The grub. The legend of the Curry Mile. Vinnie Fitzgerald is a writer, and he needs to be a part of that lambent snatch of time before night settles, before the pavements are flooded with the spice-seeking vagrants from suburbia. That magical Happy Hour, filled with the gleeful shouts of traders who've done well, whistling and laughing as they dismantle the tubular frames of their stalls and stow them away for another day. The sounds and smells pour forth, of the street winding down; a mellow, contemplative moment in time before the next act bellows into town. This is the Rusholme that buzzes Vinnie's head with stories.

Sometimes he will barely blink as he silently observes the city coming back to life again – Saturday night fever in this wondrous metropolis. He sees them all prowling, purring, eyeing each other up – all the different tribes sliding and darting in and around each other, part of each others' worlds for this one short spasm of time and space. Rusholme is a pan-Asiatic curry of Goans, Kerali, Pakistanis, Bangladeshis, Persians, Punjabis, Tamils. But the spice that gives it its kick are the white folk. The goths with their alabaster faces, the weekly pilgrimages of Smiths fans, the punk revivalists, the myriad students in all their scruff and pomp. And then there are the Rusholme Ruffians in all of theirs – dressed-down casuals from Wythenshawe up for the night to have a go at Moss Side's Young Guvnors. There's a weird little crew of old-time skinheads, tight white jeans, braces dangling down from beneath their petrol-green flying jackets, boots and shaved heads and questioning, disappointed faces. They prowl up and down, letting everyone know they're there, a bitter, watchful minority.

Abdul's is the only restaurant along the stretch that affords the ideal vantage point. Sometimes Abdul himself will come and sit with Vinnie during those twilight hours, making smiling, faltering small talk as he, too, tries to pick out whatever it is on the street below that causes Vinnie's eyes to dance and sparkle. Vinnie only ever orders a coffee, but Abdul lets him stay until the table is needed, refilling his cup while Vinnie's pen scorches across the page like the crazed indie speed freaks outside. Sometimes Abdul will watch him from the kitchen with his cooks, their tittering faces crammed into the small grid of glass. They're endlessly amused by the tall, skinny waif with his girl's fringe and thick wedge of eyeliner. Abdul assumes he's a hard-up student, so shockingly thin is young Vincent. He lavishes him with samosas and yesterday's naan bread, half hoping he might one day immortalise his busy little eating house in fiction.

'On Abdul's!' he announces as he places the plate in front of Vinnie. His tone is as proud as it is paternal. 'Just remember me

233

when you are famous worr-*rryte*-ah, yeah?' He pronounces the 'w' in writer as though he's using it to tune up for all those rippling 'r's. Vinnie makes a big thing out of feigning embarrassment and gratitude at the gift of food, swooping on the steaming parcels of pastry and mince as though they were brand new vinyl. But as soon as Abdul turns his back, the food parcels are mummified in tissue and stashed in his raincoat, ready for his grateful friends. He just hasn't got it in his heart to tell the lively little man with the clever brown eyes no thank you. It's not that he can't afford to eat – he's just not big on food.

As he approaches the bus station he sees the nose of the Manchester bus edging out. He can still make it – if he runs.

Just past Wythenshawe a nasty little crew in Jazzy B clobber pile on and instinctively Vinnie touches the welted, double-stitched pocket of his blue raincoat and reaches out for his notebook. No sooner had he heard the gorgeous lilting refrain of the Leonard Cohen paean than he knew that song was for him. That would be him, one day. A writer in a loft. A place on Clinton Street where there'd be music drifting up to him, all through the evening. And he wanted to start living that life, now. He was already someone who wrote, compulsively, wherever the inspiration gripped him. Finding that raincoat, though – that was the making of him. His pals already looked up to him as a muse, a loner, a true original, and the raincoat – the famous blue raincoat – was his totem.

Taking himself out of the line of fire Vinnie lowers his head to his notebook and transcribes their broad-vowelled argot. They can't be fifteen yet, but these scrawny white kids decked out in Moss Side garb are well aware of the fear they generate. They revel in it – the instant clamming-up of conversation, the ducking of heads behind newspapers – they know it's all down to them and the menace they exude. Vinnie feels for the young lad in front of him. He's now studying the route map on the window, desperate not to provoke the mob of hyenas eyeing him up, waiting. If he catches their eye, he's fucked. If he has to, he'll stare at it all the way into town – anything to avoid the accusatory 'what the fuck yoh lookin' at, cunt face?'

Even just imagining that harsh accent in his mind cajoles a shudder of lust from Vinnie, an inner shiver. Kenny.

Kenny talks like that. His sweet, tender hooligan, glamour thug Kenny from the warehouse, talks the talk of these baby hoodlums. He's only been working there three weeks – twenty-two days if you count today, seeing as he did his induction on a Friday. Vinnie smiles at the recollection, the first time they met. The dirty-blond, hard, cripplingly handsome townie, eyes averted, ever so slightly apologetic in his faded Cocteau Twins T-shirt. Vinnie knew the form well. In a place like Kwik Save in a town like Warrington in the coldest week of the year, to wear a T-shirt like that to work is to say: 'Don't bother. You won't get me.'

So Vinnie, for all his indisposition to small talk, struck up a break-time camaraderie with the taciturn shelf-stacker. And Kenny, in the manner of the born again, was unflinchingly upfront about his reasons for pitching up in the Kwik Save stockroom. Over ciggie breaks out back, Vincent swooned at the romance of his story – which Kenny was at pains not to romanticise. He merely stated the facts: passed from pillar to post. Most settled memory was seven years with his granddad up in Eccles. Granddad died. Various homes in and around Salford and Eccles. Running with big, wild gangs. But it wasn't this that saw him doing twelve months at Hindley. It was a crime of passion he went down for – his books. One of the lads tried to show him up as a ponce, a poof for reading all the time, and one day Kenny flipped. And that was it for Vinnie. When he heard that bit – how Kenny had stabbed the lad with a fork for calling his book habit 'gay' – he was gone. He was utterly, agonisingly

235

hooked on Kenny, yet knew too well he could never say a word about it. It would be for ever the love that dare not speak its name. He has an instinct Kenny may well come tonight. His stomach is vaulting to the thought.

The bus swings a corner and there it is, scooping its gold-crêpe tunnel right through the red-brick soul of Manchester. Rusholme. Beautiful, vibrant Rusholme. Vincent checks his time-piece, its antique face splintered down the middle by a jagged crack. The bus is late. He hasn't got time to make Abdul's tonight and, feeling a little cheated, he heads straight to the Plough to meet his friends.

He's never quite lowered himself to the tiffs over who discovered Rusholme first. Dan is fond of telling the gang he stumbled upon Didsbury Road before 'Rusholme Ruffians' was released, and at a time when the rest of them were still pressing their cheeks up against the brickwork of Salford Lads' Club. Zoe claims she and her dad have been hitting the Curry Mile for years. Vinnie doesn't feel the need to get involved. For the longest time, Rusholme was a guilty secret that Mum kept from the family. But after Dad went, and as he grew into his role as Mr Jones, he and Mum shared many a Saturday afternoon wandering the strip. While Ellie was indulging her then-love of rugby league, Vinnie was coming alive to the sights and aromas of Manchester's micro-Asia. It was, in so many ways, the making of him. Rusholme and the Smiths were the things that showed Vinnie what was really out there and what could be done. Both had compelled him to write. Yet Rusholme was something he preferred to keep to himself. The Smiths changed all that.

Like everyone who falls for the Smiths, Vinnie fell hard and heavy. He can still recall his first kiss from them with the utmost clarity. He can remember the background acoustics that percolated around the bathroom where he was sunk shoulder deep in scalding hot water. Beyond the perky, upbeat voice of Peter Powell he could hear Mum stacking away dishes in the kitchen below; every crash and clang reverberating the sting of Dad's absence, and outside, the perverse refrain of the ice-cream van cutting through his mother and sister's grief. He was thirteen years old. Dad had come and gone, and gone again, and this time he'd been gone a month. Vinnie was in his bathroom lair, fleeing the pall that hung over the house. And he was thinking, No, it's good that Dad has gone. Mum is sad, but we'll be happier, soon. We'll all be better off without him. And suddenly Peter Powell wasn't talking and those jangling, indelible, ultra-bright, scaling chords chimed out, seeming to send the radio rocking. He can remember it so clearly now. He cranked up the volume as high as it would go. He didn't care who heard. Everything he did, Vinnie did quietly, on the low. But this he had to hear! He had to immerse himself, surrender himself to it in just the same way as he let his fathomless bath claim him, day after day. He loved this band. That voice just punched him bang in the heart – fresh, fraught, wise and wistful, soaring above and below the jaunty guitar, defying and renouncing the synthesised melodrama of the charts. It was like nothing he'd ever heard.

'I would come out tonight. But I haven't got a stitch to wear . . .'

The poetry shivered his skin, its clever camp conceits prickling goosebumps all over him. He laughed and smiled and shook his head at the comic aptness of the lyrics – yet there was so much of himself, all his own sorrow and loneliness wrapped up in those bittersweet couplets that his laughter gave way to tears.

'It's tragic, it's gruesome that someone so handsome should care . . .'

Vinnie was smitten. Gone. He sat there trembling all over, anxiously waiting for Powell to reveal the identity of this charming young man. And he didn't let him down. The Smiths. How perfect.

He smiles again as he enters the Plough, happy at the pleasure his arrival will bring.

Vinnie elbows his way to the bar, fighting his way through an all-white cast of indie kids, goths, yet more Morrisseys, a few skins, a gang of foppish professor types trying to stay with the pulse, and a smattering of non-denominational students out for a Saturday night drink in a safe pub. Vinnie drags deep and hard on it, reeling back from the sticky, pulsating magic of that initial buzz of the bar. Right now the youth of Manchester is sliced in two – narcissism versus nihilism – with one side blissed up on E, the other blitzed on weed and drink and contemplating the end of the world. Apart from the young Asian homeboys who cruise the drag in their souped-up X3is, cheesy gansta rap thumping out from their cabriolets' sub-bass, Rusholme is Indie Kingdom. Its innocuous blend of musical tribes, students, arty types and downbeat intellectuals seems to seal it off from the bug-eyed bacchanalia of Madchester and he *loves* it for that.

Vinnie orders a Jameson, tosses off the dram in one slick shot, then orders another and scans the scrum of bodies over the rim of his glass. The smoke prickles his contacts. He loves this place. He could get drunk on the stink alone – that fleecy mingle of fags and weed and sweat and cheap hairspray. Some Sundays he hides last night's garb under his bed so Mum can't wash away the stench. He'll wear his clothes again to write in and, perhaps, while he pleasures himself. He shoulders his way past a couple of skins, looking them straight in the eye. Nothing to worry about. If they're in here, they're gay. One of them slips him a wink and jerks his head in the direction of the toilets. His face is blank. He's good-looking enough, sure, but that steel-hard, musclebound thug look doesn't really do it for Vinnie. He prefers the poet-ruffian, the hardened vagabond. Kenny's look. He wonders now if he'll actually show up tonight.

He spots his little crew over in their regular corner and his heart lurches. Stooped towards them and laughing hard is Kenny. Vinnie is almost on top of them before they notice him. There's lots of over-the-top guffawing, especially from the girls. There's no doubt about it – Kenny is a hit with the clique. He's a star. But he isn't so starry-eyed as to miss the envy flickering his friend's face.

'Late again, Dorian Grey?' Kenny smiles, getting his defences in first. In revealing his clever pet name for Vinnie he clearly thinks he will show them both in a good light. Vinnie bristles and for a brief moment steers away from the group, as though he's about to walk off, but just as quickly he turns back and smiles, first at Kenny, then at the others. He's forgiven him already. Kenny makes a space for him and Vinnie stoops to conquer.

'So,' he says, tossing his fringe, knowing Kenny's eyes are on him but carrying on unawares. 'Seduce me.'

And as though it was the funniest thing anyone ever said, they guffaw again.

'Hey!' beams Dan. 'Stone Roses are on at the Boardwalk. They're shit hot, man.'

Vinnie leans back in his seat and eyes his eager pal. 'Daniel.' He just says his name – hardly any stress or intonation – but they all lean forward. They know this is going to be good. Vincent smiles thinly. 'Lose the hot. Actually, no. Lose the man . . .'

Appreciative chuckles from his acolytes, but Dan resists. 'They're all over the music press.' He blushes. 'Everyone says they're top, man . . .' He tails off, aware he's delivered himself on a plate.

Vinnie smiles again, almost apologetic in his put-down. 'To be popular one must be a mediocrity.'

Zoe chimes in. 'Nah, Vin. On this one, maestro, you are wrong. Have you heard them? They rock, maa . . .'

'Man? You women love with your ears, just as we men love with our eyes.' A glance at Kenny. He's watching the sideshow, amused.

'That is your fatal error, Dorian. You value beauty far too highly.'

Vinnie swoons for an instant as he soaks up his warm, generous mouth and the hard vulgar accent at odds with the beautiful soul within. A beat – and then he strikes back. 'It is only shallow people who do not judge by appearances.'

Laughter plays its way around the table. Kenny sits back, hands him the floor and just twinkles and grins at him. Vinnie widens his eyes in mock horror and affects a Richard Pryor accent.

'And they is one band of pig-ugly motherfuckers!'

And that, the switch from arch-Vincent back to normal pub-joker just slays them. Sometimes it still takes Vinnie by surprise the level to which he's not just accepted but loved by his gang. These are the people that used to batter him – not them exactly, but their type. A type forever compensating for the ills they perceive in themselves. He knows in his heart of hearts that this wouldn't work as well if he weren't a brown boy; their pet Paki.

'OK, so they're not the greatest looking band,' Dan ventures.

'Say that again! The lead singer looks like fucking Gaylon.'

'Whatever, *The Face* did a huge spread on them. That must count for something.'

Kenny twinkles at Vinnie, knowing he's going to say something good.

'The road to hell is paved with other peoples' opinions. Here's mine – for what it's worth. I have, thank you, both seen and heard the Stone Roses' blend of pang and twang. One is aware they flirted with cursed goth not so very long ago . . .' He can see Kenny wants to intervene – sees him choke the impulse. Vinnie continues. 'Go see them, by all means . . .' He leans right back, taking two legs of his chair with him. His raincoat falls right open the further back he leans and his stomach is tensed. He's aware that his lean, brown torso is now exposed, just, and

240

he gets a rush from how it must look. He runs a hand through his thick black hair and brings the chair back down again. 'But you'll hate them.'

It seems to bring a downer on them, briefly. Vinnie's quick to make amends. Having distanced himself from this half rock, half Byrds symbol of the new Madchester indie-dance vibe, he's quick to let them know it's fine for them to like the Roses.

'It's just me.' He grins. 'I hate everything.'

At this, Kenny laughs louder than anyone, giving Dan his cue. 'What d'you think, Kenny? You up for it?'

'I dunno,' says Kenny. 'I have to . . .' He looks to Vinnie. Is it OK to say? Indeed, he's fine with it himself, but is Vinnie going to be embarrassed? But this time, Vinnie is silently urging him to spill the beans. Kenny looks into his glass as he's talking. 'I'm sort of on probation. Not probation exactly – but it's better that I do certain things voluntarily, if you see what I mean.'

They all nod solemnly, not knowing at all what he means. Zoe puts words to what they're all feeling. 'Wow!' she says. 'That's so—'

Vinnie intervenes, grinning. 'If you utter the overused and under-meant epithet "cool", Zoe . . . I'll slap you!'

Zoe goes red. 'I wasn't—'

Vinnie holds up a hand. 'I know. It's just that I was, and I needed to deflect my deep, deep shame elsewhere.'

Hearty, heartfelt laughter – Kenny, too. Vinnie can't hide his pleasure at this. He makes them laugh. They love him. He should quit while he's ahead. It's tough, keeping up the standards they've invested in him. His glass is empty, faded to a slip of ice. Crowd pleased, palate whetted, loins loose and easy, he finds himself craving that sweet tangy kick of another whiskey. But he weathers the urge, knowing it'll jeopardise what lies ahead. He's all nerves, now – nervous and itchy as hell. Hungry to get going. He's backed away from the conversation. He no longer worries about

Kenny. He's certain that, once he's gone, Kenny won't wish to stay with the others. He feels mean, but he has to tend to his hunger. He doesn't tell them he's going – he never does, never can. He heads towards the loo and exits through the saloon door.

There's a long train of buses edging bumper to bumper all the way down Didsbury Road. Without having to break his stride, he catches the one furthest up the road just as the last passenger is boarding. The doors swoosh shut. He slips his headphones on and presses his nose against the cool pane and makes stories out of the people on the street.

Vinnie doesn't see him sprinting alongside. He almost draws level with the window before the bus lurches out into the main stream of traffic. Kenny stands there panting for a moment, then hops on board the next bus along.

Four

Ellie dangles a long, slender leg out of the passenger door, hesitates, then leans over to graze her mum's cheek. It's barely a kiss, but it's enough to make Sheila smile.

'What about tomorrow, Elsbells? Do you need me to pick you up?'

'Not sure, you know, Mum. Can I call you in the morning?'

An expert would have picked up on her overtly gay, upbeat tone; the dissembling use of 'you know'; and, most obvious of all, the fob-off promise of the phone call tomorrow. But Sheila isn't ready to let go just yet.

'I can pick you up around eleven if you like? I've got a couple of patients over this way in the morning . . .'

'*Mum!*' Ellie cuts her short and compensates with her very best 'stop worrying' smile as she tries to bring the routine to a close.

'OK, honey.' She leans out of the window for another peck. Their lips hardly touch. She squeezes some joy into her voice. 'Have fun!'

'I will!'

Sheila watches her daughter's bright-red puffa jacket disappear down the dark, muddy dirt track. She finds herself choking up the way she always does at this Saturday night juncture – her little girl making her way in the big, wide world, wading further away from her, deeper and deeper into the flats of adulthood. Oh, but she's gorgeous, though! Those caramel-brown legs and the lightly freckled face and those staggering, bright-green eyes. She should just be thankful Ellie hasn't discovered – or been discovered by – boys yet.

It's odd to think now, but she felt the absolute opposite when adolescence finally drew Vincent out from his clenched little conch. There aren't many mothers who'd say this of their teenage sons but Sheila was delighted that first time he came home bolly-eyed and garrulous, stinking of drink and smoke. She was just relieved that her shy, bookish son was developing at last into a normal, healthy teenage boy.

In contrast, she finds her daughter's take-off difficult to reconcile. As she grows into her limbs and breasts and devastating good looks, she moves further away from the mother and daughter intimacies of which her friends at work boast, and to which Sheila herself had so looked forward. Far from bringing them closer together adolescence has cast a husk around Ellie that Sheila simply can't slough off. And the changes have happened almost overnight. Her bolshy little tomboy left the house one evening and returned a reclusive and beautiful young woman.

This is nice though, being a part of her Saturday night. In dropping her off, she's involved at least, if only on some peripheral level. She stays there staring at the empty dirt track for a while, awaiting Ellie's signal. She'd prefer to take her right to the door, but her own peace of mind isn't worth the embarrassment their battered Lada would cause to Ellie. If not for Vinnie's intervention, Sheila would never have twigged.

'Mum! Come on! How many other girls at Culcheth Hall request their mums to pick them up a mile away from the school gate?' he teased.

The truth of it coshed Sheila hard, but as ever, she cast herself as villain more than victim. Had she really been that remiss? How could she have missed all the signs? As Vinnie gently chided her, how could she fail to notice Ellie never asked anyone back for tea? This was so Sheila – forever the wide-eyed girl in the crowd, waving excitedly as the royal procession troops by.

She'd been exactly the same when choosing a school for Ellie.

When she'd first flicked through the school prospectus for Culcheth Hall, that was it for her – sold. So swept away had she been by its prestige, its glamour (and, truth be known, by the gold-leafed spears on the school gates) that she scarcely paused to consider the social chasm between Ellie and her classmates before signing her away. She was smitten by air-brushed images of girls in royal-blue blazers and boater hats, and the thought that her own little girl could be like them. And on some subconscious level she saw Culcheth as no different to Vinnie's grammar school, with its varied social intake. The reality was that Culcheth Hall cost an arm and a leg to its fee-paying patrons and, in the perverse way of such things, a scholarship girl was not an icon of learning but an object of ridicule – especially one whose mother drove a livid-orange Lada.

Sheila swallows a sad smile. At least this is just a sleepover tonight. In the run-up to Christmas the girls have gone on sorties to Pizza Hut, the ice-skating rink, the cinema – sometimes all three in one day, and it is starting to wear her out. She dearly wants Ellie to have all this – lovely friends from good families – but the overtime she has to work to keep it all going is gruelling. Only yesterday Ellie reminded her about the first down payment for the school trip to Rome – no way is her little girl missing out on that, thank you! And then there are the clothes she needs to keep up: Fila boots, Kickers, black lycra shorts, a royal-blue Michiko Koshino fleece and that awful stripy Adidas beanie hat. It was all very well and good for the Cartwrights of this world; they could indulge their little princess with an entire new wardrobe on Friday and she'd discard it on Sunday, from what Ellie was saying, but for Sheila, well . . . it's January and she's stone broke. Still, the little frisson of pride she experiences each time she sees her beautiful girl leave the house in her regal blue school uniform more than compensates for all the juggling and scraping and sleepless nights. That is her clever girl, there. Her beautiful, clever girl.

Ellie comes charging back down the lane without her bag, her eyes dancing with happiness. Sheila struggles with the window. She tries to wind it down quickly and smoothly to give the impression of it being electronic, but the handle is stiff and she's breathless from all the fruitless effort. Ellie sticks her snout in through the inch of space she's cleared and grins. 'Sara's dad'll drop me off tomorrow. Might even soft-soap him into taking us to Mackies for our breakfast.'

Sheila laughs, curbing the impulse to poke her fingers out and touch her daughter's face. 'OK, darling. You girls have fun – d'you hear?'

'Dunno 'bout fun, Mum. Babs is entertaining, *darling,* which means we'll all get shunted upstairs. That's if she doesn't rope us into carrying around salvers of duck's bowels or whatever it is these people eat . . .'

Feeling her eyes start to smart, Sheila throws her a wave and cranks the window back up. Ellie stands at the foot of the dirt track and watches her mum turn the car round. She finger-waves one last time, turns and heads for Sara's house.

Sheila tracks her daughter in the car's wing mirror, her heart thumping with love and pride as she watches till she's out of sight. She swallows down a huge lump in her throat, but there's nothing she can do about the tears that steadily fall.

Five

Vinnie moves quickly through the queer twists and alleys of club-land, limbs burning at the treat that lies ahead. As he peels hard onto Canal Street, he has that eerie sensation of being followed. He bobs his head over his shoulder, slats his eyes against the tight jam of bodies. Nobody. Everybody, but nobody. Outside the Rembrandt there's the usual greasy knot of leather-clad octo-genarians, feasting their vulture's glare on the tide of nubile flesh. Their prey are willing performers in the dance. Vinnie takes it all in through the drape of his fringe – the hamster wheel of skin and sex and drugs and boys and endless possibility. It intoxi-cates him. It disgusts him. He hates the queer bar clones. He hates the shameless uniformity – the handlebar moustaches, the tacky checked shirts, each one a slightly more ridiculous parody of the last.

A long line coils back from the door of one of the booming dungeons. He has no choice but to cut through and as he jostles past, face set, he feels himself being drawn into the spotlight of a dozen conversations. They can't work him out. The tall skinny indie kid in his long blue raincoat and his girl's fringe and his big, pretty brown eyes – they see him down there every Saturday. They know where he's heading and it breaks their hearts. Such a waste. Such a tragedy. Everyone on Queer Street knows that the only people paying for sex are the priests and queer-bashers. But a pretty young thing like the boy in the raincoat? A crying shame.

Vinnie tries not to smile as he passes within earshot.

'Aaah, just look at him! Don't you just want to take him home and feed him up?'

'Oh my God, wouldn't you just!'

Much hilarity among the preening queens. Vinnie rolls his eyes, picks up his pace. A couple of chubby transvestites mince past. One of them's wired, doesn't see him, but her friend stops dead in the middle of the street, eyeing Vinnie hungrily as he passes. Hands on ample hips, she shakes her head in thwarted lust. 'D'you see him? Did you see the lips!' she shrieks. Her voice is loud and hysterical, playing to the crowd. 'Get those gums around my plums, lovie!'

'Ooh no!' Her mate grimaces. She, too, stops in the road and fans herself down. 'I don't do brown.' She pauses just a beat, then delivers her pay-off. 'I've got an addictive personality.'

Harsh, drug-addled laughter ripples its way down the queue. Vinnie slows his pace, waits for the sniggering to abate, turns to the crowd and delivers the Parthian shot. 'And I don't do fat, darling. I'm anorexic.'

The laughter rings out louder than ever, accompanied by miaowing and applause.

Vinnie exits the drag and follows Sackville Street away from clubland. Within seconds, all is silence. The bawdy vulgarity of Queer Street is a distant murmur over the other side of the canal. One of the huge billboards up ahead by the flyover has been given over to a big Don't Inject campaign. It's been targeted at the burgeoning gay scene round there, a standard government AIDS scare long after the horse has bolted. But the irony never fails to draw a little chuckle from Vinnie. While gay Manchester parties into the night a few blocks away, this demi-monde of empty warehouses has long been the haunt of bagheads. The money would be better spent taking the message out to future captains of industry in Didsbury or Wilmslow where the brown menace hasn't quite dug its tramlines yet.

Vinnie waits for his boy. Every now and then the breeze parts his hair, bringing with it a drift of laughter or the ardent thump of a bass line, rippling the moon-flecked puddles. Time passes. That slow-burning desire in his loins is cranked right up now – urgent, voracious, itching under his skin. But he waits. He knows the boy will turn up. His need is even greater than Vinnie's – he needs to get paid. He squints over at the billboard, amused all over again at how hopelessly wide of the mark the agency had got it. The hollow-eyed actor they'd rigged up as a baghead looks more embarrassed than wretched. His shamed, badly made-up face is that of an adolescent caught in the bathroom wearing his sister's bra. And the way they've backlit the syringe, making it glint like an instrument of torture, is just laughable. As for the cheesy, scaremongering 'One Shot and You're Dead' strapline – it was simply not true. He's been jamming for months now, and he can take it or leave it.

For Vinnie, honey is the ultimate decadence. His record collection is a shrine to the great, eternal heroin ballads, his bookshelves a monument to Algren, Burroughs, Selby. But for him it's a weekend indulgence, nothing more. It has never been about escaping from pain or inner torment. For Vinnie, it's all about beauty. He cares little these days for the debates and dogged causes of his friends. He's found the purest resin of beauty and it fills his world with wonder. With heroin, his dreams are possibilities. And there's nothing he loves more than lying flat on the roof of a multi-storey car park with a dauntless ink-blue vault above and the honey swooning through his veins and the white, drifting moon and the sounds of the city spinning him the sweetest lullaby. 'One Shot and You're Dead'? No. One shot and you're alive. It's fucking beautiful.

Car headlights approach. Even the car has a regretful, stuttering slouch now it's all done. Vinnie can make out the silhouette of his boy in the passenger seat – the tragic peak of his baseball cap. It always makes Vinnie sad, clapping eyes on that cap. He never takes it off. Somehow, and today Vinnie can sense this better than he's ever made sense of it before, his baseball cap is a thing of pride to the boy. He cuts a forlorn figure, the kid, lent more pathos by his eternally jaunty outlook. His rapid-fire delivery is always accompanied by a big, leery grin and back-to-front handshakes and shouts of 'sorted' and 'wicked' and 'let's 'ave it!' It's too sad. The driver, a shortish man with a large head, half mounts the pavement and barely stops as his vehicle spits the boy out. Vinnie can't risk losing him to another punter. Straight away he steps out from the shadows and wolf-whistles the lad over. He ducks and squints against the darkness and crosses the road, his movements jerky and exaggerated. He hesitates. For this boy, each and every transaction is a judgement call. One wrong shot and he's dead. Vinnie whistles again. Surely he knows the call by now? One low note, one high. One low, one high. There's a delayed reaction as the sound registers in his drug-dazed skull and then he's bouncing over, all jerky skaghead shuffle, leaning forward on the balls of his feet.

He bounces under the yellow street light and Vinnie winces. While the eyes are alive and burning, the soul has gone. His skin is scabbed and scaly and that face – the pleading expression, the denial. How could anybody make a sex act with this creature? He can smell the fresh paste of semen on the lad's breath. He wishes he could do this without him.

They cross the road without saying a word and head towards the multi-storey. Vinnie struggles to keep up with him. They hover in the stairwell. The jaundiced pall of a broken light picks out the deathly grey of the lad's complexion. His skin is so thin it looks like you could blow it away. Yet he can see it now – lurking behind the junky cast is a face that would have been pretty, once. He drops the fiver bag in Vinnie's hand. 'Careful yeah if yoh crankin' up. It's proper lethal, this, man.' *Lee-fol,* he says it.

Vinnie hands over the money. Almost on autopilot, the lad

holds it up to the murky light, seems to forget what he's looking for and stashes the note in his sock.

'Be good, yeah?' he mumbles and then he's off, that madly syncopated, forward-leaning lurch. Vinnie's glad he's gone. He goes to the roof of the car park and scans it quickly, satisifed there's no one there. He likes the lonely ritual almost as much as the nirvana of the thing itself. He unpacks his kit, the syringe and the little ampoule of sterile water straight from his mum's car boot. He feels bad about taking from her like that, but what could he do? Make himself known at the needle exchange? He binds the tourniquet tight and finds a line.

The rush smashes up against the top of his skull, swelling, crashing, and soaring then fading to a smouldering coal. He screws his eyes shut, humbled by this bliss, and lies back flat, then opens them up to a sky that is suddenly spattered with stars moving closer and closer towards him. He reaches up to pluck one but it burns away, reducing him to a tingling cord dangling in the heavenly breeze.

Six

Ellie squats in the scratchy undergrowth where she's stashed her rucksack. Teeth chattering madly, she strips down to her panties and pulls out her Saturday night uniform: rib-crushing yellow vest and black lycra shorts worn beneath a black, all-in-one skintight catsuit. She puts her fleece and red puffa jacket back on, and stuffs her jeans and hoody into the rucksack. She fishes out ciggies from her side pocket, where she stashed them while Mum was making tea.

Ellie feels bad, putting her through all this – lying to her, blatantly having her off for money that she absolutely needs but which she knows her mother doesn't have. But if she truly didn't have it, how come she always manages to come up with it? She'd know if she was pushing her mum too hard. She'd know. And in the meantime, it's not as though she doesn't get a kick out of all this – dropping her daughter off outside one of the grandest residences in Stockton Heath, home of Sara 'My Little Pony' Cartwright. It's sick, but her mother loves all this. She holds out hope that Ellie's going to start stepping out with Sara's bovine brother, or one of his square-jawed mates. Hah! As if. But still she feels badly about her mum. She can't help herself.

The chicanery of this ritual leaves her dizzy sometimes – the lies, the lies – but the end more than justifies the means. The weekend has just started. Within an hour she'll be in there, up there, having the time of her fucking life. And after that? Who cares! This is it, here and now.

She sparks up and casts a backwards glance at the Cartwrights' mansion. She loves the buzz of smoking right here in the undergrowth, right in the eye of their safe, chaste lives. She can see the silhouettes of girls' heads in one of the bedroom windows, hear their affected shrieks as they pillow fight and bounce on the beds. Most of them are older than Ellie, but they sound so girlish. So very young. Not too long ago, she would have given anything to be up there herself, play-fighting and comparing breasts with the golden ones. Every one of them was beautiful, in that flawless, burnished-blonde way. Every one of them devoted to their horses. Ellie cringes as she recalls her own eagerness to penetrate Sara's inner sanctum, her first few weeks at Culcheth. Everyone flocked around Goldilocks, everyone fought for her affection. The truth of it was that Sara Cartwright – and she had to hand it to her – had real style. She had a Mulberry satchel where others had workaday school bags; she wore Red or Dead brogues and Boy underwear; and she got her hair done at Toni and Guy. It was a whole new exotic world to a single-parent alms case like Ellie Fitzgerald – and didn't they make damn sure she knew it. Not so much Sara herself, but the others' barbs about her market shoes, her North Warrington accent, her boyish cropped hair and her inability to distinguish 'of' from 'off' – it had all been part of the ongoing process that made Ellie the girl she was.

She sucks hard and deep on her ciggie, holding the smoke down as though it's a joint and as she exhales hard, she blows away the memories. She smiles to herself as she pads away down the lane. Those awful first two years at Culcheth are almost forgotten now, overgrown by the new skin of a new life. Those giggling little girls back there – they don't know anything. They haven't even a sense of what lies beyond their electronic gates. They haven't lived. Perhaps they never will.

She tosses the smouldering coal into the undergrowth. She hits the main road and turns and throws one last lingering look at the silhouette of Goldilocks' castle. She pictures the teenage mulch that litters her floor – chocolate wrappers, *Just 17* and *Smash*

Hits magazines, a DIY ouija board and maybe even a bottle of Cinzano. She finds herself laughing out loud now as she flashes forward to an image of herself, up on her regular speaker, arms in the air with a big Ecstasy grin, lapping up the carnival of the dance floor.

Ellie huddles up at the bus stop. In the near distance, the rumble-thump of a bass line gets louder as distant headlights weave closer and closer. The muffled throb of the bass beat breaks her out in goosebumps. These are kindred spirits and that car can only be going one place. It swings into view. Ellie steps out in front of the car's shrill glare, balls her hands into fists and punches out her own syncopated rhythm, arms in the air. The silver Fiesta blares right past, doesn't see her, its windows steamed up from the party within. Ellie's stomach is doing backflips – she's almost throwing up with excitement. She's always like this, from the moment she drags her eyelids open and her mind catches up and realises it's Saturday, she's a landslide of nervous, impatient nausea.

Ellie becomes aware of the car's engine rumbling up ahead in neutral. She squints up the road. The red eyes of the brake lights wink back at her, then there are two white lights, two bright white shooting stars streaking towards her as the car reverses, veering madly from side to side, a scaling nasal whine as it picks up speed. She jumps back onto the pavement. The screech of rubber against concrete as the back tyre hits the kerb. A lad jumps out of the passenger seat. The music bangs out into the cold, suburban air. 'You going Legends?' The lad is small and skinny and decked out in clubbers' garb – beanie hat, puffa jacket, tracksuit bottoms and trainers. Ellie grins and gives him the thumbs-up, nodding her head to the pulverising beat. He grins – already on one. 'Come on then!'

'Ta, mate!'

The car's tiny shell is crammed full. There are five bodies in the back and three in the front. Ellie hops in, slams the door.

She's become a dab hand at folding her lissome frame into tiny spaces. Many a night she's moulded herself into the footwell or lain flat in the dark confines of a boot while the car ploughed on in hot pursuit of the flimsiest rumour of a comedown party or a post-club rave. She wedges herself between the legs of a pretty boy and hooks her legs up over the seat in front. The boy looks like some strange cute bush creature, all hunched up inside his fleece with his cricket hat tugged right down. He locks his fingers around her, clips her in tight as the car lurches out and speeds off. Ellie can feel the lad's knees trembling. He's waited all week for this, all of them have. They've been hauling the secret of their wondrous universe around with them for days and now they're teetering on the brink of explosion. Ellie has been wanting to spit it out – holler it from the rooftops. How she is dying to tell the world about the small pocket of magic she's stumbled upon! One accidental, magical night has changed her life, changed her for ever. Legends has turned her life, her every-thing upside down and in the space of six weeks the little club has become the tide and the lunar cycle by which she sets her clock, her calendar, the very beat of her life.

Ellie sits in one of the wash basins of Legends' toilets, her body limp and leaden as she struggles to push herself back up against the crackling shortwaves of pleasure that have strafed and stroked her nerves to riot. It's heaven, and she doesn't want to move. Gradually, she regains consciousness and becomes aware of a boy and girl standing in front of her, each one of them strad-dling either knee. Their faces are rapt, intent with the utmost concentration and love they're transmitting through their subtle fingers. They're scratching Ellie's arms up and down, massaging and stroking and gently scraping her skin from shoulder to fingers. All around, bodies are flitting in and out of the toilet cubicles, vague smears of slow-motion colour, slowly blinking the night back to life.

More bare torsos pile in, seemingly swept through the door by the blast of a swooping bass line. Ellie's number one rave buddy is in the thick of them. Cal. His broad grin widens on seeing her. He springs over and envelops her in a bearhug. 'Where'd you go, Ellie babe? Been looking all over for you.'

Ellie just grins, unable to speak. The massage has taken the edge off her funk and at long last she can feel herself slotting into the easy rhythmic waves of the tablet. Her thoughts are lean and beatific, her arms light and agile as the music from outside takes her away with it, prompting her limbs to impulsive arcs and dives.

'You on one, babe?'

Ellie widens her grin a couple of inches.

'Come on, you. Me new girl's dying to meet you. Been talking about you long enough.'

As they push through the delirious heat of the club, Ellie, the tablet and the bass line meld into one. She stops stock-still, pulling Cal back. There is a warm surge of pleasure pumping out from some inner coil deep behind her lungs. She can feel her neuro-transmitters at work, shooting little darts of glee around her body, zipping in and around her heart and her fanny like fire-flies around a fire. But she doesn't dance. She just stands there, letting the bass thrum right through her. Cal makes a fist around her hand, squeezing so tightly that tomorrow when she wakes up, her skin will bear the bruise-tattoo of his nails. He pulls her along behind him, weaving a path through the dance floor chug. Ellie revels in it. It's magical, every beat, every step. Everyone nods and grins and raises thumbs at her as she passes. She pauses to hug waxy old bodies and kiss liquid young faces. The music lifts her, levels her, then lifts her again. Her head rolls back and her eyes hit the shimmering apex, a glimmering collage of strobes and glitterballs spinning dream-like reflections of faces she's seen in the toilets, in the queue, in the car park before the doors even opened, and the night doubles back on itself and comes full circle as she catches a snatched fragment of the bush-baby boy with the huge eyes from the car that gave her a lift there.

Ellie can feel the place rocking under the weight of pure delirium. She looks out across the rapt sea of bodies and shakes her head, incredulous. 'Look!' she shouts. 'Cal! Just look at it.'

The pair of them stand and stare from the fringe of the dance floor. Cal is older than Ellie and not so easily seduced, but he too is blown away by the sheer spectacle of the crowd bouncing as one to the bang of piano and bass. And they both know it – this is one of those moments when the congregation touches something bigger, purer, more astounding than anything they've known before. It goes beyond friendship or love. Only those there at that precise second where the sound drops out to silence and the piano kicks back in and their souls hit the roofs of their skulls will recognise the starblaze, that awesome, fleeting glimpse of something magnificent and profound. Ellie feels it deeply, and she knows that Cal is feeling it too. She draws him in close, digging her fingers into the small of his back and running her palm over the muscular jut of his arse. She can feel his cock hardening. His dick is stabbing into her hip and then they're kissing – their tongues probing, lapping, seeking out the wrinkled roofs of each other's mouths.

The music changes tack and hardens. They both pull away at exactly the same moment, laughing, recoiling at the sheer absurdity of what just happened. Cal shoots a nervous glance over her shoulder towards the back of the room. ''Kin' 'ell, El! Where'd that come from?'

She grins and shrugs. He's beautiful, Cal, he'd more than do for most girls, but he's too . . . nice for Ellie. He's Cal. It's that little crew up by the speakers that lights Ellie's fires. Gary Miller. She's just riding out the wilder waves of her tablet, then she'll make her move. Cal, awkward now, asks Ellie if she wants a bottle of water. She scans around for Miller and his boys while he's gone. Their nut-hard, shaven heads stand out next to the bobbing mop of hair on the dance floor. Miller himself has a rock-hard stomach, his tattooed chest packed and muscular. Ellie can feel her fanny spasm as she watches him, dancing minimally, eyes never leaving the crowd. He dances without joy – if dancing it is. He has his hands behind his back, barely swaying from side to side, perfectly on the beat and yet perversely removed from the ritual. Ellie takes in the taut, simian sneer of his face – the high-cut cheekbones, the corners of his eyes stretching upwards, almost oriental. He's beautiful. This is the boy she's going to give it to.

She's right in the hub of the dance floor now, writhing in front of Miller. He's raking his eyes all over her, doesn't even seem to mind the brace. She winks at him then turns away, swaying her bum gently to the slow build of the piano refrain then slams it as the bass kicks in, working it like a piston. She flips her chin over her shoulder, and she's got him. He's transfixed, staring at her arse. She drags his eyeline up to hers. 'I. Want. To. Fuck. You,' she mouths.

He's too stunned to move for a second, then he steps towards her. He's coming for her. She smiles to herself and turns back to the speakers as though she couldn't care, either way. She feels Miller's arms lock around her from behind, feels his cock gouge into her backside. They stay entwined like that for a while, swaying under the dominion of one, shared subconscious.

Miller lights up a ciggie, pulls hard on it, looks at the glowing ember and plants it between her lips. He strokes her flat stomach with one hand and she groans – it's too gorgeous. She feels his fingers prise beneath the elastic hem of her shorts. Ellie is on fire. 'Come on.' She grins. 'Take me back to yours. I'll take them off. I'll take everything off . . .'

*

258

Ellie steps out of the taxi and her face widens at the great hulk of concrete looming over her. She squints into the tiny bars of prison windows zigzagging the stairway. One forlorn light is humming on-off, on-off, giving the impression of a giant insect flickering around its bulb. Even to those loyal to the Grasmere Estate, this low-rise is an eyesore, but to Ellie Fitzgerald, it's gut-wrenchingly beautiful. It's the real thing. She clings to Miller's arm, a yearning, saturating kinship with him taking her over. 'I was born here, me,' she beams.

'Shithole,' he mutters.

She mock-kicks him. 'Don't say that about my birthplace!'

He grins back at her, without soul. 'Used to be all right. Before the smackheads come.' He grinds the key in the lock, pushes the door. 'And the Pakis.' He sniffs the air. 'Dirty twats.'

Miller's flat smells of stale, cloying chip fat. What Ellie can see of the tiny kitchen as they pass is a maelstrom – every surface littered by open tins and grime and pile upon pile of unwashed dishes, ready to collapse at any moment. It's filthy in there and she has to steel her stomach against the lurch of vomit as her fingers trail something viscous on the wall. He snaps on a light. The living room is just as bad – worse. A dozen dirty mugs clutter the floor and the arms of a tatty sofa. Ellie clears a couple to make room to sit. Cigarette butts float in the dregs of fungal, days-old tea. Miller boots up a big black hi-fi system. It spurts stripped-down drumbeats around the room.

Ellie shrugs off her puffa jacket, folds it into a cushion and perches frigidly on it, trying to shut her mind off to the squalor. She reaches for a cigarette, hoping it might override the stench in here. Miller, rooting through his record collection, has his back to the proceedings. She tries to fight down a growing sense of unease.

'And the Pakis . . .'

He said that. All the lads round Orford said it – she wasn't green. Yet since house music, since Legends, since tablets . . . and it wasn't that, even. It was something in the way he said it. She looks up. He's just standing there, staring at her. No feeling, just looking right through her, like he hasn't quite decided what to do with her. He makes her shudder.

'Get some knives on the go, ay?'

He steps out of the room. She reaches for her jacket, slips it back on, ready. She can hear him firing up with that dirty old gas cooker in the kitchen. A stifled curse, a muttered something she can't make out, then he's back holding two blackened butter knives. He nods at her, trying to be conversational, exuding menace.

'Cold?'

She mugs a timid grin. 'Little bit.'

He shows no concern, no reaction at all. He balances the hot knives, crumbles the pot and sets to working the blades together, releasing the thick pungent smoke. He doesn't offer Ellie any, sucking the first yield down himself, holding the smoke inside and, eventually, leaning his head back and blasting the fumes out at the ceiling.

'Here.' He's a bit squiffy as he offers the works. 'Get on it.' He flops back down onto the sofa. That cold, expressionless gaze has been melted away by a sleepy, heavy-eyed demeanour. Ellie just sits there. She looks into his face – the boy who just said those things. She takes a deep breath and she can't stop herself. She wants to go for him.

'Do you not like blacks, then?'

He thinks on it, makes a pained, knit-brow expression as he thinks. 'Don't mind niggers. Least they'll stand and fight . . .'

OK. That'll do. Ellie shifts position, coiled, looking for her out. Miller raises his head, finds it too heavy, drops it back down onto the arm of the couch again.

'What about yourself, like? Look like you gorra bit o'summat in yoh . . .'

She can feel her heart thumping hard. She stands up. 'Need a piss,' she offers.

'I'll come wiv yoh.' He drags himself up, all stoned and soppy, and starts to lurch towards her. For one sliver of a second she's going to ram her boot into his balls. Sense overrides fury.

'Er, don't think you're gonna like it – if you know what I'm telling you.' She gives Miller her best sultry look, promising there's more to come, and takes herself out of the room, down the little hallway, past the bathroom and straight outside down the stairwell. She doubts he'll come after her but she takes the stairs three and four at a time, eager to get right out of there. She stumbles out of the low-rise and heads towards town, numb to time and temperature.

Streaks of burnt copper rage out across the fading grey sky, drawing back the new day. There are still a few lights burning on through the low wash of dawn as nightcrawlers make their way home. By the time she reaches town the sky is the colour of a love bite, casting strobe lights across the filthy river. She's drained and exhausted and her mind is lurching – yet there's still a flake of her that wants to stay up, stay out. She knows that if she waits here, soon enough a car will pass by, crammed full of whey-faced revellers squashed up against the windows, out of it. But no, sack it. Eyes mesmerised by her own feet she trudges on, each step taking her further away from yesterday, closer to tomorrow. These are the hours she fears most, when her subconscious sets up tripwires for her, throwing her back and forward from the hub of the dance floor, so she has no real notion of what's memory and what's happening now. The bus station is right ahead of her, and she hears the engines cranking up. Her thoughts burn themselves out, stop playing games with her. The realisation that it's Sunday leaves her shuddering – from the eerie chill of cold first light, and from the deathly whisper of the comedown blues. Once she's allowed the thought, she's floored by it.

That's it. It's over. The shutters have been pulled down for another week. Tomorrow, school. How she longs for yesterday, but the night's already locked up and sealed away for another six days. In flats and forests and on the forecourts of a hundred service stations out there, snatches of it still throb on. But for Ellie, spotlit in the rising fireball of a winter sun, that's all gone now. The night is already dead.

She crosses the empty road to the bus station. From here she will take a bus to the launderette in Latchford village where she will wash the chemical stink from her clothes. In the toilets of the café next door she will hunch over a sink and scrub the smoke and sweat from her hair, then she'll squat under the hand-dryer and blow herself back to some semblance of girlhood. Again, the butterflies in her stomach, the flirting deception of the pill kicking itself back to life, instantly vanquished; the usual Ecstasy depression.

As she crosses round the corner, the green single-decker is pulling away. It's another hour until the next one. The lights are changing to red. If she runs she might just catch it at the next stop. Nerves blunted by fatigue, and the drugs and the countless fags, she can't get much of a pace up and, just as she's getting close enough to touch the bus, it lurches forward and swings a corner. There's a boy huddled up on the back seat. She knows she knows him before she sees who it is. The dangling black fringe, the defensive hunch of the shoulders, the famous blue raincoat – she'd know her brother a mile off, anywhere. For that stilled moment there's an unbidden delight at seeing him as the bus picks up speed and eases away. She watches him go, wonders where he's been. How she'd love to just snuggle up with her own brother on the back seat of that bus, spending the journey home in meandering confessions about their Saturday nights. As the tail lights disappear out of sight, Ellie feels herself starting to fall. She heads back to the town centre. She's exhausted and disorientated and she badly needs to get her head down, but she can't go home. Not just yet.

She holds the postcard gingerly between finger and thumb, unsure now whether she'll post it. It started out as a line, a thought – just a nice little spontaneous thing, saying: 'How are you? Thinking of you. Miss you.' But as she sat down in the shadow of the neglected cricket pavilion, hand shaking as she wrote, she found the need pouring out with the words. The postcard is ancient and dog-eared, but it's one of the old types that folds out to give you more writing space and the woman wanted twenty pence for it – so Ellie zapped a biro from the box by the stationery, right from under her nose. Feelings of confusion and loss and a dull, listless statelessness dragged down on her as she crossed over to the deserted cricket ground and sat down and wrote to her dad.

Standing here now, she's slotted fifty pence in the stamp machine and stuck them all on, just to make sure. She's still not sure she should post it.

Seven

The intrusive clang of the letter box jolts him from his sleep. Robbie tries to sink back down beneath the bed covers, shut himself off from the coronary throb of light banging at his temples, but his thirst won't let it lie. He reaches out across the bulk of a slumbering body. He can recall with pellucid clarity the full pint tankard of water he perched by the bed last night – yet he can't quite place the companion he's landed. He quails at her face, twisted into a drunken, snoring leer. Who is she? How did she get here? He pulls back a sheet to see bloated, freckled white breasts and he knows it's all his own doing. He can picture her clothed now – deep, inviting cleavage clad in a tight red dress. The oldest, most effective of honey traps, the plumped-up bosom – and one he's powerless to resist. He manages to retrieve the pint glass without waking the heaving walrus. He doesn't care how stale the water may be. His windpipe is choked and dry and gluey with mucus. He gobbles into the glass, already gulping on it before the water comes – but it doesn't. He tilts the glass right back, slowly computing its weightlessness with the stupefying fact that it's empty, but insistent nonetheless on finishing what he's started and upending the glass completely. His busty companion has drained the tankard in the night. She hasn't even saved him one tepid bastard drop.

He's fully awake now, recoiling from the rinsed-out metallic sour of whiskey and fags that clogs his palate. He clambers over the white chump of thigh that's had him pinned to the wall all night, cursing her as she rolls over, wafting up a stale dairy odour. He steals through to the kitchen, aggravated further at having to sneak around in his own flat – but there's no way he can face

264

her. He'll leave a note, and do one. He slakes himself in bellowing gulps, straight from the tap, then relieves himself in the sink, powerful jets of browny-orange piss making whirlpools round the plughole. He stands there in the kitchen, sleep-starved and wretched, plotting his next move. He can't go back to the stinking pit of the bedroom, no matter how weary he's feeling. He rolls a fag and falls back on his old dependable. He'll wrap up and walk off his hangover; a good, long walk too, depending on the gust out there. He'll set himself Bispham as a target, then catch the tram back and pray she's gone.

He plucks out last night's clothes from the laundry basket in the bathroom and slides the latch out from its groove, careful not to wake her. He catches sight of the morning's post splayed between his feet like a spilt deck of cards and remembers what it was that pulled him from his sleep. There's mail and bills and reminders from everyone, but as he scoops it all up and sets it on the ledge, one card snags his attention and holds him transfixed. His heart races away from him on sight of the ragged scrawl. He grins to himself. That's our Ellie, that writing. Who else could it be? Who else knows he even lives there? It's got to be our Ellie! He tucks it in his inside pocket, zips the windcheater right up to his neck – wincing at the noise it makes – pulls up his hood and tiptoes out of the door, grinning to himself.

He heads straight down to the prom. Even on a mild day it's windy down here, but he wears his hood up whatever the weather, to deter smitten pensioners or punters who've seen him on stage. The water is choppy, the wind bitterly cold. It feels good, the raw elements on his face, nipping and spraying and sloughing off the grime from last night. He sits on a bench, watching the seething white roil slam full force into the pier's stanchions, inhaling deep and hard on the salty diesel stink of the Irish Sea. It's beautiful. He prolongs the moment before he fishes out Ellie's card, runs his hand across the urgent hunch of capitals, smudging

265

them with the sea-sprayed damp of his fingers. It's a huge moment, for Robbie, this. A letter from his little girl; the first he'll be able to read by himself. His guts are swooping as he fingers it. He opens it up and squints to take it all in.

Daddy,

Hiya, how's it going? I've really, really missed you. Things are fine but sometimes I just miss our walks and the things we used to do. I got no one to talk about the things you know all about. And hey, I've gotten really interested in all our Irish heritage and the songs you used to sing me. The older I get, the more Irish I feel. It doesn't seem to me like I have any link with Mum's side, though of course I love her to bits. She says hello.

I'm doing fine. I have loads and loads of different friends, all sorts of different things. I go to a kind of youth club, and that's where I feel most at home. Even with that, I have a terrible feeling that it's already over. Do you ever get that? That everything good is coming to an end? I'm sorry if I'm waffling on but hey, I am your girl after all and you've done it to me enough times (only kidding!).

I think Mum misses you, too. She never really goes out. She sits in watching videos (and Terry Wogan – cringe!), but she seems happy enough. I know we'll never be a family again, and that makes me sad. Vincent also needs someone to kick him up the backside, now and again. He's doing really well at school and all that, but he's not been writing much of late, and arrrgh! It frustrates me so much, because if I had a half of his talent then, well you know what I mean. But whatever, hey? I'd love to see you, even if it was just a flying visit or something. I've got no money to get up there, so what I'm going to do and I'm smiling and grinning as I write this 'cos the thought has just popped into

266

my head. Next weekend, I'm going to cook Sunday grill, except could we make it Saturday grill instead?! If you could make it, just this once, just for old time's sake, that'd be just brilliant. If not, it can't be helped and I'll think of you as I scoff all that mmmmmm lovely grilled grub!

I love you, Daddy. I always will.

Your baby,

Ellie xxxxxxxxxxxxx (one for each year of me!)

By the time he's folded it back into his pocket and staggered to the promenade railings, Robbie is sobbing freely.

Eight

Vinnie is loafing in the bath when Sheila calls up to him. He doesn't hear her at first, her voice drowned out by the slap of the water and the modulated gravitas of Radio Four. The rap of knuckles against the door sits him up and, instantly guilty, he plunges his needle-scarred arm below the foamy surface. It's becoming more and more tricky trying to hide this flake of his life from her, and come summer, when he no longer has the luxury of hiding away in long sleeves, he'll have to be extra vigilant. He should go back to chasing. If the hit were as good, and the ritual of cooking and jamming not so profound, so poetic, he would.

'There's a postcard here for you.'

Vinnie feels a sudden bounce of relief and happiness. Kenny. It will be from Kenny. He hooks his clean arm around the bathroom door to accept delivery, then pushes the door shut. He dries his hands, fumbles around for his reading glasses and wipes the steam from them. Outside the door, his mother still lurks. 'Hey! Don't be making any sudden plans, you! It's our video night!'

'I won't.'

'I'm only teasing. You go out, if you want. But let me know in good time, will you? I'm cooking your favourite – toad in the hole. À la vegetarian of course.' Her voice trails off downstairs.

Vincent shouts after her. 'Mater! You do me a disservice. I shall be there, on time, as usual – Kleenex at the ready.' He smiles at the pleasure his words will be bringing down there, right now, and returns to the postcard. It's a black and white portrait of New Brighton in 1875. So Kenny. Restrained good

268

taste in every choice he makes. He's missed him. He wasn't working on Monday or Tuesday – and Vinnie felt weird about drawing attention to their friendship by asking the assistant manager about his rota. He knew that Kenny would be in touch, though. He knew that one of these little billets-doux would drop on the mat, sooner or later.

Dear Dorian,
    Relieved of my duties at work. Sure you've heard all about it. Need to see you, bad. Howbout Saturday? Forget Rusholme for once – let's say 8 bells at the Dry Bar for cake and ale.
    Love
    Rene

Of course, Vinnie hasn't heard all about it, but the thought chases a little shiver of amusement down his spine. He reads it again and again, reading huge significance into every little inflection. 'Need to see you bad'. Every time he reads it there is a gladdening of the heart as his gaze swoops on that one little word. Love. He can't stop staring at it, over and over. He hasn't felt so high, so absolutely, ecstatically, laughably merry about a message through the post since the time he won the writing prize. He tries to keep a rein on his feelings – he's followed this path of balmy optimism before, only to be deceived by it. So he breathes slow and deep, tries to steady the lurch of his heart and tells himself this is nothing – a careless slip of the nib; maybe even a blundering apology for his offhand manner last time he saw him, Sunday afternoon. Kenny wasn't unfriendly as such, more remote, or awkward. Different to how things were, anyway – and Vinnie had every intention of going to front him about Rusholme. Had Kenny just hated his pals? Or was Vinnie being a phoney that night; or was it that he just got up and vanished?

269

But Kenny didn't show for work the next evening or the evening after that and, gutted though he was at the time, now that he knows the reason why, Vinnie is glad he didn't make a fool of himself.

Vinnie hooks a toe around the chain of the plug and tugs. He lies there staring at the card until the bath drains empty. Just a few lines, but what magic when transcribed by Kenny's hand. If he stacks up all the hours they've spent together it's less than a day – yet he knows him so well. He smiles at the recollection of them perched out on the steep steps by the loading bay, smoking, circling one another. And then there was that first, sudden, avalanche of conversation where both of them caved simultaneously, barely able to wait for the other to pause so they could jump in and add their bit; it felt like they'd been put there to find each other, to be with one another, to be big friends. Vinnie smiles – weeks, mere weeks, yet it seems a lifetime ago. He'd looked Kenny in the eye and told him: 'Without beauty, there can be no love. And without youth, there is no beauty.'

Kenny had smiled, taken a drag on his cigarette and cocked his head back as he blew a pillar of smoke straight up into the silver-grey sky: '*Dorian Grey*,' he'd murmured. And Dorian he had stayed.

Ellie and Vinnie leave the house together. Ellie pauses at the bottom of the road, hitches her skirt right up, then tucks the hem under so it's grazing her arse. An old lady looks on, jowls wobbling in self-righteous disgust. Ellie grins and spears her tongue at her. Vinnie drags her away towards the bus stop, but he can't keep the smile off his face. He's still on a high, but he knows that if he doesn't confront her now, he'll bottle it later on. 'Listen Ellie.'

She's onto him straight away. 'Please don't start sentences like that, Vin.' She rakes him with a playful eye. 'I don't need a

270

lecture about the perils of drug-taking from someone who swans home with the dawn chorus . . .'

'I wasn't . . .'

'Give us a break hey, Vin. It's a weekend thing. I'm fine.'

He smiles at the irony, but he just can't bring himself to push on. He wants to help, but he can't. Meantime, he'll be there in the background, keeping an eye out. They're starting to gel at long last, him and Ellie. He can be there for her in other ways. He lets out a nervous giggle. 'I was just thinking . . .'

'Oh God. Sounds gooey.'

'No, 'ang on . . . it's only gooey if being taken away on holiday by your hard-working big brother is considered gooey these days . . .'

She's all eyes. 'Serious? Where?'

'Dunno. I was thinking maybe we could get off to Brighton or something.' He articulates the proposal as casually as possible.

'*Brighton?*' she almost spits the word out.

Vinnie makes a decent fist of dissembling his hurt. 'Well . . . doesn't have to be Brighton. Could go to London if you want?'

She grins, eyes alive. 'How about Ibiza, more like!'

Vinnie shakes his head, laughing. 'The hedonist's club paradise, known for its liberal slant on all things bacchanalian, with a particular yen for the mind-bending designer drug ee-*stas*-ee.'

She twigs the affectionate poke at their mother. 'Ah, but what about Mum? Won't she be hurt?'

Vinnie shakes his head, half grins. 'Hurt? About getting a break from us two loons?'

'You sure about this, Vin?'

'Sure? I couldn't be more sure! Besides . . .' He drapes an arm around her, feels awkward, withdraws it and continues, stepping on and off the pavement as they go. 'Mums just love it when their kids spend time together. Serious. She'll be ecstatic.'

'*Ec*-stat-ic.'

271

'And we'll still go to KL, whenever, yeah?'

Ellie groans, rolls her eyes.

Vinnie feels exactly the same way – the thought of spending three weeks in a blistering hot climate, while being interrogated by Mum's brothers and fussed over by her sisters doesn't conform to his ideal of the great vacation. They eat, Mum's relatives. They eat, always, and when they're not eating they're planning a meal, preparing it, talking about food. He conjures up a grin for his sister. 'It'll be fun, you know. Me and you, we'll take a train up to Thailand. I'll take you to one of those full moon parties.'

Ellie seems vaguely appeased. He gives her a peck as she starts to peel away from him towards the park. She pauses at its wrought-iron gates, wraps her fingers around a rusty bar and calls out to him, swinging herself from side to side. 'OK. We'll go for Brighton – but I'm not staying in some sweaty B&B. And we're not going to see any of those wrist-slitting bands of yours.'

He grins broadly and waves to his sister.

'*Luego*!' she says, and with that she hauls herself round the gate and off into the park.

'*Luego*,' he echoes fondly, watching her go. She's already halfway across the grass, walking her speed-fire walk, head down as she forages her bag for fags. The sight of her naked legs and swishing mane plants something awful in his stomach and he scolds himself for his own self-pity, for locking himself away at a time when she needed him, or somebody, more than ever before. Where did she go to, Ellie? And where has she been? He needs to get back in her life. He has a queasy misgiving that come Brighton, London, or even Ibiza, it will already be too late.

Ellie gets on her bus, but jumps off at the next stop – an irritating but mandatory precaution to throw her canny brother off the scent. Not that she believes for one moment he'd shop her for skiving, but it would leave her prey to another of his paternal tête-à-têtes. Only the other day he'd left a hopeful little bundle of books outside her bedroom door. It made her sad, somehow – as though he'd left them there fully expecting rejection, like you'd leave a bone for a scolded dog. She shuffled through the books, wanting to like something. He'd left her George Orwell's *1984,* Sylvia Plath's *The Bell Jar*, William Burroughs' *The Naked Lunch*, Bret Easton Ellis' *Less Than Zero* and Salinger's *The Catcher in the Rye* for her spiritual enrichment. There were a few photocopied passages from Timothy Leary and Guy Debord, and a couple of postcard prints of Bacon and Munch. Finally, he'd copied out a Philip Larkin poem about parents and left it on top of the pile. Only the cover of *Less Than Zero* even vaguely grabbed her, but by the third page she'd drifted off, absent-mindedly doodling the lurid squiggly Legends logo. It was good that Vin was more normal these days, but she didn't want him all over her.

As the bus pulls away, a diminutive lad squeezes his face through one of the slats on the top deck. He whistles down at her. He's older than her, cute enough too, but at the end of the day, he's still a boy and boys do nothing for her these days. She plays the game nonetheless – flicks back her hair and juts out her chest without so much as glancing upwards, even once. The bus rumbles away along with the lad's chances. She crosses the road, buries herself deep into the lee of the shelter and waits for the town bus. She sparks a fag and carves out a rough plan for the day. She flirts with the idea of bunking a train to one of the big cities – Manchester, Liverpool, Leeds – or she could just mooch around the town centre in the hope of stumbling upon some of the Legends heads. But before she makes any firm decisions, she needs to pack in an hour's graft. Funds are running on empty and she can barely scrape change for a ten pack, never mind her Saturday night rider of Es and whizz. The weekend starts here.

Ellie heads over to the market. It's early and the shopkeepers are hauling up their shutters, starting to primp their stalls to life. The Asian stallholders already stand poised and expectant, eager for trade, eyeing each browser and passer-by as a potential sale. This first half-hour or so is usually good for business – early-bird shoppers who know what they want, while most of the other traders are still half asleep. Ellie takes a seat at one of the outdoor tables in the market café and waits for things to get busy. It's futile trying anything while it's this quiet. She stands out anyway with her brown face, green eyes and flame red hair, but in a royal-blue, micro-skirted school uniform she might as well tie bells to her shoes.

The air's already fat with the cloying smell of rendered-down lard and tobacco. It makes her hungry for the filthy buzz and she scans the caff for a John. She spies one inside, by the window. His hands are shaking so badly he can barely put his cigarette to his lips. She goes in and plonks herself down at his table – it's just assumed that a chap that old and that lonely will be grateful of her company. She's a past master at this. She rolls her eyes. 'God, just imagine – what must it have been like to come to town on market day when this place was a real hub, hey?' She hits all the right buttons.

'Forget Chester!' He gleams. 'Capital of Cheshire was Warrington! Oh aye . . .'

She injects just the right level of deference in replying, 'Oh, I know. We're just doing it at school . . .'

His eyes are grey and glazed, but he's still able to work his features into a twinkle. 'How come you're not in today, then?'

Ellie thinks about bullshitting him but decides to give the old boy some respect. She beckons him closer, twinkling back at him. 'Because I'm a carefree, chain-smoking teenage truant enjoying the very best years of her life.' She winks and gestures to his cigarette pack. 'About the chain-smoking bit . . .'

He slides them over without hesitation, dips in his pocket, pulls out his lighter. She steadies the quiver of his wrist as she leans in to the flame, sucking hungrily on the fag. They chat. He's easy to talk to, regaling her with tales of derring-do in his days as a 'one for the ladies'. He checks his watch and, hands trembling hard as he uses the table top to lever himself up, tells her he has a hospital appointment. He gives her three cigarettes and a kiss on the cheek. She's actually quite sorry to see him go.

Ten o'clock and the market is alive. She makes her way to the back of the market where she weaves in and around the Asian rag stalls, pausing to roll her skirt up another hitch, willing their contempt. They take the bait; the women are the worst, tutting, cussing, elbowing fellow vendors to alert them to the spectacle. She knows the drill of shame, and she plays to it, grinding her hips and flipping her bum as she passes.

Ellie spots her mark – a woman in a fake fur coat buying fabric from Khan's. Her bag is wide open and – it never ceases to amaze Ellie the way women will persist with this – her purse is lying right on top. She's forever chiding Mum about it. She doesn't feel great about it but it's there, it's easy, and Khan is one of the most odious little men in the market. This is one sale he won't be making.

In the market toilets, she squats down in a cubicle, empties out the contents into her skirt. It's pay day – there's a twenty spot and a good few fifty pence bits. That's Saturday night sorted, then. There's a couple of cards, too. She's way too young to weigh the kite in herself, but two spanking new credit cards – an Access and a Visa – will be worth a few bob to her if she gets rid quick. She slots them in the sole of her shoe, then jams the pillaged purse into a sanitary bin.

As she's coming out of the market, Ellie spots two lads lolloping down the road with the inimitable Legends gait – the blithe, slack-shouldered slouch, roughly treading a straight line as they almost dance along the pavement. She runs to catch up, latching on to them as they peel right onto Market Street and disappear inside a pub. She hesitates outside. She'll never get served. She peers in through the window. There's a big gang of them – ten or twelve faces she recognises, Legends' hardcore, all the older ones, the full-on full-timers. She's got to go in there.

'I swear to you, Billy, there were a great big rabbit outside the patio fucking leering in at us.'

'How come it's always a fuckin' rabbit, though? Serious! How come no one ever sees, like, a sloth or something? How come a big, mad hamster never materialises in these situations . . . ?'

She stands off by the swing doors, staring at them. They look amazing in their bright array of fleeces and cricket hats tugged down over blanched faces. Lunchtime drinkers look on nervously. Ellie laughs to herself – it's that familiar, giddy, diving-in feeling. She doesn't know and doesn't really care how this is going to pan out. School uniform or not, she's going in there. She sashays into the lounge, goading the regulars with her tiny school skirt. She keeps her eyes straight ahead and pretends she doesn't know the inner circle are in there.

'Hey! Ella! Here she is!'

It's nothing, but it's everything to her. She tries to mask her big, flattered, delighted blush. It's like a Panini stamp collection of top heads in there. She knows all their names, their drug history, their scrapes with adventure and death. She nods as coolly as her red face and wire braces allow, and squeezes herself down on the half-moon banquette between Marnie and Crazy Larry. Marnie gives her a sad little look but, just as quickly, makes more room for her and puts an easy, protective arm around her. Ellie notices for the first time the glazed flush of their sleep-starved eyes. Her first impression is that they're stoned. Then Crazy Larry folds a beer mat into a sharp point and stabs it between his teeth. He yelps out loud, flinging the offending object

276

across the floor. He dabs his gums, nods once as he sees he's drawn blood. Larry addresses the table. 'All right. That were fuckin' shit, that. Who's got any dental floss?'

It's a stupid remark but the entire table are creased up laughing. Ellie feels obliged to join in the merriment – and then, it hits her. They're playing Fight the Barb – an everyday diversion for the giro wayfarers round these parts. Ellie's no ingénue to this, either. What better way to fritter a dull Tuesday and help chivvy the week towards the weekend? Temazzies are ten-a-penny in Warrington. Depending on the strength and colour, most pensioners will sell you three for a quid, though one of the Legends shagbags, Lauren from Bewsey, once told her there's a cripple up there who gives her five green eggs for a nosh as though she were letting Ellie in on some clan secret.

The first time Ellie played Fight the Barb she just rolled off Cal's couch, slapped the floor and slept for fifteen whole hours. He'd warned her to space them out but, keen to impress her new Legends buddies, she necked the lot. A bottle of beer or cider can help buffer the soporific kill of the jellies. But for first-time users it's difficult not to yield to the cavernous slumber they unfurl. If it's Monday or Tuesday and you haven't slept for days and your head's still banging to some subliminal sonic echo, those little ovoid capsules are heaven sent. But in order to play Fight the Barb properly you have to first override the initial balmy tiredness that washes over you. If you can stay up, fight through it and ward off the doldrums' sweet succour, it's a pretty beautiful buzz.

She gives the young lad minding the jellies her best sultry look. 'Giz a couple, then.'

He dips into his pocket, pulls out a money bag stuffed full of yellow and green eggs. 'Oner each,' he says, bored, holding them out on the flat of his hand. Ellie goes to take them. His hand wraps shut around the eggs, and the tips of Ellie's fingers. He's

277

foul, this spotty little dealer, but he thinks he's got it. He rakes his lazy eyes all over her. 'That's two quid. Even to you.'

Very firmly and with a minimum of fuss, she releases her fingers from his grip. She reaches inside her shoe. 'I'll take the lot off you,' she sneers, and slaps her kite down on the table. The lad stares at the credit cards, suddenly lost for words. Ellie makes the most of it, turning to Marnie, then Larry with a cutesy-pic shrug of the shoulders. 'If your friend'll take plastic, that is.'

There's a groundswell of wild applause and mad, unnatural laughter. One of the girls gets up and moonwalks backwards across the room, pointing at Ellie and nodding her head in tribute as she goes. Marnie nudges Ellie, all smiles, impressed. 'Just how hot are these, Els?'

'Scorching,' says Ellie, almost swooning at the attention. 'They're literally not even an hour old.' She pauses, draws herself back for added impact. 'So. Twenty jeds and five eggs.'

The lad suddenly finds his voice again. 'Koff, will yoh! I'll give you a tenner and two barbs.'

Ellie whips the plastic back off the table top. One of the cards is stuck firm in a suction trap from spilt cider. Ellie tries to look at the lad, hard. 'It's twenty.'

He stuffs the bag of jellies back in his pocket. 'Forget it then.'

Ellie glances at Marnie. She nods. Ellie blows the air out of her cheeks, folding her arms across her chest. 'Go on then. Only cos I'm in a good mood, mind.'

He allows himself a horrible, yellow-toothed smile as he slots the cards and passes her a crumpled tenner and two green eggs. She holds the note up to the light, unsure of what she's supposed to be looking for, but wanting him to know she's streetwise, not just some daft schoolie with a pretty face and tricky fingers. The lad drains his glass and stands up. He jabs a finger at her. 'Any problem with these, Metal Mickey . . .' Having got his quip out, he seems stuck for words.

'Yeah-yeah, nice grid yourself, Topex.'

Again, the table collapses in riot. They're easy to seduce, these. The lad just points at her. 'I'm right back at you, you hear?'

Ellie smiles back as sweetly as she's able. Marnie drapes a sisterly arm around her, her fingers lightly grazing Ellie's chest. Moonwalk Girl throws her a fleece to cover up her school uniform and marches over to the barb dealer. 'Except she won't give a fuck by then.' She turns smartly to Ellie. 'Will you, hon?'

Ellie very deliberately cocks her head at him, places two eggs on her tongue and swallows.

Nine

Vinnie lifts his face into the late winter sunlight as he waits for his boy. There are already one or two hopeful businessmen cruising the drag, trying to look as though they're not here for sex. It amazes Vinnie, it does. He's no stranger to fantasy, but to do this, to come here straight from work looking for rent, these men must have been obsessing about sex all day. How can anyone be that fucking desperate as to come here at the height of rush hour, solely to head off to some backstreet with a hollow-eyed wraith and get drained? And then they go home to the wife and kids and tuck into sole meuniere. Or cottage pie. Shocking, it really is.

A couple of beefy biker clones walking down towards the Rembrandt see him in his school uniform and make the obvious conclusion. 'Here around seven?'

Vinnie winks back, eyeing him up and down. 'I'll wait all night for you, love,' he purrs, letting them believe. He watches them walk off, his come-on adding an affected grind to the flattered queen's walk.

The melting sun is now a big fat disc, burning on the edge of the world. It pulses a dramatic red before it slips away behind the city skyline. Within minutes a noxious fog is weaving its way through the rush-hour headlights and drifting at knee height, creating a noirish film set of Manchester's seedy backstreets. Vinnie becomes restive. What if his boy doesn't come? The thought thrashes around his guts, strangling him. Vinnie tells himself it won't be the end of the world – he'll just have to head out even earlier on Saturday.

The moon pulls itself up from the belly of the sky and the

cityscape shifts again. These moody byways take on a dislocated, looted feel. Vinnie gags on the stench sweating out from the walls and back alleys, the stink of incontinence. Still no sign of his boy. Vinnie starts to accept it's hometime.

He hovers on the lip of the carriageway, waiting for a gap in the crazed Grand Prix mêlée. He tells himself he's in no hurry. Let them belt back to the lives they think they have at home. Let them sit in silence, another night in suburbia. He lights up a rollie. The cold night air quickly kisses it down to the roach. He lights another. He squints into the blurred strafe of traffic and sees a gap. He'll have to be quick. He's ready to dash when he sees someone coming at him from the other side of the expressway. It's him. It's his boy. He hasn't seen him yet – he's all fixed on getting across the road, head bent into his crazy mechanical lurch. Vinnie's heart gives a joyful flutter. He calls over to him. 'Oi!'

He's been buying from him since before Christmas and he still doesn't know his name. The lad freezes, raises his shoulders into a protective hunch as he squints into the soup. He hacks, sniffs and spits. Vinnie calls to him again and this time he sees him. He comes bounding over, his mouth curling up in a tragic stump-toothed leer. He's beyond delighted at this unexpected opportunity for trade. 'Sat deh!' he gurns. 'You usually come Sat deh, don't yoh?'

Vinnie smiles. 'I can resist everything but temptation,' he says.

'Say 'gain?' he says, eyes jittering up and down the street.

Vinnie is shot through with a sad kind of affection for the lad. He pats him on the shoulder, leaving his hand there. 'Nothing,' he says. 'Forget it.'

The lad remembers where he is, and who. 'I can do you a good deal on some narc if you want it?'

'Narc?' Vinnie's said it before he can stop himself. He curses himself for the slip, showing himself up as a tourist. The lad hasn't picked up on it though – he just thinks Vinnie needs convincing.

'Case yor oh dee, like. The ambos can take all night coming if they know it's smack.'

Vinnie nods gravely, piecing it together.

'Sort yoh right out if yoh gerrin a mess. Up to you, our kid. Fresh from casualty these.'

Vinnie wonders if it's worth asking him how you'd self-administer the antidote if you were actually overdosing. He pats his shoulder again. 'No ta, matey,' he says. 'If that's how I meet my maker, then I'm not gonna be arsed one way or the other. Nice way to go, hey?'

The lad has none of Vinnie's romance of heroin. He just stares at him, slightly alarmed, waiting for the order. 'How about some Nazi crank then?'

Vinnie doesn't make the same mistake twice. He just raises an eyebrow, inviting the lad to pitch it to him.

'It's got, like, the rush of fuckin' crack, yeah? But it fuckin' buh-lasts yoh, man. Pure wipe yorrout. Lasts for, like, free fuckin' days yeah, this fuckin' shit. It's . . . you're just like talking and buzzing and out there.' A little opportunistic glimmer flits across his faded eyes. 'Know what, our kid – bang the Nazi yeah, then bring yourself down with a bit a hatch and there's absolutely no fuckin' hangover. I swear to yoh, man – fuckin' perfect.'

Vinnie can't think of anything more terrifying. The lad's outstayed his use now. Vinnie needs rid of him. He wiggles his fingertips into his hip pocket, prises out a folded note. 'Give us a ten bag this time, yeah?'

He was supposed to be saving it for Saturday – all of it – but now that it's there within shooting distance, his loins are screaming out for the greedy thrill. Not even the knowledge that Mum will be trailing the aisles of Visions right now, excitedly sourcing out a film, can compete with its balmy promise.

The need to devour and be devoured has saturated his every fibre.

The multi-storey still has cars here and there, so he heads off along the canal. He hits a dank stretch beyond the flyover. There's a little humpback bridge ahead. He crouches and cooks up. The ground is littered with shit: rubbers and needles and spent gas canisters. He'd much rather be up on top of the roof of the city, smashed on its gorgeous night glow; but he knows that once the honey's coarsing his veins, he could be anywhere. Anywhere will do just fine.

There's a moment, just before he slides the needle into his vein, when he pictures Kenny's beautiful face succumbing to all this. He lies down flat on his back with the spike still hanging out of his forearm. 'Saturday,' he whispers. He'll love it. Saturday night they'll get drunk on honey, and Kenny will see heaven with him.

He passes out. The cold damp breeze wakes him. Reedy voices, the sound of shattering glass. His gaze swoons in and out of focus across a sky that is lean and black, little swabs of lint drifting dreamily across its surface. He grins up at the moon, a huge clown's smile, the kind that Ellie used to draw in lurid crayola: U-shaped, with the corners of the mouth nearly touching the eyes. Swimming. Soaring. He can't move.

Ten

She's still tingling pleasantly from the barbs as she lets herself in the front door. She makes a show of hanging up her blazer, dumping her school bag on the stairs. She needn't have worried. The TV's cathode glow frames Sheila's silhouette on the couch, lost in some love story.

'Ellie? That you, love? How was hockey?'

An awful jab of piteous love for her beautiful mother. She hopes she never finds out; prays she never hurts her. She wonders if Dad ever got her letter. Probably not. Probably moved flat five times since she was last there. But she'll go ahead, anyway. On Saturday, to make things up to her mum, she'll surprise her and cook the grill. 'Yeah. Good, ta,' she calls back, quickening her pace as she mounts the stairs in dreamy moonwalk sequence, clearing two at a time. She brushes her teeth, slaps cold water on her face and consults her reflection. She doesn't feel stoned, but fuck, does she look it!

The sound of Mum stirring to action in the kitchen below licks a hot flame of panic around her thoughts. She rolls up her sleeves, fixes her hair on the top of her head and sets about scrubbing her face sensible. She applies a fresh daub of make-up, shading in the whey satellite of her face with bright pink lipstick and rouge. Her mother's at the bottom of the stairs now, whisking a pan of gravy. Ellie ducks behind the bathroom door.

'Did you score, darling?'

The quip's there, waiting to be hit. And if Vinnie were within earshot, she'd probably slug it, for sure. She can't help feeling crushed by her mum's credulousness. She takes a breath, tries to kick a bit of life into her voice, give her something back. 'Nah, Mum. Tight game. Nil-nil.'

'Oh.' It's just a hitch of breath, the curtest of semicolons, but it tells Ellie everything. 'I didn't know it was a *match*.'

She hears all her mother's hurt sucked down to a gulp, and she feels wretched.

'*I* would have come,' she ventures gingerly, and the whisk slows to a scrape.

Ellie feels dizzy. She tries to say something in melioration. 'It wasn't really a match. Well it was, if you know what I mean. An inter-house kind of thing.'

It works. The whisk starts up again, beating out her mum's guilty relief as she shuffles back into the kitchen. Ellie's heart is racing away again. How much longer can she keep this up – the chicanery, the deceit? How long before her alibis backfire and shoot her down? She steels herself up to her reflection once again and it's futile: no amount of washing or daubing can shock the telltale pinholes of her eyes back to life. Paranoia creeps in, sprays a dark shadow around her thoughts.

'*Ell*-eee? What are you doing up there?'

She becomes aware of her mother calling her from halfway up the stairs. She's sitting on her window sill and there seems to have been some sort of time disconnect. She can't trace back her journey – how she got from the bathroom to the bedroom; she doesn't remember. It doesn't make sense.

'Come on! It's your favourite – toad in the hole with bubble and squeak – and it's going cold!'

Back in the bathroom, Ellie brushes some sense and order into her mane, then climbs up onto the rim of the bath, opens up the window slat and wedges her head sideways into the cold night air. She gulps hard and deep on it. One more lash of rouge, and then, with her ears banging out the rapid blood boom of her panic, she's making the descent down the stairs.

'So. Did you talk to Miss Kelvin about Rome . . . ?'

It seems to take Ellie an eternity to digest and compute her words. 'Oh. yeah. It's fine. No problem.'

Sheila fixes her daughter with a stare. 'Ellie, what's wrong with you tonight?'

'Nothing.'

Something is amiss, and Sheila simply can't leave it untouched for the sake of keeping the peace. Ellie has hardly touched her dinner – her favourite too – and Sheila can see now that it's an effort for her to focus, her thoughts zigzagging all over the place. Taking in the giddy lurch of her daughter's eyes, the weighted levers of her arms rising in snail-slow motion as she lifts her fork to her lips, Sheila leans across the table. Her heart is punching up through her throat. She's scared and shocked and she's suddenly out of her depth. She wishes Vincent would hurry home.

'Ellie, honey. I'm going to ask you something.' She stalls a moment, feeling the emotion race through her neck, stinging hot, up to her stoked and pulsing forehead. She tries to steady herself, dredging up every flake of her resolve. 'I need you to answer me honestly.'

How desperately she wants to sound stern enough to precipitate the tumbling confession she knows is locked up there. But Sheila is all too aware of the pleading in her gaze, beseeching Ellie not to answer her honestly, and instead to reassure her there's absolutely nothing for her to worry about. She gropes again for some degree of authority. 'Ellie. Did you go to hockey after school? Or were you somewhere else?'

Ellie says nothing. Her sphinx-like expression, cool and cold and challenging, gives nothing away. She's on her feet now, her hands gripping the edge of the table in preparation for flight. Sheila's stomach sinks another fraction, her misgivings vindicated. She's a fighter, Ellie, and if she was standing trial for a crime she hadn't committed, then the last thing she'd do is walk.

She'd hang in there till the final bell. She'd make you believe and then she'd make you suffer for not believing in the first place.

'You've been drinking, haven't you?' It's nothing more than a hunch. And in guessing so wildly, Sheila hands the initiative right back to her wayward child. Ellie snorts. There's something defiant and mocking in the short consonant of air. She shakes her head, kicks back the chair and flounces out of the room.

Sheila hovers at the bottom of the stairs, the creaking floor-boards singing out her panic as she shifts her weight from left to right, right to left. She tries to deep-breathe some rationale into her thinking.

It's been brewing for a while. Ellie's vaulting moods, her voids, her sullen and gradual withdrawal from their Saturday night ritual of takeout and a video were all portents that flagged up the looming storm long before it broke. If she's being honest with herself, it's not the fact that her daughter might have lied, might have been drinking in the park with boys instead of playing hockey that's so distressing. It's more about her own insecurities as a parent – as a mother. Perhaps if she hadn't been so eager to adopt the role of confidante with Ellie, if she had been more of a mother and less of an elder sister, she might have been able to quell the crisis before it hit. It's times like this that she finds herself pining for Robbie. Not that he'd be any better equipped to deal with such matters, but if he were around, she might not feel so wretched about reproaching her children. These show-downs would be less profound, less painful. A few heated words, a grand finale of tears and it would all be resolved by now. But with Robbie gone, each and every tactic of parenting has to be carefully thought out. Strategically executed. There can be no room for trial and error. A one-parent family simply cannot afford the luxury of discipline.

Sheila finds her curled up on her bedroom floor, shedding

287

torrents of tears tinged with the mess of her rainbow make-up. She goes to her, powerless to resist the soft embrace of her pipe cleaner arms, as they reach up and hook and fasten around her neck. She tries to stave off the slow wave of nostalgia and tenderness pushing through her as she remembers what she's here for. But it's hopeless. She's hopeless.

'I hate it when we fall out,' her gorgeous woman-child sobs, annihilating every fibre of her anger.

As she moulds herself to the hot, wet contours of her daughter's cheek, Sheila's soul gives out to a little gallop of joy. Ellie *is* telling the truth. There's not a whiff of drink on her breath. What there is – in abundance – is the sour paste of nicotine. Ellie hums like an ashtray, and for that Sheila is ecstatically relieved. It accounts for everything then – the dreamy eyes, the giddy cadence, the heavy-limbed gestures. Her naughty thirteen-year-old has tried her first cigarette and she's reeling from it. The bawdy stench, offset by the sweet, damp scent of her Ellieness, is curiously comforting as it floods and fills the fissures of the last half-hour. Sheila takes a deep draught, wanting to soak up and savour the moment for ever, the moment her little girl became a teenager. But then she pulls back, looks sternly into her tired eyes. 'Ellie, I know your brother makes no secret of his smoking, but for what it's worth, it hurts me very much. I'll spare you the lecture because I trust that you'll make your own decisions, but . . . every day I visit people dying of cancer. Some of them not much older than me. It's such an easy, simple trap to fall into, Ellie – a cigarette in breaktime, one after school. I was a teenager too, you know.'

Ellie accepts the gentle harangue, contrite and complicit in her mum's white lie. She knows full well her mother never tried smoking when she was an adolescent, if you could even call it an adolescence at all. 'I know. I'm sorry. I just wanted to try it . . .'

Sheila can't help but be amused by the naughty innocence this confession conjures and it's a struggle to suppress the smirk tugging at the corners of her mouth. She kisses Ellie softly on the crown of her head and leaves her to undress for bed. She's at the top of the stairs when Ellie calls her back.

'Mum?'

'Yes, honey?'

'I just wanted to say thanks. That's all. For not going off on one like other parents do.'

Sheila takes the compliment at face value, doesn't prod it or peek behind it. She takes it because she needs it and it makes her feel good. 'Know what, Ellie?' Sheila comes back into the room. 'Your granddad Jim used to have a saying.' She registers the flicker of anguish in her little girl's eyes at the mention of the Fitzgeralds, but she pushes on. She'll love the punchline. It will be worth it. 'Spare the rod and spoil the child. You know the one?' Ellie nods. 'Well, see, I always took it literally. I thought it was an instruction.'

It takes her a while, but once Ellie figures it out she's guffawing passionately, raking her tender green eyes over Sheila with so much love and hope. She throws her arms around her mum and holds her close, still shuddering with hiccups of laughter. Sheila is taken aback, blissfully overwhelmed. But as she rests her chin on Ellie's shoulder, she can't suppress the vague sense of an opportunity missed. Another crack papered over. What was happening, here? Was it just normal? Inevitable? Was it all bound up with Ellie's impossible, head-turning beauty? It was only Halloween that the two of them were out there in the yard, scrubbing her favourite Levis with pumice stones until they looked vintage. That was them; her and her little girl, distressing her denims and fixing Grolsch bottle stoppers to her shoelaces in deference to her pop idols, Bros. Where did all that go?

Sheila heads downstairs to clear away the dishes. She's barely reached the kitchen when a fat bass cranks up and rends the floorboards, setting her on edge all over again. She sees the empty place she's set for Vincent and her heart snags. She hopes he'll come home soon. Vincent will know what to do. He always does.

Ten o'clock and still no sign of him. Sheila kicks the neon yellow video box under the couch. She always wants what's best for Vincent. She hopes he's out having fun, having a tipple with his clever friends – a lady friend even – but God, she misses her little big man. She's not quite ready to wave him goodbye yet, and she loves these meals they plan together. Ellie she adores, but Vincent is the only man in her life, and he's stood her up.

She turns off the lights, and once she's in bed, she finally succumbs to the tide of loneliness that's descended from nowhere, spewing up its flotsam of familiar aches and pains she thought were long buried. She drifts into a shallow sleep.

The maudlin old song drags her back: 'The last time I saw you, you looked so much older. Your famous blue raincoat was torn at the shoulder . . .'

Fleetingly, she's happy: relieved that Vincent is home, safe, and so immersed in his own little world that he's carried it all on in his bedroom, long into the night. But the thought of her boy next door – so close, a plasterboard's width from her touch, but no longer needy of that touch – plunges her deeper into despair. Soon will come the moment of her absolute desertion. Vincent will leave for university, and hard on his heels Ellie will follow – and then she will be utterly alone. The thought burns a hole in her chest. She tosses and turns and, long, long after Vincent's record plays itself out and he's snoring gently, her soul is still unwilling to rest. She wonders if it might snow.

Eleven

Saturday morning. Vinnie has not moved since confirming his worst fears. *Dad*! What was he doing here?

He'd been lying in bed, holding off, just daydreaming about tonight, the biggest, most deliciously significant night of his life. *Tonight*! And then he heard a car, right outside the house, parking up on the kerb. It's what his father used to do. Whatever the motivation – anxiety not to offend, anxiety to avoid bumps and scratches from passing vehicles, maybe some weird proprietorial spasm that this was still his house, after all – he'd always park with two wheels on the road, two on the kerb. Surely not – it couldn't be! Not *him*. Not now. Desperately wishing it not to be so, Vinnie had edged over to the window to face the truth. To his abject dismay, crunching shut the rusty door of some creaking old banger was his father. Vinnie looked down on his vulnerable pink-freckled scalp, and ducked away as Robbie looked up at the house and wrinkled his nose – the house he'd never wanted. The household he'd terrorised. Vinnie turned his back on his father and lay back down on his bed, stunned, brutalised, the very concept disgusting him. *Father?* Him? What did he want from them now?

Those first few months after he'd left, Robbie had driven back from Blackpool every Sunday morning, without fail. These were tense, emotional affairs and Robbie's weekly devotionals gradually refined themselves to birthday and Christmas visits up until last year when he never came at all over the festive period. Christmas Day he used to turn up late, always, dragging two plastic binbags full of rubbish presents. The plastic ponies for Ellie – not even My Little Pony, but some nasty derivative he'd

291

picked up in the pub – and the jumble-sale chemistry set for Vincent bore testimony to the chasm his absence had dug between him and his kids. Ellie would make a big show of being ultra-delighted with everything he bought her, but Vinnie made no such pretence. His dad would sit there, brazenly trying to sell his boy some crap microscope he'd picked up. 'Top o' the range that, lad. Can't get them in your Woolies, you know. Have to go abroad.'

Heart throbbing with hatred, Vinnie would force a dimple-smile and, citing homework, he'd quickly disappear to his room, staying there until he heard the grating splutter of the ignition, the reluctant lurch of the gears and the first, then second tyre flop from pavement to street.

Vinnie sighs hard, waiting for the knock on the door. How will he be? Bold? Humble? He could scarcely forget the last time he saw him. Not because it was Ellie's twelfth birthday; not because his father spent the afternoon slumped over the bar of the near empty village hall they'd hired out in an unapproachable fug of his own self-pity. He remembers his dad's last appearance with indelible clarity because of Lord Morrissey. As soon as was humanly decent – as soon as his father was too drunk to notice, or to care – Vinnie had slipped away into town and bought *Strangeways Here We Come* at HMV. He'd lain back on his bed and let himself be washed away by it, soothed by Morrissey's pointed barbs, heightened by an understanding that, in his anger, in his misery and in his supreme solitude, he was not alone.

As he wipes away the kohl smudges that sleep has softened into bruises, he wonders what his father will make of the new life they've carved out for themselves. It's only just under a year since he last stepped foot in the house but they've all moved on so much. What will he make of their home these days – *their* home? Back then his presence still haunted the house in sentimental whispers.

292

His old pine stereogram was still there, hogging up the hallway, his battered banjo still in its place, propped up against the settee, dusted down each morning as though it were part of the furniture itself. And, of course, there was the totemic wedding photo that mocked them all, the smiling, moonstruck teenagers – a cutting symbol of hope extinguished.

Sheila still kept these ghosts for company. But slowly, strategically Vinnie had supplanted the old with the new, evicting his father wherever he could. He'd shunted the ugly stereogram out into the garage and, after a short period of observance, out to the garden for bonfire wood. Vinnie, ever a stranger to physical toil, had experienced a primal, transcendental joy from smashing the stereo to pieces with his dad's blunt old axe.

Now he can hear him crunching his way down the path. He's going to have to get up. He thinks of Kenny, tonight, and it gives him strength. Suddenly things aren't so bad at all. He'll go through with this as best he's able, for his mother, if this is what she wants. Slow and self-confident, he descends the stairs. But the first thing he sees is his mother, standing there agape. Robbie is, clearly, the last person she expected to ring the bell this morning. His father doesn't even try to jest with her. He bows his head slightly, waiting to be asked in. There's something in his father's eyes that says that, if she turned him away, Robbie would go quickly. His mother steps back to let him in – not a word between them – and now here he is, in the hall below him. Vinnie makes every effort not to stare, not to recoil from the splintering shock of horror that zips through him.

It's been eleven months, and in that time his father has aged. His brawny shoulders have wasted and slumped. There's none of that overconfident Robbie Fitzgerald vim and swagger in him now, and he's smaller, somehow. His head hangs low, his eyes pale lamps buried beneath the craggy folds of his skin. Vinnie steps towards him, dwarfing him, taking in the full extent of his

293

decline as he gets close up – the vile aftershock of his late-night cabaret breath, the burst capillaries that thread his nose, the smoky swatches of jaded orange hair, almost stuck on in clumps, clown-like.

Vinnie looks him flush in the eye, and his father can't help but break out into the biggest smile.

'Hello, son,' he says.

Vinnie steps forward but, before he can respond, a whirlwind of red hair and caramel limbs hurtles down the stairs, barges past him and flings herself onto him. '*Daaaaaaad*!' she shrieks. 'I knew you'd come!' Ellie clings to him with her knees, her eyes grinning and dancing with outlandish happiness. 'Cool wheels, Dad! Is it a Jag?'

He darts Vinnie and Sheila a nervous glance, and ruffles Ellie's head. 'It is, love, yeah.'

'Wow! You've done it, Dad! You've got the Jag you always wanted!'

Vinnie notices his father's eyes moistening up. He knows that his father knows the car's a wreck, but to his little girl it's the magical chariot of the stories he used to ream her. He watches his father stand back to appraise her, eyes like two waning moons. It's only last year that she went to stay with him but Robbie is seeing her for the first time as a woman. His sister is a beautiful young woman. Vinnie feels his head drop reflexively as he's cut out of the picture all over again, but only for a second. He comes up again, smiling. With Ellie there, he'd never get a look in with his father. And that's OK with him. That's just fine.

Vinnie watches his father tucking into the platter of meats Ellie has conjured up, and he feels only mild disgust. A year ago, a week ago and he'd have thrown a strop, stormed out, let them know all about his thoughts on meat, and eating. But the more he looks at this hollow man, the more he can't hate him. He, Vincent, Vinnie, the writer, has a life. He has a future

294

– an immediate, nerve-jangling, intoxicating future. He has Kenny. This man here – how can he despise him? He's nothing. This evening, Vinnie will be seeing his love. Nothing his father did back then has knocked him off the path that's brought him here, to Kenny. Nothing can bring him down. His father, the man who tried to break him, the man who would have scoured his very heart until he had no soul – is sitting right here, chewing meat. And for his mother, for his sister, and for Kenny he can live with that – he can see this through.

'So, Dad, come on – what's been happening? What you been up to?'

For a moment, Robbie forgets and swoons, lost in the wonder of his beautiful girl. She even talks like him, favouring the hard brogue of his Orford to the soft, suburban accent of her brother. 'You still doing loads of gigs?'

'Well, you know . . .'

'Dad! What about the Palace?'

She's willing the conversation forward but Robbie is starting to struggle. He can feel his son's eyes drilling him from across the table. He can't bluff here – the virile young singer is gone for ever. But equally, he can't let her down. 'Palace? Yeah. That one's done, now. Not doin' that no more . . .' He shoots her an uneasy grin, sensing her dismay like a stone in his guts. He keeps his eyes on his plate, tries to think up something. And then it comes to him. All his performer's instincts, everything he's learnt from the stage tells him his audience will roll with this one. 'But hey!'

Ellie's all eyes again. She's desperate for this to be good news. 'What?'

'I did get summat out of it.' He plays it out. Even Vinnie has softened his gaze now and is appraising him from across the table. 'I can read. Howbout that?'

It takes a while for this to sink in. Sheila, who has kept herself busy ferrying plates and cups and saucers to and from the table and sink, stops dead in her tracks. 'What do you mean?'

'Come off it, She. You knew!'

'Knew what?'

'Me . . . and the words, like . . .'

'I knew you had a bit of difficulty with the longer words.'

'Well. There you go, then. Now I don't, see? All that time when I had that residency at the Palace? Got meself an education, didn't I? Adult learning and all of that.' He shoots Vinnie a bold look. 'Just like you now, Vin. College boy!'

Vinnie forces a wan smile and Robbie feels his heart sink a fraction. Sheila stands there, tea towel in hand, stunned. 'Well. Good for you, Robbie. Better late than never.'

'And that's not all you got out of it, hey?' Ellie seizes the upturn in atmosphere. 'You got the car, didn't you, Dad? You got your Jag!'

Far from plumping his spirits, the reminder of that cruel, fateful day at the car showroom brings Robbie crashing back down again. Ellie's forgotten all about it, if she ever absorbed the detail of their humiliation at all. Dragging himself out from self-pity for his girl, he claps his hands together and beams at her. 'Yeah. I got the car, Els Bells. Anyway. What about yourselves?' He looks to Vinnie. 'When am I gonna be reading your masterpiece then, son?'

Again, Vinnie swallows a sad smile. He gets up from the table and, for an invisible moment, rests a hand on Robbie's shoulder. 'Soon,' he says.

Robbie feels a surge of elation and then a deep sadness at the rare shock of his son's touch. He flounders for a minute, unable to speak or think or breathe and when he comes to Vinnie has left the room. Sheila is smiling at him from the end of the table but it's a troubled smile, and it's all she can do not to radiate pity for the man who walked out on them. He's anxious to leave now, let them get back to it. He fixes Ellie with his sad green burn. But thankfully, it doesn't seem to register. She's oblivious to his sorrow. She's just made up to have her old man back.

'I best be off now.' He barely sips at his tea.

Ellie chases him all the way to the end of the road, grinning and waving through the car window. Robbie keeps his eyes on the road. As he starts to pull away she stops for breath and finger-waves goodbye as his creaking old Jag groans left and disappears in a puff of smoke. He's promised her he'll surprise her one Sunday, soon, turn up at the crack of dawn with a bag of scalding chestnuts. But she knows he doesn't mean it. Well, maybe he does – he *thinks* he'll do it – but Ellie knows they'll never go gambolling in the country again, she and her daddy. None of that matters, anyway. She sent that postcard on a whim, and she's so glad she did. She perches on the low wall at the corner of the drive and she can't help succumbing to a wave of self-regard. The simple fact is, she realises, that her animal intuition is of the most acute. Sometimes – she may as well just admit it here and now – she just knows what to do. With the deftest sleight of hand she's sutured her family back together again if only just for a few hours, and for now, for this bone-cold, delicious, early March afternoon, Ellie Fitzgerald is the happiest girl in the universe.

Twelve

Vinnie steps off the bus, his heart booming. The sharp night air strips the lining from his lungs and squeezes like a fist round his trachea. He bangs hard on his inhaler, holds the magic gas down and pulls his raincoat tight round his shoulders. It's numbingly cold. With blunt fingertips he rolls a cigarette and licks his lips at what lies ahead, all the pain and ugliness of earlier fading to nothing.

He's early for Kenny – he couldn't risk the later bus, tonight of all nights – so he stands back in the shadows of the city and watches the flickering sideshow come to life. He pulls up his collar and waits for the start of the biggest night of his life.

He watches a nervous young gay couple pick their way past a crew of football lads. Lads like these are as likely to hug them as headbutt them these days, but the weekend queers walk head down, a foot of space between them. Vinnie follows. They peel off down Sackville Street, cutting across the shank of wasteland littered with the tools of the trade: spent rubbers, empty wraps of speed and flyers for gay all-nighters. As the couple cross the humpback bridge, the space between them shrinks to nothing. All sense of guilt and fear is leached from their bodies as they hold hands and kick on. Vinnie perches his arse on the low wall, smiling as they go. A peroxide hooker takes him for a tramp. She opens up her palm and casts her loose change into his lap. 'Ey-are, love. Get yoh-self a cuppoh, yeah?'

He grins to himself, reaches for his pouch. A brutal wind gets right under the loose folds of his raincoat. He rolls one, taps a little roach in, sparks up, plugs in his earphones and walks to the soundtrack of the Cure. Almost on autopilot, he finds himself drifting towards the red-light peripheries of the tenderloin. Wraiths dart and flit across the horizon like bats. Two of them stop and stare. They think he's a John at first, then competition – new meat. He peels away from them and loops right round beyond Piccadilly Station, cutting along the black, unloved back-streets and onto Great Ancoats Street, then back towards the bus station. He spies a boy hunched over a cellophane cup in the window seat of the café. Thin and gaunt and pale as a ghost, Vinnie thinks it's his boy at first, sitting out the cold until business picks up. He feels the usual jangle of fearful excitement, but he's fine for honey. Enough for him and Kenny both.

Vinnie spots him straight away, stood outside the bar. He's leaning back, tight arse against the window, effortlessly rough and sexy. He's wearing a battered leather jacket, zipped right up. Vinnie stands back in the shadows and takes it all in. Even the way he shifts his weight from one foot to the other is gracefully muscular and sexual. Vinnie watches him and a slow tingling elation seeps through him as it comes to him that this boy is his.

Vinnie crosses the road. Kenny's head is bent to his papers and tobacco and he doesn't see Vinnie until he's right in his face. He grins hugely and Vinnie melts into the pavement. But then, just as quickly, he feels that sudden stab of panic, penetrating then withdrawing. The thought that Kenny might not feel the same is too much to bear.

Kenny sparks his roll-up, and pushing the big swing door of the bar open with his back, bows him in. Vinnie doesn't like it here. It may well be part of the Factory family but the loud and brutish clientele and the calculated minimalism of the decor make him uneasy. It isn't how Vinnie imagined his first date. The place is all harsh lighting, low-slung leather couches and crome-finish bar stools. The entire length of the bar is studded with mean-looking black guys and their brassy white fuck-bits. Kenny's quite at home, though. He shrugs off his leather and folds it up between

299

his feet. Vinnie keeps his raincoat on, a tacit gesture of his disapproval. He cuts a peculiar figure with his wire-thin frame and fierce sloping fringe, but the homeboys are unfazed. The Dry Bar regulars have seen hundreds of Vinnie Fitzgeralds pass through – androgynous waifs and Curtis devotees clad in the lugubrious apparel of the poet-depressive.

It gets worse. The boy serving Kenny is beautiful, sickeningly so. He has eyes the colour of ripe limes and a neat bob of vinyl black hair. Vinnie is utterly unprepared for the jealousy gushing up from the pit of his bowels. It rocks him sideways. He barely has time to steady himself on the bar rail before Kenny turns round and fixes his eyes on him. 'Vinnie. This is Rudy. Rudy, Vinnie.'

Rudy? How many white boys from Chorlton-cum-Hardy are called Rudy, for fuck's sake? Phoney! Rudy unleashes a devastating drop-dead smile on him. Vinnie's groin is already throbbing to the challenge. He nods, once, sparking up and giving nothing away.

'Rudy's studying philosophy at Manchester Poly . . .'

Kenny says this as though it's the most romantic thing he's ever heard, as though Rudy were the only beautiful boy in the world and philosophy the rare discipline of a privileged elite. Rudy rolls his eyes. 'Uni, if you don't mind, thank you. There is a difference!'

He unleashes the devastating smile again. He's talking to Kenny, but he's addressing Vinnie. There's a warring sensation: he's attracted to him, but he doesn't like him. He can't resist his charm, but he feels manipulated. And his whole act is such an act. For a moment, Vinnie is tempted to challenge him, see how much he really knows about philosophy, but as though sensing him sharpening his talons, Kenny puts a hand on his arm and diverts him. 'How's about you let Rene roll you a smoke?'

Rudy's on it in a flash. He turns to Kenny. 'Rene! Is that your handle? That's sooo romantic!' Vinnie is on the verge of walking out and heading off to his multi-storey car park, solo. There's enough horse here to smack himself into oblivion. Rudy checks over his shoulder, ducks away and comes back with two cans shaped like missiles. 'On me.' He winks. He stands back and looks at them, smiling like a curator admiring two new paintings. 'Rene. It's so cool that you guys love that book.'

Vinnie's dying to ask. He knows he can't. He takes a hit on the Sapporo. For all its over-the-top styling, the flinty cold beer is delicious. Kenny catches Vinnie staring at him, narrows his eyes and winks at him over the rim of the can. Vinnie smiles back, nervous, unsure. He wants to slow things down, hold the moment in abeyance. Did Kenny really just wink at him? It's always the same. He can never work out if he's misreading the signals, or if Kenny's misfiring. It'd be folly to try to push things on. If it's going to happen between them, then that's how it will be. It'll just happen. But what if Kenny is as terrified as he is? Just say he's playing possum, lying back in the shadows, waiting for some kind of sign from him? What if the moment passes them by? *Carpe diem*. He should make the move, seize the moment before it all moves on out of reach. But he can't. He runs it over and over in his mind, and he just can't picture how he'll ask him. He finds himself drifting back to safer seas. 'So, Kenny. Or should that be Rene?'

Kenny leans in to him. The contact sends Vinnie's cock pulsing. 'Thought you'd like that.' He pokes a match into the eye of his rollie and tamps down the tobacco.

'Yep. Love it.'

'I knew you'd get it.'

Vinnie slaps his head and concedes defeat. He laughs. 'Look. You've got me. I don't get it . . .'

'What don't you get?' He's toying with him. Their faces are scintillatingly close.

'Rene.'

Kenny jerks his head back. He's wearing a mock-confused expression, as though he thinks Vinnie must be joking. Vinnie shrugs. He's not joking.

'Rene? *The Thief's Journal*?'

'Nope. Read it like, yonks ago . . . but Rene?'

Kenny's disappointment is evident. 'Rene's the jailbird.' He pauses, scorching Vinnie with his gaze. 'The homosexual jail-bird.'

The two lads stare at one another. It's Vinnie who looks away first. Kenny jumps up, awkward.

'I'll get two more.'

Thirteen

Robbie pulls up outside the Irish Club. He sits there, staring at its bleak exterior. What had he expected of his journey back, today? He can't even say the word. Home. He shuts his eyes and tries to think well of himself, but he can't stand it. He can't abide what he is, what he's done, what he's become. How had things come to such a pass? What did he *want*? He shudders again, and in asking the question of himself, starts to understand the answer. He's a father, for fuck's sake. He'd been a husband too, and a bad one at that – but he was still a father. The question ought to be what did *they* want, his kids – and what was he still able to do for them? And that, he truly couldn't answer.

He groans inwardly, gets out of the car, locks it, and braces himself. He's been preparing himself for the inevitable here too; that, like almost every other pub this side of Orford, the Irish Club would have surrendered to the times. It'll be just like the cheapo Doubles Bar in Blackpool, all the granddads zonked on Bells and tablets – or it'll have gone under, closed down. But then he sees the name on the fascia, gleaming down from above the wind-battered doors – Helen O'Connor – and he tingles with a slender but wondrous hope. Maybe something lies within here after all. Maybe his beloved club will be just as he left it, just as it was. He takes down a deep gulp of breath and pushes through the doors, steeling himself.

Robbie stops and stares and drinks up the smell. Stew and malt and slough from the factories and the dead sweat of nicotine dripping from the ceiling – an elegiac, homely and ancient funk. It's almost too much for him; one of those rare moments where the world unravels and reveals its stark simple truth and everything is lucid and fathomable. This is him. This is who he is.

It's Helen who breaks the spell, slowly spins him back down to the tiled bar-room floor as she raises her brow and mock-eyes her watch. 'Me mam's still waiting on them fiddle players, Fitz.'

He grins, restrains the mad giddy urge to leapfrog the bar, pick her up and spin her round and round. She's already pulling him a Guinness.

'So you made it big time in Blackpool, you!'

She plants the Guinness on the bar – dark and soupy and swirling and perfect. Robbie stands back and watches, lets it settle to stone. She stands back from the bar, folds her freckled arms like a frame around her bust.

'Still as modest as ever then?' she laughs. 'It's OK. You don't have to say a thing. Me mate Megan used to have a B&B just by the tower – said your name was all over the place, lit up in big yellow neon.'

Another pint down, he might have told her the truth – that for a while, an oh-so-fleeting while, Robbie Fitzgerald was King of the Prom. Had he fetched up there a decade earlier then he might not be living in a rented bedsit, soaking away his withered dreams in the dregs of Blackpool's once-thriving live scene. But by the time Robbie arrived, not even the cabaret capital of the North was robust enough to resist the crush and swell of the stag dos that flocked there each weekend, demanding chart music, glitter balls and rave nights. He caught the last spume of a wave when the Palace took him on, and he rode it while he could. But all over Blackpool, stages were being pulled down to create more strobe-lit space for pissed-up head-the-balls to flail around in, and Robbie was too tired to fight for his throne.

He quit his Friday night residency at the Palace – sacked them before they sacked him – and settled for a little club off the South Pier, too far a stagger from the main drag to pull in anyone but the happy-hour pissheads and the brassy hens who shared his stale bed. Here was the truth, though – Robbie Fitzgerald was an Elvis impersonator. He was barely forty and already his best was behind him. But it was OK. He was making a living from the love of his life, dancing to his own tune. And the whiff of the Irish Sea air knifing through his bedroom window each morning was worth all the crumminess, just for that salty blast of freedom.

'You still at the Palace?'

Robbie nods. His job is to give them what they want, and this is what Helen wants to hear. He's ready to tell her more – the queues outside, the tearful fans, transported to the heart-break hotel by the splintered beauty of his voice, the offers of gigs far and wide. He's ready to tell Helen that, for a while, he made it. He got there, in the end. He's going to tell her all about the sweet-sour smell of success, but a throng of dejected Wires fans spill in and that's that. Helen is waylaid to the other end of the bar.

Robbie slinks through to the snug, takes his favourite fireside pew, the dust-mottled light calming his troubled soul. He rolls himself a smoke, pausing to sip on his Guinness and toast the belching smoke stacks, blasting their filth all over a mellow March sun. Only now does the sting of who he once was, what he had and what he lost, finally begin to soften and, with that, he's able to reflect upon the searing pain of today.

In their innocence, their unity, their cheerful functionality, the grief his former family brought him is deeper, more caustic than ever before. The moment he'd peeled left onto Thelwall Lane and the matchstick figure of his little girl faded back to nothing in his rear-view mirror, Robbie pulled over and battled for breath. Great, reverberating tides of sorrow engulfed him. Vincent's cool resentment – he'd done so well to keep it back, keep it down, but Robbie felt it with every carefully chosen

305

reply, each courteous parry. He was a man now, Vincent, and already more of a man than Robbie could ever be. He had choices. He was in control of his own destiny.

And Ellie. The sheer, unbidden beauty of his gap-toothed kid; still in braces yet already a heart-stopping young woman. Every time he said goodbye, he died a little. Sheila though – she was so cold now, so careful; putting her best foot forward for the kids but clearly immune to the man she'd once loved. She'd rid herself of him. It was there in the way she bid him farewell as he left the house. She'd looked at him, just for a second, in the eye, clamped her lips tight together and, with a subtle nod of her head, she let him go. That was it, over. She'd cut him loose.

He sips his pint and watches the fire dance down to embers. He can't move himself to throw more coal on. Outside, street lights flicker to life as the earth spins away from the sun. Robbie sips his Guinness and with each mouthful, he lets the truth in, too – lets it burn deep through the buffer of the drink. Sheila and Robbie. Him and her.

'You and me. We should do it, you know.'

The cinnamon girl in an all-white estate. He should never have let it get so far. Susheela. His first love. His last.

Fourteen

Vinnie starts to sink. All that blind, purple hope of this last week bleeding into Manchester's rank gutters. He's sure he's got this right – Kenny came on to him; he didn't bite and now he's gone the other way. His beautiful boy has taken his ball back in, and he doubts he'll ask him to play again. So immersed in these thoughts is Vinnie that it takes him a while to clock that Kenny is no longer by his side. He spins round, panicked, and sees him standing by the canal, the wind rippling his reflection across its moon-drenched surface. He looks agonisingly beautiful. Vinnie walks towards him, and thinks that this time he'll just put his arms around him and kiss him. But Kenny steps forward to meet him, eyes troubled. 'Vinnie, I don't wanna go home just yet.' He says it like a child who's accustomed to being told no.

Vinnie hunches himself up against the cold, trying to stop his teeth from chattering. 'OK? Where d'you wanna go? You say.' Vinnie can't keep those last embers of hope out of his voice.

Kenny searches his face with a long, questioning look. He's struggling to put it into words. 'Cake and ale, Vin.'

'Yeah. I got the pun.'

'But did you, like?'

The two of them are facing each other, inches apart, their breath gusting like dry ice in the cold night air.

'I dunno. You tell me.'

'That's what we used to call 'em inside. Cake.'

Now he sees. Now he's starting to get it.

Kenny drops his gaze to the floor as though the shame is too much to bear. Just as quickly he's back though, pleading at Vinnie

307

with his eyes. 'I want to go where you go.' He doesn't blink. 'I know where you go.' Vinnie gulps hard. Kenny turns away, but continues. 'That night, yeah? The other week when I met your pals? I followed you.'

He's facing the other way, looking out over the canal. Vinnie thinks back to the night, cutting through Queer Street, the strange sensation prickling his neck. So he wasn't imagining it.

'I know where you went, Vinnie. I want you to take me. Take me with you.'

He's crushed that Kenny might not want his love. Yet he will settle for an affair of a different sort. There's no one he would rather shoot honey with than Kenny.

They climb the stairway in silence. The tang of urine and vomit hangs heavy in the air. They reach the top floor. Kenny's face is clotted with fear and confusion. 'They don't do it here, do they?'

'Where else can they do it? It's hardly a spectator sport, is it?' Vinnie laughs and pushes open the door. Kenny follows him out onto the frozen rooftop, huddled up against the wind.

'Dorian Grey. Where the fuck are you taking me?'

Vinnie grins. 'Thought you said you followed me.'

'I didn't come this far. Where's everyone else?'

Vinnie isn't listening. He steps over to the edge. 'Come and see this sky. Fuck, but that's beautiful.' He tilts his head right back until he's almost toppling over, staring out at the paintbrush spray of tiny, scintillating stars. 'You can see the edge of the world from here,' Vinnie says. He points to the distant skyline where the lights and urban commotion suddenly fall away, swallowed up by a black slap of nothingness. They stay there, still, staring at the trembling energy of the city, their shoulders barely touching.

'If we stay out long enough, we might see Pluto.'

Vinnie squats down on the floor, starts to pull gear from his raincoat's pockets. Kenny's mouth drops wide open. 'Jeez! Vinnie! Fuck's sake, man. What's all this?'

Wholly absorbed by the task to hand, overcome by pure hunger, Vinnie has tuned out. He lays out his kit, unpacks the carefully folded squares of foil, the bog-roll tube and the ready-made conduit. There's a tablespoon, a gun and a filter and a spike for himself. 'It's probably best you chase your first head,' he says, without looking up. 'It can be a bit of a palaver getting a line when you've had a drink. Your veins shrink to nothing. Here's what we'll do, yeah? I'll cook for you first. Then I'll serve myself – and we can just lie back and stargaze together.'

Only now does Vinnie glance up. Kenny is looking down at him, utterly aghast. '*Junk*,' he finally spits out. 'That's why you've brought me here?'

It takes a moment for Vinnie to catch up. 'Uh? But . . . you know this. You followed me.'

'To the . . . gay bars.' He looks away. Devastated. 'I thought that's where you went.' He sits down, cross-legged. Vinnie crouches next to him.

'So, like . . . cake? Cakes and ale.'

'You thought I meant gear? Fuck, Vinnie.' He fights back the glisten of tears sheeting his eyes. 'Cake's what we used to call the queers inside.' Kenny's voice is grief-laden as he stands up. 'I fucking hate smackheads, Vinnie . . .'

He looks him over one last time, then disappears down the stairs. Vinnie freezes – torn between smack's sweet promise and the slap of Kenny's footsteps fading off into the night. A beat. And then he swings down the stairway taking three and four steps at a time, desperate to find him.

When he reaches the bottom, Kenny has already gone. It's only a hunch, but he senses where he'll be. Oxford Road. He could have gone anywhere, but Vinnie has a calm conviction he'll be there. Outside the station there's a knot of boot boys,

309

but they stand back to let him pass. He makes his way up the slope into the station, hoping against hope there may be one last chance to rescue this love of his.

Kenny is there. And in spite of himself, no matter what it is he's feeling, he can't keep the smile off his face when he sees Vinnie. Not for the first time, he reminds Vinnie of a child – Ellie, this time, when she's been crying or sulking and she doesn't want to make peace, but she can't help herself. He's tucked up against the café wall, his knees pulled in against his chest. Vinnie sits down next to him.

'I'm sorry, Kenny.'

'What you sorry for?' Kenny drops his head. 'I'm the one who's made a tit of myself.'

'The drug. I can take it or leave it.'

Kenny fixes his steely blue eyes on him, wanting to believe. 'I've spent my life around gear. Yeah? I know what it does.'

Vinnie nods, humbly. The wind whips around them, blowing Vinnie's hair into his eyes, obscuring his view of Kenny's sad, serious face.

'Kenny, man – if I could take back the night . . . take us right back to the bar . . . the drink, the buzz, the high . . . that moment when it was just you and me . . .' He breaks off, choking up with the sudden realisation of what this is. This is all happening, to him. He looks at his feet, and takes Kenny's hand. 'Are you with me, Kenny? Do you get me?'

Kenny pushes the hair back from Vinnie's angular cheeks and stares into his slit, beautiful brown eyes. Vinnie groans at his touch, his whole body electrified. It's now or never. The wind rasps through them. He leans right in to Kenny and kisses him, fully, with all the love in the world. He sucks and probes and flexes the nib of his starved, callow tongue. His body, his mind is exploding. He opens his eyes, wanting to see his gorgeous boy, see how this feels. There are a thousand million tiny stars above.

He looks at Kenny and he feels complete. He has lived. He has loved. He swoops to kiss him again, pushing him down onto the cold platform. They are necking, clawing and groping, lost in wonder, when the mob of skinheads troops onto the platform.

Fifteen

Sheila goes to pick her favourite, the one she's been saving, the squishy, cherry-centred one, but as her fingers encircle it she knows that, really, she doesn't want it. In truth she feels a little queasy and, glancing down at the near empty tray of Black Magic, she knows her sickness isn't all down to chocolate. It was so strange, having Robbie there again. She couldn't say how she might have expected to respond to him – it had been almost a year and in that time she had, more or less, forgotten what he looked like. In her mind's eye, he certainly didn't resemble the cartoonish end-of-pier drunk who'd sheepishly stepped across the threshold this morning. Her first reaction was shock; that it was, indeed, Robbie and that he looked so . . . wasted. She'd stood there, waiting for surprise to give way to something else, but it never came. She felt nothing for him. Nothing.

She'd persisted with the ritual for the sake of Ellie, whose eyes were dancing with delight at his very presence, his every word. When she wasn't being mesmerised by her father, Ellie was glancing back at Sheila, making sure she felt it, too. It was tragic. He'd left them, this man – and for what? For this? She'd occasionally fought back stabs of anger; that he could waste it all. That he'd thrown it all away. She wanted to make sure he knew, yet she didn't have to. It was there in his lost, glassy eyes.

For Ellie she'd kept up the show, filled in the gaps when conversation ran dry. Vincent did his bit too, but she could see it was an effort for him. At times he'd come out of himself, show a real spark and follow a thread; but it would tail off quickly enough, as though he were chiding himself for connecting with his father in any way at all. But Ellie, this was too sad. Day

312

upon day, Sheila had more than enough to cope with, to finesse. The one thing she hadn't tuned into at all was Ellie's visceral need to have her father in her life. It wasn't enough that he could saunter in and out, as it suited him, his situation, his self-worth. They'd have to work this out, between the four of them. Herself, Robbie and Ellie – and Vincent, while he was still here – they were going to have to make a plan they could all stick to, every time, no exceptions.

She looks at the chocolates again and, just for the sake of it, she swallows the cherry one whole.

She'd been on such a high all night, her good mood from this morning invigorated by the realisation that now, in Legends, she was one of the faces. Tales of her showing up at the pub in her school uniform; coating that acne-faced dealer off; carrying a load of hot credit cards; necking four, six, ten barbs – all this had been fed through clubland's rumour mangle and come out technicoloured, and everyone Ellie met wanted to hug her, introduce her to somebody, slip her a pill. She danced and writhed to every track, scarcely stopping for water, and all she could see were the wonders of her future beckoning through the shimmering truth of the strobe light. Yet it was an innocent remark from Cal that brought her crashing back down. Sat on his knee, Marnie stroking her palms as Cal gently scratched her scalp, Ellie had leant back into Cal and said, 'I love it, here. I love everyone.' He'd blown into her ear and grazed her neck with a kiss.

'Family, babes. We are family.' He'd slipped a hand under her vest top, ran his palm over her tummy. 'This is us, baby. One big family.' He'd kissed her neck more fervently, guiding Ellie's hand down towards his dick. And it wasn't the situation. It wasn't the seduction, the tender molestation. It was the words that sat Ellie up. The word. Family.

'I've got to see him . . .'

313

'Who?'

'Me dad.' Gently removing Marnie's and Cal's hands from her body, Ellie levered herself up to her feet. 'Me father needs me,' she said, stumbling to the exit, chewing hard and licking her lips.

Sixteen

Vinnie peers out through a narrow field of vision. His black, swollen eyelids can barely open a crack. Slowly, very slowly, he starts to take in his surroundings. He seems to be lying horizontal, up against the wall of a long, blue-tinged corridor. A doggedly preoccupied succession of green and white uniforms bustles around him, writing things down. One of them shines a torch in his eyes and says something, but though he registers the kindly smile and sees the lips moving, he can't make out the words. A nurse appears with cotton wool and ear buds. She dips them in some kind of solution and gently, carefully cleans around his ears. Each discarded Q-tip and cotton wool ball is stained brown from his crusted blood. Then comes a rising din in the background, footsteps and chunnering machines; the senseless squawking of drunks and junkies; the disorientated moaning of the elderly and the injured. A smiling voice startles him. 'Hello, handsome. Can you tell me your name?'

He tries to prise his lids wider open, but all he can see is her eyes. She looks shocked. No, she's beyond shock, the careworn sister – she's heartbroken. Her brown eyes bleed sadness and pity and compassion. He can't open his mouth. Panicked, he tries to grab her wrist and misses.

'It's OK, you're in hospital, darling. Now can you just . . .' She leans right down to him, enunciating each word for him to hear and lip-read without ambiguity. 'THIS IS Man-che-ster Ro-yal In-fir-mary, love.'

She stands back, waits for the message to sink in. He stares back at her, utterly lost.

315

'You're in the very best hands, love. We'll get you in as soon as can be. But I do need your name, first.'

The tight puckered anus of his mouth is only capable of bubbling formless sounds like the bleat of a newborn animal. More people arrive, cluster around, bend over him, discuss him. It's all just noise. He tunes out. The trolley swings a corner and the ceiling spins away from him.

He's dimly aware of being hefted up onto a cushioned bench. A machine starts up, its low purr soothing him back towards unconsciousness. The bench begins to slide slowly towards a brightly lit chamber, then he's being pulled out and heaved onto another bed. More faces, more little torches shining in his eyes. There's a gradual shifting in consciousness. One by one, his thoughts line up, sharpening themselves against the rising blade of pain. Two men in masks stand over him. The one with brown arms reads from a clipboard. 'Fractured maxilla, grossly deviated nose, fractured ribs . . . possible entrapment of ocular muscles.'

'Intracranial damage?'

'Just waiting on the CAT scan.'

The white surgeon steps back, shaking his head. 'Fuck's this city coming to.'

The registrar stands in silence, awaiting instruction. Vinnie is growing cold and damp and clammy but his every fibre is aflame. Kenny. He slips back out of consciousness and in his altered state the night comes back to him, horribly alive.

He's eating Kenny's lips, they're devouring each other and the whole world spins away from its axis, leaving the two of them swaying and coasting through the icy, weightless night. The kiss seems to go on for ever, tufts of Kenny's hair wedged between his knuckles as their tongues collide and dart and probe. The dark dank city air envelops them like a secret cloak, moonlight seeping under its hem.

316

Then footsteps. Voices. The dawning of terror as he drags his head away from Kenny and sees the platoon of black DMs, stomping down the platform towards them. There isn't even time to get up and run.

The onslaught is so vicious, so unrelentingly hateful that he only feels the recoil of the first boot. He goes down, and it all fades away. Blow after blow after blow, and just when he thinks that even these hyenas have had their fill, they turn him over and look into his eyes and . . .

He's lying prostrate on the platform. He can't breathe and there's a lacerating pain splintering through him, splashing stinging hot liquid across his eyes. He can hear their voices fading away into the low husky grind of the city. In the distance a car alarm whoops and whoops. Kenny bends over him, distraught. He whispers in his ear. There's a spark, the whoosh of his Zippo, then it all fades out again. Everything is woozy. Kenny, gently, carefully, lifts his head up. He can see the moon shrivelling to a yellow dot beyond the tower blocks. Kenny ducks down to kiss him, and everything levels out to black. A void – then an ambulance siren growing louder and louder, and a faint disc of light bleeding into his hazy frame of reference. He's awake now and his thoughts are dislocated. His nose feels thick and clogged, his eyes have been bludgeoned to slits and yet he can sense no pain. His whole body is strung out on a numb, floaty thread. He knows this high and a weak smile starts to tug at the torn corners of his mouth. This is a morphine high, and it feels delicious.

He's lifted up and strapped down, his head deadlocked into a brace. He's aware of the spike being fed into the back of his hand. He can hear the garbled spluttering of the ambulance radio as they call ahead. Broken ribs. Serious facial trauma. Multiple contusions. Lacerations to the eye, lip, nose. Immediate attention on arrival. It sounds bad – but he feels fine, drifting and careless. He feels out for Kenny's hand, but he's gone.

Another, horrid memory jolts through his subconscious. Dad. Dad turned up this morning. He should have known. He spoils everything, Dad. He turned up on their doorstep, bringing his curse with him.

Vinnie trails off, blanks out from the pain.

Seventeen

Sheila is writing to Rasa when the knock comes.

She'd been putting it off – the letter, the confessional – hanging fire till the last possible moment. But that thing with Robbie today, it's finally triggered closure for her. She cares for him still, after a fashion. And she hopes that one day, soon, maybe, Vinnie can take steps towards forgiving him. But she knows it now, he's gone. She no longer wants him. She can tell Rasa the truth: Robbie and she are no longer together, and next year when they come to visit, it would just be the three of them. She was putting her faith in Rasa to make sure there'd be no raised eyebrows from her sisters, no raised voices from her brothers. It's a good thing that she and Robbie have gone their separate ways, and she expects her family to embrace that. Next year, when they come to KL, she wants everything to be just fine.

There's a stentorian quality to the knock and her heart jolts on seeing the blur of uniform through the dimpled distortion of the porch window. Instinctively she knows this is going to be bad. Her first thought is that it's Ellie. Ellie has been showing off at Sara's house. She's got drunk and had to have her stomach pumped. She wraps her dressing gown tight across her chest and opens the door. The officer and his female partner both look grave. The WPC can't look her in the eye. Her colleague speaks up. 'Mrs Fitzgerald?'

She nods, once, turns and shows them into the living room. She sits down opposite them on the edge of the settee, her knees knocking together and flinching upwards. She dare not ask them what is wrong. For as long as she doesn't know, it hasn't happened.

'Your son. Vincent Fitzgerald.'

319

The words burn a hole right through her. 'Oh no, no,' she pleads. 'Not Vincent, no.'

The copper clears his throat and continues. It's as though, in making all this as formal as possible, a formal solution can be found. 'Your son has been the victim of a violent assault.'

Violent. The room shrinks away from her. She tries to pull herself together. Where has he been? Who was he with?

'He's been taken into Manchester's Royal Infirmary.'

She takes the full shattering slam of the information. It sits her back in her chair, pulls her entire animus down inside her. She peers out at the WPC. She seems a better bet. She hasn't delivered the blows, as yet. 'How bad is it?' Her voice sounds stronger. She has to face this. Has to face it now.

'He was conscious on arrival. There's been some facial trauma and they're operating right away.'

Sheila zones out, hand clamped to her mouth. It takes her a moment to come round, remember where she is, what this is. She has to ask. Has to know. 'Is he . . .' Her voice cracks now, snaps like a twig. 'Do we know the extent of the damage?'

The man looks at the woman. The WPC clears her throat, steps forward and squats down in front of Sheila. 'Mrs Fitzgerald. You're going to have to be very strong. Your son has suffered a prolonged assault. His injuries are going to be distressing.'

Once again, Sheila experiences the lurch of nausea and this time she can't contain herself.

Ellie can't remember whether it's M6 north – towards Preston – or south, to Birmingham. She's pretty sure she's passed through Preston when she's been up to Blackpool on the coach, but Birmingham rings a bell, too. Or was it Burnley? A lorry slows. The window goes down. 'Hop in!'

She looks up at the driver. He seems all right – what she can see of him. The passenger door flips open a second, goes back

320

on itself. She goes towards it. It's so high up. She can't imagine taking all those steps up, just to sit in a lorry. She bites hard on her lip, trying to snap out of it.

'Yaow getting in or what?'

He sounds harder, this time. Impatient. She can't place the accent. It's like Barry from *Auf Wiedersehen, Pet*. Her dad used to love that. She steps away from the lorry. 'You're OK, mate. I'm . . .' She turns and stumbles back along the hard shoulder, away from the lorry and back towards the service station.

Sheila chases through dark empty lanes towards the motorway. It's a real struggle to keep it together. She's worked on casualty, tended dozens of maxilla traumas and she's already flipping forward, preparing for the worst. Her baby – beaten up. Left for dead on a cold slab of concrete. Her thin, fragile boy. What kind of person would do such an evil thing? Why pick on meek, soft-hearted Vinnie? There can only be one reason. And, in allowing the thought to take flight, she dwells on the horror of her own experience, all those years ago. She, too, was pinned down, kicked, spat at. Why? For what? She can't bear it, to think that such monsters are still out there, feral, roaming in their packs. She berates herself – she has to stay in control. But it's useless, she's sinking, she has no one. A vicious, visceral anger rips through her, a violent disdain for her useless, wasteful, wasted husband. He should be there with her. She can't do it – she just can't do this alone. A desperate thought. She knows it – it's the last thing she should do, but there's nothing else for it. She has Ellie. Ellie will come with her. And who knows – maybe Sara Cartwright's father can make some calls. He must know surgeons and such people. She swings the car back and heads for Stockton Heath.

Her panic mushrooms out into the cold damp air. She leans

further into the intercom so her lips fizz against its crackling mesh. 'This is Sara Cartwright's house?'

'Yeh-es. You're speaking with Mrs Cartwright. But Sara has no friends staying over tonight. Who is this again?'

'Please. This is urgent. I need to speak to Sara.'

Through the muffled perforations, Sheila can hear her conferring with her husband and then the intercom clicks dead and the gates pull back. Sheila races up the gravel, smoothing down the kink in her hair, straightening out her jacket. Even in the demented scourge of her ordeal she is acutely aware of how this must look to a family like Sara's. She knows that the fact of her being alone, without a husband, and that orange jalopy parked up outside the gates have already conspired against her. A man with an elegant mane of silver-grey hair comes to the door. Behind him his wife hauls their teenage daughter down the stairs. She's heart-stoppingly pretty, a mass of golden hair and big, brown eyes. Mr Cartwright steps forward. 'Can you be quick, please. I'm only letting you in because . . .' He casts a disapproving look at his wife, then steps back into the house. Mrs Cartwright is austere, yet not unkind.

'So. What is this?'

'I dropped my daughter off here. Ellie Fitzgerald.'

A look of slight fear passes over Sara. Her mother goes to stand behind her daughter, drapes two protective arms around her. 'Sara hasn't had a sleepover this week – have you, darling?'

She shakes her head.

'And I don't think . . . Ella, is it?'

'Ellie's never been here. We don't really socialise.'

A whole, rapid-fire flashback speeds in front of Sheila's eyes. Her helping Ellie pack her overnight bag. Ellie giggling with her about Mr Cartwright's roving eye. How they lace all their food with garlic – even the cheese on toast. Ellie could not make these things up. She feels like she's choking here. She's going under. For Vincent's sake, she drags herself back up. She fortifies her voice, fighting to override another tearful breakdown. She places a hand on Sara's shoulder, looks into her eyes. 'Sara? Do you have any idea where my daughter might be?'

The girl shoots an anxious sidelong glance at her mother. Sheila turns her gaze on Mrs Cartwright, a desperate, beseeching look that only a mother can understand. She softens her voice and turns to her daughter. 'Sara, darling – if you do know anything . . .'

Sara looks torn for an instant, then hides her head in her mother's dressing gown. Mrs Cartwright holds Sara's head, makes her look up at her. 'You're not in any trouble, darling! Anything you know, anything that might help this poor lady . . .'

Sara peers at Sheila, still clinging to her mummy's warm body. 'I think she might be at Legends.'

Sheila gives a nervous, spluttered giggle. 'Right, Legend – do you happen to have his number? Or do you know where he lives?'

A beat, and then, 'It's a night club.' She fires another troubled glance at her mother. 'I only know that because Katie's sister goes.'

Sheila's reprieve lasts all of half a minute. Bile cloys in her throat. 'Is it . . . is it in Warrington?'

Sara shrugs, and Sheila knows she's telling the truth.

'Well. Thank you. I'm so sorry to have disturbed you like this. My son . . .' She chews down on her lip, fights the tears back.

Sara steps forward. 'I thinks it's somewhere near a garage. That's all I know. Someone told me they dance on a wall.'

Sheila drives round and round the centre of town in panicked loops, her world spinning out of control. She should go to Vincent – but Ellie is out there, too, and her maternal tug is dragging her in circles. All she can do is respond to each instinct as it comes to her. She pulls into three different garages, asks the attendants if there is a club called Legends nearby. None of them have heard of it. She heads up to the taxi rank at Warrington Central. Someone there has got to know. A group of Asian cabbies is clustered around their cars, elbows splayed across the roofs, drinking tea from polystyrene cups as they wait for the last train in from Liverpool. She knows exactly how this will go. She can't bring herself to approach the bastards. But she has no choice.

'Legends?' one of them spits. 'In't that the druggies' club?'

It's humiliating. The man has a broader Warrington accent than Sheila but once he's clocked her Western clothes, sussed her naked fingers and the awful shine of panic in her eyes he's already drawn his own conclusions. He and his workmates are luxuriating in her anguish. She refuses to give them the satisfaction of a lecture. She thrusts a fiver at him. 'Drive. I'll follow.'

He leads her to the bottom of Priory Street. She looks him up and down as he gets out of his cab and delves for change. She's seldom known such fire, such anger in her soul.

'Keep it!' she spits, and marches towards the garage.

Pale-faced revellers are already spilling out into the night. They look like some alien species, the boys stripped down to their waists utterly oblivious to the lacerating air. Sara must have made some kind of mistake. Sheila would know if this place, these people were a part of Ellie's world. And yet, even as she thinks it, her conviction is eclipsed by a full and sickening realisation that this is, absolutely, Ellie's world. She recalls her own horror at the works' night out, and her sickness goes deeper.

A huddle of them are gyrating on the pavement in solipsistic abstraction, dancing to imaginary beats. Sheila approaches the girl who seems the least out of it.

'Excuse me, dear . . .' She tries to sound bright and upbeat as she takes Ellie's photo from her purse. 'Please – have you seen this girl?'

The girl grins massively, baring both tiers of teeth. She steps from side to side then peers right into the photo of the schoolgirl. Beyond the black wells of her eyes, light bulbs are going off. Sheila's heart starts to sink. 'Ohhhh, yeah – that's Elleh, in't it? The scooleh. Good robber . . .'

Sheila shuts her eyes, reclaims her balance, focuses, hard. 'Is she still in there?'

The girl shrugs her shoulders. 'Done one, I fink.'

More instantaneous terror strangling her guts. 'OK. Thank you.'

She puts the photo back, hoping against hope she won't be needing it for the police again later that evening. She swears to herself, here and now, that all she's asking for is the safe return of her girl. She won't shout at her. She won't question her about Sara, or Legends or school, or anything at all. Just bring her back, and she'll make it all OK. She walks away from the syncopating ravers, back towards the Lada. The girl runs after her. 'Hey! Missus! Your Elleh might be at Knutsford, yeah? Giz a lift to the services an' al find her for yoh.'

Sheila ignores her, gets back into her car, fires up the engine and sits there trembling. She's torn between her babies. Somehow, she has an inclination that ballsy, bolshy little Ellie can take care of herself. Wherever she goes, she seems to have an override, a safe mode that always sees her right. The time she ran away to Blackpool to find her dad, she made it as far as the Haydock roundabout. Juggernauts and lorry drivers and camper vans everywhere, but Ellie persuaded the motorway police to bring her home. She peels off towards the M62. Right now, Vinnie needs her more.

Dawn is breaking the city skyline when the registrar wakes Sheila. Faint smudges of lilac clouds dapple the walls. He hands her a cup of tea, then sets about talking her through the work they've had to do on Vincent. The damage he's sustained is extensive: fractured maxilla, fractured mandible, fractured nose. The CT scan has shown up a temporal lobe bleed. It's too early on to assess how this might affect his speech cortex, let alone his general psychological make-up. There's a possibility he may develop epilepsy. He waits for her to take this all in before continuing. 'We had to do a free-flap reconstruction.'

Sheila knows precisely what this means. They've had to rebuild his face, or sections of it. In her experience, it's only victims of the very worst car crashes or infernos who need such treatment. She reaches for the registrar's wrist, eyes pleading. 'Oh no, please. Not his little face. Tell me it isn't bad . . .'

'We've had to take some skin and bone from his arm to reconstruct his chin. We've tried to find as close a match as possible but the skin on his arms is slightly darker than his face . . .'

Sheila drifts out. Up until this point she's been stoically absorbing the detail, each new revelation pushing her resolve closer and closer to breaking point. But this is just too much for her to bear. She can feel herself starting to split and tear under the weight of her own fear – and her fears for Vincent. She knows it, knows it well. Vincent will never recover from this. But her ordeal is not quite through.

'The ambulance crew that picked him up . . .' He hesitates, looks down at his feet. 'They found track marks on his arms.'

It takes a moment for it to register. Sheila can't speak, can't think. Not Vinnie. Not her Vinnie. She opens her mouth to defend him, but no words come.

The registrar continues. 'The ambulance men were amazed his body was able to survive that level of pain without suffering a heart attack. So at least some good came of it. The heroin saved his life.'

Sheila collapses back onto the bed with a groan.

'We've screened him for HIV and hepatitis B.' He places his hand on her shoulder, squeezes gently, then he's gone.

A slow tide of teal blue is rinsing out the pale dawn sky. The light is still feeble, the early morning sun blotted by the low wash of soapy pollution drifting in from Crossfields. Ellie is cold and low as she trudges the lanes back to Thelwall, her mission exposed

326

as a foolish pipe dream, the lighter it gets. She craves nothing more than the fleecy lair of her bed now, but there's hardly a car in sight. She takes out her last crumpled cigarette, weighed down by a hopeless pall of despair and nothingness. Other kids speak often of their comedowns, but this is new for Ellie. This is a desperate, debilitating low, and she needs to get home, shut out the world, curl up in the safety of her own hollow place.

She sparks the cigarette. Way, way on the horizon below and beyond lie the belching smoke stacks where her dad once worked. She cuts off across the fields and, choking back all feeling as she realises where this will bring her out, she passes the copse and keeps her eyes straight ahead, ignoring the whinny of the horses in their paddock. She hops down to the canal bank and follows its lugubrious trawl back home. Oh Daddy, Daddy, Daddy. How did it come to this? On the swing bridge above, a couple of cars blare past, then another and another, sub-bass thumping, each crammed tight with the fading fauna of the night – queasy faces and grinding jaws, living for nothing now but the beat. She knows exactly where they'll be heading. Wallie Res. Another time and she'd be with them in that convoy, chasing the same false dawn, trying to stretch out the night for ever. She passes under the bridge.

Ellie's legs are so heavy now she can barely stagger in a straight line. She trudges back over the wasteland, that mythical, muddy badlands where Vincent had been too scared to tread when they were kids – these final few yards strung out like a throbbing eternity. She sticks her head over the back fence. Mum's car is not there in the drive. She's left for work. It's safe to go in. Numb with fatigue, she heaves herself over the garden fence. The weak sun finally declares itself, edging out from behind the cloud cover, warming her face. She slumps down on the garden bench. She'll just lie down for a moment, get herself together. That sun feels nice. She'll be better in a minute.

327

Eighteen

'Ellie. Darling . . .'

Even in her comedown trance, Ellie can feel the emotion, the affection in her mother's voice. So careful not to startle her.

'Baby. It's Mum.'

The warm spool of sound dangles across the hazy flannels of her subconscious, briefly lulling her from the dark paranoia of her thoughts. The voice calls again, and this time it's closer. She forces a stubborn, sticky eye open. Her mum's harrowed face looks down on her, and her heart bangs wildly with fear, with pity, with crushing remorse. She sits up, and smoothes her matted hair down onto her skull. She is utterly unprepared for any kind of showdown.

Sheila peers into the bitumen craters of her daughter's eyes, fighting back tears. There is a crease on one side of her face and her hair looks like something washed up from the canal. She can smell the pungent heave of chemicals wafting up off her skin and clothes. There's a mechanical tick to her jaw as it pulverises an imaginary stub of gum. How could she not have seen? Both her babies junkies and not once, ever, did she suspect. The school trips. The piano lessons. Rome. All those extra-curricular activities and items Sheila had grafted so hard to pay for. She feels spent – hollowed out.

Ellie is bracing herself for some kind of rebuke. Little quivers of indignation are jabbing her top lip, teasing it up into her gums. She leans over, buying herself a few seconds with a fake coughing fit so that she can drum up and perfect her defence. A rim of wild green fixes around her black bulging pupils. Her eyes, her father's eyes are ready for combat.

Sheila pushes back the hurt, the anger stinging up her throat. She has to focus on now, on Vinnie. But this is almost too much. As she looks into those defiant eyes, she's dragged through the mincer of all the warring emotions. There's betrayal. The design and detail that's gone into her weekly chicanery is frightening. All those elaborate lies about her imaginary sleepovers and the sideshow of Sara's dysfunctional parents – she's swallowed it all, and savoured it, too. Above all that, above the hurt and the sense of her own wide-eyed gullibility, revelling in her daughter's high society, there's a crushing throb of love and affection, relief that Ellie is here and safe, even a slight sense of awe that this little thing, her own offspring, has been capable of such intricate duplicity.

Sheila takes Ellie's hands in her own. Their cold, bitten daintiness slays her and any residual anger fades to nothing. She still has tiny, dimpled knuckles. No matter what she's been up to, she's still a kid. She smiles into the strange, alien satellite of her daughter's face. Somehow, they will all get through this.

Once she's got Ellie tucked up in bed she steels herself to call Robbie. God knows what she'll tell him. The truth. Why spare him? Yet she's shaking as she dials his number. No answer. She checks the digits, dials again, carefully, but the phone rings out.

Nineteen

Ellie shrinks into her mother's flank when she sees her brother. She takes it all in – the fluid dripping into his veins, the weirdly human machine that's monitoring his vital signs. She stalls the inevitable for as long as she can. When there is nowhere left to look, she tightens her grip on her mother's hand and slides her eyes along the bed covers, up to his face. His head is fixed in a brace, his cheeks speared with a pair of metal rods. His swollen, blood-cracked mouth is wrapped around a plastic tube that plunges rudely into his throat. There's no disguise, no attempt at softening the blow here. They've put Vincent back together. His eyes are swollen to a pair of bulbous purple-black peaches, just a tiny gash in his right eye for him to peer out through. She nearly cries as she catches a whiff of the acid stink coming off him. The boy who lives in the bath would hate this – an obscene violation of all he holds dear.

Ellie remembers what Mum has said about bravery in his presence, how important it is to stay calm for Vinnie – but it's too much, seeing him like this. Suffering, begging, barely alive. Who would do such a thing to her shy, bookish brother? It would be like hitting a baby. He couldn't even block a punch, Vinnie, let alone throw one. She scans the butchered mire of his face, desperately seeking a glimpse of him. But he's nowhere to be found. That's not her brother lying there. It looks nothing like him, and for one blind moment she wishes that they'd finished him off. She fights back the tears welling from her soul and mouths 'sorry' to him, then to Mum.

She turns and leaves the room.

*

330

Ellie's tearful exit gives Vincent his first sense of the horrific extent of his deformity. There's been no room in his banging, slicing head for vanity up until now. A shrill and scintillating pain courses his body, driving him to the point of nausea – yet he holds off on the morphine. Around his wrist is a button-push device that will mainline a balmy, soothing opiate right through him at his will. But something compels him to own the pain. If he can take the worst, he thinks, what follows can only be better. And he needs to know exactly what that worst consists of. What remains of him, outside the throbbing trauma of his shell?

He tries to read the answers in his mother's dissembling face. She makes a big thing of looking directly at him like there's nothing wrong, but he can see the hurt in her tired eyes. Poor Mum. How he wishes he could make this better for her. She rolls her eyes at him.

Now his mother is just staring at him. She can't do this. The monster staring back at her is not her young, beautiful son. And Vinnie sees that. He's starting to understand. He closes his eyes and feigns sleep. He needs to be alone now, left to surrender to the black depression that laps at his subconscious. He pushes the button and the morphine takes him away.

Twenty

Vinnie is asleep when the police arrive two days later. On the empty bed beside him, his sister is snoring. Sheila keeps vigil over both of them, listening to the soft rattle of air circulating through their nostrils, watching their faces wrapped around their dreams. The policeman sees the intimate family vignette, holds up a hand and backs off, gestures that he'll come back later. But Sheila is up and out of her chair, summoning them back with a wild flapping hand. This is the third time in two days they've turned up, seen her son sleeping and left.

'Please. Those people who did this to my son.' Her eyes fill up as she tugs the policeman back towards the bed. 'Look. Look what they did to him. Please, let me wake him.'

Vinnie blinks weakly into the sun-dappled ward. The nurses have thrown the windows wide open and a distant birdsong glides on the cool breeze. The sound depresses him, reminding him of the world out there making demands on him, trying to wrench him from his coop.

'He still can't speak.' Sheila speaks for him. 'He can only write.'

The officer pulls out a notepad and pen.

Then as though sensing his anxiety about his stale, sick breath, his weeping eyes, Sheila buys him some time to clean him up. 'Just give us five minutes, yeah? Let me flannel him down.'

The police officer raises his thumbs at him, but he's glad to get away. Vinnie is used to it by now. The registrar, his mum, the night porter, his friends, all of them reacted the same way. Utterly incredulous. None of them can believe he survived the beating.

By the time the cop returns, Sheila has flannelled his face and underarms, moisturised his hands. He feels cleaner – more able to brave the gaze of the ordeal. And he can tell straight away it's going to be an ordeal. The thumbs-up officer is looking upon him differently now, his cooperative, commiserating stance supplanted by something else. Disdain and mild boredom drips from every drawled, robotic question.

'Mr Fitzgerald. Think carefully before you answer this one. There were traces of heroin in your bloodstream when they brought you in. Was this in any way related to the attack?'

Vinnie is too stunned to respond. He drifts out, shocked into vivid and immediate flashback: he's back on the platform, doubled up in searing, unendurable pain. It feels like his ribs have been snapped to spears, stabbing at his lungs. It's too painful to breathe and he yelps at Kenny in little sharp gasps, begging him for help. Kenny stoops over him, dripping his own blood onto his face. He tries to turn him onto his side to stop him choking on his blood and vomit, but shards of bone gouge into him and he screams out loud.

Vinnie, fading quickly, feels Kenny's hands in his raincoat pockets, then the rustle of foil. He forces an eye open. Kenny's fingers are quivering as he rubs tobacco together with smack and rolls it into a joint. He lights it, and squats right down so his eyelids are almost touching Vinnie's face. 'Here.'

He places the fat joint between the flaps of his torn, bulbous mouth but Vinnie can't inhale and his weeping gash only dampens the papers, staining them red. Kenny retrieves it, sucks down a huge vortex of sweet, sweet smoke, peels back Vinnie's mouth and blows hard, all the way down into his lungs. This way, they smoke the loaded joint right down to the nub, sucking and blowing till there is nothing between them but air.

Vinnie is back in real time. He's staring at his mum, his eyes low and contrite. She smiles meekly at him, killing him with her goodness. He feels dumb, dead, of no worth or purpose what-soever. Sensing that, Sheila grips his hand and nods for him to answer. He struggles his back up the pillow until he is, more or less, comfortable. He takes the pen and writes, 'It was my first time.'

He hates that he should have to justify himself to this insensitive, unrefined man. The officer casts a surreptitious glance at the track marks on his bare brown arm, his stare lingering until Vinnie twigs and snatches it away. He flashes his eyes at the officer and tries to convey to him just how far above this whole thing he is. The officer holds his gaze a moment then returns to automaton mode. 'So. You were alone when this happened?'

Vinnie stares at him vacantly.

'A young gentleman made the call. He wouldn't give his name. Do you know who that might have been?'

Unable to shake his head, Vinnie scrawls an N onto the notepad. He can see the cogs turning in the cop's one-track mind. His dealer, that's who made the call. The beating was over a drug debt. His dealer called the ambulance because he still wants him alive – at least until he's paid up. From his propped-up vantage, Vinnie can see the officer is now doodling as he auto-questions him.

'And would it be fair to say you've never seen your attacker before?'

Vinnie pens a Y. The officer doesn't even look at him, now. Vinnie won't give the dunce the satisfaction of telling him he was queer-bashed. Paki-bashed. Both. He stares at the bald spot on the cop's reclining dome and scribbles: MUGGED. Again the knowing look.

'Mugged? And your attacker was, what—'

'Attacker?' Sheila can hold back no longer. 'You really think it possible that one person could inflict this?'

The anguish in her voice yanks Ellie from her slumber. She

sits up, eyes all squiffy, her thoughts still sleep-balmed. She shoots Vinnie a lovely smile and his heart bangs with love. He couldn't bear for Ellie to know. It would kill her, her brother a smack-head. In the parochial mind of the acid house kid, Ecstasy was changing the world while heroin and drink were killing it. He beckons to the copper, scrawls down on his pad: 'Don't mention drugs in front of my sister. Thank you.'

The officer looks impatient, but nods and clears his throat. 'The mugging. Your attacker . . .' He glances at Sheila. 'Attackers. Do you remember how many of them there were?'

Vinnie blinks numbly. The horror, the sheer horror of all this envelops him and it's wrong, it's all so horribly wrong. This copper doesn't want to be here any more than Vinnie wants him to be there and at least there's something he can do about that. 'Drop the charade,' he writes. 'You don't give a fuck.'

The police officer sighs theatrically. Sheila cranes her neck to see what her son has written. 'Vin-cent!'

'It's fine, Mrs Fitzgerald. Your son's been through a dreadful . . .' He breaks off, folds his arms and levels his gaze on Vinnie, impatient now. He's more than ready for a fag and a cup of tea, then on to the next scumbag. 'Mr Fitzgerald.' His voice is loaded with ennui and irony. 'Please be assured that we will not rest until we have apprehended the thugs who have done this to you.' He stands, pockets his notebook, nods to Sheila and is gone.

335

Twenty-one

Kenny skulks in the storeroom at the end of the ward, as he has done every day for the last two weeks since they brought him in. He waits until Vinnie's visitors have gone, and he just sits there with him, talking. Vinnie knows he's there – he must do, because the nurses let him come and go as he pleases – but he hasn't said a word. He just lies there, dead to the world, barely breathing through his battered slab of face. It's killing him. Vinnie took the hiding for the pair of them, but how Kenny wishes it had been him. Not because he was used to beatings; not because Vinnie hadn't even known how to curl himself into a defensive ball; but because beauty mattered so much to him. It went beyond the superficial with Vinnie – it was his code for living. His religion. He often joked that the day his looks deceived him would be the day that he ended it all. Growing old was a thought that appalled him but even worse was the thought of growing ugly.

Vinnie lies dead still. If he can't see Kenny, then Kenny can't see him. But then, as he always does, he takes a little peek at Kenny and affects not to know he's being watched. Vinnie's eyes blister up, suddenly overwhelmed. He's cut his hair into a short, boyish crop and his supple neck tenses as he leans forward to kiss him, his fine-cut cheekbones grazing his face cage. The strain of the last fortnight is evident in Kenny's face. He's gaunt, but lovely. Elegantly wasted. He gets up to open the window, then just sits there looking at him, saying nothing. The words of a Cure song drift through Vincent's subconscious: 'Your trust, the most gorgeously stupid thing I ever cut.'

Vinnie pushes back the tears now as he remembers their kiss

– their devastating, life-changing kiss. It happened. It took place between them, and for that he's thankful.

Kenny seems to tune into his distress and as his eyes flicker all over his broken lover, he bites down on his lip as though deciding the time has come. 'Vinnie.'

No reply. Vinnie swallows hard.

'Vin. I know you can speak now. I heard you last night.'

It's true. Since they removed the tube from his throat, Vinnie has been able to talk. But he's been pretending that the delayed post-operative swelling has grabbed a chokehold around his larynx. His words are slightly slurred as he struggles to articulate his thoughts, but he could make himself understood, if he wanted. This semblance of mute excommunication is a necessary barrier between himself and the world – his mother, his sister and the daily trail of friends he barely knows. They turn up unbidden and just stay, reading to him, talking at him, smiling like there's nothing wrong at all. He knows he's hideous and this wall of silence is his fortress while he prepares himself for the worst.

Still Vinnie says nothing. Kenny pulls out a small, leather-bound notebook. 'I took this. I . . . I wanted to keep something.'

That does it for Vincent. More so than at any stage since he's been here, he feels helpless to defend himself. People can do whatever they want to him, and he has to lie there and take it. He opens his eyes as wide as they'll go and fixes his gaze on Kenny. He almost faints with love for him. But he's also horribly, bitterly hurt. His voice comes out, barely decipherable at first. But then the dry, staccato clucking morphs into words. 'You r-r-read my nn-n-nnnotes?'

Kenny's eyes, his mouth, his whole face is smiling. It's as much as he can do not to dive on Vinnie and hug him, hold him, squeeze him. Instead he smiles right into him eyes and tries to keep his voice even, as though they're picking up a conversation from a moment ago. 'Yeah, mate – your notes, your ideas, the everyday things you see. I read it all in one go.'

Vinnie looks away, stung.

'Vin. It's beautiful. It's the most beautiful thing . . .' He tails off and waits for Vinnie to come back, to look at him. He needs him to know. Sensing it, Vinnie turns back to him, eyes still angry but willing to be persuaded. Kenny recites from the heart. 'The winter sun glancing off the flat bitumen of the ship canal . . . trembling like the flame of a gas stove . . . the oil-slick water takes hold of it and spits it off across the surface. And the young lad watching it all from the locks, waiting, waiting . . . waiting for the big fat fireball to turn down the light, turn up the night . . . and only then is it safe for him to steal back through the streets, unseen. Unnoticed.'

Vinnie turns away. He's shaking slightly.

Kenny gulps back a heave of tears. 'That's you, Vinnie.' Then, more quietly, 'That's you.'

They sit in silence. Eventually Kenny clears his throat.

'Vin. Listen. Don't say nothing – just listen to every word and understand what I'm telling you. Yeah?'

The slightest flicker of agreement in Vinnie's eyes. OK. If you must. Talk. Kenny talks.

'I read. I read fuckin' everything, man, and . . .' He sighs and tries another tack. 'Look. I'm going nowhere. You and me – this is it. This is us. I'm staying right here, by your side.' He's breathing more heavily, the more animated he gets. 'We'll get you right. I promise we will, yeah – get you right as rain. And you and me, we'll get a little place out on the moors. And you'll write. And I'll chop wood and grow vegetables, yeah? And we'll . . .'

Vinnie looks up at him. Beautiful. Full of hope. His whole life ahead of him. He can't do it to him. He loves him too much.

It's over.

He buzzes for the nurse. He won't look at him. And Kenny

doesn't make a fuss in front of the nurse. He leans down low into his face and whispers in his ear, 'I love you. I love you, Vinnie Fitzgerald – and I will love you. Nothing can change that.'

Vinnie turns away. He says nothing. He listens to his footsteps fade away down the corridor. Even from where Vinnie lies, there's something strangely beatific about the rhythm of Kenny's stride. He still has hope. If only he knew.

Twenty-two

Such inner rage is alien to Sheila, yet with each imaginary argument, with every stark confrontation that eats up the miles the closer she gets to Blackpool, her mounting outrage at Robbie's sheer carelessness consumes her. How could he not be there, by his son's side, as he lies in pieces in hospital? How could he not be there, when she phoned? What is the point in his *having* a damn phone? Well, he isn't getting away with it. Sheila doesn't give two hoots how he chooses to piss away his wretched life, but his children still need him. And not just Vincent, either. If anything, Ellie's need for love, for safety, for comfort is even greater than Vinnie's, and where is bloody Robert when he's needed to provide some of that? He's at the exact same place he always goes when things are needed of him. Away.

She parks the Lada in a parallel street, as close to Robbie's lodgings as she can get, and, trying to keep the violent waxing and waning of her heart in check, she goes to put him right. She locks the car and marches forth. She's immediately stricken by the shabbiness of the building – its vicious, peeling orange paint, its slurry-stained windows and threadbare, dingy curtains – as she steps into the street, checks the details on her paper with the number that's just visible above the door. She takes down a slug of sea air, steels herself and rings. Nobody comes. She rings again, longer this time. She will stand here all night ringing this bell until somebody answers. But it doesn't come to that. A hunched figure appears at the inner door and shows his displeasure at the sight of a dark woman. 'No vacancies,' he spits past the Vacancies sign.

Sheila rings again, and thumps hard on the glass panel. He turns sharply.

340

'Hey! Hey! You're gonna break that glass.'

'I'll break the door down if I have to! Open up!'

He clicks the safety snip and opens up, keeping his foot in the door. 'Look, lady—'

'Save it. I wouldn't stay in this heap if it was you paying me. I need to speak with Robert Fitzgerald. He's—'

'Another one, hey?' He seems relieved that there'll be no awkward confrontation. 'It's not me, love. It's just some of the guests here are very set in their ways.' He steps back, knowing he won't have to ask her in. 'Robbie's gigging tonight.'

'Can you tell me where?'

'Dunno if he'll thank me for it.'

'*I'll* thank you for it.' She steps back, eyes beseeching. 'Please. It's nothing romantic. It just happens to be very, very important.'

The rheumy old landlord eyes Sheila again, shakes his head and directs her to the Cartwheel, way past the South Pier. 'It's a tram and still a good walk after that.'

Unwilling to waste time, and unready for Blackpool's charms, Sheila hastens back to the car.

Ellie lies on Vinnie's bed in his room at home, flicking through the guides and brochures the Sussex tourist board has sent. Brighton looks fun. She can't wait to show him the itinerary she's shortlisted. The record ends. 'Isolation'. She didn't really like that one. She goes back to the Bowie album, *Station to Station*, and puts it on again, the beautiful, maudlin song about the wind. That's her brother, that is. She sighs and smiles as she picks up *The Outsider* again. She'll have this finished by tonight, he'll see. By the time she goes to see him tomorrow, she'll be able to hold down a chat with him about the weirdo who didn't even cry at his own mother's funeral.

From the moment she takes her seat in the remotest corner of the club, Sheila is blindsided. Unable to swallow, she grips her glass of Coke and hopes, prays he hasn't seen her. But there's little danger of that. As though living out some deep, personal shame up there in the glare of the spotlight, Robbie scarcely looks up. Is this the man she used to adore? Her heart aches for him, truly. All that feeling and sympathy and the base animal desire to protect her man returns. She wants him out of here; out of this.

'Oh yes – I'm the great pretender . . .'

It's Robbie, all right. It's his voice – or a splinter of it – doing the business, making the ladies go to pieces. A group of garishly dressed, fiercely made-up women gather self-consciously at the foot of the stage, variously swaying together, tears in their eyes, occasionally nudging one another and over-laughing, reminding themselves it's all a bit of fun. One or two of them make a separate stand, doggedly sticking to their territory either side of the giddy knot, avidly trying to make eye contact with Robbie. It's not going to happen. Even in his pomp, that raw, prowling, sexual creature who used to rule his stage when Sheila first heard him sing, Robbie kept his eyes closed. Head back, eyes shut, lost in the ecstatic moment of his song, that was Robbie Fitzgerald. This is not. The man up there – the shadow of the man she'd loved – is dressed in a cheap white suit, a comical, hideous, tragic black Teddy boy wig rammed tight onto his head – so tight that stray red tufts spring out from the sides. She'd laugh if it weren't so sad, so very sordid. Behind him, an orange poster as bright and immodest as their Lada and in bold, cheap, black perma-print: 'Robert Fitzgerald is LYTHAM ELVIS'.

Not that any of this seems to bother his hardy troupe of fans. She can tell from their body language, that odd combination of coquetry and hopeful propriety, that many of these chunky lasses are regulars. Finally able to take a sip of her Coke, Sheila fights back tears of pity, tears of anguish, then tears of rage. She hooks her bag off the back of her chair and takes one last look at the spectacle. Lytham Elvis was going to be neither use nor ornament to his injured family. She could cry for him. She could cry for them.

Twenty-three

The day has finally come. Vinnie's head brace was removed over an hour ago, but still he can't bring himself to look. As long as he doesn't know, he still has hope. He feels around the unfamiliar dents and crevices of his face. One by one, he runs his finger over his new, crowned teeth. It all feels regular enough and, who knows, with the miracles of surgery these days they might even just have improved his looks. But no. This is Manchester, not Beverly Hills. And this is the NHS. They'll have patched him up as best as their budgets would allow. When it comes to the cosmetic cover-up, he won't be holding his breath.

The communal basin and the mottled mirror above it lie at the furthest extent of the ward. Finally he's ready to make the daunting trip to where his likeness has lain in wait all these weeks, daring him to come and look-see. Around him, invalid life goes on, untroubled by his ordeal. Two old men in flannelette pyjamas play dominoes while Vincent Fitzgerald straightens himself up. His muscles have grown lax and incompetent from the days spent tethered to his bed and his gait is unsteady, unsure at first like a newborn foal's. Using the various bed frames as leverage he shakily commences the journey of his life.

He reaches the sink, places a hand on either side of the basin and, head bowed, shuts his eyes before the mirror's gaze. He can feel the fault lines shivering beneath the surface of the moment and it feels like he, too, might crack. Slowly, he lifts his head. He knows the mirror is there, waiting for him.

He snaps his eyes wide open in one jolting blink. He locks in to the blackened, red-rimmed craters of his gaze and stares hard, not daring to stray off into the detail that lies below. He has to look. He has to know. And finally, when he can stand this no longer, he lets his eyes roll slowly, slowly down, and left, and right, taking it all in in one horrific striptease, peeling away the dressings with which he's bound his darkest fears.

Without emotion, he appraises the patchwork mismatch of the skin graft on his cheek. He observes the full, jutting lurch of his underbite, his elongated jaw bringing an idiotic, a slobbering, an ape-like countenance to his face. He steps right back to evaluate the wreckage as someone else might see him, as a whole, and he sees it in all its horror, fixed and permanent. His face has set slightly higher to the left. It's as though some gravitational pull has hooked his left cheekbone and dragged it up a fraction. It's minimal, but it kills him. He stands there and stares, transfixed by the horrific asymmetry, cast and set and utterly irreparable. He starts laughing, and then he can't stop. It becomes hysterical, this bellowing, dreadful, heartbroken laughter, and the old men put down their dominoes to see what's happening.

Once he's made his resolution, Vincent is overcome with an eviscerating, spiritual high – better than honey, better than anything he's ever felt. This is good. This feels right. He calls Ellie from the payphone at the end of the ward. 'Ellie . . . listen. I need you . . . to do ss-s-something for me.'

'Vinnie. You're talking.'

The shock in her voice makes him acutely aware of his all over again – flat and expressionless and utterly devoid of inflection. The speech therapist had told him that in time and with lots of coaching they'd be able to correct the robotic monotone. But his speech would always be slow and halting. He might never lose the stutter. He would never sound like Vinnie again – Vinnie the arch-joker, Vinnie the entertainer, the one in the know. But rather than sink him, her prognosis bore out the wisdom of the path he was about to take. There was only one way forward. 'Promise not to . . . breathe . . . a . . . word?'

'I promise.'

'I m-mmean it. I want you bring me my . . . m-m-manuscript. It's in a shhhhhoebox under the wardrobe. Will you d-do that for me?'

'Yes. Vinnie.'

'And d-d-don't dare look at it. Not even a peek . . . I'll know. I'll know if you've looked at it.'

'Should I bring in your typewriter, too?' Her voice skips faster, dances to the suggestion. 'Shall I, Vin? Shall I bring it in for you?

'It's ssss-still a bit early for that. I'm, like . . . I-I-I-I'm editing.'

'What about I bring some books in? I've started on *Clockwork Orange*, you know . . .'

'Just the m-m-m-manuscript, Ellie. And I'll need Rizlas and tobacco. And I'm gonna need my rrrrraincoat, too.'

'What? Have they given you a date for coming home?'

'Jimmy, the porter – he's going to wheel me out to the garden if it keeps dry tom-m-morrow.' He feels bad. He can picture his sister's face, beaming at this positive news.

'I promise I won't look, Vinnie. Cross my heart. God – this is just the best news ever!'

He blows her a kiss down the phone. Little Ellie. He realises just how much he loves that wonderful, angry creation. He'll have to write to her and tell her this. With all his heart, he adores her.

'One last thing, Ellie. Can you bring my Walkman? It might st-st-s-still be in the pocket of my raincoat. And there's a hundred quid . . . under the lid of the hi-fi. I'm going to need that for mm-m-mags and records and books . . .'

'Wow! I'm just so . . . waaagh! Back at you!'

Vinnie places the receiver back in its cradle and slides down the wall, to the cool hospital floor. His lollipop knees are quaking. He cinches them with his arms, stops them banging together, and thinks about what he's just done. 'Oh Ellie,' he whispers into his knees. 'Please forgive me'.

Twenty-four

Robbie catches his reflection in the mirror, the pale morning light laminating his ghoulish, pasty pallor. But rather than buck away from it, he confronts it, possesses it fully. 'Should be end of pier, you.' He leans closer in to the mirror, tugs at a wiry nose hair. 'Hall of mirrors. You freak.'

He sighs and flops back down on the bed. Something has to give here. How much longer can he keep up the good fight? Regaling the same gaggle of drunken middle-agers night after night with his cheesy Elvis spoof. He doesn't even go in for the sex now. Hardly ever, anyway. Nor the endless free drinks and instant new friends. He hasn't had a drink in a while. Booze, birds, none of it can temper the heaviness that now hangs in his soul. Since going back there, he's been flattened by this mounting tristesse. Somehow he has to end this deathless cycle of being and nothingness.

It's still early and he could probably sleep more – if only the seagulls would let him – but there's an even stronger pull outside. It's Tuesday morning and with the last of the weekend tourists headed back down the motorway the prom is all his. What he's going to do is wrap up, head down to the shore and let the stinging salt air batter him sensible. And then he's going to sit down to a big fry-up at the Pier End Café and hatch up a plan – a plan that will let him back into his babies' lives. This is what they need and the more he's sobered up, the more he sees of the picture.

Robbie dresses quickly, eager to get out there in the teeth of the wind and think it all through. What if he were to rent a flat in Orford? His residence here in Blackpool pays decent money and it would be tough to match that. But surely Helen and Irene could put enough work his way to carry him through those first few months, just till he was able to establish himself again? After that, who could say what might happen? Blackpool had given him a keen eye for talent. Out of all the fresh-faced hopefuls the tide dragged in each week desperate to make their mark on the moribund cabaret scene, Robbie could tell which of them were going to make it and which of them would be carried back out to sea again. What if he were to start his own talent agency? With all his nous and experience it couldn't be *that* difficult. Two things he knows in his heart, knows them absolutely. He will never again work the rat-run, the fag of the factory line. And he's going back. Come what may, he'll be going back to his kids. All of a sudden his heart is lurching at the thought of telling them, telling Ellie. Daddy's coming home.

Twenty-five

Vinnie shuffles along the hospital corridor. Head down, he keeps close to the wall and travels in short staccato steps, the left flank of his famous blue raincoat flapping out with each laboured step. With one hand, he clutches the HMV bag that holds his manuscript, while the other hauls the funnel of his raincoat up and over the wreckage of his face. Departing visitors swerve and step round him, stopping to stare at this horrifically emaciated stick-boy, inching his way towards freedom. He feels their horror, and their double takes tell him, once again, that he has to see this through. There can be no going back.

Outside, it's a windless spring night. Cars burn like coals through the falling darkness. A sickle moon hovers above. Vinnie slips on his headphones, invigorated all over again by the stink of diesel and the factory spew, mingling with the zest of cooling mown grass. He numbs himself to any nostalgia the scents bring on, snapping down the play button and yelping in anguished joy as the Jesus and Mary Chain's 'Just Like Honey' spools out. He rewinds back to that Cure song, his eternal soundtrack to the moment before everything changed. And for the briefest dance of time, the fraught, searing vocal lunges him right back. He's standing there, watching the love of his life like he's made of stone. Kenny. The most gorgeously stupid thing he ever cut. This song will always be for him. 'You never looked as lost as this, sometimes it doesn't even look like you. It goes dark, it goes darker still. Please stay.'

Heart waxing and waning, eyes pricking with the sweet-sour sting of what's to come, he flips off the song and concentrates on the task ahead. His mind is made up. There is no other way.

He pushes on through the pulsing artery of Oxford Road, students flitting like bats around him, weighed down with bags of shopping, making plans for the evening, plans for the rest of their lives. He draws his face down further into the conch of his coat, almost misses the lash of red that spins into the borders of his vision. He remembers the clutch of letters in his inner pocket and pauses to fish them out. He fingers through them and as he slips them into the post box, feels himself falling again, welling up. There's one for Mum, one for Ellie, one for Kenny and – after writing it, trashing it, then writing it again – there's one for his dad.

He cuts down onto the canal path. The queer bars are already roaring, loaded with every kind of possibility. High-pitched cackling bounces off the dead skein of the water. He feels an odd superiority as he walks away, turns his back on the hassle and grab and clamour of it. All that rejection and pain shivering beneath the surface of every affair. He's spared all of that now, all the worthless trials and affectations of love. The path he's choosing is heroic. He's taken enough. He's ending it before it ends him.

His pace quickens, his breathing eases. It feels as though he's being buoyed along on a current, some magnetic pull from the empty, gutted peripheries of rentland reining him in towards his epitaph. The seeds of a Nietzsche trope flicker on his tongue, angling to define the moment, but it eludes him and slides away, unarticulated. He smiles inwardly, sadly. All that knowledge. All those books. The mantras and aphorisms that he's lived his whole life by mean so very little now.

He finds his boy, gaunt and more wasted than ever. He doesn't recognise Vinnie. He brings the battered canvas of his face in close, showing himself to him, letting him see the horror of it up close, almost goading him to react. There are light bulbs popping in his head now, snapping through the wiped-out haze.

350

'It's you innit? The Paki lad?' he croaks. He seems pleased to see him, or maybe just pleased he can still remember things. 'The school boy. That's you innit?' He jabs his gaze closer, rakes his etiolated eyes all over his face. 'Fuck! What happened to your face, man?'

The irony's not lost on Vinnie. The boy's face is a crawling bag of boils and he stinks like a corpse. But he fixes him with a stare and tells the truth. 'Got done over. Me and me fella. Queer-bashers.'

Either he doesn't hear or he doesn't care. Maybe it's par for the course, around here. 'Fucking bad that, man. Bad,' the wraith says and shakes his head. 'You want to be careful, yeah?' He taps both sides of his eyes with his index fingers then points them like a pair of pistols. 'Keep these open. Yeah? Even when I'm fuckin' sleeping, these are always open, like two fucking glass eyes on top of me lids.'

The sprawling nose and criss-cross grid of scars tells Vinnie the lad's taken his fair share of drubbings. Standing there with the wind in his hair and the city soup thickening around them, Vinnie feels some deep visceral connection with this wretch, this urban fox. For a moment, he senses the lad feels it too but then the manic eyes lurch left and right and back over his shoulder. It's business as usual.

'Same?'

'Nah, mate. I need a ten-quid bag and a bag of the other stuff you said. Nazi crank.'

A glimmer of something akin to enthusiasm passes over the lad's face. 'Now you're talking, man. This will keep you up for fuckin' days.'

'And I need spikes too. Three of them.'

He digs deep in his old, stained Spiewak jacket and pulls out three sealed hypodermics. 'I'll give you these a quid each seeing as you're buying proper. I usually charge more for these, yeah.

These is like fuckin' gold dust, man. Me own script like, hot from Cohens.'

Vinnie hands him all of the money – ninety pounds. The lad thinks he's missed a trick at first. He waits to take his lead from Vinnie, see if he's ordering more. Did he ask for three bags of each? Is he waiting for a blowjob? Vinnie says nothing, watches the lad as he goes to pocket the money. Something stalls him – not so much a conscience as a prickly paranoia. He can't quite gauge the moment. Is this some kind of a test? Is he being played? Vinnie laughs and puts him out of his misery. 'Image is everything in your game, maestro.' He grins and holds out his hand to shake. 'Get yourself some new trainers or a coat, yeah?'

The lad stands there stumped for an instant, then grips his hand in a crazy back-to-front 'brother' shake. Then he turns sharp and takes off in rapid speed-fire march before the molten-faced Paki changes his mind.

Vinnie cooks up in the stairwell of the multi-storey. He taps out a mixture of the two transparent packets into a spoon, dilutes it, heats it from underneath and then draws it up through a cotton wool ball. He repeats this a second and then a third time then, gripped by a mighty, panicking dread now, edges up and outside into the open with his three loaded guns. A wind nuzzles around him. It feels good as it licks his ears, the sound of air in motion, eddying, stirring, cleansing. The clutch of his fear passes, and he plants himself in the middle of the concrete roof. He sits down and lays out his manuscript, holding it down with his heel. He puts the syringes in his zip-up leather tobacco pouch and places it carefully between his feet to stop it rolling away. He takes off his coat, folds it up and creates a buffer between himself and the hard floor, then reclines onto his elbows. He fixes his earplugs in and turns up his Walkman and reaches for the first syringe.

He hits a vein. The needle slides in, seamlessly. Blood kicks back into the barrel, exploding like an atom bomb. He pushes the plunger back in again. The spike slips out cleanly. Steadying himself against the thickening currents of ease washing over him, he takes the second cocktail and empties it into another vein. He's too gone to slake the third.

'Say goodbye on a night like this if it's the last thing we ever do.' The music carries him, lifts him high above the city.

> For always and ever is always for you . . .
> I want it to be perfect
> Like before
> I want to change it all

There's a moment, before he drifts out, where his teeth clench perfectly together and the whorled misfit of his face yields and realigns. Vinnie is young and beautiful again, for ever. The sky seems to rise up out of itself and pull the stars in tight. There's a flimsy cord of consciousness dangling between him and the spangling vault, begging to be cast loose. He's almost ready to let it go now, let go for good. With one final heave, he rolls over, loosening the manuscript and letting the wind take hold. Page by page, he watches his life, his whole sad life take to the wind. He lies back and watches a lifetime of secrets and anxieties coast and swoop and flicker away like snowflakes. He's drifting now, smiling and drifting, and he's so happy, so serene that he can hear his heart slowing to a stop. He's looking down on himself, trailing away with the snowflakes, soaring higher and higher into the studded firmament where his snowflakes are blown to ashes.

Epilogue

All through the morning, police cars have been coming and going but this time Ellie senses that the engine shutting down outside their house is not one of them. She pulls herself up from Vinnie's bed where she's been lying prostrate for the last few hours, unable to speak or think, willing each breath to be her last and main-line her straight to her brother, and edges to the window ledge. He's here. Dad.

The anger she felt towards him this morning, for not being there – the night when they'd needed him most – fades to nothing when she sees his wrecked, broken form shuffling up the path. He's holding a letter like he's clinging to some last hope. So Vincent wrote to him too then. The thought brings on another onslaught of tears. Slowly she makes her way to the landing and hovers at the top of the stairs, delaying time, still holding out for something, someone, to jolt her from this nightmare, tell her it's all a horrible mistake.

He hasn't knocked yet but her mother is already at the door.

Robbie and Sheila stand there on the threshold and they don't say a thing. The cruel realisation hangs above them, loaded, stock-still, and not even the rasping wind dare touch it. It's Robbie that finally breaks the spell. 'She.'

'Oh Robbie . . .' As though she's been holding everything back up until this moment, Sheila slumps against the wall, pinching her eyes with three fingers as she succumbs to a silent, passionate sobbing. Robbie smothers her with a hug.

'Shhh, now. Vincent wrote to us.' He crooks his knee, drops down and wipes her eyes. 'Where's our Ellie?'

'I think she's sleeping. She hasn't moved from up there. It's

354

. . .' Once again, Sheila collapses into the well of his arms and surrenders completely.

Ellie stays there a while, not wanting to intrude upon the tender scene: her parents, finally united in their grief. And she feels it too now, the full paralysing gravitas of the night's events. Vinnie is dead. Vinnie is gone. More than ever she needs her mummy and daddy. She descends the stairs and goes to them. Robbie squeezes her, buffering the violent quaking of her body with the tight clamp of his chest. She's almost as tall as him now and her body is leaden with grief but he scoops her up in one easy swoop and carries her into the sitting room. He sits her on his lap, rocking her like a baby. 'Shhhh now, little fella, I'm back now. Daddy's back for good.'

There's a brief lull in her crying, the faintest glimmer of hope in her hope-dead face.

The slight, sylph-like figure of Ellie Fitzgerald standing to arms draws tears from the crowd as the funeral directors haul out the coffin. She's wearing Vinnie's coat – his famous blue raincoat. Behind her Robbie stoops to whisper in her ear. She nods resolutely, her jaw set firm. She ducks under the front left corner of the coffin and takes her place. She's shorter than the other pallbearers and the imbalance causes the coffin to list to one side, but she pushes on, her slender, resolute shoulders near buckling under its weight.

A small congregation huddles beneath a span of umbrellas outside the church gate. The low groan of thunder peals out across the washed-out belly of the sky. Ellie smiles, closes her eyes and is filled with such a deep, sharp stab of finality that she almost cries out in pain. She can feel him out there in the rain; she can feel him in the sharp wind gusting under her coat, his coat, slapping at her calves. Vincent. Her big brother, Vinnie. He's out there.

Morbid, soulless music in the church. The sound of the pipe organ itself is deathly and austere. Sheila stays standing while the congregation sits – her gaze leaden and unfocused, her eyes shot forward in her skull. She becomes aware of her daughter tugging gently on her wrist and simply lets herself fall back. Her rump connects with the pew, jolting her from her maudlin trance, a fresh wave of agony crashing over as she remembers the reason she's here. Vinnie is dead. He is gone. Her little man is gone for ever.

There is a brief silence at the end of each hymn where the damp, high-ceilinged room echoes with the sorry chorus of stifled grief. Ellie tunes into the muffled keening of a male, purling out from the far recesses of the church. Gingerly she edges her head round and scans the room. A young man – a boy, really – is crying his heart out, forefinger and thumb of his right hand squeezing his temples to try and make it all stop.

Father Bradley cranks up his croaky pitch a notch, tries to drown out the sobs. His eulogy steers the mourners further away from Vinnie and on towards Christ. It's wrong. When he called round to go over the service, he sat there in earnest, scribbling notes while Sheila and Ellie regaled him with all that was special about Vinnie. The Father left with five pages of memories, and here he was condensing it down to this nonsense. 'Vincent Fitzgerald was a responsible young adult with a brilliant future ahead of him. He was sociable, happy and well-loved.'

Only one of these assertions, thinks Ellie, is true. The bile is mounting. She waits for a lull then leans in to her mum. 'Mum!' she hisses. 'Stop him. Please. Make him stop.'

Her mother looks up for an instant. Something enters her life-less eyes, but then shrinks away like a shadow. If anybody is going to rescue this for Vinnie, it's not going to be her dead-beat mother. Ellie scans the room. All these people here – they know Vinnie would have hated this. The group of quiet Asian men

356

who arrived from Manchester bow their heads. The one who introduced himself as Abdul smiles meekly at her. Dan Roth and the crowd, these she knows – but there are so many others there. The Cohen sisters are there, with their broken, pretty mother. A beautiful boy is trying to console the lad who's crying at the back. All these people – friends she never knew he had – all here for him. She's glad in her heart, but she can't let the priest spoil his memory. She turns to her dad. 'Please. Dad. Get up and say something. For Vinnie.'

And Robbie is taken over by a wondrous certainty. They need him again – and he knows just exactly what to do for them. He squeezes Ellie's hand and steps out into the aisle. Slowly, but with pride and fortitude, he makes his way up to the pulpit. The priest takes a step down, bows his head so that Robbie can speak to him.

'I'd like to . . . sorry, Father, er . . . can I get up a moment?' As soon as he's said it, he's aware of the cabaret tone. 'Sorry, Father. I'd just like say a few words for our Vincent, please?'

'Robert, yes – of course.' The priest tries to look happy about it as he stands back to let Robbie pass, but his lips are pursed.

The room falls silent, scattered threads of conversation hushed down to speculative whispers. You can almost hear Robbie's heart beating as he steps up to the lectern. He leans in to the little microphone, can't adjust it and visibly decides he'll do this raw. He wets his lips with the tip of his tongue, waits for every voice to fade to hush, then speaks. 'My boy. Vincent.'

On hearing his name, and on hearing it uttered by his father with so much love and regret, Sheila's knees go to jelly beneath her.

Robbie chokes back the emotion, goes to speak again. 'He . . .' He looks out at the congregation. Faces smile back at him. He takes strength, and goes again. 'Me and him . . .'

He has to take a breath, steady the swell of his heart. He

357

looks up at the church roof and mouths 'I love you.' He closes his eyes. There is not a sound, not a rustle of paper, nothing. He draws himself right up, takes a deep breath – and then he starts to sing.

> Starry starry night
> Paint your palate blue and grey . . .

Ellie doesn't know the song, but she's blown away by the plaintive beauty of her father's voice. She knows his voice, of course, she's heard him a hundred times, but this is something else. She bites down on her lip, grips hard on the pew in front and sits there, rocking.

> Look out on a summer's day
> With eyes that know the darkness of your soul . . .

Ellie puts an arm around her mother and pulls her in close. Robbie breathes and lives every aching pulse of the words as though he owns them, as though he'd sat there that day on the prom with the wind howling round him and written Vincent's eulogy: 'I forgive you, Dad. I hope you forgive me.'

> Now I understand.
> What you tried to say to me
> And how you suffered for your sanity . . .

Robbie spots Sheila gagging back her sorrow with both hands pressed to her mouth. She finds him with her tearful eyes. He holds her gaze, trying to communicate with his voice the strange sense of hope and liberation that's surging through him.

Starry starry night.
Flaming flowers that brightly blaze
Swirling clouds in violet haze
Reflected in Vincent's eyes of China black ...

Sheila closes her eyes and listens to the words.

For they could not love you
But still your love was true
And when no hope was left inside
On that starry starry night
You took your life as lovers often do
But I could have told you, Vincent,
This world was never meant for one as beautiful as you.

Robbie stays there swaying gently, eyes closed, detached from the spellbound awe of the room, as close to his boy as he's ever been.

Acknowledgements

I would like to thank:

The Society of Authors, and the patrons and judges of the Betty
Trask Award for enabling me to travel to Malaysia. Jonny Geller,
whose editorial nous at the very start helped shape the entire
course of this novel. Jamie et al at Canongate, the last word in
publishing. Anya, my brilliant, zealous editor – and ally – for her
absolute devotion to the Fitzgeralds. Peter Campbell, the ori-ginal
'thin gypsy thief', for providing me with the soundtrack to Vincent.
Dr Nick Roland, for his advice on facial trauma. Andrew Bennett,
for use of his magnificent library. John McBride, for sharing with
me his memories of factory life at Crossfields. Will, Deena and
Carla – my dream team, for being there to pick up the pieces one
grim afternoon in July, and dusting me down to fight the good
fight again. Gladys Sampson, for my Sherlock Holmes lamp and
indefatigable supply of scones, both of which helped burn the
midnight oil those last few months. Jeff Lambrecht and Sarah
Jane, good friends I met along the way. Uncle Rasa, Aunty Shanthi,
Joe boy, Thanu and Renuka; Aunty Malar, Seelan, Uncle Baby,
Suzi, Usha, and all my KL kith and kin – far too many to mention
– for being such wonderful hosts and for teaching me the true
meaning of a pot party. Wesley Walsh, my favourite Monday
distraction. And Leo, wondrous Leo, the perfect bookend.

And thank you:

Kevin, my frontline editor, my iron lung.
But it's different in November, with you.